Praise for *The Devil's Horn*, fi

'<u>Love</u> the book!'

'Will keep you gripped till the very last page.'
              Rose Ferry, booktuber

'The best book set in Majorca that I have ever read. There are a number of reasons for that – a strong plot, a splendid female hero, and some surprising twists and turns. It also includes delightful evocations of the countryside around Soller and fond descriptions of village life on the island.'   Donald Trelford, journalist

'Beautifully written and intelligent. Anna paints an entertaining account of life on Mallorca. *The Devil's Horn* is poignant in all the right places and funny too, sustained by swift dialogue and detailed descriptions.'   *ABC Mallorca Magazine*

'Unputdownable. The twists and turns keep you engaged to the end.' @booksnsunshine, Instagrammer & book blogger

'A very gripping story. It will keep you engaged to the end.'
             Expert, LoveReading.co.uk

'I don't think I've read a crime story as excellent as this one. It's gripping and quirky.'
        @askthebookbug, Instagrammer & book blogger

Praise for *Haunted Magpie*

This series is one of the best I have read this year. Isabel is now one of my favourite detectives and that is saying a lot as I'm an avid crime fiction fan. I was shocked by the ending! The pacing of the book was amazing – there were lots of twists & turns... The series deserves to be a smash hit and I can see this being developed for TV very easily. I adored this book. Just go and read it!'

Books By Bindu

'It's a tightly written, well-paced and highly engaging tale, celebrating the island, its people and vibrant culture.'

TheLiteraryShed

'I love Isabel. She is the perfect sleuth. The writer has given her a great personality and made us feel that we really know her. I devoured this book in just one sitting and immediately added other by this author to my TBR list.' Little Miss BookLover

'I couldn't read fast enough at times to see what happened – I can highly recommend this book and hope to read more of Anna Nicholas' work.' www.Lovereading.com expert

'The characters are inspiring and brave and the little ferret will steal your heart, believe me! This is a book to read and let you fantasise about travels to better places. I really can't wait to read the next book of the series. I am addicted!' Varietats

Praise for *Fallen Butterfly*

'This was such a thrilling book and brilliantly written.'
MirandasBookScape

'Isabel is a great character; feisty when she needs to be but cool & intelligent as required. A fabulous cosy crime thriller.'
DebsBookReviews

'*Fallen Butterfly* is a brilliant addition to one of my favourite series! Isabel has become one of my favourite characters. She really is a brilliant character – friendly, loyal, intelligent, strong, quirky and just darn right cool. Plus she has a pet ferret called Furó, how can you not fall in love with her?'
BooksByBindu – reviewer

'[Anna] has written several travel books about the island and this knowledge shines through, but most of all it is clear that she loves the place, its people and their way of life. Our heroine, Isabel, is a wonderful creation. A former detective, she is quirky, headstrong and courageous with a winning personality.'
Peter Fleming – PeterTurnsthePage book blogger

I like my detectives to have a bit of quirkiness and in Isabel Flores, Anna Nicholas goes full off the books quirky, but in a great way. No other detective I know has a ferret for a sidekick – he is a heart-warming addition. Anna Nicholas doesn't shy away from the gritty. There's a Bergerac feel about it, and at times having seen how successful, the likes of Murder in Paradise have been, I could see this taking off as a very good TV adaptation.
Adrian Murphy TheLibraryDoor

Praise for Anna Nicholas's Mallorca travel series

'Terrific!' Lucia van der Post, contributor, FT *How to Spend It*

'As intelligent as it is entertaining. From simple escapism to a much more complicated story about the difficulties of balancing life in two places...' Leah Hyslop, *The Telegraph*

'Anna Nicholas is one of those lucky swine who has dared to live the dream and write about it.' Harry Ritchie, *The Daily Mail*

'Witty, evocative and heart-warming. Another Mallorcan pearl from Anna Nicholas.' Peter Kerr, author of *Snowball Oranges*

'A beautifully written and highly entertaining account of the upside of downshifting.' Henry Sutton, *The Daily Mirror*

'A hugely entertaining and witty account of how to juggle life and work between two countries, keep fit and stay sane!' Colonel John Blashford-Snell, CBE, British explorer & author

'An enjoyable read for anyone wanting to live their dream.' Lynne Franks, OBE, broadcaster & author

'If you thought that glitz and glamour don't mix with rural country living you must read this book.' *Bella* magazine

'This is Anna's comic and observational style at its very best.' *St Christopher's Inns* magazine

'Endearing, funny and poignant. What more could one wish for?' *Real Travel* magazine

Anna Nicholas is the most prolific British author writing about Mallorca today. Her successful series of seven travel books explores the history, culture and delights of the golden isle. An inveterate traveller and experienced freelance journalist, she is *Telegraph Travel*'s Destination Writer, and has contributed travel features to *FT How to Spend It*, the *Times*, *Independent*, and other leading publications. Anna regularly participates in humanitarian aid expeditions overseas and runs an international marathon annually for her favourite causes. *Aunt Maria's Last Aria* is her fourth novel in the new Mallorca crime series.

Instagram @annanicholasauthor
Facebook @AnnaNicholasAuthor
X @ANicholasAuthor

Also by Anna Nicholas

Mallorca crime series
The Devil's Horn
Haunted Magpie
Fallen Butterfly

Mallorca travel series
A Lizard in my Luggage
Cat on a Hot Tiled Roof
Goats from a Small Island
Donkeys on my Doorstep
A Bull on the Beach
A Chorus of Cockerels
Peacocks in Paradise

Memoir
Strictly Off the Record with Norris McWhirter

Burro Books,
403, Union Wharf,
23 Wenlock Road,
London N1 7SJ
www.burrobooks.co.uk

Published by Burro Books Ltd 2024

Copyright © Anna Nicholas 2024

Anna Nicholas has asserted her right under the Copyright, Designs and Patents Act 1988 to be identified as the author of this work.

This book is a work of fiction and the characters and names mentioned are entirely drawn from the author's imagination. Any resemblance to actual persons, living or dead, happenings and localities is purely coincidental. The village of Sant Martí is also a happy invention by the author.

ISBN: 978-1-8383110-4-9
Ebook ISBN: 978-1-8383110-5-6

Printed and bound by CPI Group (UK) Ltd, Croydon, CR0 4YY
This book is sold subject to the condition that it shall not, by way of trade or otherwise, be lent, resold, hired out, or otherwise circulated without the publisher's prior consent in any form of binding or cover other than that in which it is published and without a similar condition, including this condition, being imposed on the subsequent publisher.

AUNT MARIA'S LAST ARIA

AN ISABEL FLORES MALLORCAN MYSTERY

ANNA NICHOLAS

burrobooks

LONDON

Glossary

The following Mallorcan and Spanish words and expressions appear in the book. I hope these explanations prove helpful.

Abanico – fan
Albondigas – meatballs
Ajuntament – town hall
Bocadillo –sandwich/roll
Ca rater/ratero – small Mallorcan dog breed
Cariño – Darling
Casita – little house
Cinta americana – strong masking tape
Copa – a glass
Cortado – espresso with a dash of milk
Depósito – water tank
Diga – Tell me or speak!
Ensaïmada – spiral-shaped Mallorcan pastry
Feliz cumpleaños – happy birthday
Fang – mud
Fiesta – party
Finca – country house
Furó – ferret
Gambas rojas – red prawns
Gató d'almendras – almond cake
Grande – big
Granizado de limón – iced lemonade
Greixoneras – pans

Guardia Civil – the Civil Guard, Spanish military police force
Infierno – hell
Jefe superior – superintendent
Llaut – small, traditional fishing boat
Lotería – the lottery
Masa madre – sourdough
Menu del día – lunchtime menu
Merienda – mid-morning snack
Moix – cat
Mores – blackberries
Moto – motorbike
Museu – museum
Nicho – recess for storing the deceased in a cemetery
No pasar – don't pass
Notari – notary
Ollas – cooking pots
Ollerías – artisan pottery workshops
OVNI – UFO
Pueblo – village
Padre – father
Paellera – paella pan
Pequeñito – little one
Pequeño – small
Plaça – village or town square
Porc amb col – pork with cabbage
Reina – queen, term of endearment
Ruta de Fang – the mud route
Setas – wild mushrooms
Siurell – pottery whistle
Tapas – savoury sharing plates
Tía – aunt
Tío – uncle
Tortilla – omelette
Trempó or trampó – a local tomato and green pepper salad
Tumbet – a typical Mallorcan dish of cooked aubergine, potatoes and peppers
Vino tinto – red wine

ONE

Maria finished grinding the small white pills in the pestle and mortar, and, frowning in concentration, tipped the powder carefully into one side of the heart-shaped gold locket. She slid it shut and fastened the dainty necklace once again about her neck. After thoroughly washing the implements in the basin, she threw the empty pill packet into a pedal bin and set the pestle and mortar back on a glass shelf. Revenge would be sweet. Her sense of excitement was palpable, and she couldn't wait for the assignation later that night. It would only take two milligrams of fentanyl placed in his favourite tipple, a racy negroni, to finish him off, but this powerful opioid mix would rocket him to the moon. Not long now.

Inspecting her face in the elegant mahogany mirror, Maria was dismayed by the gathering of tiny lines on her forehead and at the corners of her eyes and pouting lips. Flicking back her mane of damp black hair, she stared appreciatively into the bewitching grey eyes before her and smiled. Despite the passing years and the ruthlessness of the sun, she still considered herself a desirable woman. A quick visit to the aesthetic practitioner in Palma for another round of Botox and fillers before her impending tour, and her face would once again be as smooth and taut as the hide of a drum.

She massaged fragrant rose oil into her cheeks and used a tissue to remove a rogue droplet of water on the mirror. Despite its betrayal, she cherished the Georgian masterpiece with its bevelled plate glass and aesthetic cresting board in which a delicate gilt ho-ho bird was mounted. Her beloved father used to tell her that this Japanese version of the mythological phoenix with its curved neck, talons and flowing tail signified fidelity, good fortune, and wisdom. These days she wasn't so sure if the magic still held.

She yawned and threw on her vintage satin robe, loosely fastening the ribbon about her waist. Underneath she wore a matching ivory nightgown, embellished with exquisite embroidery and handmade lace. Barefooted, she padded over to the French windows and flung open the doors and wooden shutters, allowing lemony light and fresh, balmy air to flood the room. She draped a damp towel over her arm and glanced fleetingly at a fine white porcelain dish by the basin. It contained a heavy gold chain strung with five brass keys. As always, she had secured each of the locks on her bedroom door prior to entering the bathroom. After all, one could never be too careful.

A steady drip came from the nickel tap that took centre stage in the decadent bath. The gleaming white monster with its dove-grey wooden panels and Calacatta marble trim sat in state in a corner of the room and was the temple at which Maria paid homage with her daily ablutions.

Wafting onto the sunny balcony, she scrunched her toes, enjoying the sensation of warmth that was already radiating from the worn old terracotta tiles. Gentle undulating hills and verdant orchards saluted her from the north while an extensive garden, sun-scorched fields and brittle vineyards stretched to the east. Maria walked over to the delicate, low wrought-iron railings and spread out the large white towel, surveying the pastoral scene before her. Peering down from her lofty perch, she could see, far below, the hazy sun-kissed form of a black cat creeping through the buttery bracken and dry long grasses beyond the kitchen garden and aged greenhouse. Her grandfather, Alberto Rosselló, a Catalan entrepreneur and avid gardener, had commissioned the construction of the Victorian-style rectangular edifice back in the early thirties, when such novelties were rarely seen in the heartland of the island. It was fashioned from brick, cast iron and large glass panes and was a tribute to his English hero, Sir Joseph Paxton, who in 1851 created the famed Crystal Palace in Hyde Park in London solely for the purpose of housing the temporary Great Exhibition. Alberto would often remind his impressionable young granddaughter that the Crystal Palace was 108 feet high, contained 293,000 panes of glass and that it had taken 5,000 men eight months to complete. Though Maria was only twelve when the elderly man died, she had never forgotten his mantra, and she revered the more modest version in her own garden, even fondly referring to it as her little Crystal Palace.

Closing her eyes in quiet contemplation, Maria pondered which heroine to channel that morning. Might it be Dido, the fated queen of Carthage from *The Trojans*, or perhaps poor, wretched Magda from *The Consul*? The persistent piercing cry of a distant cockerel and the urgent hissing of cicadas caused her to tut, but soon she was immersed once more in the warm embrace of opera.

She gave an involuntary giggle. Of course. There was only one aria to suit her skittish mood that morning. She would sing "*Sempre Libera*", "Always Free", from *La Traviata*, a fitting paean to its troubled and cruelly deceived heroine, the courtesan,

Violetta Valéry. Maria cleared her throat, took some long, deep breaths, and hummed the jaunty tune to herself. Yes, like the lyrics of the song, she would always strive to be free.

A muffled thud came from the bathroom, causing her eyes to spring open. Maria turned towards the French windows with a furrowed brow. Had something fallen on the rug, perhaps the voluminous make-up case that she'd left sitting precariously on the side of the bath, ready to pack for her impending opera tour? She debated popping back inside to check but was distracted by the high-pitched screams of a cloud of passing swifts. Her eyes followed the tiny pewter bodies with their fast wings as they momentarily stained the blue sky grey before disappearing from view. She returned to her meditative state, recalling the song's upbeat and defiant lyrics. Expanding her lungs, she clutched dramatically at her ample chest as she unleashed the first rippling notes of the aria with the words "*Sempre libera degg'io*".

A thin trickle of sweat snaked its way down one of Maria's flushed cheeks as she sang with gusto, her voice quivering with emotion. In a state of euphoria, she coursed through each stanza, throwing out her arms imploringly to the heavens as she reached the electrifying climax. Trilling the final triumphant "Ah! Ah! Ah!", she let out an unintended screech. Someone had lunged at her from behind. Flung forward, Maria nearly toppled over the flimsy balustrade but managed to grab onto the rail with her left hand as she attempted to turn to face her assailant. A short struggle ensued, but despite her valiant efforts, she was quickly overcome by strong hands that ruthlessly propelled her forward and over the edge of the balcony.

And in that split second before she plummeted like a cursed phoenix, Maria glimpsed a white mask with a wide open turned-down mouth and brushed its surface with her hand. She recognised it as the weeping face of Melpomene, the Greek muse of tragedy, and fantasised that she was a sacrifice to the sky and that her body was so light that it might float away. Instead, with a thump, it struck the cast-iron frame of the greenhouse and fell with a sickening crash through one of its wide glass panes. Maria's torn and mangled form continued its bloody trajectory, hitting a stone table headfirst and scattering the tomato seedlings in their clay pots, coming to rest on the concrete floor. Mercifully, by then, Maria was already dead.

TWO

A complicit sun grinned down at the laughing, carefree trio enjoying the remnants of a robust breakfast in a discreet and shady *plaça*. Even at such an early hour in the cool back streets of Palma, the sun sizzled, because as every local knew, the heat of August was as fierce as a red-hot chilli pepper. Isabel leant back in her wicker chair and yawned.

'Well, gentlemen, much as I love your charming company, it's almost nine-thirty and there's work to be done.'

Gaspar glanced at his watch. 'Nine-twenty-eight. How do you do that?'

Tolo laughed. 'I told you. She's a witch.'

She eyed him over her tilted shades. 'So you say, but I haven't got the hang of my broom yet.'

A waiter arrived with a saucerful of small change which Tolo observed briefly and handed back to him. The man tapped his shoulder gratefully and, with a smile, sauntered off.

'I guess you're crazily busy with renters now,' drawled Gaspar, running a hand over his smooth, dark, sun-kissed head.

Isabel nodded. 'It's always full on in the summer, but with Idò off work recovering from a hip replacement, Pep's had to spin a lot of plates.'

Tolo shrugged. 'It's good for him. He's young and he likes challenges.'

Isabel rose from her seat and twisted her mane of dark curls into a makeshift bun, securing it with a random plastic peg she plucked from her pannier.

'Hm, Pep didn't find removing lively young frogs and a random terrapin from a swimming pool such a fun challenge yesterday. All the pools in our properties need constant topping up with chlorine in this heat or they turn green, and without Idò, he's on his own.'

Gaspar puffed out his cheeks. 'I don't envy the poor guy. Mind you, working in the homicide team under your boyfriend here isn't such a dream ticket.'

Tolo gave a growl. 'I've just bought you breakfast. What more do you want?'

'A break from poring over cold cases and sorting out fights between drunken tourists in Arenal.'

'You love it all,' Tolo replied, giving him a kick under the table. 'Besides, at least we've only had one murder and a few stabbings this summer.'

'True,' Isabel replied. 'And Magaluf has cleaned up its act, so there's little trouble brewing over there. And I get a break from police work.'

Tolo clicked his teeth. 'Don't speak too soon, *cariño*. Remember, in this job you never know what's around the corner. Before you know it, we'll be knocking on your door for backup.'

Isabel tapped her chin thoughtfully. 'What are the cold cases?'

'A couple of prostitutes found knifed to death in Palma back in 2010. The killer was never found but some new DNA evidence has come to light. We're also reassessing the disappearance of a bar owner back in the late nineties. Seems that he had a thriving cocaine business on the side and upset a few local drug barons. One of them has entered into a plea bargain and handed over some crucial information.'

Isabel frowned. 'Awful for the families not to know the fate of their loved ones for all these years.'

He sighed. 'That's why we need to keep these cases open and give them some air.'

Gaspar looked up at Isabel. 'And how's Florentina?'

'Dear Mama is still in Valencia with my neighbour, the good Doctor Ramis. They're at some new film festival until Saturday. The founder is a close friend of his.'

'Are they officially an item?' Gaspar asked with a wink.

Isabel made invisible speech marks in the air. 'Just friends.'

'Yeah right,' he replied with a smile.

Tolo wiped a bead of sweat from his forehead and gestured towards a long queue of tourists at a nearby taxi rank. 'Can't get a ride for love nor money here in Palma this summer. Mind you, it's far worse in your neck of the woods.'

Isabel nodded. 'You're more likely to see an OVNI than a taxi in Soller.'

'Well, the last sighting of an unidentified flying object in Spain was in Soller, of course.' He smirked.

'I remember the story well,' Gaspar replied. 'I love anything to do with OVNIs. One night back in November 1979, a local mechanic named José Climent Pérez was leaving a cinema with a chum when he snapped a luminous object hovering over Puig de L'Ofre. Around the same time, a plane departing Palma airport had to be diverted to Valencia due to the same disturbance. The captain claimed that he was being tailed by unidentified objects emitting a green and red glow. Nothing was ever proven, but it was an eerie story.'

'The military confiscated Pérez's photo negatives too. Something fishy about the whole episode,' Tolo concurred.

Isabel burst out laughing. 'You two! It was probably just a meteorological phenomenon.'

Tolo scrunched her arm and grinned. 'If you say so.'

'A shame we don't have a cinema anymore in Soller, though.' Isabel gave a wistful sigh.

Tolo sniggered when a man wearing little more than a pair of swimming trunks and flip-flops crossed the street. 'Now there's an alien phenomenon. See that?'

Shaking his head, Gaspar leant back in his chair and watched the bulky figure disappear around a corner. 'True. Where are the beat cops when you need them? He should be fined just for exposing that big white beer belly. Not our call.'

'He'd never get a cab dressed like that.' Isabel snorted with laughter.

Tolo's mobile rang. He sprung from his seat. '*Diga*!'

Gaspar rose and followed Isabel to a nearby shady plane tree where they waited for Tolo. She fumbled in her bag and quickly unwrapped a Chupa Chup lolly and stuck it in her mouth.

He feigned disgust. 'Still eating those horrible things?'

'You bet,' she said, elbowing him hard. 'They keep me sweet. So I tell my dentist.'

Gaspar observed his boss pacing around the exterior of the café, a pained expression on his face as he talked animatedly into his phone. Finally, he shoved the mobile in the breast pocket of his blue linen jacket and approached them. He ran a hand through his dishevelled grey-brown locks.

'That was the commissioner. The opera singer, Maria Rosselló Morales, has been discovered dead in her garden in Moscari. Most likely suicide.'

'What? Tía Maria?' Isabel looked visibly shocked. 'But the papers reported only yesterday that she was about to go on a European tour. She was at a press conference a few days ago, laughing and talking about the trip.'

Gaspar turned to Isabel. 'Tía Maria?'

'I'm guessing it was a nickname awarded her by students at the Conservatori de Opera in Palma where she taught. The media often affectionately refer to her as Tía Maria.'

Tolo offered a bleak expression. 'According to the commissioner, she was known to suffer from severe depression. The incident happened about an hour ago.'

'Presumably the Guardia Civil has been alerted?' asked Isabel.

'Oh yes. Apparently, our chum Capitán Gómez is already at the house, and the medical examiner, judge and court registrar are on the way.'

'How did she do it?' asked Isabel.

Tolo shrugged. 'It appears that she leapt from a bathroom terrace on the top floor of the property. She'd bolted the door from the inside, so the husband had to break it open. I need you over there, Gaspar.' He issued a sigh. 'Given her public profile, the commissioner would like us to handle this matter, but for now, let's keep an eye on Gómez. You know what an oaf he can be.'

Isabel squinted up at the sun. 'They're securing the scene?'

Tolo frowned. 'There's no suspicion of criminality, but I argued the case anyway. The commissioner has agreed to allow Nacho and the forensics team to examine the body in situ, though he doesn't want a circus over there. Naturally, there'll be a post-mortem.'

They began walking towards La Rambla. Isabel was thoughtful.

'I'm on my way to Inca to see a guy who makes ferret runs. I could pop by the scene with Gaspar as it's en route.'

Tolo shook his head. 'Ferret runs? Are you serious?'

She tutted. 'Deadly serious. Furó needs a run in the garden to stop him getting bored and eyeing up the hens. He's been stalking a few of late.'

'How come you've only just told me?'

'He's not your ferret.'

Gaspar coughed loudly. 'Okay, sparring partners, can I cut in here? I'd like Bel along, especially if Gómez is there. Safety in numbers.'

Tolo nodded and pulled out his mobile. 'Agreed. I'm heading back to the precinct. I'll WhatsApp you both the location now. Keep me in the loop.'

He gave Isabel a light kiss on the cheek and, with hands in pockets, strode off towards Avinguda de Jaume III.

Isabel and Gaspar walked along La Rambla and turned into the underground car park. She had left Boadicea, her powerful Ducati Monster, on ground level, while Gaspar had found a space on the upper tier. Her beloved Pequeñito, a canary-yellow Fiat 500, remained parked outside her terraced home back in her village. Isabel felt a stab of guilt for choosing her powerful motorbike over Pequeñito for this particular sortie, but she would make it up to him the following day. They would go to Can Repic together in the early morning before the tourists awoke and make the most of the warm sea, empty beach and still, aromatic air.

She turned to Gaspar. 'Statistically, there are one hundred suicides in the Baleares every year.'

'One hundred and one now,' he quipped.

'Maybe.' Isabel offered a fleeting smile. 'You know the town with the highest suicide rate in Spain is Alcalá la Real. They only have about twenty thousand residents and yet in the last thirty years, they've had ten suicides annually.'

Gaspar clicked his teeth. 'It's such a beautiful rural idyll too.'

'As they say, *pueblo pequeño, infierno grande*. Hell is a state of mind, not a place,' she replied and punched his arm. 'Bet I'll beat you there.'

He laughed. 'Knock yourself out, but if you do get there first, play nice with Gómez. I don't want to have to pick up the pieces.'

Without replying, she headed towards the sleek and gleaming motorbike, a playful grin on her lips.

Isabel set off, carefully navigating the narrow streets of Palma. She joined the MA-20 and finally took the MA-13 towards Inca, the fastest route. Providing the traffic wasn't too heavy, she estimated that she'd arrive on the outskirts of Moscari in around thirty minutes. She revved the engine and smiled once she was coursing along in the fast lane as free as a bird, the breeze caressing her face.

So far, the summer had passed quite uneventfully in the village of Sant Martí, in the rugged northwest of the island. Her holiday rentals agency, Hogar Dulce Hogar, continued to flourish, with weekly bookings from holidaymakers right through to the end of October. As soon as November came, with its cooler and rainy weather, there would be few tourists about, a time to take stock and slacken the reins a little. Isabel had taken over the ailing agency from her mother, Florentina, at a time when she had grown weary of her work as a detective inspector with the National Police in Palma, and prior to that on the mainland. She had loved her job, but as a rule-breaker, she had loathed the bureaucracy and the constant need to conform.

There was also another reason why she'd thrown in the towel. Some years previously, her beloved Uncle Hugo, a fearless investigative journalist and her deceased father's twin, had disappeared off the streets of Barcelona late one night and was still missing. One crucial eyewitness, a prostitute, who was later found dead in suspicious circumstances, had maintained that she had seen him bundled into a dark limousine bearing a Colombian flag. Isabel had scrambled to find answers from the local Mossos d'Esquadra, the Catalan Police Force in Barcelona, with whom she'd worked, but she was met with a cool, if not hostile, response. Her father, a retired police superintendent of Castille-La Mancha on the mainland, had died of a broken heart, never knowing what happened to his twin brother. Meanwhile, her mother no longer had the will to continue running the rentals agency, so Isabel quit her high-profile police career and took over, turning the enterprise into a great success. Frustrated at the lack of answers regarding her uncle's whereabouts, Isabel had hired Emilio Navarro, a Barcelona-based private investigator, to pick up the trail, and recently there had been a shocking development. It appeared that her uncle was still alive and had been sighted in Colombia in the company of a notorious drug baron. She had no idea what it could possibly mean.

Meanwhile, Tolo Cabot, the unconventional homicide chief of the National Police in Mallorca, and her former boss, had lured her back into detective work, assisting his team with puzzling island crimes. Always close friends, their relationship had since blossomed and they had become romantically involved, much to the delight and amusement of their colleagues at the Palma police precinct.

Isabel steamed ahead and took exit 30 in the direction of Cami Vell de Pollença. She had a strange sense of foreboding about the sudden death of Tía Maria, who until that morning's fateful event had been the most famous living opera singer in Mallorca. Something didn't feel right, and she trusted her instincts, as always. Perhaps that was why she'd offered with such alacrity to attend the scene of the incident with Gaspar. Was it the need for a little excitement following a long and listless summer without police work, or the growing sense of unease that pricked her senses and made her heart thump? As she neared the grand entrance of Can Rosselló on the outskirts of Moscari village, she was sure she'd find out soon enough.

At the gate, Isabel was flagged down by a green-uniformed military police officer manning a makeshift checkpoint. Hastily, she pulled out the National Police badge that Tolo instructed her to carry when working on a case. The young Guardia officer gave it a cursory glance and pressed a button partly obscured by creeper on a nearby wall. The lethargic gate came to life and slowly slid back on its rail. The young man smiled at her.

'Always wanted a Ducati. How does she handle?'

'Like a dream,' Isabel replied. 'Give you a quick spin later if you like.'

He pulled a face. 'I wish. Stuck here until eight p.m.'

Isabel clicked her teeth. 'Too bad. By the way, is the gate usually closed?'

'No, we asked the husband of the deceased if we could activate it for security reasons today.'

As she coursed up the leafy, winding driveway, she saw ahead of her a large courtyard flanked by bougainvillea, palm trees, and orange trees. Isabel parked close to the elegant, ivy-clad porch that was flanked by two snow-white oleander trees and gave a low whistle as she pulled off her helmet. She'd seen many a country pile in her time, but the beautifully proportioned, honey-stoned property was exquisite. Set across three floors, the house had large windows framed by stylish white shutters, while rooms on the upper floors spilled out onto pretty balconies with dainty wrought-iron railings. Isabel secured Boadicea and briefly surveyed her surroundings just as she heard the distinctive energetic step of Capitán Gómez crunching on the gravel. Bracing herself, she looked up brightly and smiled as he approached.

'So, Bel, are you the advance cavalry? I'm disappointed to see that Tolo has once again left you to handle a highly sensitive matter when one of his own team should have been present.'

'I am one of his team,' she replied frostily.

'*Si, si,* but you are just a consultant to the team, and it is Tolo's responsibility to...'

A car rolled into the driveway and Gaspar's cheery face appeared from the driver's window.

Isabel turned to Capitán Gómez with an arch smile. 'So, Álvaro, you were saying?'

He folded his arms tightly and offered a curt nod in Gaspar's direction. 'Saved by the bell. Frankly, I am happy to leave Tolo to sign off on this unfortunate tragedy. I have far more pressing matters to deal with currently.'

'You do?'

'As it happens, Isabel, I am investigating a series of aggravated robberies in the Llucmajor area. No doubt foreign residents are to blame. What we sow, so shall we reap.'

Isabel frowned. 'And we Mallorcans are angels, of course.'

'With all due respect, you are only half Mallorcan.'

'Ah, then I'm truly damned,' she replied.

Gaspar sauntered towards them and punched Isabel on the arm. 'You win.'

She nodded. 'Naturally. Should have had a wager.'

'No way! I'm not that stupid.' Gaspar turned to the military captain and smiled.

'Good to see you, Álvaro. Just wish it were in happier circumstances. Where are we at?'

The Guardia Capitán wafted a dismissive hand through the air. 'It appears straightforward. The deceased locked herself in her private bathroom on the second floor and, after showering, threw herself off the accompanying balcony. Most regrettably, her body crashed through a greenhouse window and landed on concrete. An unpleasant end for such a talented singer.'

'Can I just verify that the door was bolted from the inside, not locked with a key?' asked Isabel.

'That is correct. Does it matter?'

'Yes, because if someone had a duplicate key, they could have entered the bathroom, killed Maria Rosselló, and locked the door after they'd done the deed.'

He gave a snort of laughter. 'I do love your vivid imagination, Isabel. Let's not get ahead of ourselves.'

'Has the medical examiner arrived yet?' Gaspar asked.

'They're all here and that includes Nacho and his forensics team. He's already started examining the body.'

'Has the bathroom been secured, Álvaro?' Isabel asked.

He shook his head impatiently. 'It's not a crime scene, Isabel. Besides, every man and his dog has walked through there this morning.'

'Tolo said that the husband had to break down the door.'

'Correct,' he replied, fixing her with his gimlet eyes. 'Roberto Pons, the gardener, was in the orchard and saw something that resembled a body floating down from the top floor, so he called Pepe Serrano, the husband, on his mobile. Señor Serrano and Raquel Tur, the maid, were in the cellar sorting fruit and immediately rushed upstairs. They found the door locked so the husband forced entry.'

Isabel frowned. 'It takes some strength to smash down a door, unless it was old.'

Capitán Gómez nodded. 'It's a rather ancient mahogany door. He managed to break the lock and gain access.'

'Where is he now?' asked Gaspar.

'He is downstairs with members of my team and will be expected to answer detailed questions shortly in Palma. The attendant judge and court examiner will want to see statements from the maid and gardener too. Understandably, all are in shock.'

Gaspar sighed. 'What a waste of a life.'

'Indeed,' he replied. 'I always think those who die by suicide are very selfish. Do they ever stop to think what trouble they'll cause?'

Isabel stifled an impatient growl. 'Did she leave a suicide note?'

'Not that I know of.' He glanced at his watch. 'Well, my job here is done. As my superiors have granted your force jurisdiction, I shall leave you both to it.'

Gaspar patted his shoulder. 'Thanks for doing a great job. We'll tie up any loose ends.'

Isabel watched as the Guardia captain climbed stiffly into his official military vehicle and sped off along the gravel track.

'Why does he always have to be so objectionable?' Isabel asked.

'Second nature, I guess. So, what next?'

Isabel headed towards the porch. 'Let's take a look at the upstairs bathroom. It should have been sealed off.'

'True, but Gómez has obviously ruled out foul play and the powers that be seem to want this case put to bed quickly.'

Isabel gave a grunt as both slipped into their white forensic suits and booties. She snapped on her latex gloves as they walked into the silent hallway. The perfectly preserved historic stone flooring was constructed from grey and white pebbles that ran in concentric circles. Elegant mahogany antique furniture and occasional tables, crammed with framed gilt-edged photographs and small objets d'art, were placed imaginatively about the room. Isabel walked towards the majestic marble staircase that curled up towards the roof. A slice of bright blue sky winked at her through a vast skylight.

'The ceilings in this place are so high.' She stood on the first step and looked over a banister pointed downwards. 'There's a steep staircase leading to a lower floor, presumably the cellar where the husband and maid were sorting out the fruit together. Bucolic bliss or plain weird?'

Gaspar grinned. 'How the other half live, eh?'

Isabel began climbing the stairs two at a time.

Gaspar cleared his throat. 'Maybe we should let someone know we're here?'

'We already have, and he's left. Come on.'

Somewhat hesitantly, he followed her, whistling at the sombre historic portraits that lined the ample stairwell. 'This is like a museum. Actually, it's a bit creepy.'

Isabel caught his eye. 'The house is supposed to be haunted. It's an emblematic property that dates back five hundred years.'

'How do you know that?' he puffed, stopping to catch his breath.

'I googled it,' she replied with a wink. 'It has a grisly history.'

He narrowed his eyes. 'You're just trying to wind me up.'

As they reached the first floor, Isabel turned to him. 'There's a separate narrow wooden staircase to the upper floor. It's probably where the servants would have had their quarters in a bygone era. I'm guessing this leads to Maria's bathroom.'

'How do you know?'

'Well, Gaspar, she was supposed to have fallen from the top floor of the house, remember?'

He shrugged and followed her up the creaky wooden staircase. On the gloomy landing, they were greeted by the sight of an open door whose lock had evidently been smashed. Wood splinters and debris lay about on the tiled floor. Before entering the room, Isabel tried the handle of a polished mahogany door on the right-hand side which gave onto a large, oak-floored studio. Inside, there was a grand piano, microphone and rows of chairs. Various music stands and a podium stood in a huddle by a white wall.

Gaspar looked around the large space. 'This was probably her practice room.'

Isabel nodded. 'Maybe she held rehearsals and small concerts here.'

She put her head around a door which led into a poky, airless room with floor to ceiling shelves of sheet music. A cream sofa with plump cushions and a blanket had been squeezed into a corner. Isabel took in the scene for a few seconds, closely examining the cushions and sofa, and closed the door.

Returning to the landing, she tried the handle of the door on the left, but it wouldn't budge. Her eyes opened in surprise, and she nudged Gaspar.

'There are five locks on this door. A bit bizarre.'

'Maybe the couple keep valuables in there.'

Isabel focused her attention on the broken door ahead of them. The brass bolt on the inside had buckled and come loose from the wood, presumably when the husband had smashed the door open. There was no lock so that ruled out the idea of duplicate keys. Stepping over the debris, she walked inside. She stood in the chic, serene bathroom and looked about her.

'No sign of any kind of struggle.'

Gaspar opened the wardrobe door and examined the luxurious cream silk negligées and cotton waffle bathrobes inside.

'Expensive garb in here. Italian and French labels.'

'Well, as our department's style icon, you should know.'

He chuckled. 'Designer brands are way above my pay grade, Bel. Besides, silk nighties aren't really my thing.'

As Gaspar strolled out onto the balcony, Isabel took her time checking the shower and bath area and examined the contents of the bathroom cupboard and shelves. She took out a box of unopened pills and read the label, taking an image of it on her iPhone. Next to the basin was a dish containing a gilt chain adorned with five heavy keys. She frowned. Presumably they fitted the locked door off the landing. Surely Maria wouldn't wear such a heavy necklace, though? Who was she trying to keep out? A small stone mortar and pestle caught her attention. Carefully lifting it off the glass shelf, she sniffed it and ran a finger around its interior. She photographed it and set it back on the shelf. Gaspar called to her from the balcony.

'Bel, are you coming?'

'Give me a sec.'

She bent down and opened a small pedal bin and pulled out its contents. It contained some used cotton pads and a spent pill packet. She turned it over and studied the tiny, typed script that ran across its foil wrapper, popped it into a plastic specimen bag along with the pads, and wandered outside. Gaspar was leaning over the balustrade, a pained expression on his face. Isabel joined him and winced at the destruction below. Broken glass and splintered wood covered the ground, while white-suited forensic officers pored over what appeared to be a corpse inside the damaged greenhouse. Isabel grimaced, thinking how like a mannequin the unnaturally pale, immobile form seemed. She gripped the railing.

'This is pretty flimsy. It would be easy to push someone over the edge.'

Gaspar stood up straight and shrugged. 'Or throw yourself over. No evidence that anyone pushed her, Bel.'

She nodded. 'I know. Just covering all the options.'

Gaspar frowned. 'Maybe she fell over the edge by accident.'

Isabel pressed her body against the railings and then used her hands to raise herself up. 'She'd have needed some ballast to do that. The railings aren't low enough to simply flip over unless you are fairly strong and athletic.'

Gaspar nodded. 'True, so we can probably rule that out.'

She held up the bag containing the empty pill packet. 'I found this in the bin. It's an empty packet of fentanyl. I wonder if a doctor prescribed it as a painkiller or she got it elsewhere. Pretty lethal stuff.'

'True. As synthetic opioids go, it's one of the strongest.' Gaspar took it from her and squinted at the script. 'Maybe she had some medical condition. Wasn't she a depressive too? Perhaps she took a cocktail of drugs before jumping to her death.'

Isabel seemed thoughtful. 'There are unused antidepressants in her medical cabinet. The expiry date was two years ago. If she took anything, it would most likely have been the fentanyl since we have the evidence. Then again, the pestle and mortar were wet, so maybe she used them shortly before her death to grind the pills, possibly with other substances, and then rinsed it out.'

He stared at her. 'What are you talking about?'

'There's a pestle and mortar on the bathroom shelf.'

'Missed that.'

Isabel tutted. 'We need the forensics team up here. The room should have been sealed immediately. Gómez cocked up.'

In the garden below, a familiar figure in white garb shielded his eyes and stared up at them. She waved at Nacho, and he returned the gesture and beckoned for them to join him.

They returned to the bathroom.

'Let's seal off the room for now. We'll get the forensics team to give it the once over,' Isabel said.

With her gloved hand, she picked up the chain with the five keys.

'These have to open the locked door on the landing.'

Gaspar stared at her. 'We don't really have the right to poke about in any of the rooms here without a warrant. What's so interesting about that room?'

'Well, I'm guessing it belongs to Tía Maria. Maybe it's her office.'

'It could be the couple's bedroom.'

'But the bathroom was only used by Tía Maria, so maybe she had her own room. If that's the case, why did she lock her own bedroom when the bathroom was only a few steps away?'

'There are lunatics everywhere,' he replied. 'Maybe she had valuables in there and didn't trust the maid.'

Despite Gaspar's protestations, Isabel picked up the keys and headed for the room in the hallway. She spent time unlocking all five locks and finally pushed open the heavy mahogany door. Gaspar gave a weak shrug of the shoulders.

'We don't have jurisdiction.'

'I just want to have a quick peek. Maybe she left a suicide note here?'

The large room was dominated by a voluptuous double bed adorned with an extravagant gold and cream satin cover embellished with embroidery and tiny pearls. The opulent bedspread had been peeled back on one side and was strewn with crimson and gold velvet cushions and large and small decorative lace-trimmed white pillows. Light poured in from elegant French windows at the far end of the room where a narrow balcony cast its gaze over the rear gardens and orchard.

Isabel bit on a nail. 'If she'd wanted to commit suicide, why didn't she use the balcony here? Unless she shares the room with her husband, but it doesn't look like it.' Isabel inspected the bed carefully. 'She sleeps here alone. The other side of the bed is untouched. I wonder where the husband sleeps. This bed linen must have cost a fortune. I'd guess that it's fine Egyptian cotton.' She looked about the walls and gave a low whistle, while Gaspar stood uncomfortably in the doorway. 'This art is the real deal. It's very dark and gothic.'

Gaspar puffed out his bottom lip. 'Who'd want to sleep surrounded by all that religious and operatic stuff? Some of those portraits are really sinister.'

'They're probably her ancestors,' she replied with a grin. 'See that portrait of an elderly man facing the bed? He has her eyes. I'm guessing it was her father or even grandfather.'

Gaspar pulled a face. 'That's a bit odd.'

Isabel walked over to an elegant chaise longue and ran her gloved hand along the tapestry upholstery. She approached an elaborate mahogany wardrobe built into the wall. It was embellished with carvings of animals and birds, and inlaid flowers were fashioned from mother of pearl. She frowned when she found the door firmly locked.

'Why would she lock her wardrobe?'

Gaspar gave a sigh. 'I have no idea, but as we shouldn't be in here, let's head out to the garden and catch up with Nacho and the forensics team. They'll be wondering where we are.'

Isabel examined the mahogany bedside cabinets with their gold-tasselled handles and checked the drawers of an elegant desk crammed with photographs in elegant frames. She sighed. 'Well, no obvious sign of a suicide note here.'

She used her mobile to take images of the photographs on the desk and locked the door behind them. Taking a plastic sample bag from her pannier, she slipped the keys on the gilt chain inside.

'I think we should take these. We don't want anyone entering the room until forensics have taken a look. That's providing there isn't another set.'

'This isn't supposed to be a crime scene,' Gaspar protested. 'Besides, I don't have any tape with me.'

Isabel smiled. 'I do.' She fumbled in her pannier and took out a roll of yellow and black sticky tape which had the words *'escena de crimen – no cruzar'* running throughout. She taped a section across both the bedroom and bathroom doorways, biting off the ends with her teeth.

'Classy,' remarked Gaspar with a shake of the head.

Next, she took out two large red stickers that read *'NO PASE'*, peeled off the backing and stuck one firmly across each of the door's locks and corresponding frame.

'It's just a precaution, Gaspar. We still don't have the whole story.'

He shrugged. 'Okay, but Gómez won't be happy.'

'He's no longer working the case,' she argued. 'Besides, we need to speak with the husband and staff to find out exactly what happened here. If they're being interviewed in Palma today, I can come back tomorrow.'

'Good plan. Tolo and I are at a meeting with the authorities in Arenal all morning about a recent stabbing incident, so if you're happy to question them alone, it would cut us some slack.'

'Of course.'

They walked back downstairs and made their way to the garden, where Nacho stood writing on a clipboard. He stepped forward and greeted them, clicking his teeth.

'Hope you haven't had breakfast. It's not pretty.'

'It never is,' she replied softly.

THREE

Isabel sat in her swivel chair, sucking on a Chupa Chup and wearily eyeing a screenful of unread emails on the computer, her thoughts miles away. An arthritic fan whirred monotonously but insistently on a bookshelf, fluttering a pile of papers on her desk that she'd secured with a limestone rock, a memento from one of her local mountain hikes. She was still haunted by images of the shattered body of Tía Maria, a woman at the peak of her career with seemingly everything to live for. She had left the forensics team to examine the opera singer's bathroom and bedroom in the vain hope of finding a suicide note or a clue as to how and why the woman had fallen to her death. Once she'd got the okay from Tolo, she would return to the house the following day to interview the husband, maid and gardener. Hopefully, they might shed some light on the matter. Idly, she looked across at Furó sleeping in his basket and had a sudden desire to bury her face in his soft warm pelt and hold him close. The phone rang, shaking her out of her sombre mood.

'*Diga?*'

'I wasn't sure you'd be back home from Inca yet. A success?'

AUNT MARIA'S LAST ARIA

Isabel smiled. 'I've ordered Furó a run, if that's what you mean. It's going to have lots of tunnels and games and even hammocks and bunks. After all, he might want to invite some ferrety friends here for sleepovers.'

He laughed. 'Please tell me you're joking?'

'Of course not. Only the best for Furó.' She sighed. 'Actually, I needed the distraction after visiting the crime scene.'

Tolo offered a sympathetic grunt. 'Gaspar's just debriefed me. He said it was a gruesome spectacle. By the way, I've arranged for the husband and staff members to meet you at the house tomorrow afternoon at five. The maid, then the gardener, followed by Pepe Serrano. Gaspar tells me you're not convinced that this is a suicide.'

'There's something not quite right about this case. Gómez is keen to wrap it up, but I feel there's a lot we still don't know.'

'Gómez is finalising his initial report, then we officially take over. What's on your mind?'

Isabel sighed. 'A few things. Why was there an empty packet of fentanyl in her bin and who might have prescribed it? It's such a powerful opioid. It's got about a hundred times more kick than morphine, as you know. The pestle and mortar I found on a bathroom shelf had recently been washed so we might assume that she'd smashed up the pills and downed them before jumping. All the same, what if Nacho finds no trace of fentanyl in her system?'

'He hopes to get us the post-mortem results this Thursday, so I guess we'll find out soon enough,' he replied.

'In the meantime, I'll do some digging. Are you coming over here tomorrow night?'

'Wild horses wouldn't stop me. Didn't you say you'd be doing risotto with *gambas rojas*?'

'Sometimes I wonder what attracts you most: me or my cooking.'

'I'll leave you to decide,' he replied. 'Happy digging, *cariño*, but be discreet and please don't wind up Gómez. I've got enough on my plate.'

Isabel finished the call. Smiling, she walked over to her open window and breathed in the hot and humid air. At the end of the month the storms would come, bringing cooler temperatures and much-needed rain. The tourists would be disappointed, but locals welcomed the inclement weather, grateful that the parched water channels running through their orchards would be filled, brittle soil softened, and thirsty plants revitalised. She watched as her hens, shielded by imperious Salvador the cockerel, chortled and clucked as they gathered under a shady orange tree. A pair of doves cooed from a stone wall and flitted off into the sky. Isabel turned as the door to her office banged open. A hot and bothered Pep stood before her clutching two large panniers full of laundered towels. His thick, black glossy hair fell across one eye.

'I'm going to take these over to Ca'n Verde as the new guests arrive tonight. The cleaning team need them now.'

Isabel waved her lollipop in the air. 'Sorry, Pep. Mama will take over when she's back on Saturday.'

He exhaled deeply. 'It's just a bit frantic without her and Idò, but we'll manage.'

'Can I do anything?'

'You're already handling guest enquiries and future bookings. And now you've got this new police case.'

'I can still help out here.'

'Well, I've just picked up a whole load of used sheets and towels from three of the *fincas* in Fornalutx. Any chance you can leave them at the laundry?'

Isabel looked past Pep and into the central office where several large bags of crumpled linen sat by his desk.

'No problem. I've got to answer a few urgent emails and then I'll go.'

Pep dropped the bags by his side and pushed the hair from his face. 'By the way, we've got competition.'

'Oh?' Isabel replied, looking up from her computer.

'There's a South African guy called Adam Markham who's setting up a rival holiday rentals business in the valley. Jesus was talking about it in Bon Día this morning. It's called Woning Luxury Living Real Estate Group.'

'That sounds more like he's selling properties. I thought you said he was doing holiday rentals.'

'He's doing both. I was at the post office this morning and Señora Coll whispered to me over the counter that he's been leaving calling cards all over the place. Apparently, he's offering to handle holiday lets and refurbish and sell properties. The agents in the valley are keeping an eye on him.'

Isabel stretched her back. 'There's room for everyone here, Pep. We have more than enough work, so let him do what he likes. The marathon runner looks straight ahead, never at those running beside or behind him.'

Pep frowned. 'What's that got to do with anything?'

'Life is about striking your own path, Pep, not being distracted by what others are doing around you. Envy is like an insidious ivy that grips you by the neck and won't let go. Better to be creative and a pioneer, rather than worrying about potential rivals.'

He clicked his teeth. 'I get that, but say he starts nicking our clients? Jesus says he's already signed up three clients in Soller.'

'Good for him. Meanwhile, I suggest we get on with our work and stop hypothesising about what may or may not happen. Adam Markham may turn out to be a breath of fresh air in the valley.'

Pep tutted impatiently and headed off into the office as Isabel's mobile rang. She groaned when she saw Josep Casanovas' name flash up on the screen and crunched on the last sweet morsels of her Chupa Chup. The editor of *El Periódico*, the island's leading newspaper, wore two hats these days, but she had a feeling she knew which he'd be wearing on this call.

'Well, if it isn't the esteemed mayor of Forn de Camp.'

He gave a titter. 'It is indeed, although I'm calling with my editorial cap on.'

'You surprise me,' she replied crisply.

'It's about the tragic suicide of Maria Rosselló Morales.'

'The opera singer?' exclaimed Isabel in mock surprise.

'Come on, Bel.'

'It hasn't been officially announced yet. How do you know about it?'

He laughed. 'I have my sources, and before you ask, an old friend called me this morning with the news. She happens to be one of her neighbours in Moscari. Quite a scoop.'

'When are you publishing the story?'

'Tomorrow morning.'

Isabel rolled her eyes. 'Can't you wait until the official announcement is issued by her family?'

'I'm running a newspaper, Bel. I could have issued something online today, but out of decency, I decided to wait.'

'Aren't you a hero.'

'I just wondered if Cabot had filled you in on anything. There's speculation that she was taking antidepressants.'

'Even if I did have such privileged information, I'd hardly be broadcasting it, Josep. I thought you knew me better.'

'It was worth a punt. If you hear anything, you know where to find me.'

Isabel threw the mobile onto her desk and walked into the main office. Pep had already left with his bags of laundry but had left a note on his desk for her. It read: *Trempó salad, coca and a tortilla in the fridge. Cake in pantry. Thank Rosa.* Isabel clasped her hands together in delight. Pep's mother was an excellent cook and had fretted that she and Pep would starve when Florentina was away. The fact that Isabel was an accomplished cook herself cut no ice with Rosa. She was a traditional housewife and simply couldn't grasp how Isabel could competently juggle work and kitchen duties at the same time. Frankly, Isabel rather liked being cosseted in this way by the older women of the village. As a lover of homemade dishes, especially Mallorcan specialities, how could she resist? Besides, it would be insulting to refuse such thoughtful gestures.

Isabel decided to deal with her emails later. With a brief smile in Furó's direction, she grabbed the bags of linen and walked downstairs to the *entrada*. The internal shutters on the French windows were closed to keep out the intense heat so the room was dark and cool. Isabel switched on the light in the shuttered kitchen and opened the fridge door to get a bottle of water. To her delight, she saw several foil-covered dishes lining the shelves. What a feast she would have later. Hastily, she closed her front door and strode along the garden path, wincing to see patches of yellowed grass on her lawn. Flower heads drooped and only the oleander, rosemary and bougainvillea bushes appeared perky. Luckily, her basil, mint and coriander plants had so far survived the heat as she'd kept them under the shade of her porch. Clicking the gate, she piled the bags into the boot of her beloved vintage Fiat 500 and jumped into the driving seat. She revved the engine and gave the dashboard an affectionate pat.

'Forgive me for ignoring you, dear Pequeñito, but life has been busy.'

She flicked the indicator and frowned when Pequeñito gave a squeal and began to chunter.

'What's that you say? We need to discuss the elephant in the room? I take it you're referring to why I chose to ride Boadicea to Palma and Moscari this morning instead of travelling with you? A good question.'

She turned out onto the empty cobbled street, sensing that it was about three o'clock, *siesta* time, when thankfully, local roads were mostly traffic-free.

'I apologise, but you know how congested it is in the summer. Sometimes taking a *moto* to Palma is much faster and I can weave in and out of traffic. Of course, you will always be my first choice, and Furó's too.'

The little car grumbled and gasped but was soon coursing happily along the mountain roads, invigorated by the fresh air and exercise. Isabel hoped she'd been forgiven. Resting her elbow on the edge of the open window, she sang raucously and drank in the glorious views. No matter how stressful life could be, just the sight of the verdant Tramuntanas and the fragrance of fresh thyme in the balmy air filled her heart with hope and joy.

Later that evening, Isabel sat on her candlelit terrace, sipping on a glass of ruby-red wine and admiring the clusters of stars in the sky. Furó snuffled around her bare feet beneath the table and whimpered when a gecko escaped his clutches and shimmied up a nearby pillar.

'He was too fast for you, Furó,' she said. 'Just think, soon you'll have your very own playpen out here. You could even invite some ferret friends here for sleepovers. What do you think?'

Furó jumped onto her lap and began burrowing under her linen serviette. Yawning, she pulled his head free and stroked his soft furry ears and whiskers. There came the sound of loud splashing and croaking from Isabel's *depósito* at the far end of the orchard. Isabel loved her chorus of ebullient frogs who came to life as soon as dusk fell. She knew they'd be partying into the night while her resident barn owl looked on with disapproval. Gently tipping Furó onto the ground, she rose and stacked up the empty dishes and carried them carefully into the kitchen. She washed up and, making sure that Furó was safely inside, locked the kitchen door and headed for the stairs with the remnants of her wine.

No sooner had she switched on the hall light than her mobile purred from her back pocket. In some irritation, Isabel saw that it was Josep Casanovas calling.

'I am popular tonight, Josep,' she said.

'I'm sorry for the late call, Bel, but I thought you might be interested in something.'

'Go on,' she replied without enthusiasm.

'It's about Tía Maria. I was doing some research for tomorrow's paper and happened upon an old news story which I'd forgotten about.' There was a pause. 'Apparently, three years ago, someone sent her poisonous mushrooms. They were delivered as a gift in a nice box, but she was suspicious and had them analysed. It turned out they would have made her extremely ill or even killed her.'

Isabel was alert. 'I don't remember reading about it.'

'The story was more or less knocked on the head by my boss at the time. He was under pressure from the Conservatori de Opera and local politicians not to publicise it. In the end, it was buried at the bottom of a page and received no other coverage.'

'Did they find out who'd sent them?'

'It was assumed that it was a disgruntled student. Maybe a prank gone wrong. Anyway, the culprit was never found.'

Isabel breathed heavily into the receiver. 'Please tell me you're not going to mention this in your news story tomorrow?'

He laughed. 'Of course not, Bel. I'm not that fickle. All the same, let's keep in touch. Maybe there's more to this suicide than we know.'

After she'd killed the call, Isabel stood in the *entrada*, her mind a whirl. Who had sent Tía Maria the mushrooms and why? Increasingly, the opera singer's sudden death seemed to be throwing up more troubling questions than answers. Tomorrow, she would meet with the husband and staff members. Perhaps they would shed more light on the matter. Until then, she would get some shut eye. Isabel had a feeling it was going to be another long day. So much for it being a quiet summer.

FOUR

A plump orange sun floated on the horizon like a giant beachball on a calm, azure sea. Isabel whisked a damp curl from her forehead as she studied a copy of *El Periódico* on the upstairs terrace of Bar Castell. She finished the article by Josep Casanovas and gave a deep sigh of relief. He had been true to his word and not written about how the opera singer had once been sent poisonous mushrooms. If her death was proven to be suspicious, the less information in the public domain, the better. She looked up when a baby dove flew onto the table and began pecking at crumbs on her plate. Having enjoyed an early swim with Furó at Can Repic beach, she had returned to Sant Martí for a robust breakfast at Bar Castell. Rafael, the longstanding owner, had presented her with a fluffy *ensaïmada* pastry and a *cortado* while he busied himself in the kitchen preparing her scrambled eggs and tomatoes. To Furó's delight, Rafael had also treated him to a small bowl of raw steak, which he'd demolished in a matter of seconds. Now he pattered about beneath the table, his fur still glistening with briny water, waiting patiently for his mistress to finish her breakfast. Replete and at peace with the world, Isabel observed the dove's soft downy feathers and innocent brown eyes.

'Be careful, my little friend. Not all humans will welcome you to their table.'

The dove cooed in reply and, having had its fill, fluttered away. Isabel folded the newspaper and stood up. She wandered over to the railings and looked down onto the quiet and shady *plaça*. As usual, Jesus was puffing on a large Cuban cigar under the awning of Bon Día, the village's grocery store. Freshly delivered boxes of brightly-hued vegetables and fruit were piled up at the entrance, awaiting his attention, but Jesus took his time in the morning, enjoying his first puff of the day. Soon enough his shop, a mecca for locals and visiting hikers and cyclists, would be buzzing with life, but at this early hour, it was empty. Jesus stepped forward onto the sunny pavement and looked up at her. Isabel smiled.

'I've had a delivery of Chupa Chups, if you're interested.'

'Of course,' she called. 'I'll be down in a minute.'

As she turned to pick up her pannier, with Furó hot on her heels, she noticed a man observing her from the open doorway. He was lean and tall with boyish good looks and an impish grin.

The man lowered his gaze to Furó. Bending down, he extended a hand in his direction. To Isabel's surprise, Furó sniffed him warily and allowed the stranger to stroke him.

'What's your name, little fella?'

'Furó.' Isabel squinted at him in the sunlight. 'You're honoured. He's not usually so accommodating with new friends.'

He laughed. 'I grew up on a farm and had two pet ferrets. I take it you're the famed Isabel Flores. I'm Adam Markham. I've recently moved to the valley.'

Though not a native English speaker, Isabel picked up on the South African accent, one she had always found attractive. She shook his hand.

'A pleasure. I've heard a lot about you.'

He grimaced. 'Not all good, I bet. I seem to have ruffled a lot of feathers with local real estate agents.'

Isabel offered him an enigmatic smile. 'We cannot please all of the people all of the time. I think that's what the English monk, John Lydgate, was supposed to have said.'

'I wouldn't have a clue.' He laughed. 'But it's true. All the same, I just want to assure you that I have no intention of stepping on your toes. I'm a great admirer of your rentals business. You've got a great brand and formula.'

'Really? I always think it's rather unformulaic.'

'Sorry, what I mean is that you have a great reputation, and everyone respects your agency.'

'That's nice to hear. So, what brought you to Soller, Señor Markham?'

He ran a tanned hand through his glossy, sun-streaked hair. It fell in soft layers to the collar of his baby-blue linen shirt.

'Please, call me Adam. I'm not one for formalities.'

Isabel smiled. 'Neither am I.'

'So, Isabel, I come from a family of long-established realtors in Cape Town. We refurbish old houses and sell them on, as good as new with stylish interiors and fittings. When my old man was alive, the family used to come here on holiday during the summer. We rented places in Biniaraix and threw ourselves into village life, so I've always had a love of this valley. My girlfriend, Liv, suffers from psoriasis and finds that sunshine really helps the condition.'

'You have a lot of sun in Cape Town.'

'True, but we also have a lot of crime, and Liv has become really stressed about it, so I suggested we move here instead.'

'She isn't South African?'

'Liv is Dutch. She was working for an NGO in Cape Town. That's how we met.'

Isabel nodded. 'So, what kind of business are you setting up here?'

'Fewer rentals and more refurbishment of old and grotty buildings with potential. We're looking to attract the luxury market for holiday rental and purchases. Of course, we'll manage everything from start to finish to take the pain away for householders. No offence, but you seem to aim for more middle-income folk and family groups.'

'We don't have a lot of Hollywood A-listers on our books, if that's what you mean.'

He offered her a coy smile. 'Exactly. Those are the guys we're aiming at, and of course local residents who want someone to elevate their properties to sell at an enhanced profit.'

'And who are your ideal purchasers and renters?'

'Foreigners with big bucks who are looking to grow their property portfolios or rent. Most of these guys are looking for sound investments, though some simply want a holiday place in the sun.'

'The majority will leave their homes vacant for most of the year while locals struggle to find fair-priced accommodation in the valley.'

He grinned. 'Sadly, the way of the world, Isabel.'

She offered him a blank stare. 'Well, I wish you good luck.'

Adam stepped away from the doorway to let her and Furó pass. 'Actually, I could do with some luck. We've been met with some hostility and even threats.'

Isabel frowned. 'What do you mean?'

He shrugged. 'Put it this way: when someone leaves a dead seagull outside your office door, you know you're not exactly Mr Popular.'

'I'm really sorry to hear that. Have you any idea of the culprit?'

'No, but frankly, it could be one of several agents who've warned us off.'

'I'm surprised to hear that. I've never had a problem with competitors around here.'

'But you're a local.' He winked. 'Anyway, it's worse in South Africa. Once, a rival realtor threatened to kill my dad and even turned up at our house with a shotgun. It can be like the Wild West down there.'

'Maybe,' Isabel replied. 'But we don't tolerate Wild West behaviour here in our valley.'

He reached into a leather portfolio and planted a shiny brochure in Isabel's hands. 'This'll give you an idea of my new business model.'

Isabel thanked him and winced inwardly at the strapline on the cover: *Get off to a flying start finding your perfect home. At Woning Luxury Living, we make dreams come true.*

They walked through to the bar area, where Rafael stood arranging a display of gin bottles. He wore a cynical smirk on his face as Adam Markham bid farewell effusively to Isabel and jogged down the stairs to the street.

Isabel turned to Rafael with a raised eyebrow. 'He's an interesting character.'

He gave a snort. 'A pretty boy in a fancy suit. Watch him, Bel. He's after your business, whatever he might tell you.'

Isabel reached over the counter and patted his arm. She was always touched by how protective the villagers were of their own.

'Don't worry. I'll be keeping an eye on our South African friend. He may surprise us all.'

Rafael shook his head and leant forward confidentially. 'You don't seem to know about Juan.'

Isabel pushed out her bottom lip. 'Juan Jaume? What about him?'

'Late last night, I arrived back from seeing my mother in Es Pla and saw Juan and his boy having a right set-to in the *plaça*. They were shouting at one another, and Manuel was blind drunk, as usual. I tried to calm the situation, but they were going at it hammer and tongs, so I called Pau. Thankfully, he was still on duty and took Manuel home.'

'We're lucky to have such a dedicated local police officer as Pau, but what were they arguing about?'

'It seems that Juan has signed a deal with that South African guy to refurbish and sell his home and Manuel evidently was hoping to get his hands on it when his old dad died. Added to that, Juan told Manuel that he intended to change his will.'

'It's his money,' Isabel replied. 'Besides, Manuel is in his forties now. Time he fended for himself.'

'True, but he's living in that shack on the edge of the village without a job and has accused his dad of neglect. A bit rich when you consider that Juan gave him a lump of money a few years ago and the idiot blew it all on drugs and alcohol. That lad is a nasty piece of work.'

'But what's your point?' asked Isabel.

'That the South African guy is causing family divisions. I've also just heard that mad old Irish woman, Bridget Kelly, who lives up by the *torrente*, has signed her house over to him for a refurb and sale.'

Isabel gave a sigh. 'I don't think we can blame Adam Markham for the fractious relationship that exists between Juan and his son, and if Bridget wants to sell her house through him, that really is her decision.'

'You're too trusting,' grumbled Rafa. 'That's your problem.'

'Quite the contrary, Rafa,' Isabel replied. 'But I like to give everyone the benefit of the doubt.'

Despite Rafael's protestations, she left a handful of coins on the counter and headed for the *plaça*. After stocking up on Chupa Chup lollies and sunflower seeds at Bon Día, she strolled over to the fountain and took a draught of water. Moments later, someone tapped her on the shoulder. She swivelled round. It was Padre Agustí. He wore a troubled expression and fiddled with a set of rosary beads.

'Is everything alright, Padre?'

He shook his head. 'A terrible thing has occurred, Bel. The bells of Sant Antoní have given up the ghost.'

Isabel looked up at the façade of the Baroque church looming over the square and gave a sympathetic murmur. 'It seems that the clock has stopped working too.'

'What?' he exclaimed in horror. 'Double trouble.'

'I'm sure it's easily fixed.'

'Not so, Bel. The mechanism in the bell tower is complicated. It's very old and so is the clock face. I have an engineer coming all the way from Manacor today, but the last time he visited, he warned that the pulleys were showing signs of wear and tear. I fear that we have a broken wood stay too and as for the clock, who knows.'

'Why not wait until he comes before jumping to conclusions?' She pointed towards the sky. 'Maybe it's time to have a private word with the big man upstairs.'

He nodded slowly. 'Ah, yes! Whyever didn't I think of that? Thank you, Bel. I will pray to our Almighty for a solution. Now

I must visit Señor Rubiol. He has bronchitis and is very poorly. I shall be reading him pages from the New Testament, which will hopefully lighten his mood.'

Isabel smiled encouragingly and lifted the ferret into her arms. Once the priest was out of earshot, she giggled.

'Did you hear that, Furó? Poor old Señor Rubiol. A captive audience, unable to escape from his bed. As if being ill isn't bad enough!'

Furó sneezed and made clucking noises.

'Okay, you want your kibble and basket. Let's go home and find out what Pep has been up to.'

Isabel sang softly as she walked along Calle Pastor, admiring the flowering pink and white oleander bushes that lined the quiet cobbled street. When she reached the gate of Ca'n Moix, she turned to face the mighty Tramuntanas that dazzled in the distance, emblazoned by sunlight. As soon as the summer heat subsided, she looked forward to getting back to hiking and enjoying the peace and beauty of the hills once more. Pep looked up as Isabel strode into the central office and turned down the music playing on his smartphone.

'Llorenç called. He says you're having lunch with him today.'

'Correct, though I almost forgot.'

'Isn't Tolo coming over here for dinner tonight too?'

Isabel observed her assistant with narrowed eyes. 'Just because I'm having three square meals today does not mean I'm pigging out.'

He tittered. 'At least you left me some of my mother's scraps for lunch.'

'Don't give me that, the fridge is groaning with food, thanks to Rosa. Your wonderful mama's cooking is fantastic. I need to buy her a thank you gift.'

Pep shook his head. 'No way. She'd be offended. She feels it's her duty to stand in for Florentina while she's away. It makes her so happy.'

Isabel groaned when her mobile rang and the name 'Gómez' flashed up on the screen. She walked slowly into her office, where Furó was already tucking into his bowl of kibble.

'Álvaro, good to hear from you.'

He gave an irritated cough. 'Yesterday, my duty officers over at the house of Maria Rosselló Morales told me that you'd sealed off the bathroom and the couple's bedroom. Whyever would you do that?'

Isabel inhaled deeply. 'Until we know conclusively that she committed suicide, I'd rather act with caution. The bathroom is a potential crime scene and the bedroom too. We need to search both thoroughly for any clues.'

'Clues to what? The bathroom door was bolted from the inside. Unless a murderous ghost was in there, I think suicide is a fairly obvious conclusion.'

'But we only have the husband's word that the door was locked.'

Capitán Gómez gave an exasperated sigh. 'The maid was with him and also confirmed that was the case. What further proof do you need, Isabel?'

'I shall be interviewing them both later today and will form my own opinion. Besides, we need to wait for the forensic report and results of the post-mortem.'

'The truth is that the president and various local ministers feel that it would be more dignified for the family if the funeral could go ahead as soon as possible. The last thing they want is idle speculation about how the poor woman died when it's painfully obvious. The event has been arranged for next Wednesday at the cemetery in Inca and both the president and the minister of culture will be present.'

'That seems a little premature. Isn't it best to wait for the forensic results?'

'I'm not sure what Tolo Cabot feels about this case now that he's in charge, but we are all under pressure to bring the matter to a speedy close. The Señora was evidently a sad and very unstable woman. There are so many in this world, Isabel.'

She rolled her eyes and reached for a Chupa Chup. 'Gaspar and I found a gold chain with five heavy brass keys on it in the bathroom. We subsequently discovered that they fitted five locks on a bedroom door off the same landing. It definitely belonged to the victim. Don't you find that odd?'

'People are odd, Bel. Just because some couples have five locks on their bedroom door proves nothing.'

'I don't think the husband sleeps there. Only one side of the bed had been slept in.'

'So what? Countless couples have their own rooms. I speak from experience.'

Isabel ploughed on. 'There was an empty packet of fentanyl in the bathroom bin. We need to know if she took an overdose before her death or perhaps it held another purpose.'

'My advice is to put this sorry case to bed as soon as possible. As I explained, I have a far more pressing criminal investigation on my hands. The last thing any of us needs is the president on our backs. I'm sure Tolo feels the same.'

'As head of homicide for the National Police, I'm sure Tolo can justify to him why we need to look more closely at this case.'

'It's not that simple, Isabel. The president has made it clear to both our forces that he wants to cause the family as little pain as possible and to give Maria Rosselló a quick and decent burial away from the prying eyes of the media. In September, a dignified memorial will be held in her honour.'

For some minutes after the call, Isabel sat at her desk sucking on a Chupa Chup, deep in thought. Why was the president keen to have poor Tía Maria buried so hastily? Was there something more to this case than met the eye?

It was three o'clock when Isabel and the mayor of Sant Martí finally left Can Busquets, the village restaurant, after a light and scrumptious lunch of grilled seabass and *trempó* salad, washed down with a glass of cool rosé. They had discussed the upcoming sixtieth birthday of Alfonso, the village's resident artist, and resolved to hold a surprise party for the much-loved member of the community later in the month. He now lived alone, having lost his long-time husband, and would never think himself worthy of such fuss. As they walked slowly along Calle Amar, Llorenç stopped abruptly and threw out both arms, his eyes glued to a large billboard on one of the walls of Taller Bernat, the local mechanic's garage. The poster sported the logo of Woning Luxury Living with its white seagull motif, and the image of a spotless contemporary kitchen. Underneath were the words, 'Aim high, and live your best life.'

Llorenç mopped his brow and turned to Isabel. 'What does that even mean?'

'If you're an aspiring chef, it might have resonance,' she teased. 'That's quite a cool kitchen.'

'As I said to you over lunch, these rich foreigners are taking over our valley. Look at Deia. You'd have to use a magnifying glass to spot a local these days. We even have Germans opening a hiking shop here in Sant Martí.'

'Actually, Hans and Romi are Swiss, and we do need a shop for hikers and cyclists. They've restored a dingy abandoned property and given it purpose.'

Llorenç grunted. 'The worst are the greedy speculators and investors. And what about all these young holidaymakers taking pictures of themselves with mobiles on metal poles and getting drunk in the *plaça* at night? They drink and shout until the early hours, keeping law-abiding citizens awake. While they sleep until midday, the rest of us have to get up for work.'

'Fair enough, but it's the same every summer. The person most to blame is Jordi for keeping his bar open so late and ignoring the law. Besides, they're not that disruptive. By midnight, they've all left.'

Llorenç sniffed indignantly. 'We need to keep control of our village, or it will become a circus here. As for this Markham bloke, we don't need any more estate agents in the valley wooing residents with promises of big profits. It'll go to their heads.'

In the *plaça*, Isabel leant forward to kiss him on both cheeks.

'Don't worry about Sant Martí. We'll never let it become a circus.'

'I hope you're right,' he grumbled.

She patted his arm. 'By the way, those metal poles are called selfie sticks. *El palo selfie.*'

He pulled a face. 'A terrible, egotistical invention. They should be banned.'

Isabel watched as Llorenç scuttled over to the town hall building and, with effort, pulled open one of the arched wooden doors. She cast her gaze upon the clock face of Sant Antoní, whose black hands remained frozen in time at just past five-thirty. Isabel hoped that the engineer would find the root of the problem. Both the village mayor and priest were out of sorts today, but soon everything would be resolved. The church bells and clock face would be repaired, and the hot and sticky summer would soon be over, allowing Sant Martí to revert once more to its sleepy and peaceful state. She smiled to herself and headed for Calle Pastor, where Pequeñito sat quietly under a plane tree. Once she'd polished off some emails back in the office, they would set off together for Moscari. Isabel was eager to interview Tía Maria's husband and staff. Whether they would be able to answer the many questions swirling in her head she couldn't say, but even one small revelation or clue might be enough to determine whether the opera singer's death was by suicide or whether more sinister forces were at play.

FIVE

Isabel arrived in Moscari as the sun was waning in the sky. It was still humid but sullen. Grey clouds had gathered on the horizon and drops of rain landed heavily on the windscreen.

'Hurrah!' she cried, patting the dashboard. 'Just what we need after all this heat, Pequeñito. Let's hope it's a downpour.'

As the little car came to a juddering stop at the gates, a bored-looking Guardia officer gave Isabel's police badge a cursory glance and waved her on. She parked up by the porch and checked that she had her notebook, pen and phone in her pannier before leaving the car. A solemn young woman in a black dress observed her from the front door and came forward to greet her with an open umbrella.

'Are you Señorita Flores? I'm Raquel Tur. I work for Tía Maria and Tío Pepe.' She extended the umbrella to cover both their heads. 'Well, not Tía Maria anymore…'

Isabel nodded. 'You are the housekeeper?'

The woman shook her head and led her up the shallow steps of the porch. 'More a maid than housekeeper. Aside from the weekends, I come in every day to help with cooking and cleaning.'

They walked into the cool and sombre *entrada*.

'Your boss's death must have come as a terrible shock to you.'

Raquel's eyes filled with tears. 'It was so unexpected. I still can't believe it happened. Can I get you some lemonade or coffee?'

'Lemonade would be lovely. Where can we chat?'

'The kitchen is quiet.'

'Perfect.' Isabel smiled. 'I'm also here to see your gardener, Roberto Pons, and the Señora's husband, Pepe Serrano.'

The woman nodded. 'Yes, Roberto knows to come here after we've spoken. The police officer who rang suggested twenty minutes for each interview and that you would want more time with Tío Pepe. The Señor has asked us to call him when you're done with us.'

They walked into the kitchen.

'Let's get started, then,' said Isabel gently as she took a seat at the kitchen table.

As she sipped on her cold drink, she looked around. The room had a large gleaming stainless-steel cooker and contemporary fittings and fixtures. One wall was given over to elegant wooden cupboards and a dresser decked with stylish earthenware pottery. The buttermilk-hued woodwork blended seamlessly with the creamy marble worktops, all offset by warm terracotta floor tiles. Raquel sat opposite her, nursing an espresso.

Isabel offered a reassuring smile. 'I notice you referred to your *jefes* as Tía Maria and Tío Pepe. Is that an affectionate name for them both? It's kind of funny given the association. Was that intentional?'

The woman eyed her intently, a lack of comprehension in her eyes. 'It's what everyone calls them locally. They're affectionate nicknames. I don't know of any association.'

Isabel smiled. 'You know, the sherry brand Tío Pepe and the coffee liqueur Tía Maria.'

'I'd never thought of that,' she replied awkwardly.

'Really? Must be just the way my mind works. So, tell me about yesterday morning. What time did you get here?'

'Around seven-fifteen, as usual.'

'That's early.'

'The Señora always likes – I mean liked – her breakfast ready by eight-thirty. Señor Serrano is an early riser too, so he and I would sort through the vegetables and fruit left by Roberto before I made her breakfast.'

'What did the Señora usually eat?'

'It was always the same. Blueberries and raspberries with coconut milk chia pudding and mixed seeds followed by two poached eggs, sauteed spinach and grilled mushrooms.'

'Sounds delicious.' Isabel felt her stomach rumble and quickly tapped her pen against her chin. 'And what about her husband?'

'He makes himself a coffee and waits to eat until lunchtime. He's a good cook so we often prepare dishes together.'

'What happened yesterday morning?'

'I was in the cellar sorting through a big basket of fruit when Roberto suddenly rang my mobile to say he'd seen something white floating down from what seemed to be Tía Maria's balcony. He sounded anxious and told me it looked like a body had fallen. He said he was on his way from the orchard to the side garden below Tía Maria's bathroom.'

'What time was this?'

'It was just before eight. Not long before, I'd checked my watch as I needed to prepare the Señora's breakfast.'

Isabel raised an inquisitive eyebrow. 'What did you do?'

'I told Roberto that I would let Tío Pepe know and that we would go and check on her.'

'Where was the Señor at that moment?'

She hesitated, her brows knitted in concentration. 'It all happened so quickly but he'd been in the kitchen with me until I went down to the cellar to sort out the fruit.'

'I thought you usually did that together?'

'Yes, we do, but Tío Pepe said he had to go to his room first.'

'The couple's bedroom on the second floor?'

'They have separate bedrooms. His is on the ground floor.'

'How long was he away from you?'

Raquel shrugged. 'Maybe ten minutes. To be honest, I was quite absorbed with my work. I can't say exactly. Not long.'

'So what happened next?'

'I ran up the stairs to the kitchen and called out his name. Then he appeared at the door and asked what the matter was. I told him about Roberto's call.'

'How did he react?'

'He was quite calm and suggested we go immediately upstairs to investigate. We got to the top floor but found the bathroom door locked. He started banging on it and shouting out, 'Maria! Maria!' but nothing happened. In the end, he put his weight against it and finally the door burst open. He was shaking and gasping with the effort. He's got a bad back.'

'Did you try the door handle yourself?'

Raquel frowned. 'No. I saw Tío Pepe turning the brass handle both ways, but it didn't seem to budge. He entered first and showed me that the bolt had broken away from the wood on the inside.'

'What did you find in the bathroom?'

The young woman bit a nail in agitation. 'Nothing. It was empty, but the French windows were wide open. We rushed onto the terrace and that's when we saw down below that something had crashed through the greenhouse.'

'What did you both do?'

She dabbed at her eyes with a shaky hand. 'We rushed downstairs to the garden and found glass shards lying all around the greenhouse. The Señor was as pale as milk and told me to stay back while he went inside. Then I heard panting and Roberto arrived. He was out of breath and asking what had happened, but I didn't know. I remember that he looked terrified when he saw all the glass and also ran inside the greenhouse. Minutes later, they both came out and told me that they'd found Tía Maria, and that she was dead.'

She burst into tears. Isabel sprung to her feet and pulled out a chair next to her. She placed an arm around her shoulder.

'You've had a terrible trauma. It's natural to cry.'

Raquel sobbed in her arms.

'The worst thing is that I didn't like Tía Maria. She was always so mean to me, but I never wished her dead.'

As Isabel endeavoured to comfort her, she heard footsteps and an affable, bearded face appeared around the door.

'Sorry to disturb you, but I was told to be here for an interview?'

Isabel stood up slowly. 'And you are?'

'I'm Roberto Pons.'

'Great. Just the man I wanted to see. Take a seat. Raquel and I have just finished.'

With a watery smile, Raquel rose to her feet, thanked Isabel, and hurried out of the room.

Roberto turned to her.

'Poor girl. She's been in such a state. Well, we all have.' He shook his head. 'I still can't believe what happened. It doesn't feel real.'

Isabel nodded. 'Of course. This is painful, but can you take me through what happened when you arrived here yesterday?'

'I got here at six-thirty as I do in the summer to avoid the heat. I walked to the orchard and as usual on a Tuesday and Thursday, picked the ripest fruit and left it in a basket outside the kitchen door. Raquel takes it in when she arrives and washes and sorts the fruit out with the Señor.'

'You only collect fruit on those two days?'

'Sometimes it's vegetables too. I spend the rest of the week working on the land. There's a lot to do.'

'I can imagine. Is it far to the orchard on foot?'

'About fifteen minutes.'

'What did you do then?'

He shrugged. 'I returned to the orchard and took the tractor around a patch I'm cultivating. It must have been getting on for eight o'clock. I stopped to have my *merienda*, a *bocadillo de jamon*, which I'd brought with me, and I was looking towards the house. Suddenly, something caught my eye. It was a biggish white object falling fast from the second floor.'

'Did you suspect then that it was a body?'

He breathed heavily. 'I was too far away to be sure, but I had a bad feeling about it. I knew that Tía Maria's bathroom was upstairs on that side of the house, so I quickly rang Raquel and asked her to check on the Señora. Meanwhile, I got off the tractor and ran to the garden.'

His face became pale, and beads of sweat broke out on his forehead. 'I'm sorry, but it's horrible to replay everything again. I had flashbacks last night.'

Isabel got up and opened the door of the huge fridge. She found the lemonade jug in the side bar, plucked a glass from the draining board, and placed both in front of him. He poured himself a drink and ran a handkerchief over his face.

'Normally, I have Brut, my young Labrador, with me, but he was poorly and at home yesterday. I had to take him to the local vet the night before as he had an upset stomach. I'm glad he didn't have to see the Señora in that terrible state.'

Isabel leant forward confidentially. 'And so you ran to the garden?'

'Yes, and just as I got there, I saw Raquel standing by the greenhouse. There was broken glass and split wood all over the ground and the roof had caved in. I asked her what had happened, but she was in complete shock, so I ran inside. I found the Señor crouching over the body of his wife.' He closed his eyes for a second and gripped the table edge. 'She was unrecognisable. Just a bloodied mess and her limbs were at odd angles. Her white nightdress was saturated in blood and in shreds and what was left of her head was just pulp. Horrible.'

'How was Señor Serrano?'

'He was very quiet and just stood looking at the ground.'

'Who called the police?'

He gave a sniff and wiped his eyes with the back of a hand. 'The Señor did that. We were all just standing there in shock, but after a few minutes, he took out his mobile and rang our local village police officer, who must have alerted the Guardia Civil.'

'Is there anything else you remember or think is important to mention?'

He was quiet for a moment. 'A silly thing.' He gulped hard. 'But the only way I really knew it was her was by the gold heart locket that still hung around her neck. She always wore it.'

For some time after Roberto had left the kitchen, Isabel sat and scribbled into her black notebook. The gardener had promised to alert Pepe Serrano to her presence, so she awaited his arrival. Moments later, the door sprang open, and a tall and wiry figure came into view. Isabel took in the thick pewter hair, swept back from the face, the faded jeans and old white linen shirt that exposed the dark olive skin of his arms. She noted that the fingers were long and elegant, the nails groomed. She extended her hand.

'Señor Serrano, I presume. I am Isabel Flores. I am so sorry for your loss.'

The large, impenetrable eyes rested on her face. He offered a cursory nod and pulled out a chair across from her. 'Thank you, but please call me Pepe. I don't stand on ceremony. It's been a troubling time.'

'I'd imagine so. I won't keep you too long.'

He shrugged. 'I have all the time in the world these days. Ask what you like.'

'Are you retired, then?'

He offered a ghost of a smile. 'I work in a cash and carry near Inca. I'm the stock controller, but my life is unhurried.'

Isabel absorbed this information carefully. 'Is the job manual?'

'Not so much now. I have a small team that use mechanical equipment to do most of the lifting and carrying of stock. I'm sixty-five, so I have to watch my back.'

'Why is that?'

He looked surprised. 'I had a herniated disc in the lower back some years ago, so I try not to overdo it. The joys of ageing.'

Isabel smiled. 'I'm curious about your current job as I believe you were once a lawyer.'

'You've done your homework, I see. Yes, I studied at La Universidad de Navarra in Pamplona. My practice there specialised in tax law, and laterally, criminal law.'

'When did you come to Mallorca?'

He puffed out his bottom lip. 'Fifteen years ago, I was a guest at one of Maria's concerts in Pamplona. At the after party, we were introduced to one another by mutual friends, and we struck up an unlikely friendship.'

'Why unlikely?' Isabel asked.

'We had opera in common but little else, though I was attracted by her beauty. I was divorced and my daughter, Juliette, had gone to study in Cape Town and I was lonely. We got together shortly afterwards, and I agreed to move to Mallorca. This is Maria's paternal home and where generations of her family lived. Sadly, her grandparents died when she was a teenager and her parents passed away in a boating accident in Italy when she'd just turned thirty. I always think it gave her a sort of vulnerability.'

'Moving here must have been quite a big change for you.'

He nodded. 'Maria was very persuasive. I love opera so I was lured by the idea of her giving me personal performances every day.'

'And did she?'

A wry smile crept across his face. 'If she was in a good mood, which was rare.' He gave a cough. 'But no marriage is perfect, is it?'

'I wouldn't know.'

'Maybe keep it that way. Freedom is undervalued.'

'Did you give up law?' Isabel asked.

'Not at all. I opened a practice in Palma which I ran for some years. When I turned sixty, I decided on a new career.'

Isabel arched her eyebrows. 'In a cash and carry?'

'Why not?' he retorted. 'Every job has its worth. I like it there. There are neither expectations nor stress but plenty of benefits.'

'Such as?'

He laughed. 'The pay is terrible, but I don't need money. Do you like fish?'

Isabel eyed him curiously. 'I'm a foodie.'

He pulled back his chair and rose quickly. 'Come, I want to show you something.'

Somewhat warily, Isabel got up and followed him out of the room. He strode along the sun-dappled corridor and opened the door of what appeared to be a large and cool pantry. At the far end of the dingy room lay another door, which he opened with a key from his pocket. He turned on a light and beckoned her inside.

'This is my bedroom,' he announced with an air of pride.

Isabel's eyes darted around the poky claustrophobic space that resembled a monk's cell. A narrow bed with a simple white pillow and cotton sheet stood against a white-washed wall, facing the door, while a makeshift bedside cabinet, in the form of a wooden crate, sat at its side. A teetering pile of books, an old lamp and several pairs of reading glasses obscured the dusty surface. Isabel followed a beam of sharp sunlight up to a small window with a wrought-iron grille. The walls of the room appeared to be constructed of plasterboard and were lined with heavy-duty boxes and crates. Isabel's eyes rested back on the bed. Now, she noticed that the mattress was supported not by a bedframe but crates and boxes. She turned to him.

'It's certainly got novelty factor.'

He laughed. 'My wife always had an eye for the finer things in life, but I am a simple man at heart. I moved down here five years ago when Maria threw me out of the matrimonial bedroom. The pantry was huge, so I created this little room within. It's perfect for me as I love cooking and to be near the kitchen and back garden. It's also very peaceful.'

Isabel eyed him intently. 'What are in all those crates?'

'That's why I invited you here. They are mostly *anchoas* and jars of *bonito del norte*. You asked about the perks of my job and here they are. Every time I purchase two crates of tinned or bottled fish at my cash and carry, I get one virtually free of charge. Can you believe it?'

'I take it you eat a lot of fish?'

He shrugged. 'A fair amount, but I like to have an ample supply. You can never have enough, in my opinion.'

'Clearly,' she replied.

Excitedly, he lifted the mattress at one corner. 'See. They serve another purpose too. Tins of Anchoas de Cantabria and *bonito*, the very best quality. Who needs a bed frame?'

Isabel squatted by the bed and surveyed the rows of shiny flat tins inside one of the crates.

'You particularly like La Reina del Cantábrico?'

'That's just one of many excellent brands. I have others such as Mingo and Arroyabe piled up here.' He swept an arm across one side of the room. 'All of these are iconic anchovy brands. A lot of the best *bonito* and anchovies come from Santoña in Cantabria. The fishers use mostly purse seine nets at night to surround whole schools of the tiny fish. Millions are caught annually, usually in the spring, but it's a time-consuming business.'

'Is that so?'

'First, they beat the fish to expel the blood and then they're descaled and gutted and placed in brine. After that, they're cured and packed in oil or salt. I once went on a nighttime anchovy fishing expedition. It was exhilarating. The fish looked like darting stars or luminous fireflies in the darkness of the ocean, but sadly, the majority are snared and beaten to death: an ignominious and tragic death. It's a shame really, as they are beautiful, almost celestial little creatures.'

Isabel watched as his face took on an animation she hadn't seen previously. Her eyes wandered to an old hardback sitting aloft the pile of tomes by his bed. It was *The Giant Golden Book of Elves and Fairies*, a beloved vintage English title from her childhood. She picked it up and examined the contents page.

'I had this book as a child. It belonged to my father. It dates back to the fifties.'

He nodded enthusiastically. 'I used to read it to my daughter. It has one special story.'

'"The Cannery Bear" by Ray St Clair.'

'How did you guess?'

'You sleep on a pile of fish tins, so it didn't take a lot of deduction. I always loved that story too. A bear with wings and radar to help fleets find fish in the sea. A crazy concept.'

There was a glint in his eye. 'Imagine, though, if you could be that bear, flying high over the sea, free from the cares of the world.' He blinked. 'You know, salted anchovies date back to the time of the Phoenicians, and yet they weren't truly commercialised until the late eighteen hundreds. I make it my business to keep a good stock here,' he said.

Isabel replaced the book and perched on the edge of the mattress.

'If I ever run out, I'll know where to come,' she replied.

He fixed his dark eyes on her. 'For sure, but remember, there are always more fish in the sea.'

A silence hung in the air. Isabel rose slowly and leant against a tower of *bonito* crates.

'Where were you around eight a.m. yesterday? Raquel said you had gone to your room while she was sorting fruit in the cellar.'

His face suddenly sagged. 'I was in here.'

'Doing what?'

'A stock take.'

'Of these tins?'

'Yes. I do one every week.'

'Always at eight o'clock on a Tuesday?'

He gave a sigh. 'Not at all. I normally count them on a Monday night, but I was distracted by a rumpus between my wife and

Fermin Janer, her belligerent cousin, who came here unexpectedly. He's been in litigation with Maria for years over the inheritance of this house and other family assets.'

'So what did he want?'

'Just to rattle the cage and remind us that he was still pursuing his legal case against Maria. He believes he was entitled to half this house, which was owned by Maria's grandfather, Alberto. The old man had two sons, but he clearly left the house to Maria's father, the eldest, and it was passed down to Maria. Fermin inherited money, as it's the law in Spain not to cut a child out of the will, but he had his eye on the house.'

'Who inherits now?'

He gawped at her. 'I suppose I do. We left everything to each other in our wills, unless she changed hers without my knowledge, of course.'

'Why would she do that?'

He shook his head. 'Maria was mercurial. I am waiting to hear from the lawyer.'

'Tell me why Maria had five locks on her door and threw you out of the bedroom.'

Pepe Serrano stood by the open door with his head bowed. 'Why indeed? I simply have no idea and never asked. About five years ago, I came home from work to find the locks on the door and all my personal belongings placed in a spare bedroom on the lower floor.'

'You never asked Maria why?'

'What was the point? We'd been growing apart and she'd become increasingly remote.' He shrugged. 'Maybe she just got bored with me.'

'Were you ever violent towards her?'

He gave a hollow laugh. 'I wasn't the one throwing the shoes, if that's what you mean.'

When they were in the corridor, Isabel cast him a long look. 'Now we need to talk through what happened yesterday morning, step by step. Shall we return to the kitchen?'

Half an hour later, Isabel walked out onto the porch while a subdued Pepe Serrano followed in her wake.

'I'm going to miss Maria. We were an odd couple, but we bumbled along.'

Isabel stood by Pequeñito. 'Do you think she committed suicide?'

Pepe issued a sigh. 'It's the only logical explanation. As I told you, the bathroom door was bolted from the inside. She had been out of sorts and volatile for several years. More recently, I think she was seeing a therapist of some kind and was on medication for depression.'

'How do you know?'

He gave her a blank stare. 'Georg, one of her students, suggested it, thinking I already knew. Maybe she confided in them. A few had regular lessons here.'

'Do you have their names?'

'Gemma Palau and Georg Bisbal, but I don't have their contact details. Matías Camps, the director of the Conservatori de Opera, will surely know.'

'When did either of them last visit?'

He shrugged. 'I saw Gemma's bike leaning against the porch on Monday, so she must have been here. I was on my way to Inca. Georg hasn't visited for some time, but a little while ago he mentioned that he was going on holiday to the mainland in August.'

Isabel nodded. 'But returning to the subject of Maria, why commit suicide on the eve of a European tour when, by all accounts, she was on excellent form? She'd got out her toiletry bag, and her cases were virtually packed.'

He appeared lost for words and wearily shook his head. 'I was her husband, but frankly, I'm the last person you should ask.'

'Who else, then?'

He stared at her. 'Maybe one of her lovers.'

'You have their names?' she asked with a pert smile.

'I have no evidence that she was unfaithful to me, but it's likely. She was very secretive and had countless admirers.'

'Did you love her?'

He looked taken aback. 'Once upon a time, but over the years, I realised I'd married a stranger, an imposter. Someone I no longer knew.' He held her gaze. 'But then, do we truly ever really know anybody, least of all ourselves?'

Isabel walked slowly to her car, her thoughts jumbled. As she reversed, she shot a look back at the house and saw Pepe Serrano observing her steadily from the porch. She may have imagined it, but she could have sworn she saw a playful grin on his lips.

SIX

Somewhere in the shadowy trees, a scops owl emitted a persistent and eerie single note call while a fowl screeched indignantly from the corral. In the inky darkness, Isabel strained to see what had caused the kerfuffle, surmising that one of the hens had been pushed off her perch by another bossy and feathery matriarch. Tolo and Isabel relaxed in wicker chairs on the patio, enjoying the last of their red wine and listening to the sounds of the balmy night. Tolo touched her hand across the table where a candle cast ambient light about them.

'What a meal. That has to be one of your best prawn risottos ever.'

She gave a mock frown. 'You said that the last time. Maybe you've forgotten.'

'Not at all. That's because every time you cook it, it gets better and better.'

She gave his bare foot a playful kick under the table. 'What about my lemon pie? Is it as good as my mother's?'

He sucked his teeth. 'We're getting into murky territory, *cariño*. If Florentina were here, she'd be standing behind me with a rolling pin, daring me to answer. As she isn't, I'll say they are neck and neck.'

'Hm. I'll accept the compliment.' She gave a sigh. 'I keep thinking about the encounter I had with Pepe Serrano this afternoon. It was quite surreal.'

'Altogether very fishy.' He smirked. 'The man's evidently got a screw loose.'

'But does that make him a murderer?'

He yawned. 'No one's accusing him of that. I think all the evidence points to this being a suicide. From what you've told me of your meeting, his marriage to Tía Maria was a sham and they lived separate lives, though seemingly peaceably enough. All the same, Gaspar and I will be checking on their life insurance policies and her last will. We'll also run a check on that cousin that Serrano mentioned to you.'

Isabel pushed away her spent dessert bowl and eyed him intently. 'Aside from Pepe Serrano, and Fermin Janer, Maria's cousin, what about the person who sent her poisonous mushrooms?'

Tolo gave an impatient grunt. 'That idiot, Casanovas, probably dredged that up in the hope of creating a news story from nothing. It was probably a disgruntled student playing an irresponsible prank.'

'But the media has always led us to believe that Maria was loved by all her students.'

'Even the English paper, *Majorca Daily Bulletin*, described her as an island treasure. Mind you, the Tía Maria and Tío Pepe dual sobriquet is quite funny. I wonder who dreamed that up,' Tolo said.

'Some wag. But about the mushrooms, if the prank had gone wrong and she'd actually eaten them, she could have died. Nothing funny about that.'

'True, but let's not get fixated on a side show. At the moment, there is nothing to suggest this was a suspicious death, and the two incidents happened a few years apart. Don't let Casanovas lead you down a rabbit hole.'

Isabel tittered. 'And don't let your dislike of Casanovas blur your vision.'

She began stacking up the plates. Tolo blew out the candle and, tucking the mats and serviettes under an arm, walked with her inside with their glasses. Carefully he put everything down on the kitchen table and placed a hand on her shoulder.

'I'm prepared to keep an open mind on this case, but let's wait to see what Nacho and the forensics team discover before we jump to any conclusions. As you know, Gaspar has arranged for you to meet Matías Camps, the director of the Conservatori de Opera, tomorrow morning, which should prove useful.'

Isabel nodded. 'I'm also going to arrange to meet Eva Salas, Tía Maria's agent. I did a quick online search earlier and see that she represents quite a few musicians, including Catalina Grimalt, the only other well-known local opera singer here.'

'I can't say the name rings a bell.'

She laughed and gave him a hug. 'That's because you don't like opera. If it was a jazz pianist, you'd know the name of his hamster.'

'Or possibly his ferret. Speaking of which, where has Furó gone?'

'He's asleep upstairs in the office.'

Isabel's mobile chirruped from the kitchen table. Tolo raised an eyebrow.

'I'll go and check on Furó and see you upstairs.' He sauntered off with his half-finished wine glass.

'*Diga*,' Isabel said curtly.

She was surprised to hear a South African lilt. Adam Markham sounded agitated.

'Sorry to ring so late, Isabel, but I came back to my rented place in Biniaraix a little while ago and found a dead seagull outside the front door. It had been gutted and blood had been smeared on the porch and doorframe. It's kind of freaked me out. The office is one thing, but whoever did this knows where I live too.'

'Of course, everyone will. This is the Soller valley. People talk.'

'They're trying to drive me out, but it won't work. Intimidation and threats are a coward's tools.'

'I'll pop by tomorrow afternoon. Please can you put the dead bird in a clean plastic bag and keep it for me – and do use gloves.'

'Too late. I've already disposed of it and cleaned up. It gave me the creeps.'

Isabel sighed. 'Well, in that case, my best advice is to lock your doors and go to bed.'

When he'd hung up, she stood for a few minutes deep in thought until she heard Tolo calling to her from upstairs. She switched off the kitchen light, wondering where one might snare and kill a seagull, or better still, locate a dead one.

It was barely eight-fifteen and yet the sun glowered in the infinite blue sky. Once Tolo had set off by car for the precinct in Palma, she had taken Furó for an early swim at Can Repic. To her chagrin, as she'd manoeuvred out of a tight space near the beach, she had grazed Boadicea against a stone wall. Back in Sant Martí, she had dropped the bike off at Bernat's workshop and sworn him to secrecy. Heaven forbid that Tolo and Pep found out. They'd rib her mercilessly and never let her forget such carelessness.

Now she stood in a queue of locals by the counter of Bon Día, chatting with her friend, Marga, and Brazilian next-door neighbour, Juliana.

'This heat is unbearable,' exclaimed Marga as she thrust a hand through her damp red hair. 'Running a salon in the summer is no joke with the dryers blaring all day, but what can I do?'

'Have you air conditioning?' asked Juliana sympathetically.

She eyed her dolefully. 'I can't afford it. The rent and taxes are crippling enough. I just use fans.'

Juliana clicked her teeth. 'Tell me about it. I fling all the doors and windows wide open in the studio, but it's still baking. My ladies are flagging during my yoga classes, but air-con is too expensive.'

'My poor friends,' said Isabel. 'I must buy tickets for the *lotería* today.'

Marga laughed and slung a tanned arm about her shoulders. 'And if you win, *cariño*, you must install air-con in my salon and pay for the running costs.'

'And my studio,' cut in Juliana.

'Of course,' Isabel replied with a wink. 'In the meantime, let me treat you both to *ensaïmadas*. I've got to buy some for Pep and Idò, who are back at the office awaiting their breakfast.'

'Don't spoil them or they'll get lazy,' admonished Marga. 'Pep is always happy to put his feet up and your Uncle Idò is a sly fox. He's milking that hip replacement for all it's worth.'

Juliana screeched with laughter. 'It's true, Bel. The other day, as I reached home, he hobbled past with his stick. We had a brief chat, and he carried on, but I had forgotten something in my car so came back out onto the street. Imagine my surprise to see him happily walking along, swinging his stick!'

Isabel stared at her in disbelief. 'The old codger. I shall have words with him.'

Jesus faced them all. 'Poor old Idò. Give him a break.' He leant in confidentially. 'Any news on Manuel Borras? That guy's a real troublemaker.'

Isabel kept her voice low. 'Rafa told me that there had been some trouble, but let's keep an open mind.'

Jesus shook his head. 'A bust-up between him and his old man and that South African guy hasn't helped. He's stirring things up here.'

Marga winked. 'Markham's quite a catch, though, and I bet he's loaded.'

Jesus was disapproving. 'We don't need his type here, flashing the cash and promising folks more money than they've ever had. Money only brings sorrow.'

'Not always,' remonstrated Marga. 'Frankly, Luis and I could do with a little extra cash, and if Adam Markham offered us a bundle for our home, we might be tempted.'

'You could have air conditioning at the salon,' teased Juliana, sweeping back her mane of hennaed hair.

Isabel turned to Marga. 'That house has been in your family for more than one hundred years. You'd never sell it.'

Her friend laughed. 'You're right, but sometimes I dream of having a little nest egg for a rainy day. Everything is so pricey these days, even Sofia's nursery costs a small fortune. Luis and I do our best, but it's a struggle.'

'*Poc a poc*,' soothed Jesus. 'You and Luis are young and work hard. You'll get there. At least we all have roofs over our heads, so we're luckier than many in this world.'

Marga paid for her goods and graciously accepted the fresh *ensaïmada* proffered by Isabel. She placed a kiss on her best friend's cheek and, munching on her pastry, strode along the street, swaying her ample hips, her gold bracelets tinkling joyously like sheep bells. To Isabel's amusement, the crumbs that fell to the ground were quickly gobbled up by a band of opportunistic doves that followed her every step.

Isabel walked back to Calle Pastor with Juliana, while Furó nimbly pattered along behind them. A water truck trundled past, reminding Isabel of the shortage of water in the village during a particularly hot and dry summer. As she reached her front gate, she kissed Juliana goodbye and smiled to herself. How lucky she was to have such warm and vibrant Brazilian neighbours on one side and trusty Doctor Ramis on the other. She opened her front door and immediately heard Pep's voice and the rich familiar laugh of her uncle emanating from the office. Over breakfast she would take Idò to task about the state of his new hip. Surely it was time to lure the old rogue back to work. She contemplated the holiday rental requests for the following year awaiting her attention and uttered a small groan. Guests were booking further ahead these days as the valley became ever more popular with overseas visitors. At noon she would drive to Palma to visit the director of the Conservatori and later Tía Maria's agent. With any luck, both might shed some light on the opera singer's character and recent state of mind.

By the time Isabel pulled into the car park of the Conservatori in Palma, the sky had turned pewter, and rain began to pitter patter steadily on Pequeñito's bonnet.

'How wonderful, *amigo mio*,' said Isabel. 'At last, we have a little respite from the heat.'

She turned to her right and noticed a shiny, cherry-red Fiat 500 parked close by.

'Avert your eyes, Pequeñito. That's one of the new boys on the block. You are an original, the real deal. Always remember that.'

Unfurling her umbrella, she stood on the damp tarmac and surveyed the austere building before her. The Conservatori was housed in a magnificent period building with art nouveau flourishes and an elegant set of stone steps that led to a grand porch and polished mahogany front door. As she entered the cool *entrada*, Isabel's eyes explored the detailed frescoes that decorated the walls and the magnificent stairwell, coming to rest on a dramatic crystal chandelier that hung from the high ceiling.

A voice piped up from behind the reception desk. 'That's a turn of the century masterpiece. It was produced in northern Italy in 1902. The Mallorcan who built this house emigrated to Sète in 1880, where he made a pile from trading oranges, and then came back home and built five properties in the capital, all in this style.'

Isabel smiled at the fair-haired young woman. 'You're very well informed.'

She laughed. 'I'm a sucker for history. You know that chandelier is worth €50,000?'

'Really? In that case, I wouldn't like to be the one that cleans it.'

'True. It's a very delicate task. I assume you're here to see Matías? He told me to expect you.'

Isabel nodded. 'Have you worked here long?'

'The past three years. I'm Elena, Matías's niece. I'm studying for a master's degree in music in the States but work here every summer to earn some cash.' She smiled. 'I'll call my uncle and let him know that you've arrived.'

When she'd finished the call, Isabel turned to her.

'I suppose you must know all the students and tutors here.'

'Sure, it's a small college. They're a good bunch.'

'All of you must have been so upset by the death of Maria Rosselló.'

'Tía Maria?' Elena sighed. 'We're all still reeling. It's a terrible loss for the opera world.'

'She must have been adored by her pupils.'

'I'm not sure about that, but the students certainly revered her.'

'She wasn't popular?'

The woman took on a confidential tone. 'I don't want to speak ill of the dead, but she could be really mean and temperamental. I did some voice training with her a year ago and at times she made me feel so small and stupid. All the same, she was a perfectionist and made you aim high.'

Isabel frowned. 'So a bit of a diva.'

Elena laughed. 'You could say that, but she was a brilliant performer. As long as you didn't take her words to heart, it was okay.' She paused. 'Here's my uncle.'

A man appeared on the stairwell and cast a stern look in her direction. 'Not gossiping, I hope, Elena.'

Isabel stepped forward. 'Not at all. Your niece has been telling me all about the history of this beautiful building.'

'I'm pleased to hear that.' He extended a hand. 'Señorita Flores, I presume? Let's go to my office.'

Once on the first floor, Matías Camps led her into a large office with views to Palma's old quarter and La Seu Cathedral. He offered her a seat.

'This is about Maria?'

In the harsh light from the window, Isabel noted that his face took on a haggard appearance.

'I'm sorry for your loss, but yes, I wonder if you could tell me a little about her. I believe she tutored here for many years.'

'A decade, to be exact. She was not only a colleague but a close friend, so this has hit me hard. Maria taught only our most talented students, those with potential to become the opera singers of tomorrow.'

'What kind of timetable did she keep here?'

His fingers danced on the rim of his desk. 'She worked here from Monday to Thursday during term time, though now and then she had to go on tour.' He paused. 'She took a kind of sabbatical five years ago after she'd returned from one particular tour on the peninsula. The tour was three months long and had left her physically and mentally exhausted.'

'How long was she away from the college?'

'About a year, but then she came back and was on great form.'

'Did she get on well with other staff here?'

His eyes flickered and he cleared his throat. 'She was admired by many but expected high standards from everyone and that included her colleagues.'

'What about the students?'

'She was like a caring aunt, and they loved her. That's how she got the affectionate nickname, Tía Maria.'

'And what about her husband's name, Tío Pepe?'

'The students came up with that too.' He smirked. 'It was a little bit of harmless fun.'

'And were the poisoned mushrooms that were sent to her here also just a bit of fun?'

His face darkened. 'Listen, we never discovered who sent those mushrooms, but Maria adored wild *setas*, so it was obvious that it was a gift gone wrong.'

'How so?'

'The gift box contained immature death caps, otherwise known as *Amanita phalloides*, which are highly toxic and dangerous but look very similar at button stage to puffball mushrooms, which are edible.'

'Have you ever tried them?' she asked.

'Yes, they are actually quite delicious. I forage for wild mushrooms in season. That's how I know it's easy for a novice to make the mistake.'

Isabel processed this information slowly. 'If that were the case, why didn't the perpetrator come forward to admit the near fatal error of judgement when it was discovered that they were poisonous?'

Matías Camps waved his hand in the air impatiently. 'We didn't want a media circus over here, so we tried to defuse the situation. Of course, the incident was reported in one or two local papers, but we played it down. Frankly, if it had been one of our students, I imagine they would have been mortified and relieved that she'd not eaten them. Who'd ever want to admit to having done such a foolish thing?'

'Someone who felt they should make an apology.'

'It was three years ago. It's all in the past.' He shook his head irritably. 'Is there anything else?'

'Can you arrange for me to meet Gemma Palau and Georg Bisbal, two of Maria's students?'

'Why ever do you need to see them? Georg is still away on the mainland, but Gemma has gone through enough trauma with all this.'

'I believe they had private classes at the house in Moscari. Both might be able to help us with the case.'

He looked alarmed. 'Isn't this just a straightforward suicide?'

'Is suicide ever straightforward, Señor Camps?' she replied.

'Maria was very highly strung and frequently suffered from depression and severe anxiety, so suicide is not out of the question.'

'Do you know if she was seeing a therapist? Presumably, as her close friend, she would have confided in you.'

He raised an eyebrow. 'Not necessarily. She was a very private person. All the same, she did once mention that she was having some kind of therapy from someone in Santa Catalina. I don't know anything more than that.'

A silence fell between them until Isabel cleared her throat.

'When can you introduce me to Gemma Palau?'

'Monday at around eleven o'clock would be best, after the students' morning meeting.'

'I will need Georg's mobile number, and I'd also like to catch up briefly with staff members. Can I do that on Monday morning too?'

He nodded curtly. 'They have a break period at nine-thirty. You can meet them in the staff room, but I'm not sure what you're hoping to achieve.'

Isabel resisted the urge to get up and pull his ears hard. 'I'm sure they'll all have memories of Maria.'

'Suit yourself, but none of them knew her well.'

'But you did, even though she held things back from you?'

He dropped the pen he'd been fiddling with and winced as it clattered and rolled noisily across the desk.

'I knew her better than most.' He stared at her with belligerent eyes. 'That's why I still can't accept that she's gone.'

In the reception, Elena smiled and passed Isabel a piece of paper with the mobile number of Georg Bisbal. She thanked her and headed for Mercat Olivar. She wanted to have a chat with one of the market's mushroom sellers, who was an expert on foraging for wild fungi. While there, she decided to have a quick snack. After all, who could resist the *tapas* and seafood bars that lured shoppers like gastronomic sirens with their heavenly displays?

Isabel stood in Plaça de Sant Francesc, admiring the vast sandstone façade of the basilica before her. It was early afternoon, and she was feeling at peace with the world having consumed a generous portion of red prawn risotto and a side order of crispy *padrones*, washed down with a glass of cool Albariño. Despite Isabel's weak protestations, her favourite bar owner at the market had also persuaded her to polish it all off with a *crema*

Catalana that sat on a scrumptious base of marinated peaches and cherries. Now she studied the arched portal of the Baroque church with its impressive tympanum. She was tempted to stop by the Gothic cloisters, as it was some time since her last visit and the tranquillity in the shady garden with its bushy citrus trees was always a joy during the heat of the summer. However, time was not on her side. She walked past the landmark statue of Juniper Serra, an austere Franciscan friar and evangelist from the eighteenth century who had set up missionaries in Alta California and colonised the indigenous people. He was a controversial figure by modern standards, and Isabel had a feeling that should time travel ever allow their paths to cross, she would give him a piece of her mind about his evangelical ways. She crossed the street and walked into the cool lobby of Hotel Sant Francesc, a luxury bolthole away from the fray. In the elegant patio, she spotted a solitary customer, a stylish, middle-aged woman with a neat blonde chignon and voluptuous red lips, who was nursing a glass of water. She felt that it had to be Eva Salas, Tía Maria's agent, and headed for her table. The woman offered a well-practised dazzling smile.

'Isabel Flores, I presume? I'm Eva. Do join me.'

'This is such a beautiful hotel,' Isabel said as she looked around her.

'It's where I come for all my meetings. You can be assured of discreet service.'

She beckoned over a member of staff, who swiftly took Isabel's coffee order and left them to talk. Eva Salas fixed her with a steady gaze.

'Tell me what you want to know about poor Maria. She was my client for fifteen years, so you can imagine how distressing her death has been for me.'

Isabel took out her notebook and pen. 'Presumably it came like a bolt from the blue.'

The woman shrugged. 'Well, yes and no. Maria was a depressive and self-medicated on and off for years.'

'Do you know if she was on medication at the time of her death?'

Eva shook her head. 'She did seek help from a private doctor about five years ago and was prescribed antidepressants, but she told me she'd weaned herself off them completely. Of course, she could have been lying.'

'Do you know his name?'

'I'm afraid not, but he was based in Palma. That aside, she had a volatile nature and an unconventional marriage.'

'In what way?'

'Maria and Pepe lived increasingly separate lives, and yet she told me that she'd never countenance a divorce. She was like a tempestuous wave, always having huge ups and downs. I had a feeling that she might end her life one day.'

Isabel was silent for a moment as she accepted her *cortado* from the waitress.

'At this stage we're not certain whether it was suicide.'

The woman gave a cynical guffaw. 'What else? She was alone in a locked bathroom, by all accounts, and evidently threw herself over the railings. Or are you implying that it might have been an accidental fall?'

Isabel took a sip of coffee. 'Tell me about the tour Maria was about to embark on.'

'It would have embraced ten cities across Spain over a two-month period and then she was to travel to venues in Germany and France. Such a wasted opportunity. She seemed so excited about it, but she must have been nursing severe anxiety. Heaven knows what was going through her head. It's been a nightmare untangling everything and it's involved so much work and loss of revenue, of course.'

'I believe that you represent Catalina Grimalt?' said Isabel.

Eva nodded. 'Indeed, and I have several well-known tenors on the mainland.'

'Would it be possible to have your current client list?'

The woman gave a sullen pout. 'I'm not sure why you need it, but sure, I can email it to you.' She made a steeple with her fingers. 'Frankly, regardless of whether Maria fell by design or accident, we need to put this heartbreaking episode to bed for all our sakes. I've discussed the need for a memorial service with both Pepe and the regional president's press secretary. We've agreed to hold it at Bellver Castle next month and opt for a low-key, private funeral at the cemetery in Inca next Wednesday.'

'The forensic report is still pending, so that can't go ahead without court and police approval,' Isabel replied.

Eva whisked a dismissive hand through the air. 'Isn't that just a formality?'

'Was the Balearic regional president a good friend of Maria's?' asked Isabel.

The agent eyed her coolly. 'Maria had influence and knew both the minister of culture and the Balearic president on a professional and personal basis. All of us want to commemorate her life in a positive way. I intend to reissue her greatest works for the enjoyment of all her fans.'

'You mean commercially?' asked Isabel.

'Of course. Naturally, Pepe will want to capitalise on his wife's success. Why not? She's gone and this is a fitting way to preserve her memory.'

'Presumably both of you will gain financially from the venture?'

She tutted impatiently. 'Life goes on, Isabel, and we all have to earn a living. I need to recoup my losses from the cancelled tour and Pepe has to think about his future. He's not getting any younger and Maria's crazy cousin, Fermin, might have him thrown out of that house if he wins his legal case posthumously against Maria.'

'Do you know Pepe well?'

She shrugged. 'Ever since he married Maria. In fact, I went to the wedding. It was a lavish affair in Barcelona, followed by another celebration in Palma. I'd only just taken Maria on as a client, but we had quickly established a good relationship. Pepe was quite an eccentric even then. He's got worse with age.'

'In what way?'

'Put it like this: he's a great collector of masks. One night I came for dinner, and he was wearing some creepy white theatrical mask and a Grecian robe. That's hardly normal, is it?'

Isabel resisted the urge to smile. 'Did he take the mask off?'

'Only when we sat down to dine. It was peculiar, and all the other guests were in formal suits and rather embarrassed. He offered no explanation and neither did his wife.'

'How did he and Maria get on?'

'In the early days they seemed to get on famously, then about five years ago their relationship deteriorated quite inexplicably. Maria told me that they no longer shared the same room and that he slept near the kitchen. Neither could be described as angels. Pepe used to be blisteringly sardonic with Maria and she had a temper. Once she hurled a shoe at him when I visited, and the stiletto cut the back of his head badly. It was streaming with blood and needed stitches. That's artists for you.' The woman threw back her head and laughed. 'He lived to see another day, so there was no harm done.'

AUNT MARIA'S LAST ARIA

As Isabel got up to leave, Eva leant forward in her seat with an earnest expression. 'We don't want suicide to define Maria. No one is perfect. Let's celebrate her life and talent instead.'

After her meeting, Isabel returned to Pequeñito, waiting patiently in the underground carpark by Plaça de la Reina. She spent a few moments reliving her conversation with Eva Salas. If she hadn't been convinced before of something untoward about Maria's impromptu death, she certainly was now.

SEVEN

Isabel and Gaspar sat at the conference table in Tolo's office at the precinct. Both were munching on slices of almond cake that had been lovingly presented to them by Corc, Tolo's neurotic male assistant. A brilliant blue sky grinned at the pair from outside while a fan whirred monotonously from a sideboard. Tolo continued to pace about the room, examining a file of notes that had been delivered to him by Nacho.

Gaspar took a last gulp of coffee and set his mug down on the table. He had a smile on his face. 'So, Bel, let me get this straight. Eva Salas told you today that Maria and Pepe had a peculiar marriage and hadn't shared the same bedroom for five years. Aside from sleeping on tins of fish in a kitchen pantry, the guy also dresses up as a Greek god at dinner parties for no apparent reason.'

'Just because he's a nut doesn't prove anything,' interrupted Tolo as he joined them at the table.

'True, boss, but I agree with Bel that something's very odd about that household. We're waiting to hear from Maria's lawyer about her will, but it's highly likely that Pepe will inherit everything. Her cousin, Fermin, stands little chance of winning his case against her now, so Pepe gets the lot. Quite a motive for murder.'

Isabel stared at them both. 'Pepe might dress up as a Greek god and eat far too many anchovies, but it proves nothing. Besides, why wait until now to bump her off? Have you had time to investigate his own personal finances yet? He told me that he doesn't need money and only works at the cash and carry in Inca for fun.'

Gaspar shrugged. 'He's got a private pension which pays him a reasonable whack, but it's certainly not enough to lead a luxury lifestyle.'

Isabel laughed. 'Remember that you're talking about a man who sleeps in a cell with only dead fish for company.'

Tolo frowned. 'What about the mushrooms?'

Isabel finished the last morsels of her cake and licked a sugary finger. 'Matías Camps believes that the death caps sent to Maria were intended as a gift, possibly from a student who'd confused them with edible puffballs. I checked that out with a mushroom expert at Mercat Olivar, who thought it unlikely that even an amateur could get it wrong.'

Gaspar opened the file in front of him.

'Nacho's initial forensic report doesn't point to anything but suicide. There was slight bruising on both of the victim's shoulders that could imply external pressure, but he consulted with Pedro Massip, director of the Forensic Institute in Palma, who dismissed it. Pedro felt the bruising could easily have happened when she hit various hard surfaces as she fell through the greenhouse.'

'What about any DNA?'

'None, but Nacho has sent her clothes for quite a revolutionary analysis in Barcelona. These days they can lift finger and glove prints from fabric, so he thinks it's worth a punt.'

'They can lift them from skin too,' Isabel replied. 'What about the force of the impact and velocity when she hit the ground?'

Tolo nodded. 'Nacho's on the case. All we know at this stage is that she fell face forward, which seems to corroborate the theory that she threw herself over the railings. They've also lifted prints from the railings which have proven to be Maria's. The implication is that she propelled herself over.'

'Or maybe gripped them as someone tried to propel her over,' Isabel replied.

Tolo's eyes flickered over the file he was holding. 'Forensics will feed us more information as they conduct further tests.'

Isabel drained her coffee cup and stretched her arms. 'Despite there being no suicide note, everything the maid and gardener witnessed points to a self-inflicted death. The maid was insistent that the bathroom door was locked when she and Pepe arrived, but of course he could have pretended to turn the handle rigorously as if it wouldn't open before kicking it down.'

Gaspar scratched his chin. 'That sounds a bit far-fetched, though. Besides, aside from the door handle, forensics found none of his DNA at the scene. Though I admit, Gómez and his team had been tramping about in the bathroom before it was sealed off, so the scene was contaminated. Tomorrow afternoon, Nacho is conducting a thorough forensic sweep of Maria's bedroom before he goes on holiday to Formentera.'

'I was planning on popping over there in the morning as I have a few more questions for Pepe. I'd also like to have another peek at Maria's bedroom, without disturbing anything, of course.'

Tolo nodded. 'That's fine by me. Take the strong box and the chain with the five keys before you go today, and make sure to leave it for Nacho at the house tomorrow afternoon.'

'No problem. How long is Nacho away?' asked Isabel.

'A week. He leaves with the family on Saturday and returns next Friday, so Pedro Massip will handle the results.'

Isabel nodded. 'He's a bit dour and unimaginative, but I suppose we'll just have to make do with him until Nacho returns.'

'Pedro's okay, but he's all for an easy life,' Tolo admitted.

Gaspar turned to her. 'Backing the suicide theory, Maria was in some floaty white number when she fell, as if she wanted to look her best before she did the terrible deed.'

Isabel gave him a playful wink. 'Pure speculation but a romantic notion. What I do find puzzling from the forensic report is that she had no drugs in her system, and yet I found that used pestle and mortar and empty packet of fentanyl in the bin.'

'It could have been in the bin some days and we don't know what she'd used the pestle and mortar for,' Gaspar countered. 'Maybe she'd been smashing up spices.'

'Fair enough,' Isabel conceded. 'All the same, I can't help but think it's important. We're missing something.'

'Like what?' Tolo replied impatiently.

'The big question is why she would want to commit suicide on the eve of a tour she was by all accounts excited about. True, we don't know what state of mind she was in that morning, but something doesn't add up. We still don't know where that empty packet of fentanyl came from or who might have prescribed it to her.'

Tolo and Gaspar eyed her thoughtfully.

'There is one other thing. According to Pepe and Matías Camps, Maria was seeing a therapist in Santa Catalina. Is that something your team can follow up on?'

Gaspar nodded. 'Sure.'

'If we can't come up with anything concrete, the funeral will go ahead in Inca next week,' Tolo said resignedly.

'I know.' Isabel stood up. 'Meanwhile, I'm heading home to see Furó and to find out what Pep's mother, Rosa, has left me for dinner.'

Tolo grinned and kissed her on the cheek. 'You are so spoilt by the matriarchs of Sant Martí. Talking of which, what time does Florentina get home on Saturday with Doctor Ramis?'

'About lunchtime. Since you're staying over tomorrow night, you might get to see them.'

He shook his head. 'I'm on duty at the children's home in Palma on Saturday, but I'll see them soon enough. Aren't you and Pep training for the Peguera Triathlon on Saturday?'

'Of course, I nearly forgot.' Isabel wrinkled her nose. 'We're cycling all the way to Lluc late morning. Pep is a taskmaster. The kids at the home will love seeing you.'

'How long have you been volunteering over there now?' asked Gaspar.

'Six years,' Tolo replied. 'I've organised a football match for them on Saturday – staff and volunteers against all the kids, followed by a big *paella* and ice cream.'

'They'll kick you into touch,' Gaspar goaded.

Tolo grinned. 'Too true. We'll be crushed.'

He punched his shoulder. 'Whatever state you're in, don't forget my birthday party on Sunday. My mother's already started cooking some Guinea-Bissau specials. The whole family will be there.'

He looked across at Isabel, who had made her way to the door.

'Bring a big appetite with you.'

Isabel laughed. 'You can count on that, Gaspar. I love your mother's cooking.'

Tolo stood by the door with a wry smile. 'As you seem to be on a constant "foodathon", *cariño*, that triathlon couldn't have come at a better time.'

Isabel giggled and was about to leave, but a thought suddenly struck her. 'Did the forensic report mention a gold heart locket fastened around Maria's neck?'

Gaspar shrugged. 'I'm not sure. We'll check with Nacho.'

'If there is a locket, I'd like to see it,' Isabel said. 'The gardener said she always wore it.'

Tolo eyed her quizzically. 'Is it significant?'

'Who knows,' Isabel replied. 'But we should leave no stone unturned.'

A dazzling blue sky accompanied Isabel all the way to Sant Martí. She had spent the journey from Palma ruminating about Tía Maria and was convinced that the opera singer's untimely death was not voluntary, but how so? All the evidence and witness testimonies pointed to suicide. She would need to employ some lateral thinking. As Pequeñito gasped on the final bend before reaching the village square, the Baroque clocktower of Sant Antoní loomed large in front of Isabel. It was six o'clock and Isabel smiled to see that the hands on the clock were displaying the correct time. The engineer must have fixed the problem, or a certain celestial being had answered Padre Agustí's prayers. But what of the faulty bell tower? Time would tell. Minutes later, Isabel arrived in Calle Pastor. Having squeezed Pequeñito into one of the few remaining parking slots on the sunny street, she jogged to Bernat's yard, which he kept as an overflow for clients' cars at the end of her street. Inside, she found the mechanic recumbent under an old white van. His head poked out like that of a wary tortoise.

'Your poor Ducati. Luckily for you, she's as good as new. A deep nasty scratch, though.'

'What an angel you are, Bernat. How much do I owe you?'

'You wouldn't take any money for dog sitting my Paca last month when the wife and I went on holiday, so let's call it quits.'

Isabel was very fond of Bernat and his old mongrel and had gladly looked after her for a week. Luckily, Furó was thrilled to have a playmate in the house and the two had got on famously.

'Come on.'

He winked. 'You'll find Boadicea in the yard. Let's keep her little accident between us.'

'I'd appreciate that. I'll pick her up now.'

To Isabel's relief, the gleaming bike showed no evidence of a dent. Just as she revved the engine, Hans, the Swiss owner of the village's new hiking shop, emerged from a car. He smiled genially.

'*Hola*, Bel. Was your bike in for repairs?'

Isabel faltered. 'Now and again, I leave it here when there's nowhere to park.'

He nodded. 'Good thinking. In the summer season, it's a problem here in Sant Martí. Trust Bernat to let you keep it here. He's such a nice guy.'

Isabel nodded cheerfully. She rode the *moto* back to the house, hit by a wave of guilt for telling a fib, and in the absence of a space, parked the bike in the front garden. As Isabel entered her cool and dark *entrada*, she heard loud music emanating from the upstairs office. No doubt Pep was enjoying his private disco. During the summer months, Isabel kept most of the outside shutters firmly closed during the day to keep out the intense heat, but she found the house a little gloomy. Still, it was a necessary evil, and as soon as the sun waned early evening, she flung open all of the shutters and drank in the views of the Tramuntanas from her front and back windows.

Pep smiled up at her from the floor as she walked into the office. He was squatting by a large clear plastic tube attached to

AUNT MARIA'S LAST ARIA

a fabric pit filled with small, coloured balls. Isabel watched as Furó wriggled along the tube towards her and stuck his nose out, whiskers all a quiver.

Isabel whisked Furó into her arms and began stroking his sleek head. 'What's going on?'

'Angélica was visiting a friend in Es Pla yesterday who used to keep a ferret and was getting rid of its old toys. So, she thought of you and took a few home for Furó. It'll keep him going till his new run arrives.'

'What a thoughtful fiancée you have, Pep,' Isabel replied. 'She's one in a million.'

'She certainly is and is still not my fiancée, so you can cut that out!'

Isabel giggled as she placed Furó on her shoulder. 'What a spoilt little ferret you are, but we all love you.'

Furó made little snuffling noises and pushed his head under her mane of dark, curly hair.

Pep got up and observed her keenly. 'So don't keep me in suspense. What are the results of Tía Maria's post-mortem?'

Isabel flung herself in a chair disconsolately while hunting for a Chupa Chup in her voluminous pannier. 'I'm afraid there's no evidence to suggest it was anything but suicide.'

Pep snorted. 'What, you'd have preferred poor Tía Maria to have been murdered?'

'Put yourself in the shoes of the great Sherlock Holmes. Would he have taken this calamitous event at face value? It's about justice, dear Watson.'

He grew serious. 'You think she was murdered?'

'I do indeed, but I have no evidence to suggest that and no idea who the culprit might be or of the motive. Everything currently points to the husband, of course, but we have to be sure.'

'That's exciting. So, we're onto a new case?'

Isabel eyed him sternly.

'There's nothing remotely exciting about murder, Pep. Now, if you want to help me, please first sort out the new bookings that I've received for next Easter and pick up the laundry from the cleaning team.'

He sat back in his chair with a complacent grin. 'All done.'

Isabel clapped. 'Well done, deputy sleuth. In that case, you can research the clients of Tía Maria's agent, Eva Salas. She has emailed me a huge list of them – past and present. I want you to find out whether any of them had a connection with Maria.'

'Why?'

'I'm just trying to join the dots. Five years ago, something happened to Maria while on an operatic tour on the mainland. She subsequently had some kind of breakdown.'

'But what has that got to do with her death?'

'Maybe nothing at all, but nevertheless, I'd like to be sure. Then you can do some subtle checks on Maria's cousin, Fermin Janer. What kind of person is he? What do his neighbours have to say about him?'

Pep's eyes were bright. 'I'll get right onto it.'

'Let's discuss it all in my office.'

'Fancy a *cortado*?'

'If you're offering,' she replied.

Pep hesitated at the door. 'My mother brought round an enormous cake full of juicy *mores*, but it seems like you'd prefer to suck on one of those horrible lollipops.'

Isabel glanced at the Chupa Chup in her hand and quickly rewrapped it.

'Cake it is!'

Pep grinned as he left the room. 'A wise decision, dear Sherlock. There's nothing better than cake for helping to solve a puzzling case.'

It was early evening, and the soft blue sky was still streaked with pearlised golden light. Isabel headed to Bar Castell, her mind whirring. She had heard that the refurbishment of Juan Jaume's property had already begun, so she took a detour and strolled up the hill towards the *torrente*, where bright yellow diggers and a crane were jostling for space on the congested road. Before she had even reached the main gate, a large sign on the front wall caught her eye. It read: *Woning Luxury Living, Real Estate Group. Making dreams come true.* She noticed the seagull motif above the logo and her thoughts strayed to the dead bird that had been left at Adam Markham's front door. That was something she found deeply unsettling and so out of character for the valley. Certainly, there were old enmities in every community, but this sort of sinister stunt was very rare. A voice interrupted her thoughts and she turned to see Pau, the local police officer, strolling towards her. He had a bright orange cone under one arm.

'I'm trying to keep local drivers pacified. I've had a few grumbles about the hold-ups on the road with all this heavy equipment around. It won't be for much longer.'

Isabel nodded. 'Who has Adam Markham got to handle this work?'

Pau grinned and pointed to a corpulent, jovial-looking man in a hard hat at the controls of a digger.

'Xavi from Soller got the contract. He was over the moon. Apparently, Markham didn't quibble about price and has been really pleasant to work with.'

'That's good to hear. I get the impression not everyone in the valley is so pleased about his arrival, though.'

Pau raised an eyebrow. 'Too right. You know the real estate agent Tomeu Tous?'

'Sure, he's a big fish in the valley, though I've never had dealings with him.'

'He's been bad mouthing Markham to anyone who'll listen. Says he's going to ruin the market for all the local agents by offering such high prices to sellers while charging exorbitant rates to renters and buyers. I told him that competition was a good thing, but he wasn't having any of it.'

Isabel frowned. 'Has he met Adam?'

Pau shrugged. 'I doubt it, and I wouldn't recommend it either. He's a real hothead.'

Isabel wiped a bead of sweat from her forehead, aware that a slice of sun was still stubbornly peeping from the tips of the Tramuntanas.

'I'm off to Bar Castell to see Idò and the gang. When do you knock off?'

'Not for another hour. I'll come and join you all when I'm finished.'

As Isabel was about to set off, she suddenly became aware of a glowering presence on the far side of the street and saw Manuel tracking the workmen's every movement. He had a wild look in his eye and was shaking uncontrollably, his hands forming tight knots at his side. Instinctively, she thought of approaching him, but Pau gripped her arm.

'He's been on a bender, Bel. He's not safe. I'm keeping an eye on him.' He paused and sighed deeply. 'I tell you something, though. Tomeu Tous might not be a fan of Markham, but Manuel is a simmering pot of rage. He hates Markham with a passion and that goes for his own poor old dad since he decided to refurbish and sell his home. It all comes down to money and greed and I've got a feeling that this whole project isn't going to end happily at all.'

The sound of raised voices and laughter in Bar Castell hit Isabel before she'd even opened the door. A few of her more timorous holiday rental clients confided in her that they were nervous about entering the local village bars because of the boisterous nature of the conversation. Often, they assumed that a terrible argument was taking place between locals, and Isabel had to reassure them that it was nothing of the kind and that Mallorcans simply loved lively conversation and debate. Rafael stood behind the counter, pouring glasses of rosé, a damp tea towel resting on his shoulder. He smiled and offered her a complicit wink.

'Llorenç is sounding off in there about the foreign food that Jesus is now selling at Bon Día. Frankly, if that's what visitors want, you've got to play the game.'

Isabel nodded. 'It's not just visitors. There are many foreign residents who want a few home comforts. I like to try new foods too. There's an English salty spread called marmite. I love it in *estofados*.'

He pulled a face. 'It's horrible! I was given it on a piece of toast by an English customer. It just tastes of salt. Yuk. Anyway, can I get you a *copa*?'

'*Tinto*, please, and plenty of olives and almonds.'

'Coming up, señorita.'

Isabel wriggled through the throng of tourists and locals, stopping to share greetings as she made her way to Llorenç's table. The doors to the terrace were flung wide open and a fan whirred, but there was little breeze, and the heat was still palpitating despite the late hour. Pep brightened up when he saw her and pointed to a spare seat at his side, a look of relief on his face. As she squeezed past Uncle Idò, she planted two kisses on his cheeks and stroked the head of his elderly dog, Perro. Llorenç sat across from him, with Bernat on one side and Alfonso on the other. He was holding forth about Bon Día, offering a lengthy pronouncement about the perils of pickled herrings, marmite, crème fraiche and baked beans. Isabel and Alfonso exchanged weary looks as Llorenç's diatribe showed no signs of abatement. He was halted mid-flow by Rafael, who appeared with a tray of fat green olives, salted almonds and a generous glass of *vino tinto*.

Isabel took a sip of her wine and popped a few olives into her mouth as Llorenç ordered another round of drinks. Pep gave her a nudge while Alfonso offered her a pleading glance. She quickly took the hint and turned to the diminutive mayor.

'You're so right about all the new foods at Bon Día. The other day I noticed a product called Quark in the cold cabinet and there are jars of sauerkraut and a big selection of French cheeses and wines too.'

'Indeed, a nonsense,' said Llorenç, tutting. 'Especially when you think of our peerless cheeses and local wines.'

She nodded enthusiastically. 'Do you recall the platter of pâté and smoked sausage I brought round last week when I popped by for a drink?'

Llorenç clapped his hands together. 'Joana and I loved it. Delicious local fare. Was it from Es Pla?'

'Actually, the wild boar pâté was French and the smoked sausage a German speciality. I bought them from Bon Día.'

He frowned as laughter broke out around the table. 'Well, I suppose there are always exceptions to the rule. All I'm saying is that we must uphold our own gastronomic cuisine and not let new arrivals stage a takeover.'

Alfonso took a glug of white wine. 'I must admit to buying German and French mustard, and who can resist a bit of Brie?'

'I most certainly can,' Llorenç replied huffily. 'Manchego for me all the way.'

'You've got to move with the times, Llorenç,' yelled Idò as he helped himself to a big handful of almonds. 'Talking of which, any news on how Juan Jaume's refurbishment is going?'

Bernat groaned. 'Don't mention that Adam Markham to me. He placed one of his posters on the wall of my garage without even asking me, so I've torn it down. I don't want to advertise his company to all my clients.'

'I did notice it when I came by your workshop this afternoon.' She bit her lip. 'I mean, when I last popped by.'

With the enthusiasm of a pig sensing a nearby truffle, Pep's eyes sparkled.

'This afternoon? Why were you at Bernat's? You haven't scratched Pequeñito, have you?'

'Of course not!' Isabel exclaimed heatedly. 'Bernat can back me up.'

'True,' said Bernat. 'There's nothing wrong with Pequeñito that I know about.'

Pep eyed them both with suspicion. 'If you say so.'

Isabel was keen to change the subject. 'Just before I came here, I walked by Juan's home and the refurbishment is well underway. Paul told me that Xavi got the contract.'

'He's a good builder is Xavi,' replied Idò. 'All the same, you have to wonder what kind of deal Markham and Juan have. Presumably, Markham is paying for the refurbishment, and they'll split the profits when they get a sale.'

'Something like that,' said Llorenç. 'The house will go for a fortune once it's given a facelift. It's got a lot of land and some of the best views in the village.'

Alfonso gave a sigh. 'I hope his son doesn't cause trouble. I was giving an art class at the town hall yesterday and Manuel barged in, looking the worse for wear. He told me he'd just seen his lawyer and needed to talk to the council's architect about his father's house. I led him to the right office.'

'What did he want to know?' asked Isabel.

Alfonso shrugged. 'I've no idea, but he looked surly.'

'He always looks surly,' said Pep. 'I reckon he wants to hold up the work somehow and stop the sale.'

'A bit late for that,' said Llorenç scoffingly. 'The only way he could halt the project is if he killed off either Markham or his dad.'

A nervous silence descended on the group. Isabel crunched on a nut and frowned. Someone was threatening Markham, and Manuel was proving to be increasingly erratic. The sun still shone, and happy tourists continued to amble through the cobbled streets, but she felt instinctively that something rotten was eating away at the heart of Sant Martí.

EIGHT

A sultry sky accompanied Isabel and Furó all the way to Moscari. She had decided to take Boadicea for a ride now that the *moto* was back to its former glory and had carefully strapped her beloved ferret into his carrier at the back of the bike. Furó loved the speed and motion and spent his time peering out at the fast-disappearing roads, the wind fluttering his whiskers. Isabel soon arrived at Can Rosselló and parked up on the gravel drive. The front of the *finca* was surrounded on three sides by fruit trees and mature pines, and as Isabel breathed in their hot woody aroma, she closed her eyes and took some long deep breaths. It was good to be back in Es Pla, the peaceful agricultural heartland of the island. She walked past the blossoming white oleander bushes and orange trees and made her way to the porch, where moments later she was greeted by Pepe Serrano. She took in the Nehru-style white linen shirt and crisp navy shorts, complemented by tawny-hued moccasins. He appeared relaxed and pleased to see her.

'What have we here? A ferret?'

'This is Furó,' Isabel replied. 'Do you have a problem with him entering the house? I'd like him to see Maria's bedroom.'

He gave a deep laugh and peered at Furó in his carrier. 'Be my guest. Why are you so keen to see my late wife's bedroom, my little friend? Are you an opera buff?'

Isabel pulled Furó to her chest and fondled him. 'He's a very cultured ferret and is an invaluable help to me in my work.'

He grinned. 'I hope he likes dogs because we have Brut with us today. He's the Labrador pup owned by my gardener, Roberto. Come, please join me for a coffee.'

They settled in the sunny kitchen, where Raquel greeted Isabel warmly and began making their coffee. Furó sniffed noses with the frenetic Brut and they played happily together, chasing balls across the kitchen floor. Moments later, Roberto entered and, laughing, picked up Brut.

'I'll get him out of your hair now. He could do with a run around in the garden.'

When he'd left, Furó jumped onto Isabel's lap. His brown eyes settled on Pepe's face and his whiskers twitched as Isabel stroked him. Raquel wandered over and placed a tray of homemade biscuits and slices of almond cake on the table. Isabel's stomach rumbled heartily.

'You poor thing,' exclaimed Pepe. 'Did you skip breakfast?'

Isabel helped herself to a biscuit and a piece of cake. 'Not at all, I'm just exceptionally greedy.'

'I like honesty,' he replied. 'So why did you want to see me?'

She took a sip of coffee. 'A few quick questions. How well did you know Maria's regular students, Georg and Gemma?'

He shrugged. 'I rarely engaged with them. Young people aren't interested in old fogies like me and besides, they were here for their music lessons.'

'And when was the last time Gemma visited Maria? You mentioned seeing her bike on Monday.'

He was silent for a few seconds. 'Indeed, her bicycle was parked near the porch so I can only assume she'd come for a class with Maria.'

Isabel took some notes, the pen paused above her pad. 'In that case, she saw Maria the day before she died?'

He nodded. 'That would be the logical conclusion.'

'Presumably you and Raquel sorted the fruit left by Roberto every morning? Would anyone else have known about this routine?'

'Actually, we only sort the fruit on Tuesdays and Thursdays when Roberto collects them. Sometimes it's vegetables too, of course. The other days he's busy working on the land.' Pepe turned to observe Raquel. 'Can you think of anyone?'

The young woman shrugged. 'Possibly the students. The front door is always open, so Georg and Gemma used to come and go as they pleased and often came in the early morning to practise.'

'They didn't have set times for their lessons?' asked Isabel.

'Yes,' Raquel replied, 'but Tía Maria invited them to use the practice room on the top floor whenever they liked. She was often at the Conservatori or running errands.'

Isabel smiled. 'That's very helpful. And now I must have another quick glimpse of Maria's bedroom.' She turned to Pepe. 'As you know, the forensics team will be here shortly to examine it, but I just want to have a very quick check on something myself.'

Pepe rose to his feet and opened the kitchen door. 'Would you like me to accompany you?'

'That won't be necessary.' Isabel drained her coffee. 'Thank you for the delicious cake and biscuits. It's set me up for the day.'

Raquel came forward with a small foiled wrapped package. 'Here are some more of my homemade biscuits. There are too many for Pepe, Roberto and me.'

'How kind,' Isabel replied, tucking them into her pannier. 'Furó and I won't be long, and I can let myself out.'

Her host gave a braying laugh and wagged a finger. 'Oh no, no, no. You might steal the family silver, so it will be my duty to bid you farewell before you go.'

Isabel returned to her *moto* and removed the portable safe that contained the five keys to Maria's bedroom. She opened it and put the keys in her pocket, walking briskly in the direction of the greenhouse and side garden.

'Come on, Furó. Let's go for a brief walk. I need to check something out.'

Her companion darted ahead, weaving through the long yellowing grasses at the side of the lawn, exploring every rocky crevice.

Some fifteen minutes later, she returned to the house, having picked up the portable safe from her bike. She left the heavy item in the *entrada* and made her way upstairs. As she reached the top landing, Furó sniffed about the door and gave a low growl. Isabel carefully inspected the yellow and black sticky police tape and red sticker with the words '*NO PASE*' and placed her hands on her hips.

'Ha! You are spot on, Furó. This police tape has been removed and replaced. Whoever did it probably used steam. Someone has been here before us, but who?'

With gloved hands, she carefully pulled back the tape and unlocked the door using the five keys and entered the room. Despite everything appearing to be just as she had left it, Isabel felt that in some way the room had been violated. She wandered about and stood lost in thought by the shuttered French windows. She examined the photographs on the desk, peering at each in turn.

'These pictures have been moved about, Furó.' She took out her mobile and flicked through some images she had taken of the room during her visit on Tuesday. 'Yes, they have definitely been swapped around.'

She picked up a gilt frame at the front and took a closer look at the handsome, costumed male with his arm placed around Maria's shoulders. As she too was in a dramatic velvet ensemble, Isabel surmised that they had both been performing in an opera. The man's face seemed very familiar to her, so she used her mobile to take an image and returned the frame to where she had found it.

'Someone placed this here deliberately, Furó. Whoever it was, they wanted us to find it.'

As she scrutinised the man's face, she was distracted by the ferret scratching frantically at the door to the extravagant wardrobe.

Isabel tutted. 'Stop that or you could damage the wood.'

Furó ignored her and began hissing and growling. She came over and wrestled with the handle. She looked at him. 'Is there something inside that you want me to see?'

The ferret whimpered and began scratching again at the locked door. Isabel picked him up.

'Okay, my little friend. Let's find out what is inside, shall we?'

She left the room and returned to the kitchen. Pepe and Raquel were still there, both occupied with different tasks.

In surprise, Pepe stared at her. 'Back so soon? That was a quick visit.'

Isabel addressed both of them. 'Have either of you entered Maria's bedroom since my last visit?'

'No.' Raquel bit her lip. 'I simply haven't had the heart to go up to the top floor.'

Isabel persisted. 'Do either of you have the keys to Maria's bedroom or the wardrobe?'

'Obviously I don't,' Pepe replied smoothly. 'Remember that Maria threw me out and had all those locks fitted. I most certainly haven't been up there since you last came to the house.'

Raquel wiped her hands on a tea towel. 'I don't know anyone who had a set of keys to her room, but I do know where Maria kept the one to the wardrobe.' She looked a little embarrassed. 'She allowed me to clean the room every week and once I saw her place the wardrobe key in her jewellery box on the dresser. I pretended I hadn't seen.'

'Do you have a local key cutter around here?' Isabel asked.

Raquel nodded. 'Well, Ferretería Bordoy in Inca can cut most keys. It's certainly the best known.'

Isabel nodded. 'Why do you think she was so secretive about the contents of her bedroom?'

Pepe yawned. 'I wouldn't read too much into it. She was always very private and dramatic, as if living in a scene from one of her operas.'

Raquel gave a sigh. 'I've no idea, but she became really strange after she returned from her opera tour on the mainland five years ago and had some kind of breakdown. She wouldn't come out of her room for nearly a year and when she did, she was hollow-eyed and jumpy.'

Pepe nodded. 'For appearance's sake, we all called it her sabbatical. Raquel had to leave her meals and even clean bed linen outside the door. Only her private doctor was allowed inside once or twice a month to check up on her.'

'Was she on medication?' Isabel asked.

'The doctor would tell us very little, though he did admit that she was depressed, and he'd given her antidepressants and sleeping pills.'

'Do you have his name?' Isabel asked.

'Doctor Blando. He had a private practice in Palma. That's all I can recall.'

Isabel stood by the kitchen door. 'If your wife had a mental crisis, have you any idea what might have set it off?'

'Her agent, Eva Salas, thinks she just had a personal meltdown brought on by all the pressure. Who knows?'

'One other thing,' said Isabel. 'I believe you collect masks?'

Pepe was slow to answer. 'That was a long time ago. I keep them in a glass cabinet in the study on the first floor. Who told you that?'

'A little bird.' Isabel winked. 'Do you mind if I take a look at them on my way to the second floor?'

He was hesitant. 'They're not particularly interesting, but by all means. It's the first door on the right at the top of the stairs.'

When Isabel reached the first-floor landing, she found the study door shut, though a key sat in the lock. She turned it slowly and walked into the dark, cool room, switching the light on as she closed the door behind her, the key in her hand. To her surprise, the glass and mahogany cabinet ran along the entire length of one side of the spacious room and contained hundreds of papier mâché masks, all seemingly colour-coded. Some were exotic and colourful African and Asian varieties while others were distinctly creepy and sinister. One particular sample, shaped like an enormous eagle's head, caught her eye. It had real white and silvery feathers and clamped in its painted bloodied beak was a limp grey rodent made of wood. As she explored the cabinet with her eyes, she noticed a gap between two white masks. She frowned. Had one been removed?

Isabel returned to Maria's room and discovered her elaborate antique mahogany jewellery box on the dresser. To her frustration, that, too was locked. She sat on the floor with it and pulled a hairpin from a small purse in her pannier, which she straightened out and used to wiggle in the lock. Furó watched her avidly, grunting and whimpering as she failed to open it.

'Cut me some slack, will you? It's a knack.'

After a few minutes, the lock clicked and the lid opened. Inside she found well-ordered rows of glitzy earrings, rings, necklaces, and pendants. In a separate area in the box's deep interior were a few broaches, keys, ribbons, and hair clips. She beamed at Furó and held up an ornate key, which she guessed, by its size, might fit the wardrobe lock. As soon as the wardrobe door creaked open, a musty sweet fragrance, perhaps rose, snaked its way into the room. Furó leapt inside, growling and sniffing as he wove about the exotic gowns and coats. Isabel separated each hanger, raising an eyebrow at the expensive couture labels. She felt inside the pockets of coats and dresses, and even the shoes lining the wardrobe, but found nothing of any significance. Somewhat disappointed, she stepped back while Furó continued to scamper about in the shadowy space. She was about to drag him out when, of his own volition, he appeared with something small in his mouth. He dropped it at Isabel's feet but continued to growl threateningly at the wardrobe. Isabel picked it up and locked the door, returning the key to the jewellery box. It was a glass button shaped like a red and white spotted ladybird. She looked at Furó uncomprehendingly.

'It's pretty, but what's so important about it?'

As Furó sneezed and growled unhappily, she stashed the button in a small sample bag and shooed her insouciant ferret out of the room. Next, she locked the bedroom door and returned to the *entrada*, where she secured the five keys in the portable safe. Pepe was waiting for her in the kitchen and seemed amused when she placed the safe on the table.

AUNT MARIA'S LAST ARIA

'Please can you give this to my colleague, Nacho, when he arrives this afternoon? As you know, he will be examining Maria's bedroom.'

A smile lingered on his face. 'My pleasure. I shall guard it with my life until he gets here. Can I offer you a drink before you go?'

Isabel shook her head. 'Thanks, but I need to head off.'

Pepe accompanied her to the courtyard and stood squinting in the sunlight as she got out her helmet and secured Furó in his carrier on the bike. Isabel turned to him.

'Do you know the man in this photo?'

She flashed him the image on her mobile that she had taken in Maria's bedroom.

'Of course, don't you? It is Enrique Diaz, the most famous tenor in Spain.'

'Was he a good friend of Maria's?'

He shrugged. 'I wouldn't go that far. In the past they performed together on the mainland. He and Maria had the same agent.'

'You mean Eva Salas?'

'That's right. If you want his details, Eva will have them.'

Isabel nodded. 'By the way, I liked the masks, though one appeared to be missing.'

He stiffened. 'Oh?'

'I'm guessing it was white, since you appear to have arranged them by colour. There's a gap among the white masks.'

'That is curious. I will have to check. Let's hope one hasn't run away.'

Isabel held his gaze. 'And have you heard from Maria's lawyer yet about her will?'

'It appears that I will inherit everything, including this house.'

'You must be relieved. It will be difficult for Maria's cousin to contest the will.'

Pepe folded his arms. 'I've no idea, but my lawyer and I will meet soon to discuss the best way forward for all parties.'

Isabel stared at him for a second. She wondered what he meant by that.

As she mounted the bike, Pepe came forward as if suddenly remembering something.

'I have a small request. Maria always wore a heart-shaped gold locket that I gave her. It was my mother's, so it has great sentimental value. It was on Maria's person when she died and I'd dearly like it back.'

Isabel nodded. 'I'm sure it will be released as soon as forensics have finished examining it. I'll find out when.'

Pepe gave her a wave as she drove off, a sudden sombre expression printed on his face.

It took Isabel barely fifteen minutes to reach Ferretería Bordoy. A young man at the counter listened to her request and disappeared to the back of the shop to find the owner. The shop was empty, save for an old hound that eyed Furó curiously. An elderly man appeared and grinned when he saw Isabel clutching Furó in his arms.

'He's a beauty. I used to have a pet ferret as a lad.'

Isabel smiled encouragingly. 'Really? How lovely.'

'You want to know about the keys for Can Rosselló?'

Isabel slid her police badge across the counter. He examined it for a few seconds before returning it.

'Well, Señorita Flores, you've come to the right place. We've cut the keys for the Rosselló family for many years. Such a tragedy about Maria. I knew both her father and grandparents. Sadly, her parents passed when she was young.'

Isabel offered him a sympathetic look. 'Really my question is whether you know anything about five keys that fitted the locks of a particular bedroom?'

He nodded. 'Indeed I do. Maria had them cut about five years ago, as I recall. Two sets were made.'

Isabel perked up. 'Did she say who they were for, by any chance?'

'She told me that she wanted one for herself, and a spare set too. I assumed they were for her husband. Is it important?'

Isabel wrinkled her nose. 'I'm really not able to discuss that, but I am so grateful for your kind help.'

The shopkeeper checked that his assistant was not in earshot and whispered, 'This conversation will go no further.'

As Isabel left the shop and returned Furó to his carrier, she turned to him. 'I love that generation. They understand the importance of discretion.' She pulled down her helmet. 'It's understandable that in normal circumstances, the shopkeeper might assume that Pepe would have had a set of those keys, but of course, there is nothing normal about this case, is there?'

Furó gave a loud grunt as if in agreement and promptly sneezed.

Before setting off for Inca, Isabel called Nacho to warn him that someone had broken the police tape on Maria's bedroom door and entered the room. She told him about the button Furó had found and which she had placed in a sample bag inside the portable safe, along with the five door keys. She was keen to know if his team could track down its provenance.

She smiled at Furó. 'Early this afternoon, I've arranged for us to visit Catalina Grimalt in Ses Salines, so we've got time to visit Pere in Inca to see how he's progressing with your run. Pleased?'

Furó began chuntering and broke into a happy dance, puffing up his tail and pawing excitedly inside his carrier.

'While we're there, Furó, we must pick up a special wine for dinner tonight. I'm making Tolo baked cod with *tumbet* and it's all prepared back at the house. Perhaps we can stop in the village of Biniamar for a spot of lunch at Bar Mayorga and then take a walk to the village's unfinished church, which is a wonder to behold. In truth, it was a bit of a vanity project by a Mallorcan politician named Antoni Maura. They started building it in 1910 but Maura never managed to raise the finance to finish it.'

Furó yawned heavily and rolled sleepily onto his side. Isabel laughed.

'Okay, enough history. Let's hit the road.'

By the time Isabel and Furó reached the rough track leading to the *finca* of Catalina Grimalt, the air had cooled, and a light sea breeze had replaced the dense and humid air. Sleepy Ses Salines lay in the southeast of the island, close to the sea, and even in the heat of the summer, the salty air seemed fresher than in other coastal enclaves. Isabel dismounted her bike, shook out her hot damp hair and clipped Furó into his harness.

As she approached the porch, the arched wooden door opened and a handsome woman in full make-up appeared, clutching a handkerchief.

'Isabel Flores? Do come in. I am Catalina.' She stopped to look down at Furó, a look of undisguised disgust on her face.

'What is that creature?'

'A ferret. His name is Furó. In my email to you I did ask if it was okay to bring him along, and you said it was fine providing he was harnessed.'

Catalina frowned. 'My assistant would have replied. I had no idea these vermin were now pets. Is this a new trend?'

Isabel tried to control her breathing while Furó gave a low hiss. 'They are incredibly loveable and intelligent animals. In fact, they make perfect detectives as they have a keen sense of smell and remarkable instincts.'

AUNT MARIA'S LAST ARIA

The woman stared at her in silence. 'How fascinating.'

'I can keep him in his carrier, if you prefer.'

Catalina forced a smile. 'No, bring it in, but please keep it on a lead.'

The living room was as frosty as its owner thanks to a large air-con unit that rumbled in a far corner. The woman suddenly dabbed at her dry eyes.

'It's so heartbreaking to talk about Maria. Such a great talent and a very dear friend of mine.'

Isabel nodded. 'So you weren't in any way rivals?'

'Not at all! She was a soprano, and I am a contralto.'

'I'm not an opera buff, but am I right in thinking that contraltos usually play villains?'

Catalina eyed her coldly. 'Contraltos sometimes have villainous roles, but I tend to play strong, iconic characters. Talented contraltos are a rare breed and more sought after than sopranos. We're not the divas.'

'Did Maria concur with that view?'

'It wasn't something we discussed.'

Isabel smiled. 'Kathleen Ferrier was an exceptional contralto who died far too young. She had a beautiful voice.'

'So you do know about opera.'

'Not really, but I love all things English, and she was a famed opera singer during the forties who was greatly loved and admired in the country.' Isabel paused to stroke a fretful Furó, who was blatantly baring his teeth at the contralto.

'Your ferret looks very aggressive,' Catalina said uneasily.

'Not at all. It's his way of smiling at you.'

The woman shifted in her seat. 'You must understand that Maria was deeply unstable, and it was probably only a matter of time before she took her own life. She had a terrible marriage, and her husband was a brute.'

'She told you that?'

'Not in so many words, but they slept in separate rooms. Everyone knew in our circles. And she was always desperate to get off the island to go on tours.'

Isabel observed her quietly, and how her hands constantly clutched at the handkerchief that sat like a well-placed prop in her lap. 'Where were you on Tuesday morning?'

Catalina frowned. 'Here, practising for an upcoming concert at La Seu Cathedral. My neighbours can confirm that. Why do you ask?'

'Until we know for certain the manner of Maria Rosselló's death, we need to track the movements of her close contacts, such as yourself.'

'But it was suicide.'

'Maybe,' Isabel replied. She stood up. 'Did you ever perform alongside Maria?'

'Yes, several times here and in the mainland.'

'Were you by chance on the tour she made five years ago?'

The woman shook her head. 'No, but that was the tour that proved her undoing. She simply couldn't handle the pressure of so many venues in Spain and Europe. When she returned, she was in a terrible state emotionally and withdrew from the world.'

'As you were such a close friend, I imagine you must have visited her during that period?'

The woman hesitated and sighed. 'I would have done, of course, but I really felt Maria wanted to be alone and I respected her privacy.'

'I see,' Isabel replied.

Catalina beamed at her. 'Next month, Eva is going to organise a memorial service at Bellver Castle in her honour with the president in attendance. Naturally, I have agreed to perform and waive my fee.'

Isabel didn't know whether to laugh or cry. Instead, she maintained her composure.

'How very magnanimous of you.' She stood up. 'I shall be in touch if I need anything more.'

At the front door, Catalina offered her hand and began theatrically dabbing at her face. Furó gave a long and steady growl and hissed as Isabel tried to push him sharply behind her legs.

Catalina watched Isabel manoeuvre the bike onto the track and with the handkerchief in the air, waved a half-hearted adieu.

Isabel rode northwards and parked on the side of a country road close to the tranquil salt marshes of Es Salobrar on the outskirts of Campos. It was a stone's throw from the long blond beach of Es Trenc, a magnet for summer tourists, and yet, it felt a million miles away from the bustle. She decided that Furó deserved a long run after his unpleasant encounter with the disingenuous contralto and released him from the carrier, laughing as he ran like the wind. As she headed up the rural path after him, she turned to admire the peaceful Hotel Fontsanta which housed the only natural hot springs in the Balearic islands. Once she had treated Marga to a birthday spa day at the rural haven and both had emerged squeaky clean and glowing. They had continued the fun back at Bar Castel with a few glasses of *cava*.

Now she and Furó made their way through the wild and deserted terrain, listening to the call of the birds and breathing in the still, aromatic air. The sky had dulled and the sun was slowly dipping below the hills, creating a blood-orange fringe on the horizon. Furó undulated happily through the long sun-bleached grasses of the nature reserve, racing back to Isabel whenever she called to him with her familiar two-fingered whistle. To her delight, a small gathering of pink-feathered greater flamingos stood by a shallow stretch of muddy water, their long and graceful necks bobbing up and down as they drank. There was a colony of at least three hundred in the nature reserve but sightings were rare until late summer. Isabel spotted Furó darting about in a muddy pool. Instinctively surmising that it was close to eight o'clock, she pulled him out. Just an hour earlier, Tolo had called apologetically to say that he was stuck in a meeting and wouldn't get to Sant Martí until at least nine-thirty. Isabel didn't mind. It was the nature of police work, and in the sizzling summer, dining at a late hour was the norm.

As she and Furó headed back towards the car, she distinctly heard light footsteps. She stopped abruptly and, breathing softly, cocked her head in the direction of the sound. Furó gave a low hiss, speeding off towards the path that led back to the car. In some fright, she sped after him, worried that he might dart onto the road. As Isabel emerged from the path, she heard a car door slam and spotted a lone red Fiat 500 parked further along the road. To her dismay, she watched as Furó raced madly towards it just as it pulled away from the kerb. The car accelerated and, with its headlights on full beam, headed straight towards the hapless ferret. For a terrifying moment, Isabel watched as Furó, stupefied by the lights, stood stock still before he regained his senses and jumped out of the vehicle's path. As it roared past, Isabel was able to read the last letter of the registration number. It was a Z, the same letter that she remembered seeing on the number-plate of the red Fiat 500 in the car park of the Conservatori in Palma. Was it pure coincidence? Shaking with adrenalin and shock, Isabel embraced Furó and secured him safely in his carrier. With a deep breath, she revved the bike and set off on the fifty-minute journey back home to Sant Martí.

It was past four o'clock in the morning and although still dark, the cockerels had already begun to crow. Isabel crept down the stairs, using her iPhone torch to guide the way. Tolo had arrived in the late evening and they had enjoyed a candlelit dinner out on her terrace, but she had been distracted and unnerved by her experience at the nature reserve. Keen not to worry him, she had played down the incident, and they had spent the evening discussing the ongoing investigation into the death of Maria before, exhausted, Tolo had gone upstairs to bed. Isabel had joined him an hour later, but she was wired and ill at ease. All the windows were flung wide open, but the heat was intense and unremitting. Isabel had tossed and turned, and had been tempted to resort to air conditioning, despite the ruinous expense, but finally got up and decided to read instead.

She sat out on her garden patio, enjoying the balmy air, and listened to the cry of the scops owl and awakening birds. Nature's early morning chorus was something that Isabel relished, and she would spend time identifying each bird call as she sipped on a coffee before leaving for her daily swim. She picked up her dog-eared copy of the novel *Cold Comfort Farm* by Stella Gibbons, one of her favourite British authors. Even though the book had been written in 1932, its messages still resonated with her, and she was tickled by the humour. Despite its comic value, and its satirical take on the alleged wonders of rural life, Isabel still felt unease whenever she read the book's immortalised refrain: 'Something nasty in the woodshed'. Momentarily, she placed the book in her lap and repeated the phrase out loud. She thought about Maria's ornate wardrobe and the tiny ladybird glass button that Furó had found inside. Her ferret certainly felt there was something nasty in the wardrobe, something disturbing that for now remained a mystery. Perhaps the little ladybird button would hold the key.

NINE

Isabel and Tolo sat under a cream parasol outside Café Jordi in the *plaça* of Sant Martí. As there were so many tourists during the summer season, Jordi, the eponymous owner, had set up a large table permanently reserved for village residents. This meant that his elderly customers in particular would always have a place to enjoy their coffees and *menu del día* and no one could moan about visitors snaffling all the tables. Isabel and Tolo had enjoyed a hearty breakfast of scrambled eggs and mushrooms served with fresh brown sourdough bread. This was an unusual diversion from the usual white crusty baguette served by Jordi, but he had recently been seduced by the delicious offerings from the newly installed Uruguayan bakery in Fornalutx. Señora Coll, the postmistress, sat opposite Isabel, fanning herself with a lace-edged *abanico* while she sipped on a *granizado de limón*. Next to Tolo, Pep savoured a coffee, waving to his many young female admirers who passed by on their way to Bon Día.

'Where's Angélica this morning?' asked Isabel.

'At the market in Soller with her mum. She's seeing some girlfriends this afternoon, so I'll have some peace to watch football after you and I have done our cycle ride to Lluc.'

Tolo grinned. 'Ah yes, *cariño*, you have your triathlon training later this morning.'

Isabel scrunched her nose. 'I don't mind running half a marathon or swimming, but I'm not so keen on the ninety-kilometre bike ride. It's a long way.'

Pep sat back in his chair and tilted his sunglasses. 'Don't be a wimp. It's good exercise and with all the Chupa Chups and cake you eat, probably a lifesaver.'

Isabel laughed and thumped his arm. 'That was mean.'

'*Madre mía*! I can't imagine doing anything so energetic,' exclaimed Señora Coll. 'But as Doctor Ramis knows, I have a very delicate disposition and must refrain from frenetic activity. Without his pills, I'd be a goner.'

Isabel stifled a grin and nodded. 'Indeed. Miguel is a lifesaver. Talking of the good doctor, he and Mama are arriving home this afternoon. I've missed her baking.'

'Hopefully you've missed her too,' said Tolo with a wink.

'And what about all the cakes and buns my mother's been doing for you in her absence?' protested Pep.

'Very true. Rosa has been an angel, and I am so grateful.' She slid a smile towards Tolo. 'Of course, I miss my darling mother, but she is, you must admit, an exceptional cook.'

Tolo nodded. 'Her *porc amb coll* is fantastic, and let's not start on her *paella* and *albóndiga*s.'

Jordi, as portly as ever, approached the table, wiping his big red hands on an old apron.

'Like the bread? It's from that new bakery in Fornalutx. I was a bit sceptical at first, but it tastes so good. That Uruguayan family can show us Mallorcans a thing or two about baking.'

'It's delicious,' Tolo replied. 'I'm going to drive past the village on my way to Palma and pick up a few loaves.'

'Their almond croissants are scrumptious too,' Isabel replied. 'Best to avoid the shop if you're on a diet.'

Pau appeared under the awning of Bon Día and strolled over. He took off his police cap and ran a hand through his damp hair. 'This heat gets to you. What I'd do for a swim.' He smiled across at Isabel. 'Everything okay with your Ducati now?'

Pep narrowed his eyes. 'Aha! I knew you were hiding something, Bel. What happened to Boadicea?'

Tolo gripped her arm. 'You had an accident?'

'Is nothing sacred in this village?' Isabel huffed. 'I had a minor skirmish with a wall while reversing my bike after a swim. Bernat promised to keep mum.'

'It's my fault,' Pau replied. 'I saw him working on the bike in his yard and asked what had happened. Sorry, Bel.'

'As long as you're okay,' Tolo replied. 'You must always tell me about these things. I don't care about you bumping the Ducati, your life is more important.'

'Bel is the clumsiest woman I know,' goaded Pep. 'She managed to wrench the handle off the door of the town hall which has been there for centuries without incident.'

'You don't know your own strength, my girl,' tutted Señora Coll. 'Now I must be off. Frans is manning the counter for me back at the house and he's got to leave by nine-thirty.'

Isabel found it touching that such an unlikely friendship had formed between the elderly postmistress and the eccentric young German artist and eco-activist who lived a bohemian life in the mountains.

Isabel got to her feet and pushed some notes into Jordi's hands.

'All the drinks are on me. Come on, Tolo. You've got to get to the precinct.'

Jordi wandered off inside the café and returned with some coins in a bowl. Isabel left it on the table and set off across the *plaça* towards Calle Pastor with Tolo.

When they were out of earshot, he said, 'Any news about your Uncle Hugo? I know I shouldn't ask, but has Interpol been in touch again about his whereabouts?'

Isabel gave a sad shake of the head. 'Emilio Navarro called me the other day. He said that the matter was delicate, and I should sit tight. I don't have a clue about what's going on, other than that Hugo appears to be alive.'

'That is a comfort.'

'Is it? I don't know if he's a wanted man and that's why he's under surveillance by Interpol, and I feel bad not being able to tell my mother about what I know.'

Tolo pulled her close and gave her a hug. 'It will all become clear in the fullness of time. For now, put it all out of your mind and focus on your work and the people you love.'

Isabel nodded. 'I want to get to the bottom of Tía Maria's death, even if everyone keeps assuring me that she committed suicide. Pepe mentioned that five years ago when she had a breakdown, she was seen by a private doctor in Palma. His name was Blando, but I can't find any trace of him on the medical register.'

'Maybe he left Mallorca.'

'That was my thought. He might be retired or is practising elsewhere.'

'Leave it with me. I'll get Gaspar and the team onto it.'

'There's something about that little ladybird button that Furó found that troubles me too, and who broke into Maria's bedroom? And why? Why place that photo of Enrique Diaz in front of the others on her desk? It was intentional.'

They arrived at Tolo's car. 'I've no idea, but don't read too much into it. As for Furó's find, you have to admit that he does sometimes just enjoy hunting and retrieving things. The button might have no significance at all.'

Isabel hunched her shoulders. 'You're right. All the same, I want to keep an open mind on this case. It would be good to know who left Maria those mushrooms and find out more about her cousin, Fermin.'

Tolo nodded. 'Fine, but we also must accept that this could be just a sad case of suicide.' He smiled. 'What are you up to after your bike ride?'

'I'm going to pop by the cash and carry in Inca to talk with Pepe's boss. Hopefully, I might get to meet some of his co-workers.' She shielded her eyes from the harsh sun. 'What about you?'

Tolo exhaled deeply. 'I've organised a press conference about the cold case involving the two murdered prostitutes.'

'How is it going?'

'We're close to tying up loose ends on that case and also one involving domestic child abuse. Later, I have a meeting with our favourite Guardia captain, followed by dinner with the police commissioner.'

'Why do you need to see Gómez? Please keep him off my back.'

Tolo laughed. 'He hasn't got time for you, *cariño*. He's totally preoccupied closing in on a massive drug ring that extends from the sink estates of Palma to Cala d'Or and Alcudia. He wants my advice. In fairness, he's done a great job.'

Isabel grinned. 'Now there's a thing! A friendship between you and Gómez.'

'Steady on,' he replied with a chuckle as he bent forward and kissed her.

He got into his car and, revving the engine, leant out of the window.

'Please give a hug to Florentina and Miguel tonight. I wish I could join you all for supper but I'll see you at Gaspar's birthday bash tomorrow. That's going to be fun.'

'Can't wait,' Isabel replied.

As he drove off, Isabel heard someone calling her name and turned to see Adam Markham hand in hand with a pretty woman.

'Can I introduce my girlfriend, Liv Bos?'

Isabel shook the woman's hand. 'How are you finding life in our valley?'

'I'm loving it. The weather is amazing. It's doing wonders for my psoriasis already.'

'Glad to hear it.' Isabel turned to Adam. 'Is everything okay with the refurbishment of Juan Jaume's house? I saw Tomeu Tous hanging around outside the other day.'

He shrugged and looked at her over his shades. 'He'd wanted to sell the house, but I offered a better deal, so the best man won, right?'

Isabel puffed out her lower lip. 'Well, keep an eye on him. No more dead seagulls?'

Liv Bos frowned. 'What dead seagulls?'

Adam stiffened and with his girlfriend's back to him, placed his right index finger to his lips. Isabel took the hint.

'Oh, it's nothing. Just with the hot weather, some poor gulls have been found dead.'

The woman looked concerned. 'You found one, Adam?'

'Yes, while I was on a walk. I guess it's too hot for some sea birds.'

As they walked away, Adam turned back and gave Isabel a surreptitious nod.

She walked slowly up her garden path, spending some time sniffing the rosemary bush with its heady aroma and admiring the cool velvety petals of the oleander bush. She felt a prickly sensation on her arms and shivered despite the hot air. Opening the front door, she heard a loud chuntering and her heart melted to see Furó standing on his hindlegs in anticipation of a cuddle.

AUNT MARIA'S LAST ARIA

The town of Inca was bustling with people and cars, but it was Saturday, a day when everyone did their shopping. After weaving her way around a long queue of cars, Isabel found a parking space close to the commercial park. She hopped off Boadicea and made her way to a large faceless building protected by heavy gates. A perfunctory sign indicated that this was Inca's cash and carry. Having reached the reception area, she showed a sleepy young staff member her police badge. He picked up a phone and gave her a tentative smile.

'The boss will be with you in a minute.'

Isabel nodded. 'Is Pepe Serrano in today?' She knew very well that he didn't work at the weekend, but she was keen to see what reaction his name elicited from his colleagues.

'No, he's only here on weekdays.'

'Has he worked here long?'

'For as long as I've been here,' he replied. 'He's like everyone's favourite crazy uncle.'

'Really, why do you say that?'

The young man tittered. 'He's a bit eccentric, old Pepe. We have this deal where you buy two boxes of cans of fish, and you get one free. He has loads of them. He and his wife must eat nothing else.'

'That is strange.'

'All the same, he's a nice bloke and the guys who work for him say he's very laid-back. I've never seen Pepe lose his temper. In the lads' breaktime he often plays salsa and flamenco music in the warehouse and gets them all to dance. As I say, an eccentric.'

'Did you ever meet his wife?'

'As if someone that famous would come here!' His forehead puckered. 'The boss told us that she'd topped herself last Tuesday. Poor old Pepe. He'll have taken it hard. Apparently, he's coming back to work next week.'

A door opened and a hefty man in blue overalls appeared. He extended a hand.

'Señorita Flores. I'm Arturo Pina. Please come to my office. It's a bit scruffy, I'm afraid.'

When Isabel was settled in a plastic chair with *cortado* in hand, she looked around her. 'Your office seems rather tidy.'

He laughed. 'Luckily you can't see inside the cupboards. So how can I help? We're all devastated to hear about Pepe's wife. Such a big name too.'

Isabel nodded. 'I suppose I'd just like your honest thoughts about Pepe. He's not in any trouble. This is just a formality in cases of suspected suicide, and I'd appreciate your discretion.'

'Of course, though I can't tell you too much. Pepe is a bit of a closed book. He comes to work, does his job, and gets on well with his team, but he rarely talks about his home life.' He tutted. 'I know little about him apart from his wife being a famous opera singer.'

'Is he good at his job?'

'He's such a clever chap. He could do my job standing on his head, but he has no ambitions. It's probably his age. When he applied for the job some years ago, I thought it was a joke given that he'd been a big shot lawyer, but he was very modest. He's proven to be a real asset.'

'Has he ever mentioned a man named Fermin Janer, his wife's cousin?'

He shook his head. 'The only other family member he once mentioned was Juliette, his daughter from his first marriage. One day we got talking about kids, and he told me that she lived in Cape Town, and that they had no contact. I got the impression that she and Maria didn't get along. He seemed very sad about it.'

Isabel finished her coffee and politely accepted a mini tour of the premises.

'Pepe certainly loves his anchovies,' Isabel said with a smile.

Arturo laughed. 'He's one of our best customers.'

As Isabel walked back through reception, the young man at the front desk smiled at her.

'Don't worry about Pepe. The lads will keep an eye on him. We're like one big family here.'

It was late evening and Isabel sat in her mother's garden, relishing the last spoonful of a chocolate mousse. Doctor Ramis sat back in his chair with a satisfied expression.

'Your *estofado* was delicious, Bel, and your mousse, a triumph.'

Florentina nodded. 'My daughter is a good cook, but she spends far too much time running around after dangerous criminals. One day I pray you'll settle down, Bel.'

Isabel laughed. 'You might be disappointed. Anyway, I'm so happy you're home safe and sound. Cooking you supper here was the least I could do.'

Florentina tapped her hand. 'I don't think attending a film festival posed much danger.'

'Maybe not, but it's good to have you both back in Sant Martí.' She winked at Doctor Ramis. 'Señora Coll will be over the moon to see you. She was talking about the lifesaving properties of the magic medication you give her.'

He shook his head. 'I hope she never finds out that they're just sugar pills. I'll never get to heaven.'

'I've heard it's overrated,' quipped Isabel.

Her mother gave her a disapproving look. 'What a thing to say! Well, my dear daughter, it's been a long day, and I need my bed.'

'Me too,' said Doctor Ramis with a loud yawn. 'We'll help clear up.'

Together they washed and dried the dishes. At the front door, Isabel kissed her mother on both cheeks and stretched out her battered limbs. Her long cycle ride with Pep earlier in the day had left her with stiff legs.

'Are you sure you should be doing that triathlon in October? It's a terrible strain on the muscles,' fretted Florentina.

Doctor Ramis pecked her on the cheek. 'Nonsense, my dear Florentina! It will do Bel the world of good. I'm a doctor, trust me.'

Isabel and Doctor Ramis ambled through the streets of Sant Martí to Calle Pastor. The air was still pulsating with heat despite the hour. A few merry stragglers were leaving Bar Jordi while a fan-tailed dog gave chase to a cat as they headed up through a lean cobbled alley. The streetlights cast an amber glow on the ancient dry-stone walls and highlighted the scampering geckos that ran stealthily between the dark crevices and hanging ivy. As they turned into the street they shared as neighbours, a swaying figure appeared before them in the gloom, clutching a half-empty bottle. Isabel saw to her dismay that it was Manuel Borras. He wore a menacing smile and mumbled incoherently to himself. With half-closed eyes, he lurched past, but a few paces away he stopped and called after them. His voice took on a sudden clarity.

'If you see my father, say I'm coming for him. He's going to wish I'd never been born.'

TEN

Isabel sat on her knees in the corral with a bloodied baby dove in her hands. In a disorientated state, the young bird appeared to have flown inside the henhouse only to be attacked ferociously by her matronly hens. She eyed them all with fury.

'Shame on you! I cannot abide pack mentality. It has no place in a civilised society, and you have bitterly disappointed me, and on a Sunday too. Instead of showing this poor baby dove any mercy or love, you brutally attacked it and left it for dead. No treats for the rest of the day.'

Somewhat contrite, the hens stood still with eyes averted, making soft clucking noises. She stood up and, gently stroking the head of the bird, stared at them all.

'Did none of you ever read about the demise of the Roman emperor, Julius Caesar? He was attacked by a group of conspirators led by Brutus, a man he trusted. They had their reasons, but you are just a spiteful, bloodthirsty, and cowardly bunch. I have no more to say on the matter.'

She slammed the corral door and bumped straight into her elderly uncle. Idò's face crumpled with laughter.

'I'd have recorded that if I knew how to work my mobile. Perhaps you'd have been better on the stage instead of doing all this police work.'

Isabel smirked. 'Well, I'm mightily cross with them. Look at this poor baby.'

Idò pulled a face as he examined the half-dead creature. 'That's life, my dear Bel. Survival of the fittest. It's Darwin's law. I think he's a goner.'

Isabel walked with him towards the kitchen, carefully nursing the bird in her left hand. 'Where's Mama?'

'She's in the *entrada* sorting out the fresh laundry with the cleaners and Pep and I are off to Casa Elena in Biniaraix. Seems like the pool pump is caput and they've got an ant infestation too.'

Isabel gave a groan and turned on the coffee machine.

'Didn't they call Pep about the bats too?'

'Yes. The wife is always on the blower to Pep. If you ask me, she's got the hots for him.'

Isabel gave a guffaw. 'She wouldn't be the first. Anyway, how's your hip now? Are you okay to go over there?'

He nodded. 'Actually, I'm quite enjoying being back at work. I got a bit bored sitting around with Perro at home. It's not like I could take him for long walks and so we just sat around eating cake.'

'Idò, you mustn't give him cake. All that sugar and fat isn't good for dogs.'

'I only gave him a little. Besides, you're a fine one to talk with all those lollies you eat.'

Florentina bustled into the kitchen and dumped a huge bag of towels on the table.

'You can make me a coffee too, Bel. My legs are aching. Miguel and I went to Juliana's Pilates class early this morning and it was quite a challenge at my age. Yoga is easier.'

AUNT MARIA'S LAST ARIA

Isabel laughed and placed a cup in front of her. 'Has the good doctor gone home for a rest?'

'As if. He's seeing a patient,' her mother replied with mock scorn.

'On a Sunday?' cried Idò.

'It's old Mateus. He's got bronchitis very badly and asked if he could pop by. A doctor's work never ends.'

She sipped on the cup of piping hot coffee and added some cream from a small jug.

'How about a slice of orange cake?'

Idò brightened up and headed for the pantry as his sister called after him.

'It's under a cover and next to the fresh *magdalenas* I baked this morning.'

Isabel returned to the table, having carefully washed the dove's wounds with a mild saline solution in the sink. She placed a hot water bottle under some soft tea towels inside a wooden box and gently put the bird inside.

'Poor thing,' said Florentina. 'Did Furó bite it?'

'Of course not,' Isabel replied. 'It was my wicked hens. I shall ask Miguel to take a look at it.'

'The vet might be better,' added Idò. 'Tomeu will know what to do.'

Isabel got up and put the wooden box on a shelf in the cool dark pantry.

'Maybe, but I don't want to disturb him on a Sunday. Besides, I've also got to get to Gaspar's birthday lunch party in Calvia so don't have much time.'

'Calvia?' exclaimed her mother. 'That's so far! Just for a lunch.'

'It's only forty minutes away by *moto*.'

Her uncle grinned. 'Go easy on the wine if you're on the bike, Bel.'

She rolled her eyes. 'Really? I was thinking of knocking back a few bottles.'

Pep emerged from the *entrada* and surveyed them all. 'The cleaners have just left. I see everyone's eating again. Come on, Idò, we've got to get going.'

The elderly man stuffed a last morsel of cake into his mouth and rose to his feet, reaching for a wooden stick that was propped up against a wall. Pep frowned.

'And you can forget about that sympathy stick, Idò. The game's up. I saw you walking quite easily without it late in the *plaça* last night. You've been milking that hip replacement way too long.'

Isabel and Florentina giggled as Idò shuffled to the door, wearing a gruff expression.

'The pain comes and goes, Pep. You wait till you're my age.'

Pep gave him a friendly nudge. 'With the amount of work Bel gives me, I'll be amazed if I make old bones.'

And with that, Pep placed an arm around Idò's shoulders and, chuckling, the pair set off for Casa Elena.

It was six-thirty in the evening and Isabel, Tolo and Giselle, Gaspar's Mexican girlfriend, sat on the bright red sofa in Gaspar's parents' living room. They were watching the animated older couple perform a traditional Balanta dance while Gaspar strummed a kusunde, a gourd lute. Gaspar's father, Maalam, a native of the Balanta community of Guinea-Bissau, was proud of his heritage, as was his Mallorcan wife, Neus. She had spent many years working as a doctor in the country before returning with Maalam to the island of her birth when Gaspar was a toddler. Neus loved the people and traditions of her husband's birthplace and not only spoke Creole and the Balanta dialect but also knew how to perform many of the community's spiritual dances.

Earlier, Neus had prepared a lavish lunch of traditional Guinea-Bissau Creole cooking, and Isabel had eaten more than her fair share. When she'd been invited to dance by Gaspar's elderly West African uncle, it had taken a great deal of resolve not to just collapse on the nearest couch. All the same, she and Tolo had got into the spirit and shimmied around the house as various family members and guests showed them the ropes of the most famous dances.

When Maalam and Neus finished dancing, everyone clapped and whistled. Isabel turned to them.

'Tolo and I would love to visit Guinea-Bissau. It's on our wish list.'

'If you come to my village in Bolama, you will be treated like a princess,' Maalam promised with a radiant smile.

'Don't do that or it'll go to her head,' teased Tolo.

Gaspar laughed. 'If you do visit, you'll be stuck with my extended family for the rest of your days. They'll never let you leave.'

'If they stuff me with Creole cooking, I won't want to,' Isabel replied.

Sometime later, a yawning Tolo and Isabel finally took their leave, remembering that both had early starts in the morning. At the door, Gaspar hugged them warmly.

'Thank you for the stylish shirt and cufflinks. I love them. Almost too good to wear.'

'You are the office style icon, after all,' Isabel laughingly replied.

Tolo gave a snort. 'He's still got a long way to catch up with me.'

Isabel planted kisses on Gaspar's cheeks. 'It was the best birthday bash ever and I adore your family. Now I need to diet for a week.'

Tolo thumped Gaspar's arm and winked. 'Be warned, tomorrow morning the team will be expecting leftovers from Neus's cooking.'

As Isabel and Tolo walked slowly to their vehicles on the dark street, she fixed him with a serious expression.

'Sorry to talk business, but tomorrow morning will you let me know about whether Nacho found a locket on Aunt Maria's corpse?'

Tolo frowned. 'Do you ever switch off? Don't worry. Gaspar is on it.'

Isabel clicked her teeth. 'I've also placed a call with a South African police contact to find out where Pepe's daughter, Juliette, lives. Be good to touch base. According to his boss, Arturo, the two are no longer in contact.'

'How is that relevant to this case?'

'I'm intrigued to know if and why they had a falling out. It might prove another piece in an ever-expanding jigsaw.'

Tolo gave a weary yawn. 'I'll trust you on this one. Meanwhile, try and get some rest.'

He kissed her goodbye and flinched when she revved the engine. 'Please take care on the road, *cariño*,' he yelled as she rode off with a roar into the night.

It was late evening by the time Isabel killed the ignition. Helmet in hand, she patted Boadicea goodnight. She hadn't been able to find a parking place close to the house so had used Bernat's yard, knowing that he wouldn't mind. The street was quiet, which was normal for a Sunday night even at the height of the tourism season as the village restaurant and two bars closed early and there was little to do as a visitor. As she neared C'an Moix, she was amused to find Doctor Ramis wrestling a rubbish sack to his front gate. He was wearing a long white nightshirt and a pair of red espadrilles.

'A most fetching outfit, if I may say so, Miguel. You're up late.'

He gave a small gasp of surprise and pushed a hand through his thick white locks. 'Ah, Bel, don't sneak up on me like that! How was the party?'

'Wonderful, and now I'm looking forward to a good night's sleep. I've eaten far too much.'

'That's exactly how it should be. Well, night, night, dear girl. I am off to watch a medical documentary for half an hour. Lights out before midnight.'

Upstairs in the office, a sleepy Furó padded over to greet her, yawning heartily. She whipped him up in her arms and headed for the bedroom and placed him in his cosy basket. Before turning off her bedside light, she sent Tolo a brief text message to assure him that she'd got home safely. She knew he worried. An hour later, she awoke with a start as the phone began to trill, its screen illuminating the room. Rubbing her eyes and yawning, she reached out to answer it.

'Bel? Are you awake?'

She wondered why Capitán Gómez should be calling her at gone midnight. 'I am now, Álvaro.'

'I'm afraid an unfortunate incident has occurred in your village, and I would appreciate your cooperation.'

Isabel ignored the pomposity of the tone and sat up, suddenly wide awake. 'What's happened?'

'An elderly man named Juan Jaume has been found dead in his kitchen. It appears that the man tripped and hit his head on the floor, but the circumstances are a little unusual.'

Isabel gave a shiver when she heard the name. 'What do you mean?'

'Better if you come over.'

'I'm on my way.'

Furó looked up from his basket and whimpered as she switched on the light and hurriedly got dressed. Much as she didn't welcome the disruption to her sleep, she was pleased that the Guardia captain had sought her help. Perhaps he was begrudgingly beginning to trust her judgement. She ran down the stairs and out into the empty street, her mind aflutter as she recalled the threatening words of Manuel, the elderly man's son, the night before. Had he killed his father? The thought was abhorrent to her.

In the sticky heat, Isabel strode up the hill to the house, suddenly aware of the bells of Sant Antoní offering a single chime. If they had been mended, they wouldn't be ringing at such an hour. The bells always ceased at midnight and resumed at six o'clock in the morning. Something was awry. Isabel stopped at the tall wrought-iron gates to show her card to a solemn Guardia Civil officer. She donned her white forensics suit, plastic booties, and latex gloves, and headed for the large tiled *entrada*. She didn't know the victim well, but they had always politely greeted one another in the street, and she felt sad that the elderly man had died on the eve of signing a deal on his property. Just when he could have spent his twilight years without a financial care, his life had been cruelly ended. At the kitchen door, a po-faced Capitán Gómez beckoned to her.

'Thank you for coming, Isabel. You'll find the body over here.'

Isabel stepped into the brightly lit and dishevelled room and looked around at the tired furniture and assorted clutter strewn on the scuffed wooden sideboard. The sink was full of dirty plates and glasses, and stained tea towels sat in a heap on a worktop by a grimy cooker. A lone glass by the sink caught her eye. Warily, she sniffed the contents. Beyond, the inert form of Juan Jaume rested on the tiled terracotta floor, face downwards. Both arms were stretched out in front as if he'd been attempting a waterless crawl while dark gore pooled about his head next to a bloodied tea towel. Isabel noted that a long smear of blood ran from the table to the place where he lay. She crouched on her knees and quietly examined the corpse as Guardia officers carefully picked their way about the room, sombrely photographing the scene. After a few minutes, she rose to her feet.

'Despite the blood flow, that head wound appears to be superficial. Perhaps he had a heart attack or seizure and fell.'

Capitán Gómez eyed her keenly. 'Hopefully the post-mortem will tell us more.'

She ran a gloved hand along the old wooden dining table. Two empty glasses stood opposite one another next to a chipped bowl. She smelt them both and held the empty bowl up to the light. She returned it to the table.

'Two empty glasses that contained whisky and a bowl that is smeared with salt and grease, so probably crisps. It seems like Juan had company earlier tonight. I wonder who that was. What do you know so far?'

The police captain led her over to the French windows which opened onto a large and wild garden full of yellowing grasses and hungry, parched olive and citrus trees. A huddle of people, some in night attire, sat on a flight of stone steps, speaking in hushed tones.

'That's the Ronda family who live next door. The two teenage sons claim that about two hours ago they returned from a night out in Palma and noticed that all the lights were on in this house, yet the elderly man usually went to bed early. They say that they sat in the garden drinking and smoking until about eleven o'clock when they heard a sudden crash here. At first, they didn't pay much attention, but then they thought they heard groaning coming from the kitchen. Enric, the older boy, rang the doorbell, but Juan Jaume didn't answer, and the door was locked.'

'Was that so unusual?' Isabel asked.

'According to both boys, Juan Jaume always left it open. The lad climbed over the back fence instead, and that's when he found the old man bleeding profusely and lying in a delirious state on the kitchen floor.'

'The back door was open, then?'

Capitán Gómez clicked his teeth. 'Evidently it must have been if the boy is telling the truth.'

'What happened after that?'

'Raul, the younger brother, woke the parents, who then called the Guardia in Soller. They'd tried to reach Pau, but he was off duty. He's now been alerted and is on his way over here with Llorenç.'

'I know the Ronda family well. The boys are seventeen and nineteen. Both of them can be trusted.'

Capitán Gómez gave a sniff. 'We shall see. I notice that they both have those dreadful tattoos on their arms and legs.'

'Last I heard, sporting tattoos wasn't a crime,' Isabel replied. 'Did Juan say anything to either of them before he died?'

He gave an impatient shake of the head. 'The older boy, Enric, said that he was muttering a number. He wondered whether it was the combination to a safe.'

'What was it?'

Capitán Gómez consulted his notebook. '7033. It means nothing to me.'

Isabel frowned. 'I'll go and talk to the family. Have you called forensics?'

He nodded. 'Until we know for certain what occurred here, I have decided to treat it as a crime scene. Forensics are on their way.'

'Good. We need to know if there are fingerprints on those glasses and a toxicology report is essential.'

'I know how to do my job, Isabel.'

She smiled. 'Of course, Álvaro.'

'Llorenç mentioned that the victim had a troublesome son named Manuel. He is certainly a person of interest.'

Isabel nodded. 'He and Juan had a bad falling out over the house sale.'

Outside, she found Enric and his brother, Raul, smoking agitatedly, while their parents and two older sisters attempted to comfort them. They were all visibly shaken and seemed relieved to see Isabel. She offered them her condolences and listened quietly while the boys repeated what had happened. She turned to the parents and sisters.

'Did you hear any disturbance coming from the house earlier in the evening?'

The wife nodded. 'I heard Juan yelling at someone around eight-thirty. I didn't take much notice as it all died down quite quickly, and I heard a door slam soon after. I assumed he was having a row with his son. He and Manuel have been hammer and tongs since the old man agreed to that sale.'

'When did Juan normally go to bed?'

'The lights were usually out by nine-thirty,' her husband replied.

'We got home around ten o'clock, but they were all on so Raul and I thought Manuel must have company,' said Enric.

'Capitán Gómez told me that you spoke with Juan before he died,' Isabel replied gently.

He nodded. 'It was horrible, Bel. When I saw him lying on the kitchen floor, I ran over and touched his face and spoke with him. He opened his eyes, but he didn't seem to know who I was. He kept telling me that it was the wrong number and that it should have been 7033. He said he'd been tricked.'

'What did you do?'

'There was a lot of blood, so I wrapped a tea towel around his head.' He gulped back tears. 'Then I called my mum and told her to get an ambulance, but when I looked back, he'd crawled away from the table. He was shaking all over like he was having a fit and his eyes looked glazed. I tried to put the tea towel to his head, but he pushed it away. Then he lay down and stretched out his arms and everything went still.'

Isabel patted his shoulder. 'I think you should all go home. You must be exhausted. You can give statements to the Guardia in the morning.'

Isabel re-entered the house and found Capitán Gómez on his phone. She took the opportunity to have a quick look around the house. Upstairs, three of the four musty bedrooms were empty save for drab double beds with sinking mattresses, stripped bare of sheets. In the fourth room, Isabel was surprised to find an elegant antique mahogany double bed with ornate hand-turned spindles at the headboard and base. In a bygone era, they were common in middle-class Mallorcan homes, and she remembered with fondness her grandmother's *finca*, where they sat with pride in every bedroom. She surmised that this had to be Juan Jaume's room, as she found a wardrobe of men's trousers and old threadbare shirts, some of which she'd seen him wear. The simple bathroom along the corridor had whitewashed walls, a lavatory, basin and basic shower with plastic curtain. Isabel poked around the chaotic contents of a mirrored cabinet. There were half-empty bottles of mouthwash, dried out toothpaste and brushes, packets of cotton wool and plasters, and exhausted metal tubes of antiseptic cream. A cardboard box of pills labelled Nembutal grabbed her attention. She studied the label and dosage and took an image. She returned the box to the cupboard and made her way back downstairs, where she found Llorenç and Pau. Their faces were pinched and pale in the bright light of the hallway.

The mayor made the sign of the cross and fixed his sad brown eyes on Isabel.

'Poor Juan. Who would have thought it. Of course, he had a bad heart.'

'He did?' she asked.

Pau cleared his throat, seemingly overcome with emotion. 'He took various pills. I was over here one day, and he told me they were for low blood pressure. Miguel Ramis will know.'

'Interesting,' Isabel replied. 'I shall speak with him. Hopefully, forensics will be here soon, and we'll know more after the post-mortem.'

Llorenç gave a start. 'You're not suggesting that there could be foul play involved?'

'It's still too early to say,' she replied quietly.

'You think Manuel might have killed him?' he asked breathlessly.

Isabel tutted. 'I wouldn't put that around, Llorenç.'

There was the sound of a car engine and doors slamming and a few moments later, a tired and frowning Pedro Massip arrived, already kitted out in forensic garb. He eyed Isabel wryly.

'Trust Nacho to take a break as soon as the first suspicious death happens this whole summer. He owes me.'

Isabel led him down the stairs to the kitchen where Capitán Gómez was still pacing around with his mobile to his ear. She gave Pedro a curt smile and pointed to the corpse.

'He's all yours.'

'Any hypotheses before you go?'

'The victim had company this evening, but we don't know exactly when. There are traces of whisky in two glasses on the table and one by the sink. Perhaps the glass by the sink implies he had an earlier visitor followed by another later with whom he shared a bowl of crisps. We need to know whether they were innocent social get-togethers or whether one of his visitors intended him harm. Hopefully, you can help with the timeline. He's got a deep cut and a bump on his head, but I don't believe that was the cause of death. He was apparently fitting before he died so perhaps unwittingly ingested something that killed him.'

He stared at her expectantly. 'You think he was poisoned?'

'I'll let you be the judge of that.' She paused. 'Another thing. Pau, our local police officer, said the victim was suffering from low blood pressure, but I haven't found any meds aside from a packet of Nembutal upstairs in the bathroom cupboard. As you know, it's sometimes taken for insomnia but not advisable if you suffer from low blood pressure.'

Pedro Massip nodded. 'True. It can help with seizures, but it would be irresponsible to dish it out with heart meds. Who's his specialist?'

'I think my next-door neighbour will know. He's Miguel Ramis, the village doctor.'

'That's handy. Find out what you can from him, and in the interim, we'll organise a toxicology report.'

Isabel headed back down the hill towards the dark and silent *plaça*. She may have imagined it, but there was a sudden chill in the air and a fretful breeze shook the leaves on the plane trees. She looked up at the clock tower. It was already nearly two o'clock. As she passed by, the bells of Sant Antoní suddenly rang out. She gave an involuntary shudder at the ominous sound. Padre Agustí would have an uncomfortable awakening the next day – unruly bells and the untimely death of a faithful parishioner.

ELEVEN

A golden sun followed Isabel and Furó all the way from Calle Pastor to Bar Castell. It was early morning, and both had enjoyed a quiet swim in Soller bay while the hotel guests in the port continued to slumber in their beds. Isabel pushed her curtain of damp curly hair behind her ears and greeted Rafael at the counter. He eyed her gloomily.

'What a night! Poor old Juan.'

Isabel rubbed her eyes, still feeling the weight of fatigue from the night before. 'You've heard the news.'

He cocked his head towards the interior of the premises.

'Llorenç told me. He's on the terrace trying to calm down Adam Markham. He's in a real state. I'll bring you a coffee and my eggs of the day.'

Isabel brightened. 'What kind of eggs?'

'Scrambled with chives and Manchego.'

He bent down and stroked Furó's head.

'I'll prepare some raw egg for my little chum here too.'

Isabel smiled and walked through to the terrace, where Adam sat with his head in his hands opposite Llorenç. They both looked up as she took a seat at the table and settled Furó by her side.

'Good morning, gentlemen. A sad night indeed.'

Adam appeared pale and wired. 'It's a catastrophe. I'm really saddened to hear about Juan's death, but if I'm honest, it could sink me financially. I've already invested heavily in the refurbishment of his house as we needed to get it shipshape for a potential sale, but the legal formalities were due to take place today.'

'You mean you hadn't already signed a contract?' asked Isabel.

'I feel like a bit of a fool, but Juan and I shook hands on it. It was a verbal agreement.'

Isabel puffed out her cheeks. 'In that case it might be a good idea to speak with Juan's lawyer about how you might recoup your losses.'

'I intend to do that.' He drummed his fingers against the table. 'Listen, Llorenç has just told me that someone had been drinking with Juan earlier last night. Could it have been Manuel or Tomeu Tous?'

Isabel eyed Llorenç sternly. 'I don't think we want to make idle speculation at this stage.'

He sat back in his chair and covered his face with his hands for a second. 'And what about the bird?'

'What bird?' asked Isabel.

Llorenç wore a guilty expression. 'Sorry, Bel, maybe I shouldn't be mentioning this publicly, but after you'd left, a dead seagull was found by the forensics team behind the kitchen shutter. They took it away in case there was DNA.'

Isabel's eyes widened in surprise. 'I see. Well, I am sure forensics will let us know if it has any significance. In the meantime, I'd advise keeping this information between yourselves.'

Adam nodded. 'But do you think it's the same person who left a seagull outside my home?'

Isabel shrugged. 'There's no evidence of that. By the way, when did you last see Juan alive?'

His lip puckered. 'Only yesterday morning. He was on good form, and we agreed on certain plans to the upper level of his property. We confirmed the signing of the contract would happen today at the *notario's* office at noon.'

He rose wearily, ruffling his fair hair with an impatient hand.

'Look, guys, I'd better head back to the office and get onto Jaume's lawyer and cancel the *notario*. This whole thing is a mess.'

When he'd left, Isabel leant forward confidentially. 'Llorenç, please don't provide information about the crime scene to anyone else. Or have you already?'

He patted her hand. 'My apologies. Markham collared me as I walked in here and as it was his client, I felt I should tell him the truth. I only told him and Rafa.'

At that moment, Rafael appeared with an enticing tray of eggs, fresh crusty bread, a saucer of scrambled raw egg and coffee, which he placed on the table. Furó leapt from his seat and awaited his treat on the tiled floor, eliciting a laugh from Rafael.

Rafael tucked the empty tray under his arm. 'So, what were you saying about me?'

'Bel's just been ticking me off for revealing too much to you and Markham about last night's crime scene. I was just overwrought, but she is of course right. It was unprofessional of me.'

'Don't worry, Llorenç,' she said with a wink. 'By now, the Ronda family will probably have told half the village about last night.'

Rafael tapped her shoulder. 'I won't say a word to anyone, Bel.'

She helped herself to the coffee and smiled at him. 'I trust you. Let's just try to keep an open mind.'

'All the same,' said Llorenç, 'this doesn't look good for either Manuel or Tomeu Tous. They both had an axe to grind. That dead seagull worries me.'

'But why leave a calling card that might implicate you?' she asked.

Rafael scratched his chin. 'I reckon it's to warn off Markham. After all, his logo is of a seagull. That's no coincidence, is it? I doubt they'll find out who left it there. No murderer is stupid enough to leave DNA on it.'

'You'd be surprised,' Isabel replied.

As Rafael headed back to the bar, Llorenç took a sip of his coffee and hungrily watched as Isabel devoured her scrambled eggs.

'Anyway,' he said. 'It's not as if Markham hasn't any assets. He can always lean on his old man in South Africa to lend him some cash. He told me his father had a big real estate business there. Don't forget he's already got contracts with that wealthy Swedish couple in Fornalutx and Bridget Kelly.'

Isabel poured olive oil onto a chunk of bread. 'That's true. I don't know anything about his father's wealth, but those two properties are gold mines.'

Llorenç offered a sly grin. 'Mind you, Markham might regret taking on Bridget Kelly. She's a typical Irish expat, drinking too much and falling over her cats all the time.'

'Come on, that's unfair on the Irish. She's just a dotty elderly woman who can't cope with all the steps in her house and garden. It's a huge house and there are no handrails. She has few lights on her land so it's no wonder she falls so much.'

'It doesn't help that she's always sozzled. You know how often Miguel and the clinic in Soller have had to stitch up her cuts.'

Isabel shrugged. 'Perhaps she's just lonely and takes comfort in the bottle. It must have been hard for her when her husband died. Now she's elderly, it would be better if she could find a smaller, cosy home with fewer hazards.'

'I suppose that's why she's selling up. It makes sense,' Llorenç replied.

Furó suddenly jumped on Isabel's lap and began to paw her arm.

'He wants to go home for a kip. We both had a disruptive night.'

Llorenç patted Furó's head. 'Before you go, Bel, you should know that Álvaro is bringing Manuel in for questioning today.'

'What time?'

'He said he'd be there most of the afternoon.'

'A good idea,' she replied. 'Even if it's just to eliminate him from the enquiry.'

Llorenç nodded stiffly and together they joined Rafael at the counter. The mayor insisted on paying for Isabel's breakfast.

'You went beyond the call of duty last night, Bel. Álvaro and I appreciate your support. Let's hope that together we can get to the bottom of this unfortunate incident.'

Isabel and Furó headed quickly back to Calle Pastor through the *plaça*. She had a meeting with the students at the Conservatori in Palma and didn't want to be late.

Isabel sat in one of the empty classrooms at the Conservatori crunching on sunflower seeds, a bottle of tepid water and a whirring fan at her side. She had interviewed all of Maria's academic colleagues, who, without exception, had politely expressed sadness at the diva's demise while at the same time pointing out her many faults. With one voice they accused the opera singer of being cold, egotistic, and ruthlessly ambitious, but conceding that she had a rare musical talent and got the best results from her students. Now she awaited the arrival of Gemma Palau, one of the students who regularly visited the home of the opera singer. Panting, Gemma Palau threw open the door, her eyes flitting to the growing mound of sunflower husks on the desk in front of Isabel. She took a few deep breaths and apologised for being late, explaining that she'd been delayed in a previous class and had run from the lecture theatre. Isabel studied her face and offered her some sunflower seeds.

'Thanks, but I've just had a *merienda*. I used to eat those a lot when I was a kid.'

'I don't know about you, but I still do.'

She giggled shyly and then turned serious. 'So you're a policewoman? You wanted to see me about Tía Maria?'

'I sometimes help the police out with cases when they're busy. I believe that you frequently visited Maria Rosselló at her home.'

She nodded. 'Every week. Usually, I'd go for private lessons on a Monday and Friday, but as it's the holidays, I've not visited very much of late.'

'I can imagine. It's so hot in the middle of the island at this time of year. So did you visit last week?'

The girl picked at a nail. 'No, I had a busy week and Tía Maria was preparing for her opera tour.'

'I see. How did she get the sobriquet "Tía Maria"? The media say it was a term of endearment by her students.'

The girl shook her head. 'One of my friends here came up with it. We called her Tía Maria and her husband Tío Pepe. You know, just a stupid joke based on the drink brands. No one liked Tía Maria, to be honest.'

Isabel smiled. 'And which of your friends thought up the name?'

The girl shrugged. 'It was Patricia Clos. She left the Conservatori last year as she needed to earn money – she supported herself. There were five of us scholarship students, now just Georg and I are left. He's still on holiday, but I rang him to tell him the news. He was very shocked.'

Isabel tapped her chin with her pen. 'So what is Patricia doing now?'

'Apparently, she's a music teacher at a secondary school in Palma and works in a children's theatre. I lost touch with her.'

'What about the others?'

Gemma frowned. 'Lucia Berganza left and joined a dance group a few years ago and then committed suicide. It was rumoured that it was a drug overdose. The Conservatori hushed it up, but the director admitted to us that she had died. As for Juana Ballister, she moved to the mainland.'

'Do you have any of their details?'

She shrugged. 'Not anymore, but the director will have them.'

Isabel took a sip of water. 'Tell me about the poisonous mushrooms.'

The girl froze in her chair. 'I don't know anything about that.'

'But you know the story, right?'

Gemma shot a glance at the door and began playing with some frayed threads on her shorts. 'Everyone heard about it. The director said someone meant to give them to Tía Maria as a gift and hadn't realised they were poisonous.'

'Do you believe that?'

'Sure, why not?'

'You said Tía Maria was disliked.'

'She was, but I don't know any students who'd have wanted her dead. It was just that she gave us loads of homework and was always critical.'

The girl suddenly jumped up. 'Look, I'm sorry, but I have a lecture now.'

Isabel rose and scooped up all the discarded husks and threw them in a bin along with the empty plastic bottle. Just as they reached the corridor, Isabel turned to face her.

'Just one last thing, Gemma. Why did you tell me that you hadn't visited Maria on Monday? I have proof that you did. You came on your bike that day.'

The girl's mouth dropped open and she gaped at Isabel.

Isabel touched her arm. 'It's okay. Why not tell me what really happened?'

Gemma slumped against a wall. 'Okay, I had a lesson with Tía Maria that afternoon, but I swear I didn't do anything to her. She was in a foul mood and yelled at me for fluffing my rehearsal for a public performance at the Conservatori next month. I told her to get lost and that I didn't want her to teach me ever again.' Her eyes filled with tears. 'I didn't mean it and now she's dead.'

'Why would I assume you'd done something to her?'

She folded her arms and gave her a defiant stare. 'I've stayed over there at the house without permission. My mum and I argue a lot and I don't like my stepdad, so sometimes I've cycled over there and snuck into the house. They always leave the front door unlocked, even at night, so now and then I sleep there. However, on Monday night I went home to Inca as I had to babysit my stepsister who was staying over. My mum can confirm that.'

'Good.' Isabel walked with her towards the reception. 'You used to sleep on the sofa in that small room leading off from Maria's music studio.'

'How could you know that?'

Isabel chuckled. 'When I visited the room, I could smell a sweet perfume that had lingered on the cushions and blanket. It's the same perfume you're wearing today.'

'Wow. There's no fooling you.'

On the front steps, Isabel smiled at her. 'Is your stepdad ever aggressive towards you?'

Gemma shook her head. 'Not really. It's just that he and my mum think I should work and earn money rather than study to be an opera singer. They don't get why this scholarship is so important to me. Now I feel like giving it all up. What's the point? Tía Maria's dead and all the other students have money and normal families. I feel like a freak here.'

Isabel took her firmly by the shoulders. 'Freaks so often become bright stars and stand out from the mundane and predictable. To be normal is so overrated – trust me. Be different and never try to be anyone but yourself. Honour Maria's memory and follow your dreams to be an opera singer. What is the opera you're performing in next month? I'd like to come.'

Gemma blinked back tears. 'It's called *La Fanciulla del West*, the Girl of the West, by Puccini. I play Minnie, the lead soprano. It's set at the time of the Gold Rush in California and Minnie is a tough tavern-keeper. It's about love, money, and betrayal, but Minnie triumphs in the end and takes control of her own destiny.'

Isabel smiled broadly. 'In that case, isn't it time to take a leaf out of Minnie's book?'

It was with some relief that Isabel arrived back in Sant Martí. Although Palma was bustling with happy tourists, she was pleased to be away from the heavy traffic and noise of the city. She had popped by the police precinct to brief Tolo and Gaspar on her meetings at the Conservatori. Both were baffled by her interest in the three scholarship students who were no longer at the opera school and felt that the case of the poisonous mushrooms was proving an unnecessary distraction. Nonetheless, Isabel's curiosity was piqued, and she stubbornly resolved to cover all bases. While there, Gaspar had given her Maria's gold locket to return to Tío Pepe, since it had proven to be of little interest to forensics. The team had reported finding black and white images of a man and woman inside that had been identified as her grandmother and grandfather. No prints were on the locket, aside from Maria's own.

She found Pep hunched over a file while Furó padded about on his desk. Pep looked up.

'Have you had lunch? Florentina has left you a huge bowl of *trempó* in the fridge and there's a fresh sourdough loaf in the pantry. She also made vegetable *coca* and a lemon cake. It's all too good.'

'I picked up a *bocadillo* in town, but I'll tuck into all that for my supper. Mama's only been back a few days and she's cooking like mad.'

He grinned. 'She's probably a bit miffed that my mum took over in her absence. You know how she likes to be needed.'

'Don't we all. Your mother and Florentina are both such talented cooks and I am the luckiest woman in the village.'

He nodded. 'Plus, you have the most handsome guy working as your assistant. You hit the jackpot.'

She punched his arm and sat down in a chair close to the whirring fan. All the windows were open, but the air was stifling. 'Shall we put on the air-con?'

He threw out his arms. 'I thought we were trying to save costs! No way.'

'When you first came to work here, you were always begging to have the air-con on, but suddenly you've become Mr Thrifty.'

'Now that Angélica and I are sharing a flat, I get to pay for the electricity, so I know how much it costs.'

She laughed. 'There's nothing more sobering than having to pay your own bills.'

When she and Pep had settled down in her office with coffee and slices of Florentina's lemon cake, he looked across at her.

'You haven't asked about the wounded dove you found.'

Isabel frowned then gasped. 'I forgot about it. Poor thing is still in the pantry.'

'No, it isn't. It had perked up considerably and so I set it free and watched it fly away.'

Isabel smiled. 'Some good news at last. Thank you, Pep.'

'How did it go at the Conservatori?'

She gave him an account of her morning. Pep gave an irritated sigh.

'So unless Nacho found anything untoward in Maria's bedroom last Friday, the case will be closed, and a verdict of suicide given?'

'That's what Tolo told me today. He and Gaspar are unconvinced of any foul play and in truth there's no forensic evidence whatsoever. Maria's funeral will go ahead in Inca this Wednesday pending the final forensics report.'

'Why are you so interested in those scholarship students?'

She began unwrapping a Chupa Chup. 'I just feel that one or all of them might hold the key.'

'To what?'

She eyed him helplessly. 'I honestly don't know. Even if one or another gave Maria those poisonous mushrooms three years ago, what does it prove?'

Pep nodded and picked up Furó. 'What about the ladybird button our little friend here found?'

Isabel was glum. 'Tolo and Gaspar think I've lost the plot. They surmised that it was probably from an item of clothing in the wardrobe, although I didn't see one it could have come from. I left it for Pedro Massip and the forensics team in case there are any traces of DNA on it. Frankly, I'm grasping at straws.'

He offered her a sympathetic smile. 'At least I've got a bit of interesting news. I found out a little about Maria's cousin, Fermin

Janer. He's a potter and has a *siurell* workshop in Pòrtol. I think we should pay him a surprise visit tomorrow.'

Isabel brightened. 'Good plan.'

'I also popped by his village, Mancor de la Vall, and discreetly spoke with some locals and neighbours. They all seem to like him and believe he was given a rum deal in the will of Maria's father. All the same, they say he has a terrible temper. He lives with his wife in a simple stone terraced house, but it's neat and well kept. She's a teacher at a local nursery.'

'Excellent work, Pep. And have you had a chance to find out any connection between Maria and any other of Eva Salas's clients aside from Enrique Diaz?'

He nodded. 'Maria seemed to have appeared on stage with several other of Eva Salas's clients. I checked them out online and in press cuttings but found nothing of great interest. Most are now retired. Apparently, Diaz and Catalina Grimalt also appeared in productions together on the mainland. I've found media reports online about them remaining close friends. Maria and Catalina also toured together and there are images of them posing side by side in some old local press articles. It seems that they were as thick as thieves at one time.'

Isabel waved her Chupa Chup around in the air. 'So all three stars knew one another well.'

'Does that mean something?' asked Pep hopefully.

'I'm not sure, but everything seems to be connected. Someone has the spare set of keys to Maria's bedroom and deliberately put the frame of Enrique Diaz and Maria at the front of the desk.'

Pep's eyes shone with excitement. 'Maybe Catalina had the spare set if she was her friend but was jealous of Maria and Enrique's professional relationship and killed her.'

'Hm. As motives go, that seems a little extreme, Pep, but anything's possible.'

He clapped his hands together. 'What next?'

'I think it's time I had a chat with Enrique Diaz.'

'His contact details are on the client list if you need them.'

'Perfect. Thanks.'

He observed her for a few seconds. 'Why don't I try to get hold of the contact details for the other three scholarship students? Surely it would be better to find them ourselves. That director of the Conservatori sounds a bit fishy, so maybe best not to involve him.'

Isabel stared at him in wonderment. 'Excellent reasoning, Pep. I too don't want him to know what we're up to. There's something dark about that man. Happy sleuthing, Watson.'

She stood up and peered down at her parched garden from the open window. 'Meanwhile, I must also put my mind to the death of Juan Jaume. Do you know if Doctor Ramis is about? I need to speak with him.'

'He and Florentina have gone to see a film in Palma. They'll be back late,' he replied.

'As Manuel is being questioned by Gómez this afternoon at the Guardia's offices, I might pay a brief visit to his shack later.'

'You're not going to break in, Bel?'

Isabel tutted. 'What do you think? Of course not. I just want to get the lie of the land.'

Pep narrowed his eyes. 'I hope that's true. It's one of your worst habits.'

'I know,' she replied with a wink. 'But you have to admit, it normally gets results.'

TWELVE

It was early evening by the time Isabel cleared her desk and locked up the house. She wore an old black T-shirt and shorts and trail running shoes because Manuel Borras lived on a strip of wild forestland, and she needed to move quickly and stealthily. No sooner had she got onto her bike than she heard someone calling. She closed her eyes briefly, wondering what new calamity might have befallen someone in her community but was relieved to see Padre Agustí standing on the pavement.

'Bel, what terrible news about poor Juan. But he is now in the embrace of Our Almighty Father. It was his time to enter Heaven's gates, and he will now be in everlasting peace.' He shook his head sadly. 'He always had a weak heart.'

Isabel raised an eyebrow and murmured a comforting platitude.

He continued, 'Meanwhile, we've had a terrible problem with the church bells.'

'Yes, I heard them chiming in the night, but at least the clock is okay.'

'Indeed, it just had a faulty hammer.' He smiled. 'But I wanted to tell you that the bells are now functioning too.'

'You had the engineer over again?'

He shook his head. 'On Friday, the engineer told me that our mechanical system would need to be replaced with an automatic alternative at huge cost. He said he could do no more. I was at a loss, but you had reminded me to put my faith in the big man in the sky. So, last night, after mass, I prayed into the small hours and promptly fell asleep at five-thirty. When I awoke three hours later, the mechanical settings were working perfectly.'

Isabel digested this news carefully. 'Well, whatever the weather, it's great to know that the problem is solved.'

'But dear Bel, it's a miracle. And you have taught me, even at my old age, to put more faith in our heavenly Lord.'

Isabel smiled to herself and pressed the ignition. 'I remember the old sexton who used to ring the bells of Sant Antoní when I was a child.'

He stepped back from the car. 'Ah, dear Paco. Let's hope he's now ringing the bells of the Almighty in the sky.'

As Isabel waved goodbye and rode out of the village, she muttered to Pequeñito, 'Poor Paco. He hated those bells. Let's hope in the afterlife he's having a well-earned rest and doesn't have to ring a wretched bell ever again.'

Manuel's stone shack sat in a clearing on the edge of woodland. The small yard was filthy and strewn with ancient car parts, rubbish, and piles of rotting wood. A rotten, corrugated plastic roof, stained brown by dried tears of mud and covered in dry, bleached moss, had been placed over two concrete pillars at the front of the dwelling. A clutter of white plastic chairs, caked in grime, sat in desultory fashion about the small porch. Isabel had left Boadicea behind a clump of olive trees and now gingerly walked around the dingy property with Furó, peering through the windows to ensure that no one was home. Manuel's battered old car was not in the rocky parking area and the only sound was birdsong. If the shack hadn't been so scruffy and the grounds so unkempt, it would have been a peaceful place to live. With gloved hands, she tried the back door before opening it with the aid of a set of skeleton keys.

'That was too simple,' she said to Furó. 'People really should invest in better locks.'

Furó chuntered in evident agreement and slipped stealthily inside and began inspecting the rooms. There was a single bedroom, kitchen cum dining room and a small, gloomy bathroom. Isabel crinkled her nose at the stale smell that hung oppressively in the air and frowned when she heard Furó sneezing from the hallway.

'Furó, don't go running off. Let's keep together.'

With a grunt, he pattered obediently behind her as she peeked in cupboards and drawers. On the kitchen table Isabel found a notepad and a biro. She ripped off the top sheet and held it up to the light.

'Aha! What did Manuel write? We need a pencil.'

She opened a drawer crammed with old bills, stained envelopes, paperclips, and rubber bands. Furó pawed the contents with her and pulled out a yellow crayon with his teeth. Patting his head, she gently released it from his hold and began rubbing it over the indents on the piece of paper she'd torn off.

'I used to do this as a kid. Look, it's showing some words.'

Replacing the crayon in the drawer, Isabel walked to the window and held the paper up to the light.

'There are two words. They seem to be "Asturias" and "woman". That means nothing to me. What about you?'

With a yawn, Furó jumped down from the table and began sniffing around the kitchen as Isabel stood thoughtfully looking at the note. Moments later, she heard tyres on gravel. In alarm, she swept Furó up into her arms and darted for the bedroom, leaving the door ajar. She offered Furó soothing strokes and whispered in his ear.

'Manuel seems to have returned early. Llorenç told me he'd be with the Guardia all afternoon.'

Swearing under her breath, she huddled against a wall, her eyes widening at the sound of a key in a lock, followed by heavy footsteps. The fridge door was opened, and soon came the familiar tinkle of a bottle cap being pulled and the fizzing of lager being poured. Manuel's voice boomed as he spoke agitatedly into his mobile.

'What's the deal with the will and when do I get my cut? You promised it would all be okay, but it's not, is it?'

It seemed that whoever was at the other end of the line was trying to placate him.

'Shut up. You're lying. Who is this slut from Asturias?'

Isabel stood closer to the bedroom door and raised an eyebrow as Manuel continued to yell aggressively in slurred tones.

'Listen. I don't want that South African stooge getting a cent. I don't care. Sort it, you idiot.'

Isabel heard the crack of the mobile being thrown across the floor. Furó stared up at her with anxious eyes. She put her fingers to her lips and kissed his head. Some minutes later, there came the sounds of Manuel getting another lager bottle from the fridge. He turned on the television at a high volume and the cheering of football fans filled the room. Manuel began clapping and hooting whenever a goal was scored. When she felt it was safe, Isabel peered out from behind the door, and in relief saw the recumbent figure of Manuel on the sofa. He was snoring heavily, the lager bottle resting against his paunch. Very carefully, she closed the bedroom door and tiptoed to the window. She deposited Furó on the ledge and unfastened the window catch, her heart beating wildly. With whiskers twitching, Furó jumped down into the bracken and waited patiently for Isabel to lower herself onto the ground. Together, they slunk off into the woods in the direction of Boadicea. Isabel strapped Furó into his carrier, put on her helmet, and rode off along the uneven forest track that led back to Sant Martí. As she hit the main road, her eyes alighted on a lone red Fiat 500 parked up on the side of the road. She looked in her wing mirror as it pulled out quickly and turned in the opposite direction. Was it just a coincidence or was it the same car she believed had tailed her at Es Salobrar and had been parked at the Conservatori?

Once home, she settled Furó in his basket and made herself a chamomile tea. Her heart was still beating fast and her hands shook. As Isabel passed the wood-framed mirror in the hallway, she stopped and delivered a stern, disapproving glance at her double. Did she no longer have the courage for all this adrenalin, or had she just become a bit too relaxed during the long and languorous summer? Her reflection gave an emphatic nod. What she needed was action, risk and even danger. Little did she know that she'd soon be getting it in spades.

It was midnight and Isabel sat idling on her patio, admiring the clusters of golden stars, her bare feet kissing the warm tiles beneath the table. She had spoken with Tolo earlier, though she'd failed to mention her adventure with Furó up at Manuel's shack. She hadn't discussed the death of Juan Jaume with him either, so surely it would make little sense to bring it up so late in the day. He had enough on his plate with the many cold cases he was juggling and the ongoing investigation into the death of Maria. Wearily, she rose from her seat and carried the empty plate and breadbasket into the kitchen while Furó padded softly behind her. She had polished off her mother's *trempó* salad and the vegetable *coca* and was about to have another glass of red wine when something occurred to her. She still hadn't examined the heart-shaped gold locket that Gaspar had given her earlier that day at the precinct. She walked through to the *entrada* and pulled the brown padded envelope from her pannier. Inside she found a delicate gold necklace, but the heart itself felt heavy in her hand. She topped up her glass of wine in the kitchen and headed back out into the garden. The air was fragrant with rosemary and in the silky darkness, Furó watched with rapt attention as agile geckos played hide and seek in the deep crevices of the stone walls.

With a smile Isabel settled back in her wicker chair and by candlelight examined the pendant closely. The clasp opened easily and inside she discovered black and white images of Maria's grandparents. The pretty young woman had intense eyes, and her long dark hair was swept up into a bun, while her handsome husband sported an extravagant moustache and sideburns. Both wore formal attire, and she guessed that the photos harked back to the forties. She snapped the locket shut and studied the decorous engraving on its surface. It seemed sad to Isabel that Maria had opted to include images of her grandparents rather than Pepe, who'd gifted it to her. She wondered if he knew. Dangling the locket in front of her, she suddenly frowned. There appeared to be something odd about the mechanism. She moved the candle closer and examined the locket's s hinge. Furó scuttled across the table and began pawing at the chain. Isabel laughed. She stroked his whiskers and soft pink snout and eyed him excitedly.

'There's something odd about this locket. It's got a thick interior section and a bulge on both sides, which makes me wonder if it's double-sided.'

Ignoring her, Furó began to snort and shake his head as he tried to bite the chain. She gently pushed him back and tried to find a way of opening the other side, but it wouldn't budge. Puzzled, she took a sip of wine and with renewed vigour tried to slide back the rear face of the locket with her fingertips. To her utter surprise, it gradually opened, revealing a cavity packed with a white granular powder. Isabel exchanged a baffled look with her ferret and gingerly gave it a sniff. She slid the mechanism back into place and gave a long sigh.

'Look at that, Furó. I don't know for sure, but I'm guessing that before Maria's death, she crushed a load of fentanyl tablets and placed them here, and that's why we found the empty packet in the bathroom bin. But why? It's a dangerous opioid that I used to come across in some of the worst sink estates in Barcelona. It's odourless and has no taste so can be easily slipped into drinks.'

Furó grunted, his excitement waning, and pottered back to observe the geckos on the garden wall. For a while Isabel turned the pendant over in her hands, her mind working overtime. If she was correct and the substance turned out to be fentanyl, why had Maria hidden it there, and more importantly, what was its ultimate purpose?

THIRTEEN

Isabel sat on the empty terrace of Bar Castell, her bare feet resting on the railings and her damp tresses wound up on her head with the help of a red plastic peg. She had chomped her way through fried eggs and a heap of cooked tomatoes and mushrooms with garlic and now polished off a thick slice of toast, which she dipped in olive oil. Furó sat by her side licking his lips, having finished a bowl of kibble and raw beef. He pawed at her bronzed arm as she cast her eyes on the *plaça* below.

'We're going home soon. Just give me a minute.'

As she took a last swig of coffee, her mobile rang, and she smiled to see Tolo's name flash up on the screen.

'Bel, sorry I haven't got back to you yet, but I've only just got out of an early briefing. To be honest, I had to listen to your message twice to absorb the news. You're sure that powder in Maria's locket is fentanyl?'

'Forensics need to confirm that, but I'd say so. It would explain the pestle and mortar we found in her bathroom, and the empty packet of fentanyl.'

'You think Maria was using it as a recreational drug?'

'Who knows, but she obviously put it in the locket for a reason. What doesn't make sense is why she'd bother to grind up the pills in a pestle and mortar, hide the powder in her locket and then jump off her balcony. Why commit suicide after going to all that effort?'

'We're assuming that she placed the fentanyl powder in the locket. Could Pepe or another member of the household have found an opportunity to access the locket, perhaps when she took it off?'

Isabel gave a sigh. 'Pepe seemed keen to have it returned for sentimental reasons, but now I wonder. All the same, even if he had access to the locket, why would he place fentanyl in it? It doesn't make any sense.'

Tolo gave a groan. 'Her funeral is tomorrow, but this won't change anything. It has to go ahead. All the same, we'll now have to keep the investigation open and confirm what the powder is and try to discover its purpose.'

'There's something else. Pep researched Eva Salas's clients and discovered that both Maria and Catalina Grimalt had been good friends at one time, and that both knew and performed with the tenor Enrique Diaz.'

Tolo issued a grunt. 'And?'

'So, I rang Eva Salas this morning after my swim, and she told me that Enrique and Maria regularly performed together until they fell out five years ago. Eva said it was some kind of squabble after a performance in Barcelona, but Catalina and Enrique remain close friends. In fact, she told me that Enrique is currently on the island visiting Catalina.'

'I'm still not sure why any of this is important.'

'You'll remember that I sealed off Maria's bedroom, yet someone with a spare set of keys rearranged the images on her desk, with one of Maria and Enrique placed up front.'

'So you said.'

'Clearly someone did it to get our attention.'

Tolo gave an impatient cough. 'I admit that this is all very puzzling, but frankly, it doesn't alter the fact that Maria appears to have been alone in her locked bathroom and most likely jumped, or possibly fell by accident. We still don't have a case against Pepe Serrano.'

Isabel bit on a nail. 'You're right, but I'm still convinced that it wasn't suicide.'

'I trust your instincts, *cariño*, but we need hard evidence. Can you come by the precinct tomorrow lunchtime? Pedro Massip will have some further forensic results.'

'Sure. I'm waiting on some other results that are closer to home.'

'What do you mean?'

Isabel sighed. 'An elderly man named Juan Jaume died on Sunday night. It was possibly from natural causes, but the circumstances were suspicious. Gómez is handling the case.'

'Why didn't you mention this to me?'

'You've been so tied up with work.'

He gave a growl. 'I'm never too busy for you. Let's discuss it when we meet. What are you up to today?'

'I'm visiting a *siurell* whistle maker in Pòrtol this morning and then I'm home all day.'

He laughed. 'Is this to stop Furó from going astray?'

'As if. He's his own ferret. Actually, I'm visiting Maria's cousin, Fermin Janer.'

'The one who is challenging her father's will?'

'The same. I'm hoping he can fill in some gaps.'

Tolo nodded. 'Let me know what he says. Meanwhile, I'm off to see the commissioner. We're about to announce the positive results of another cold case and I'm on a roll. It's so good for relatives to have closure, however painful. Call me later and don't forget to buy me a whistle.'

Isabel dropped the mobile into her pannier and placed Furó around her neck like a stole. On her way out, she poked her head around the kitchen door behind the bar and waggled a ten euro note in Rafael's direction.

'My hands are covered in flour. Pay me tomorrow.' He smiled. 'On second thoughts, don't pay me at all. You left me all those fresh eggs. We're quits.'

Isabel winked and tucked the note back in her pocket.

'In that case, maybe I should bring you eggs every day.'

She jogged down the steps and released Furó. She picked up a prescription for her mother in the chemist and strolled across the *plaça*, with Furó trotting happily behind her, and waved at Jesus and Llorenç on the way. She looked up at the clockface of Sant Antoní and smiled to see that it was coming up for ten-thirty. Although she wore no watch, she knew without a shadow of a doubt that it was absolutely spot on.

Isabel knocked on the door of Doctor Ramis's house on the way home but received no answer. With a frustrated sigh, she shrugged and clanged the gate shut. In the office she found Pep sitting cross-legged on the floor, a heap of animal-shaped balloons bobbing around him. He offered a weary expression.

'I hope you don't mind, Bel, but Angélica has a pack of restless kids in the summer school, and I promised to deliver some animal-shaped balloons for them this morning.'

Isabel laughed. 'Is this one of your many hidden talents?'

He shrugged. 'My uncle used to make them for us as kids and he taught me. If things go belly up here, I can always become a child entertainer.'

'That won't happen, Pep. You're a Poirot in the making.'

AUNT MARIA'S LAST ARIA

'What's that?'

Isabel shook her head. 'Look him up. So, how is Angélica enjoying running the summer school?'

Pep frowned. 'She's in that school all year, so I think it was a mistake to volunteer for the summer school, even if they do pay her. It's really exhausting in this heat.'

'Everything in life is an experience. At least she has given it a go. Now, why don't I help you and then we can head off to Pòrtol.'

'No offence, Bel, but I'm not sure your talents lend themselves to balloon making. You know how clumsy you are.'

With a frown, Isabel grabbed a balloon and blew heartily into it. The balloon swelled and there was a sudden loud pop as it exploded. Pep grimaced.

'How about making us both a coffee instead?'

Sometime later, as Pep carefully loaded the balloons in a large cardboard box, ably assisted by an enthusiastic Furó, Isabel sat hunched over the phone in her office. It rang several times before a deep, impatient voice filled the void.

'*Quien es?*'

Isabel politely introduced herself to Enrique Diaz and wasn't surprised to receive a surly and stilted reply when she asked about his relationship with Maria.

'I haven't been in touch with her for at least five years. We had a falling out when she last performed with me in Barcelona, and I refused to work with her again.'

'What did you argue about?'

'Maria resented my getting top billing on all the publicity material and earning more than her. At the end of our tour together, it all blew up and we had a huge row.'

'I see.'

His voice sounded hoarse. 'I was truly sorry to hear about Maria's suicide, but frankly, she was always unstable.'

'The investigation is continuing. Suicide is one theory.'

'What are you suggesting happened?'

'As I say, we are investigating all avenues. Meanwhile, why are you here in Mallorca?'

'I'm visiting my friend, the opera singer Catalina Grimalt. It was her birthday yesterday, so I came over to celebrate it.'

'And when did you arrive on the island?'

Isabel sensed a hesitancy in the voice.

'Last Monday. I had a meeting that afternoon with my agent, Eva Salas.'

'That was the day before Maria died.'

'So I heard.'

'Can you tell me about your whereabouts last Tuesday morning?'

'I had a lie-in at my hotel and a late breakfast at about eleven o'clock.'

'And where are you staying?'

'At Hotel Son Bunyola in Banyalbufar, away from the prying eyes of the media.'

'You can't find anywhere more private on the island. My boyfriend treated me to a luxury stay there. It was a weekend to remember.'

He gave a low chuckle. 'I'd hang on to him, if I were you.'

'Thanks, I intend to. What else have you been doing while in Mallorca?'

'I don't have to answer, but if you must know, I've been seeing friends and having a bit of a holiday. I'm going to attend Maria's funeral tomorrow out of respect and will leave the next day.'

'Had you hoped to see Maria while you were here?'

'As I said, we hadn't been in touch for years.'

'Is your wife with you?'

'She's working. We allow ourselves the odd solo break.'

Isabel held the receiver in the crook of her neck as she absentmindedly drew variously shaped stars across a blank piece of paper. She tapped her foot impatiently.

'So, was that all?' he asked.

'For now. We'll both be at the funeral tomorrow, so if I think of anything else, I'll let you know.'

Having made a quick phone call to Hotel Son Bunyola, Isabel rang Georg Bisbal, the scholarship student who, like Gemma Palau, used to have private lessons with Maria at her home in Moscari. He assured her that he hadn't visited the house for a month as he had been staying on the mainland with his elderly grandparents and would not be returning until September. He appeared traumatised by the news, admitting that although Tía Maria was a harsh taskmaster, she was the best tutor he'd ever had.

Isabel walked through to the main office and helped Pep load the balloons into Pequeñito, then they delivered them to Angélica at her school. Isabel deposited Furó at Florentina's house, and they set off for Pòrtol and neighbouring Sa Cabaneta. Isabel loved visiting this small enclave in the south, famous for its red soil and *ollerías*. It lay within the municipality of Marratxí, where every spring the Fira del Fang, a huge ceramics fair, was held. Isabel, with her mother and Uncle Idò in tow, would make the annual pilgrimage there to buy *greixoneras* and *ollas* at far better prices than in the shops. Idò liked to hang out in the bar chatting to all and sundry while she and her mother visited the colourful stands. Pep sat in the passenger seat, gazing out of the window. Suddenly, he sat up and pointed to the Museu del Fang, the local pottery museum.

'Let's park here. Fermin's workshop is close by those of Ca Madò Bet and Can Bernadí Nou.'

Isabel easily found a space on the empty street. She stood in front of the museum, examining the Ruta del Fang map, which highlighted all of the pottery and ceramic workshops in the town.

'Have you ever done the route?' she asked Pep.

'I wanted to do it with Angélica, but she thought it looked too difficult.'

'Nonsense. It's a lovely walk around the town and only takes a few hours. The soil and clay used to be sourced here in Pòrtol, but now it comes from the mainland.'

'Why is that?'

She shrugged. 'The supply dried up, but at least the tradition continues. The museum has a wonderful collection of *siurells*. It's only a short visit.'

Pep laughed. 'Angélica could probably handle that as long as there was a coffee and *ensaïmada* at the end of it.'

As they passed the workshop of Madò Bet, Isabel smiled.

'This is the most famous of the *siurell* makers. Coloma is the third generation of women in her family who makes them. I must pop by to see her after we've interviewed Fermin. I promised to buy Tolo a *siurell*.'

Pep eyed her quizzically. 'How do they make them?'

'The little figures are made out of clay and then a whistle is inserted – it's a secret as to how this is done. Coloma has shown me, but I'll never breathe a word. Once the clay figures are fired, she paints them white and adds green and red brushstrokes. She also offers custom-made designs that break away from tradition. It's a time-consuming business.'

'Sounds like a lot of work for little return.'

'True, but artisans enjoy what they do. It's not about the money.'

AUNT MARIA'S LAST ARIA

Pep shrugged and approached the yard of Fermin's workshop. Ca Janer was written in bright blue letters on a sign decorated with *siurell* graphics at the modest entrance. Isabel stepped forward and rang the bell, smiling when a Siamese cat rubbed against her leg. A large man in a grubby white apron pushed open the door.

'I see you've met Angélica.'

Pep laughed. 'That's the name of my girlfriend.'

'Don't make her jealous,' the man said with a grin.

Isabel flipped open her police badge. 'Mr Janer? I'm Isabel Flores. I work with the National Police. Could I ask you a few questions?'

He nodded warily. 'This is about my cousin, Maria, I take it?'

'Yes, it is.'

His eyes roved the empty road. 'You'd better come inside.'

When they were settled with coffees, Isabel said, 'How did you and Maria get along?'

Fermin stared at her with sad eyes. 'It's no secret that we weren't on good terms, although we were very close as children. Sadly, her father's brutally unfair will changed our relationship. I have been fighting for justice for some years. When our grandfather Alberto died, my father should have been entitled to half of Can Rosselló, but the old man favoured his eldest son and so Maria's father got left the house. My father was given a modest sum of money instead, but he felt hard done by. He always wanted to own Can Rosselló. When Maria's father died, she inherited the house.'

'But your father accepted the money at the time?'

'Yes, because he was bullied into it by Alberto's lawyer, and he needed the cash. Maria's father had connections and had made a lot of money with his businesses. He was in cahoots with Alberto's lawyer. I still believe my heirs have a rightful claim to their share of Can Rosselló.'

Pep set his mug on the table and offered a sympathetic glance.

'Good luck with that one. Inheritance is complicated.'

The man's face flushed red, and his fists formed tight balls.

'It is when you're dealing with thieving crooks!'

Isabel picked up a small clay figure. 'This is beautiful. I see you've not used the traditional *siurell* colours.'

Fermin gradually calmed down. 'I like to break away from the norm. Some shop owners want them in strange colours. If they're paying, who am I to argue? Of course, some others in the town disapprove.'

Isabel smiled. 'Did you see Maria recently?'

He looked downcast. 'I had a row with Maria the night before she died. It was last Monday night. I wish it hadn't happened.'

'What was the upshot of the encounter?'

He shrugged. 'I threatened her with more legal challenges, and she just laughed and told me I'd never win. She was a very cold woman.'

'Was Pepe there?' Isabel asked.

'He left the room. To be honest, her husband seemed embarrassed about the whole issue.'

'Did you see her again?' asked Pep.

'Of course not. She threw herself off her balcony the next morning.'

'Allegedly,' cut in Isabel.

He stared at her. 'You think she was murdered?'

'Do you?' Isabel asked.

'Of course not. She wasn't well liked locally, but I can't think of anyone who'd want to harm her. All the same, her students couldn't stand her.'

'What makes you say that?' she countered.

'A few months ago, after one of our rows, I got talking to a lad named Georg who was using the piano at Can Rosselló. He was one of her students at the Conservatori and told me she was disliked by everyone there.'

Isabel stood up and looked out of the window.

'It seems that poor Maria was liked by very few people, despite being an excellent teacher. Andre Gide once said, "It's better to be hated for what you are than to be loved for something you are not."'

Pep gnawed at the corner of his mouth and frowned. 'I think I get that.'

Fermin regarded Isabel in some confusion. He nodded. 'That is a wise comment. I shall remember it.'

Isabel opened the door.

'Thanks for your time, Mr Janer. If you think of anything else, do get in touch. Here are my contact details.'

He studied the card. 'You may not believe me, but I'm sad Maria is dead. She used to be like a sister to me. I'll be at the funeral tomorrow.'

Isabel walked into the yard, where her eyes momentarily settled on an open garage at the side of the building. She frowned and strode towards the front gate as Fermin stood sombrely on the porch, his eyes trained on them. When they were out of sight, Pep turned to her.

'You looked startled back there. What did you see?'

'There was a red Fiat 500 in the garage. It was too dark to read the number plate, but the last letter could have been a Z.'

Pep stopped in his tracks. 'You think it's the same car that you saw outside the Conservatori and last Friday in Campos?'

'I've no idea. It could just be a coincidence. Tomorrow at the cemetery I'll inspect all the vehicles in the car park, just in case.'

'There was definitely something a bit odd about that guy.'
'That's the trouble, Pep. Just about everyone in this case is odd, but does that make one of them a murderer?'

FOURTEEN

The marbled sky was darkening, but a stubborn heat persisted. Isabel sat at her desk with the windows flung open, enjoying a moment of calm. Earlier, she had been for a long and sticky cycle ride and run with Pep, in a half-hearted attempt to train for their impending triathlon. They still had time on their side and Isabel looked forward to the cooler air of September, when training would become less gruelling. She listened to the call of Salvador, her fretful cockerel. It was well past his bedtime, but he and his feathered hareem became restless in the warmer weather and shunned the cosy henhouse in favour of sleeping al fresco on its roof. Even then, they took their time to nod off. Isabel jumped up and with Chupa Chup in hand and walked into the main office, where she had recently set up her faithful whiteboard. It was here that she jotted down her thoughts whenever she worked on a new police case. Picking up a black marker pen, she began scribbling on one side of the large board. She had divided it in half, one side devoted to Maria's case and the other to the unexplained death of Juan Jaume and the mysterious dead seagulls that seemed to stalk the new South African estate agent in the Soller valley.

An hour later, the telephone rang. With a distracted tut, she went to answer it. She was surprised and unnerved to hear the voice of Emilio Navarro.

'Bel, I'm sorry to disturb you on a Saturday night, but I have potentially good news.'

Isabel issued a hoarse cough. 'Oh?'

'The Mossos d'Esquadra force has recruited a new police chief. A bunch of senior officers have been suspended, pending an internal investigation.'

'How does that affect us?'

'For one thing, the new chief appears to have reopened your uncle's case. He's ordered a review of the suspicious death of the key witness who saw him being forced into a car bearing a Colombian flag.'

'The prostitute who was found dead from an overdose.'

'Correct. But there's more. Your uncle is believed to be in a safe house.'

'Why?'

He sighed into the receiver. 'It's likely he is in a witness protection programme of some kind.'

'But isn't he under suspicion himself? Remember, he was photographed recently in the company of a Colombian drug baron in Medellin.'

Emilio clicked his teeth. 'There's a lot going on that we can't understand. I've got this information from a reliable informant, but it bodes well. If your uncle is being protected by government forces, and the Barcelona force is under scrutiny with a new boss, it speaks of internal corruption.'

'You mean there's been a cover-up?' she asked.

'It's what you and I have thought all along. It would explain why we received so little cooperation from the force at the time Hugo went missing.'

'Perhaps he was working on an investigative report for his newspaper and discovered corruption within the Mossos d'Esquadra,' Isabel suggested.

'It's highly plausible.'

'But why was he abducted by a Colombian faction?'

'We don't know that for sure. What if he went willingly and the prostitute misinterpreted the scene? Remember it was late at night and dark.' Isabel crunched on her Chupa Chup. 'Or perhaps corrupt officers at the Mossos were involved in a Colombian drug ring that Uncle Hugo uncovered? But why would they keep him alive all this time? Nothing makes sense.'

'My informant says things are moving quickly. I firmly believe that Hugo will be in touch soon. In the meantime, keep this between us. Hold tight.'

For some time, Isabel sat quietly in her chair, mulling over her conversation with Emilio. She yearned to speak to Tolo but knew that he'd had a frenetic day. At least she'd see him at the precinct in the morning. She left Furó sleeping in his basket and pottered downstairs to the kitchen, where she discovered her mother's goodies in the fridge and pantry. There was a large *tortilla de patatas*, *albondigas*, a pepper and tomato salad and a crema Catalana. In the pantry, she found a fresh seed loaf and fruit cake. Isabel pottered out to the patio and placed some mats on the table just as she heard knocking at the front door. It was gone nine o'clock and she wasn't expecting company. If it were her mother, she'd just barge in as the door was seldom locked. She emerged from the kitchen and found Tolo standing in the *entrada*, a grin on his face.

'I hope it was okay to let myself in.'

Isabel rushed to give him a hug. 'What a wonderful surprise. I thought you were having dinner with your boss tonight?'

Tolo nodded. 'The poor guy has gone down with some awful bug so probably won't be in for the rest for the week. I risked coming by as you'd said you'd be home.'

'Well, your timing is meticulous. I'm just about to pig out on my mother's delectable fare.'

He followed her into the kitchen, clutching a bottle of Sío. 'I've brought a little offering that will go perfectly with it. I'm starving.'

She laughed. 'Me too. Now I've got you all to myself, I can fill you in on what's been going on in the village. You'll need that wine.'

A few hours later, Isabel and Tolo retired to her office, where she outlined her preliminary thoughts and theories about both Maria's case and the death of Juan Jaume. Tolo stood in a contemplative state, scrutinising the images and timelines.

'You've done an impressive job so far. I'm just sorry that I've been so distracted by the cold cases. I'd definitely like you to follow up on the other bursary students. If one of them can tell us who gave Maria those poisonous mushrooms, we might find out if she had any real enemies who wished her harm.'

'I agree. I feel that one of the students holds the key. Pep is sourcing their contact details discreetly. It's better that we don't involve the director, Matías Camps.'

He nodded. 'Good move. I know you've had your reservations about him. This case is proving to be an uphill struggle because of the lack of cooperation from the regional government and those close to her. Even the commissioner is urging me to put the matter to bed as quickly as possible.'

'It's obvious that Maria had powerful friends who don't want a whiff of a scandal. She was an island icon, after all,' she replied. 'But we still have a job to do. If she was murdered, they'll just have to cope with the fallout, even if it does upset their sensitivities.'

He took a sip of wine. 'But what about motive? Her cousin, Fermin, seems more of a dreamer, hoping that one day he'll get justice for the sins of the past, knowing that he has little chance.'

Isabel leant against Pep's desk with arms folded. 'He had plenty of opportunity to bump her off these last few years. Why now when he was in the middle of a court case?'

Tolo nodded. 'Maria left everything to Pepe in her will, so he's unlikely to get a slice of the house.'

'True, but he still believes that he has a legitimate right to the property.'

Tolo tapped the whiteboard. 'You've noted here that there could have been bad blood between Enrique Diaz, Catalina Grimalt and Maria?'

She shrugged. 'It may be nothing, but there's something awry there. I didn't feel either Diaz or Grimalt had been totally honest with me.'

He broke into a mischievous smile. 'So, shall we address the elephant in the room?'

Isabel frowned. 'You're talking about Pepe.'

He pointed towards the whiteboard. 'Who else? If Maria was indeed murdered, he has the best motive of all, as you have conceded here. He could have fooled Raquel, the maid, by faking that the bathroom door was bolted from the inside, having earlier pushed Maria off the balcony. After all, as both he and the maid confirmed, he slipped out of the kitchen at around eight o'clock that morning, supposedly to do a stock take of his tins, giving him ample time to do the deed and return to the kitchen.'

Isabel tapped her chin. 'Now he inherits everything, and according to Eva Salas, intends to clean up commercially with the release of Maria's recordings, although we only have her word for that.'

Tolo offered a thin smile. 'Look, this guy has been living in a cupboard with a load of dead anchovies for company for some years. Maybe he'd simply had enough.'

Isabel stood contemplatively in front of her whiteboard.

'You'd think so, but he appears to be content with his lot. He seemed genuinely proud to show me his monastic cell. Admittedly he's an eccentric, but a murderer?'

'You've got good instincts, but don't be fooled by him. You're a sucker for weirdos. That's how you've ended up with me.'

Isabel laughed. 'You've got a point.'

Tolo re-examined her notes on the board about the death of Juan Jaume.

'This is a sad case too, but the man could quite easily have died of natural causes. I get that his son, Manuel, has an axe to grind and that someone else was at the house that night, but so far, it's all pretty circumstantial.'

'I think that's Gómez's view,' she said.

'I tend to agree with him on this one. I guess he's still waiting for the forensics report.'

'Hopefully, he'll have it soon. In the meantime, I've been trying to get hold of Miguel next door to find out what medication he'd prescribed to Juan. I found Nembutal pills in his bathroom cupboard. They are usually for insomnia, but he purportedly took low blood pressure tablets, which is odd.'

Tolo's eyebrows rose. 'A bit of a heady mix, but maybe there's a rational explanation.' He paused. 'The dead seagulls are troubling, though. As you've surmised, maybe that agent Tomeu Tous is trying to frighten off Markham.'

'It could just be a decoy,' Isabel mused. 'You know, something to throw us off the scent.'

Tolo yawned. 'Hopefully forensics finds DNA on the dead birds. Why not wait and see. I'm more concerned about that red Fiat 500 you've seen. I wish you'd told me about that earlier.'

'It's probably just my imagination. This job can make you paranoid.'

He gave a weary guffaw. 'Tell me about it. Anyway, perhaps it's time to turn in. Tomorrow's going to be a busy day, *cariño*.'

Isabel nodded and wandered over to the window and looked out onto the empty street. She surmised that it must be nearly eleven-thirty, an hour during weekdays when few of the village's summer visitors remained. The weekends were another matter. As she gazed out at the smudgy silhouette of the Tramuntanas, she became aware of an altercation. A gate clanged close by and loud voices filled the silent void. Isabel shot a look at Tolo and rushed towards the office door. Together, they ran down the stairs.

'Did you see anyone?' he asked breathlessly.

'No, it's too dark. Come on!'

Isabel grabbed a torch out of a drawer in the *entrada*, and together they stepped outside into the balmy night and walked quickly along the garden path, shining the torch ahead of them. It didn't take Isabel long to discover the cause of the disturbance. In the middle of the street, she saw Doctor Ramis in his nightshirt and Wee Willie Winkie nightcap, seemingly attempting to placate a snarling Manuel who swayed before him, empty bottle in hand.

Isabel stepped forward. 'What's going on?'

Manuel's glassy gaze fell on her.

'All this old fool had to do was slip me a few pills. Something to ease the pain. I asked him nicely.'

Doctor Ramis shook his head in frustration. 'I'm not giving you drugs, Manuel. It won't solve anything. You can't come to my door at this time of night making impossible demands.'

Tolo walked slowly towards Manuel.

'Maybe it's time to set off home, *tío*, and leave the good doctor to go to bed.'

'Who are you to tell me what to do? You're all the same. That idiot doctor at the clinic is trying to imprison me…'

Doctor Ramis gave a sigh. 'Manuel, your doctor at the clinic in Palma is trying to help you quit the drugs and alcohol.'

'I'm not doing rehab, so forget that.'

Isabel slipped her neighbour a brief, reassuring smile and placed a hand on Manuel's arm.

'I'm sorry for your loss, Manuel. The death of Juan has been a huge shock for you.'

He broke into laughter. 'A shock? As if I ever cared about him.'

Despite his invective, Isabel saw that his eyes had welled up. She spoke softly to him.

'Did you see your father on Sunday night? Someone had been drinking with him before his death.'

He dropped the bottle and watched with a befuddled expression as it rolled towards the gutter.

'Yes, I was there. The old sod asked me round for a few whiskies to wind me up about the house sale. He told me that he would be spending as much of the money as he could before he died.'

Isabel stared at him. 'When did you leave?'

Manuel shrugged. 'Dunno, but my old dad was still alive and kicking when I left.'

He used Isabel's arm to steady himself and stared at her. She recoiled at the smell of alcohol on his breath but didn't budge.

'I found out today from his idiot lawyer that he only left me half of the house, and that damned South African wants his investment back too. He can go whistle.'

Isabel eyed him intently. 'Who gets the other half?'

'Some female relative in Asturias. She gets half of everything in his will. The old devil well and truly shafted me. I hope he rots in hell.'

Tolo had had enough. He pulled Isabel away and grabbed Manuel by the shoulder. 'Right, I'm taking you home. If you cause more trouble tonight, you'll be sleeping in a police cell.'

Manuel shook himself free and, cursing loudly, lurched off along the street. Isabel turned to Tolo.

'Leave him be. He'll find his way back.'

Doctor Ramis shook his head sadly. 'Thanks for intervening, both of you. I was about to go to bed but noticed him standing on my porch in the dark. He was demanding I give him naltrexone.'

'It's used for treating substance abuse, isn't it?'

He nodded. 'Yes, but Manuel is under the care of a specialist at an addiction centre in Palma. I can't interfere with his treatment plan. His father organised it, not that it's been a success so far. He's so out of control.'

Isabel stood by his gate and offered him a sympathetic scrunch of the arm.

'In the end, each of us has to want to change. It cannot be done by force.'

'True,' Tolo replied. 'Mind you, he looks like a hopeless case.'

'He used to be a happy, cheeky boy with a good heart,' Doctor Ramis replied. 'He just got in with the wrong crowd.'

Isabel turned to her neighbour. 'Just one thing, Miguel. On Sunday night, I noticed that there was a box of Nembutal in Juan's bathroom cupboard. Did you prescribe them?'

He shook his head. 'Heavens, no. His consultant prescribed him fludrocortisone, which increases blood volume. Juan suffered from Addison's disease, which is caused when the adrenal gland makes too little cortisol. On top of that he had very low blood pressure, but he never mentioned a problem with insomnia. Nembutal can be used for sleep issues but would not be advisable in Juan's case, as it can cause hypotension.'

Isabel frowned. 'I wonder why he was taking it.'

'I've no idea, but it would have been very risky. Someone would have had to prescribe it and as his doctor I know that his consultant did not. He was taking a mild painkiller for his arthritis. Nothing more.'

'When would he normally take his meds?'

'I advised him to take the two pills in the morning, but he preferred to take them in the evening.'

'What colour were they?'

'White. Is that important?'

'You never know.'

Isabel bade him goodnight and followed Tolo into her house. Upstairs, they found Furó wide awake and whimpering in his basket. Isabel picked him up and stroked his soft fur.

'It's okay, my little friend. Everything's alright. Time for bed.'

She placed him in Tolo's arms.

'I just want to check on something. I'll come up in a minute.'

Tolo patted Furó, his brows knitted. 'What are you up to?'

'I've had a crazy idea that I need to check out.'

She waited till Tolo had left and turned on her computer. She began to research fludrocortisone online, scrolling through the information until her mouse froze in her hand. She enlarged the image of a small white pill on her screen and gave an involuntary gasp. The number 7033 was imprinted on its surface. Before Juan died, he had told his neighbour Enric that he'd been tricked with a wrong number, and that it should have been 7033. He had wondered whether it was the combination to a safe but now it was obvious to Isabel that Juan had in fact been referring to his prescribed medication. On Sunday night someone must have switched his daily pills with something more deadly, and Juan had evidently realised too late, but what was it? Isabel heard Tolo sleepily calling for her. Her mind awhirl, she switched off the lights and made her way to bed. Tomorrow, she would be at the precinct when the forensics reports would be released. In the meantime, she wondered how on earth she'd be able to get a wink of sleep.

FIFTEEN

A smouldering sun glowered in the sky as Idò stood outside Ca'n Moix, remonstrating with the local council workers who cleared the gutters with noisy leaf blowers. Isabel arrived at her gate with Furó, her hair still damp from her early morning swim. Tolo had left for Palma as soon as Salvador began to crow, leaving Isabel ample time to go for her swim before the rest of the world awoke. She frowned, nonplussed to find her uncle gesticulating wildly at three young men in overalls.

'Is there a problem?' she yelled above the noise.

Idò turned to her with a scowl. 'Those wretched machines are a pollution on our streets. Besides which, it's not even autumn, so why are these goons using leaf blowers?'

One of the men turned off his machine. 'There's no need to be rude. It's not just in autumn that you get leaves. The kerbs and gutters are full of them all year round. We've nearly finished this patch anyway.'

'Thank heavens for that! I can hardly hear myself think,' he snapped.

Isabel linked arms with him and offered a conciliatory smile in the direction of the men. 'Thank you for all your hard work, especially in this heat. My cranky old uncle evidently got out of the wrong side of bed.'

They nodded and laughed good-naturedly as they slowly progressed along the street. With a defeated grunt, Idò followed his niece into the house, wiping the sweat from his forehead. In the kitchen, they found Florentina dishing out plates of freshly baked blackberry cake to Pep, Doctor Ramis and Llorenç. Immediately, Idò broke into a smile and gave his sister a hug.

'My favourite cake!'

Laughing, Florentina shook him off as she bustled about the kitchen.

'You say that about all my cakes, brother. I thought you'd be here as soon as I served up coffee.'

'As it happens, I'd just arrived when I heard those loud leaf blowers outside. Llorenç, you have to ban those things before we all go deaf.'

Llorenç chewed thoughtfully on a morsel of cake. 'Some villagers like them, Idò. As mayor, I have to take on board all opinions.'

'I'd love to know who likes them. They're a menace on our streets.'

Doctor Ramis eyed him thoughtfully. 'You have a point, Idò. We never used to have these noisy gadgets when we were growing up. My mother used to get us to sweep the courtyard until you could lick it clean.'

'Same here,' Idò replied as he accepted a cup of coffee and plate of cake from Florentina.

Isabel smirked at Pep as she bent down to give Furó his bowl of kibble, and then pulled out a chair at the table. She took a gulp of coffee and turned to Miguel.

'I wanted to tell you about my discovery after the little drama last night.'

Florentina butted in. 'What drama?'

'Around midnight I had a visitation from a drunken Manuel seeking medication for his addiction, which I'm not at liberty to give. Tolo and Isabel kindly saw him off,' he replied.

'That man's as big a menace as the leaf blowers,' yelled Idò. 'You'd think he'd lie low given that his old man's not long in the grave.'

Llorenç shook his head. 'Poor Juan. When Capitán Gómez interviewed Manuel, he admitted to visiting his father on Sunday night but insisted that he was still alive when he left. Perhaps Juan did just die of natural causes.'

'I very much doubt that,' Isabel replied glumly. 'We'll have to wait for the forensic report, but his death is suspicious.'

'Good grief!' exclaimed Florentina. 'Why do you say that?'

'And what was your discovery last night?' asked Doctor Ramis.

Isabel stared at them all, her eyes resting the longest on Llorenç. 'If I tell you, you must promise to keep it to yourselves.'

'As if we wouldn't,' replied Llorenç with a hurt expression.

Isabel told them about the potential medication switch and the significance of the number 7033, a number found on one brand of fludrocortisone tablets.

Doctor Ramis broke the silence. 'Goodness, what a terrible thought. Hopefully a toxicology report will show something up. However, if Juan mistakenly took Nembutal instead of his usual fludrocortisone tablet, it wouldn't have killed him.'

Isabel's forehead creased. 'It's not just the Nembutal I'm worried about. What if someone switched his fludrocortisone for something dangerous that, when combined with Nembutal, would have had a catastrophic effect?'

'Do you have proof of that?' Llorenç asked.

'No, I don't, but in his final moments, Juan felt he'd been duped, so he must have somehow realised that his pills had been swapped,' Isabel replied. 'Maybe when he started to feel unwell.'

'Have you told Tolo and Capitán Gómez?' asked Doctor Ramis.

'I told Tolo first thing this morning. He's already spoken with Capitán Gómez, who'll be alerting the forensics team.'

Florentina sat down heavily opposite her. 'What kind of a person would kill a lovely man like Juan? I honestly wouldn't have thought Manuel capable of such a thing.'

Isabel shrugged. 'You'd be surprised how implausible some killers are. The key is to keep an open mind.'

'So what next?' asked Pep.

'Well, I need to get to the precinct to find out what forensics have thrown up about the death of Maria, and to bend Pedro Massip's ear about my new theory on the death of Juan.'

'I wish you hadn't returned to police work, Bel. It makes me so stressed.'

'Try being me,' Isabel replied with a grin.

'That dead seagull was sinister,' Llorenç suddenly piped up.

'What?' gasped Florentina.

Isabel offered Llorenç an exasperated look. He flushed. 'Sorry, Bel. I shouldn't have mentioned it, but since I have, I may as well tell everyone. A dead seagull had been placed in Juan's kitchen. Others were found outside Adam Markham's office and home. There's speculation that maybe Tomeu Tous put them there to scare him off.'

'Whatever next!' Florentina exclaimed.

'We mustn't speculate, Llorenç,' warned Isabel.

Idò looked thoughtful. 'Old Tomeu isn't a bad person. He's scatty as anything, though. I was in his office the other day and he was searching everywhere for his jacket. He swore he'd had it on the back of his chair. Most of the properties he sells are shabby and in need of a lot of renovation, but he's well liked. He's a great fisherman too.'

Isabel interrupted. 'He must see a lot of seagulls in that case.'

'Funny you should say that. He can't stand them. He calls them the scavengers of the sea. Mind you, there are quite a few local seagull protection groups, so someone likes them.'

Isabel smiled. 'Is that so? Anyway, what are your plans today?'

'I'm off to top up more pools with chlorine,' he moaned.

'And I've got to pop by Casa Elena again,' cut in Pep. 'The wife says they've got a wasp problem.'

'A likely story,' scoffed Idò. 'That woman just fancies you. She's always on your back.'

Florentina laughed as Pep scrunched up his face.

'Miguel and I have a Pilates class with Juliana at noon followed by a painting lesson with Alfonso. When is Llorenç planning to hold his surprise party?'

'On the thirtieth of August, his birthday. It'll be in the function room of the town hall,' Isabel replied.

'How thrilling,' exclaimed Doctor Ramis. 'He's a wonderful fellow and such a talented artist.'

'Indeed, he is,' cooed Florentina. 'And did I tell you that I've found a local genealogist to help me with our family tree?'

Isabel smiled. 'I didn't know that kind of thing interested you.'

'I have a reason.' She paused. 'There's always been a mystery surrounding your grandmother on your father's side, so finally I thought the time had come to find out more about her.'

'What kind of mystery?' piped up Pep.

'My husband, Juan, knew little about his mother, Ana, who sadly died giving birth to him and his twin, Hugo. The boys asked Ignacio, their father, about her, but he was always reluctant to discuss the matter. When the boys were toddlers, he married Luna, and she was like a mother to them, but she too learnt little about Juan's first wife.'

'Why do you think that was?' Pep asked.

'Juan assumed that her death was too painful a memory,' Florentina replied. 'But it would be nice to find out more about her.'

Isabel took a sip of her coffee. 'When we were in our teens, my brother, Eduardo, and I asked Uncle Hugo if he'd researched her, given that he was an investigative journalist, but he was very evasive. Maybe he was unhappy about what he discovered.'

'What did your grandfather do?' Pep asked.

'He was a career diplomat and spent a lot of his early career in London,' Isabel replied.

Florentina nodded. 'Ignacio was a very clever man and a polyglot. That's why he made Juan and Hugo learn several languages as a child.'

Isabel gave a groan. 'And in family tradition that's why my father was insistent that Eduardo and I learnt English, French and German as kids.'

Florentina waggled a finger. 'How lucky you both were, my girl. Your language skills have brought you foreign clients.'

Isabel shrugged. 'True, but it drove us both mad as kids when he forced us to speak in different languages at dinner time.'

Pep laughed. 'What a nightmare.'

Isabel stood up and walked towards the *entrada*. 'I'm off to Palma and then I'll pop back to change into something appropriate for Tía Maria's funeral this afternoon.'

Llorenç got to his feet. 'I've a meeting at the town hall so must be off too. I'll leave you good people to enjoy your day.'

Pep followed Isabel to the front door. 'By the way, I've got hold of the phone numbers of those scholarship students you wanted.'

'You're a star. I'll contact them tomorrow when I have some time in the office. Keep an eye on Furó for me.'

He winked. 'Of course. Besides, I need someone to help answer the calls.'

Isabel sat across the desk from Tolo, a glum expression on her face. 'So, Pedro Massip still hasn't got the analysis back on the contents of Maria's locket?'

'I'm afraid not.'

'And the forensics report that Nacho wrote shows nothing out of the ordinary in Maria's bedroom, no DNA, nothing amiss?'

'So it seems,' he replied. 'I know this is frustrating, but maybe we have to accept that there may be no mystery to solve. The only real suspect is Pepe Serrano, and we still have no proof of his involvement.'

Gaspar stood by the window, enjoying the cool air emanating from a fan. 'Massip's team did identify that glass ladybird button that Furó found. Apparently, a Milanese button factory makes them for upmarket clothing lines in Europe. There is one Spanish fashion brand in the Salamanca district of Madrid that has bought supplies of them.'

Tolo shrugged. 'I'm not sure where we're heading with this line of enquiry.'

Isabel drummed her fingers on the desk. 'I agree. Maybe Furó just took a liking to it. I'm going to focus on that group of scholarship students at the Conservatori. I'm sure we're missing something there.'

'Let's concentrate first on the funeral this afternoon,' Tolo replied. 'It'll be useful for you and Gaspar to see how everyone interacts, particularly the relations between Pepe and Fermin.'

'And, of course, Eva Salas and her clients, Enrique Diaz and Catalina Grimalt,' Gaspar said.

Isabel nodded. 'Yesterday, when I called Diaz, he told me he arrived last Monday and was staying at Hotel Son Bunyola in Banyalbufar. Apparently, he slept in on Tuesday, the morning of Maria's fall. However, I called the hotel, and the manager could only confirm that he had taken a late breakfast at around eleven-fifteen. He signed his bill at eleven-forty. Staff could not confirm his whereabouts before then.'

'Meaning?' asked Gaspar.

'That he could have slipped out of the hotel earlier, driven to Can Rosselló and potentially killed Maria. The front door, according to the student Gemma Palau, is always open. It's only an hour's drive from the hotel, so he could have been back in time for breakfast. I know it sounds preposterous and we have no reason to suspect Diaz, but it's worth bearing in mind.'

Tolo scratched his stubbly chin. 'It's possible, but without a motive, we've little to go on. And, of course, there's still the small matter of the bathroom door being bolted from the inside.'

Gaspar suddenly smiled. 'Before I forget, Bel, I tracked down that therapist that Maria visited in Santa Catalina. His name is Frank Rendall and he's British. I'll text you his details.'

'Thank you. What about Doctor Blando?'

'That's the bad news. He died two years ago. A group of doctors took over his practice, Clinica Casa de Salud, but it's unlikely they'd have had any contact with Maria.'

'Can you send me the details anyway?'

He nodded. 'The office is just off Jaume III, so a quick walk from here.'

Isabel stood up. 'I'd better head back to Sant Martí to change before attending the funeral.'

'I'll see you there,' Gaspar replied.

Tolo grinned. 'You're already in a natty black suit, I see.'

'You know me, boss, always Mr Sartorial.'

As Isabel stepped into the corridor, Tolo called after her. 'Weren't you awaiting some other forensic results from Massip to do with that death in Sant Martí?'

She nodded. 'That's why I'm popping by his office before leaving Palma. I can't trust Gómez to pass them onto to me.'

'He's a bit overwhelmed with work currently.'

Isabel eyed Tolo in some bemusement. 'Backing your former nemesis, now that's a first.'

'They're besties these days. Didn't you know?' Gaspar hooted with laughter as a grinning Tolo threw a well-aimed pen in his direction.

Isabel and Gaspar stood back from the throng of mourners who'd gathered close to the Rosselló family mausoleum at Inca's municipal cemetery. The pair had discreetly sat in the back row of the Chapel of Rest during the perfunctory service, watching the smart attendees as they were shown to their designated seats. The air conditioning had suffered a malfunction so female guests had been forced to swish their fans in the thick, still air while men broke protocol and removed their jackets. Isabel had keenly observed each and every one of the thirty guests. In the first row on the right-hand side sat Pepe and Fermin and his wife. Behind them were Matías Camps and several of the tutors from the Conservatori, including Gemma Palau. On the left, filling several rows, were local politicians and some notable society figures. Enrique Diaz, Catalina Grimalt and Eva Salas sat in the front row chatting with the president and minister of culture while several senior advisers in the second row leant forward to participate in the conversation. Isabel observed the ease with which the island's political elite chatted animatedly with the opera stars. In their chic and formal black summer attire, all they needed were flutes of *cava* and they could have been guests at a cocktail party. One lone attendee intrigued Isabel. She was a young woman with shoulder-length red hair who sat in a row midway on the left. At one point she locked eyes with Gemma Palau and offered a furtive nod.

Now, as the guests began to disperse along the cypress-lined avenues of graves, Isabel and Gaspar slunk off along another path close to a tower of *nichos*. Tía Maria's family had the luxury of a family vault, so there was no thought of her remains being stored in one of these high-rise waiting rooms.

Gaspar turned to Isabel. 'I noticed there was a date of 1867 above the main gate. Is that when this place was built?'

'Actually, it was 1820. I read in the local press that archaeologists recently exhumed some bodies in a plot here, looking for victims from the Spanish Civil War,' she replied.

'Did they find any?'

'They uncovered several unidentified corpses, but one was thought to belong to Joan Mut Jaume, a nineteen-year-old artillery soldier from Llucmajor who was sentenced to death by firing squad. It was documented that his remains were moved here in 1936.'

'That's horrible.'

Isabel nodded. 'Just a boy. If forensic evidence proves it is him, let's hope he has a decent burial posthumously and it gives the family some closure.'

'So, any thoughts on the guests?' Gaspar asked.

'I noticed Pepe didn't shed a tear and hardly spoke with any of the guests. He and Fermin looked understandably uncomfortable in one another's presence.'

'But what about Eva Salas and those two opera singers? They formed quite a cosy coven. None of them looked remotely sad.'

'No surprises there,' Isabel replied. 'Did you notice the red-haired girl sitting alone? She gave a nod to Gemma Palau.'

'I saw that. Perhaps she was another of Maria's students. She left before the burial.'

'Given how many people Maria must have known, it was a very small turnout.'

Isabel raised an eyebrow. 'No doubt the guests were vetted. Journalists weren't allowed beyond the main gates, but I imagine the world will be invited to the memorial.'

'It's as if the elite wanted her buried as quickly as possible and with minimum fuss.'

Isabel eyed Gaspar intently. 'Exactly.'

He examined a grand stone monument with elaborate carvings. It read *Magin Marques y familia*.

He chuckled. 'When I die, it'll be a quick cremation and my ashes thrown to the wind. I won't be laid out in one of these swanky affairs.'

'Me neither,' Isabel replied. 'I want my ashes to be released high in the Tramuntanas, one of the places I most love.'

'What a cheerful pair we are.' He stopped on the path. 'Anyway, how did you get on with Massip today?'

'He's still awaiting the toxicology report relating to the death of Juan Jaume, an elderly man, in our village. The good news is that he lifted prints from a spent glass of whisky found by the sink which have proven to belong to Manuel Borras, the old man's son. There were two other spent whisky glasses on a table, though. The victim's prints were clearly visible on one but the other had been wiped clean.'

'That's suspicious.'

'Highly.'

'So aside from the father and son, there was one other there that night?'

'It seems that way, but who? A dead seagull was also found at the scene, so Pedro is having that forensically analysed. The others were clean.'

'What others?'

'A few dead seagulls have turned up in suspicious circumstances in our valley recently.'

Gaspar shook his head. 'I didn't know about that. You have some real weirdos in Soller.'

She winked. 'A few steps beyond our valley, you'll find a whole lot more.'

As they neared the car park by the chapel, Isabel grabbed Gaspar's arm. 'Talking of weirdos, someone's been tailing me in a red Fiat 500, just like that one. Quick, it's reversing!'

As they ran towards it, the car screeched out of the gates and roared up the road.

'Did you catch the number plate?' Isabel gasped.

'No, but I'm pretty sure the driver was female, judging by the driving.'

Isabel gave him a poke in the ribs. 'You chauvinist. Well, she hasn't got the makings of a good cop with such clumsy sleuthing.'

Gaspar smiled. 'In that case, we should be able to catch up with her soon enough.'

SIXTEEN

Capitán Gómez stood by the open window in Llorenç's office, drawing deeply on a cigarette. He was sleekly attired in his Guardia Civil uniform as usual, but the top button of his jacket was undone and beads of sweat clustered on his forehead. Isabel observed him with a wry smile.

'Strictly speaking, it's against the rules to smoke in a municipal office, Álvaro, and as an enforcer of the law, you're on pretty shaky ground.'

He walked briskly back to the meeting table and offered her a withering glance. 'I'm under a lot of stress at work and home, Isabel. There are times when even paragons of virtue cave in to pressure.'

Llorenç threw his head back and laughed. 'Come, come, Álvaro. Things can't be that bad.'

The military captain stubbed out his cigarette and threw himself into a chair. 'My wife has hired an English au pair for the children as she's decided to go back to college, and the girl is proving very disruptive.'

'In what way?' asked Isabel.

'She has filled the kitchen cupboards with unpalatable foods and is always frying bacon and eggs.'

Isabel guffawed. 'Anyone who likes food is good in my books.'

'But she has bought tins of tomato soup and baked beans and some awful-looking dried packet stuff to make brown gravy. Why not make her own soup and sauces? And she even has pizzas delivered. She'll never find a husband if she can't cook.'

'You're sounding like a snob and a sexist, Álvaro. I hear that lots of British and American people like takeaways. Many people are too busy or tired to cook these days in the cities.'

'Aside from that, she's very loud and speaks English with a funny twang. I don't understand her very well. Maybe it's because she's from the northern parts. I like peace at home, but she's always got the television blaring in the evening or is playing raucous games with the children.'

'Do they like her?'

'Of course. She's a typical irresponsible eighteen-year-old.'

'She sounds ideal. Besides, they'll learn English, which is so useful. She might be good for you too.'

'I very much doubt it,' he replied.

'What is your wife studying?'

Capitán Gómez waved a dismissive hand in the air. 'She has a ridiculous notion to retrain as a lawyer. I'm hoping she'll tire of all the lectures and assignments and go back to being a housewife.'

'You've got to move with the times,' said Llorenç.

'I'd rather not, thanks. Things were perfect before. She had such an easy life, and now she's plunged us all into chaos.'

Isabel breathed deeply and pursed her lips, while a chortling Llorenç offered her a surreptitious wink.

'So where are we up to on Juan's case?' he asked.

'Pedro Massip is still awaiting a toxicology report. He's a solid fellow, if a tad slow.'

Isabel gave a sigh. 'At least we now know why Juan mentioned 7033 before he died. If we know for certain that Juan's medication was switched on Sunday night, sinister forces were definitely at play.'

'We shouldn't jump to conclusions, Bel. That son is a bad apple, but I'm not sure whether he's capable of committing murder. I interviewed him the other day and got little out of him. He doesn't appear very bright.'

'Not all murderers are Einstein material, Álvaro,' she quipped. 'Besides, why point the finger at Manuel? We know nothing at this stage.'

'Who else would have wanted to kill him? Would Tomeu Tous really have gone that far? There was also no sign of a break-in or robbery, so we can rule that out. We'll just have to wait for the forensics report.'

'What's your take on the dead seagulls?' asked Llorenç. 'It seems to me that someone is trying to get at Adam Markham every which way.'

Capitán Gómez took a sip of water. 'Markham only has himself to blame. He barged into the valley, snapping up properties and alienating local estate and rentals agents. The dead seagull found in Juan's kitchen is unlikely to have any connection with the pensioner's death. It's more likely to be mischief making, as you say. Perhaps someone is just planting them in homes with a connection to Markham.'

'We've no idea yet how long that seagull had been languishing in the kitchen,' Isabel replied. 'Forensics will have a better idea, but it could have been placed there a few days earlier.' She turned to Capitán Gómez. 'Did it smell badly?'

His nose wrinkled in disgust. 'It reeked to high heavens. I'm sure it was just an intimidating message left for Markham. Aside from Tomeu Tous and Manuel Borras, the man probably has countless enemies.'

'As if he cares.' Llorenç guffawed. 'It seems wherever he goes, he picks up clients. They're like a hungry swarm of mosquitoes.'

'His luck may run out soon,' Capitán Gómez replied sourly.

An awkward silence fell on the room until Llorenç eyed them both.

'By coincidence, Manuel Borras still looks after the garden for the wealthy Swedish couple that Markham has as a client. I've no idea how he's kept that contract all these years given his erratic behaviour.'

'He must be doing something right, then,' Isabel replied.

'Mind you, it's a second home, so they're in Sweden most of the time,' Llorenç added.

Capitán Gómez turned to Isabel. 'How did Maria's funeral go?'

She shrugged. 'Low key. The great and the good were there and a few lecturers from the Conservatori.'

Distractedly, he glanced at his watch and stood up. 'I must leave you as I have another meeting. Hopefully Tolo can put the sad business to bed now.'

Isabel offered him an enigmatic smile. 'Don't be so sure, Álvaro. As the old proverb goes, "It ain't over till the fat lady sings".'

It was late and the air had cooled. As groups of tourists strolled through Soller's Plaça de la Constitucío, laughing and chatting animatedly, Isabel looked about her, unsurprised to see that not one table on any of the terraces was free. Summer had become extremely busy in the town and those locals who didn't benefit from tourism grumbled about the crowds, lack of parking and packed bars and restaurants. All the same, the town needed its visitors to boost the local economy, and Isabel felt that it was worth the few months of disruption, provided the extra footfall didn't impact the local environment.

She sat back in her chair at Café Sóller, admiring the underlit modernist façade of the church of Sant Bartomeu. It was designed in 1904 by Joan Rubió i Bellver, a disciple of the Catalan master architect, Antoni Gaudí, who had also renovated the Bank of Soller back in the day. She was proud of the historic landmarks of her valley and loved delving into the captivating story of the town's émigrés who left Mallorca for a better life in the Americas, Europe and France during the nineteenth and twentieth centuries. The successful ones returned to Soller with immense wealth and those who'd lived in France created art nouveau palaces along the town's residential streets such as Gran Via and Carrer de sa Lluna. Her thoughts were interrupted by Josep Casanovas, who sat opposite her nursing the remnants of a cool beer.

'As I was saying, Bel, with my mayoral duties and editing the paper, I hardly have a moment to myself these days. Everyone wants a piece of me.'

Isabel managed to maintain a straight face.

'It must be exhausting to be so in demand, Josep.'

'And then, of course, I'm being pressured to take on a much larger advisory role within the regional government. I can see how I'd be a great asset to the president, but I have to think about my own ambitions and welfare.'

Isabel suppressed a yawn. 'I was surprised not to see you at Maria Rosselló's funeral.'

'Come on,' he replied. 'You know very well that journalists were barred at the cemetery gates.'

'As someone with an ear to the president, I'd have thought you'd have been warmly welcomed.'

Missing the irony, he gave a terse shrug. 'True, but that strange husband of Maria Rosselló refused to allow any press to attend the service. As I wear both political and journalistic hats, I had no choice but to stay away.'

Isabel attempted a sympathetic smile. 'Have you any more intel on Maria?'

'Why do you want to know? I thought the case was now closed.'

'Idle curiosity, Josep.'

He grinned and leant forward conspiratorially. 'As it happens, I heard on good authority that she had an affair with the minister of culture and someone else on the island.'

Isabel fixed bright eyes on him, suddenly wide awake. 'Was that recently?'

He nodded. 'I believe it was in the last few years. What if the husband found out? Perhaps that's why she ended up headfirst in that greenhouse.'

'Or perhaps she simply decided to end her own life. I suppose you know nothing more about those poisonous mushrooms.'

'Afraid not, but now she's gone, does it matter?'

'I guess you're right.' Isabel smiled. 'I'd better head home. Tomorrow's going to be a long day.'

Josep rose slowly and slapped a note on the table. 'My treat this time.'

Hamlet, the café's owner, sauntered over and offered Isabel a huge smile. 'Where's my favourite ferret?'

'At home, sleeping. He finds this heat exhausting.'

'He and I both.'

Josep scooped up the change Hamlet had left on the table and turned to her.

'Do you know everyone in this town?'

'Only the movers and shakers,' Isabel teased as she picked up her pannier and stepped onto the cobbled pavement. As they walked through the busy square, Josep said with an air of faux nonchalance, 'And what's your beau working on at the moment?'

Isabel stiffened. 'Mostly cold cases.'

'I've got to admit, Tolo Cabot has had quite a run of luck in bringing the perpetrators to justice.'

She frowned. 'He's worked tirelessly, actually. Luck doesn't come into it.'

'Fair enough, but there's always an element of luck, Bel. Forensics are so much better these days. All the same, credit where it's due. He's done a fair job.'

Isabel felt a ripple of anger course through her and breathed deeply. She wondered when Josep would cease his immature vendetta against Tolo, built mostly on jealousy. She focused on the twin spires of Sant Bartomeu, relishing the sudden cool breeze that rattled the leaves on the plane trees. As they parted, she saw Tomeu Tous striding along the street and made a beeline for him. He seemed pleased to see her.

'Your uncle passed by the other day. He told me that you were helping the police to find out what happened to Juan Jaume.'

'Don't believe everything Idò tells you,' she said with a grin.

'Is it true, though? I only ask because Juan had promised to sell his property to me, and that Markham bloke came along and stole it from under my nose.'

Isabel folded her arms. 'In truth, Adam Markham just made Juan a better offer. You can't resent him for being a smooth operator.'

'What annoyed me was that he persuaded Juan into tarting up the property and offered to invest, which I couldn't do. He boasted that it would sell for double the price. How could I compete?'

'Why bother? You already have a good business and reputation.'

He pushed a fretful hand through his grey spikey hair. 'Manuel was really hacked off too. You know his father cut him out of half the will at the same time.'

'Who told you that?'

'Manuel, of course. His father's lawyer is on the mainland and advised him that some woman is inheriting a bundle. Manuel had never heard of her. Maybe Juan had a mistress?'

Isabel shook her head. 'It's really not any of our business.' She offered him a kindly smile. 'Look, I have competitors in the valley, including Adam Markham, but I just concentrate on what I'm best at. Why not do the same?'

His face darkened. 'Wait till he steps on your turf. He's already snatched two deals right from under my nose – Juan Jaume and Bridget Kelly. I won't be happy until he leaves the valley.'

'You might have to wait some time,' Isabel replied.

Tomeu Tous gave a cynical laugh. 'We'll see about that.'

Isabel watched as he slipped off down a dark street, a concerned expression on her face.

SEVENTEEN

A bright sun bobbed up on the horizon as Isabel strode along the beach, her hair streaming water. Meanwhile, Furó raced around the sand, his wet, glistening fur streaked with golden sunlight. Rootling about in her pannier, Isabel pulled out a towel and wrapped it around her. She scaled her favourite rock and poured herself a coffee from a flask. She sat in deep reflection, her eyes resting on the still water as seagulls circled the bay, cawing excitedly. Despite the sense of calm and the balmy air, Isabel felt instinctively that tempestuous weather was on the way. Small, worrisome quiffs began to appear on the tips of the waves and dark brooding clouds hugged the peaks of the Tramuntanas. She hoped there would be plenty of rain, as every garden in Sant Martí was parched and in desperate need of resuscitation. After his exertions, Furó scampered up the rock and snuggled inside her towel.

'Want some coffee?' she asked. 'Or maybe some kibble?'

At the magic word, he gave a whine and began sniffing around in her bag until he located a plastic container. She opened the lid and laughed as he nudged her hand out of the way and began chomping contentedly on his food. Isabel found her thoughts straying to Maria. Despite a mild scepticism on the part of Gaspar and Tolo, she was sure there was nothing natural about the opera singer's death, and yet a part of her questioned her conviction. After all, there wasn't one definitive piece of evidence to support the case for murder. Perhaps the woman was depressed and secretly stressed about the upcoming tour, prompting her to take her own life. But what of the white powder in the heart locket? If toxicology tests proved that it was fentanyl, why was none discovered in Maria's system? Did she just conceal it in the locket to take when her nerves got the better of her or did it have a more sinister purpose?

Isabel gave a gasp when her mobile rang. It was just after six o'clock by her reckoning, not the most social of hours for a call. Immediately she was alert, a prickly sensation running through her as she drew the phone from her bag. She frowned at Adam Markham's name flashing up on the screen.

'Adam, what's up?'

The man's voice sounded wan and shaky. 'Hi, Isabel. Forgive me for ringing so early, but there's been another tragic incident. Bridget Kelly is dead.'

'How?'

'I'd arranged for a pool engineer to fix a faulty pump for Bridget. He entered the property via the garden gate so as not to disturb her and that's when he saw her. She was lying motionless at the bottom of a flight of steps in the garden. He rang the Guardia first and then called me as a courtesy.'

Isabel pushed back a lock of wet hair and rubbed her eyes.

'Have the emergency services arrived yet?'

'No, I'm here with the pool engineer, waiting for them. Could you come over?'

'What about Capitán Gómez?'

'He's apparently on his way.'

She was surprised to hear a groan followed by a series of deep sobs. 'Listen, Adam. I'm at Can Repic beach, but I'll leave now.'

She heard the familiar sound of a nose being blown. Adam's shaky voice filled the line.

'I really liked Bridget. She reminded me of my grandmother who died a year ago. I really wanted to help her refurbish the house and get the best price. It's as if disaster follows my every step. Maybe I'm cursed.'

'I'm on my way.'

Gathering up her belongings, Isabel placed Furó in her pannier and walked quickly towards Pequeñito, parked on the promenade. As she reached the car, she noticed a local police officer hovering next to it. He pulled down his shades and gave her a long look.

'Bel, you can't park Pequeñito here.'

She rolled her eyes. 'Come on, Xisco. There's no one else about. Cut me some slack.'

He grinned at her and gave Furó a pat. 'You can't make up your own rules, Bel. I mean, for an ex-cop, you're a bit of a rebel.'

'A rebel? But I've always thought of myself as such a law-abiding citizen.'

He chuckled and took on a confidential air. 'You know that crazy old Irish woman in Sant Martí? She's just been found dead. Pau was contacted by emergency services. He and the Guardia are on their way to her home now.'

She nodded. 'I'm heading there too.'

He tilted his head. 'I knew you'd never give up police work. It's in your blood. Don't let me hold you up.'

She smiled and jumped in the car, allowing Furó to command the front passenger seat. As she reversed, the bronzed, smiling face of the local lifeguard appeared at her open window.

'Hey Bel, just as well you got up early. A storm's due in another hour. I'm going to keep an eye on the beach. There's always the odd chancer who thinks it's clever to take risks.'

She nodded. 'Hopefully visitors will just hunker down in their hotels with a cool drink and good book until it's over.'

As Isabel drove along the quiet port road, she heard a loud clap of thunder and the sky turned surly. Moments later, lightning flashed and rain thudded down. The lifeguard wouldn't have to wait. The storm had already arrived.

Isabel found Capitán Gómez waiting for her on the front porch of Bridget Kelly's home. The rain continued to fall in sheets and thunder growled from the heavens as, in her shorts and T-shirt, Isabel ran from the car to join him. The courtyard was filled with heaps of rubble and a solitary yellow digger stood by the gate, its wheels ingrained with wet red mud. Once under cover, Isabel squeezed out her hair and wiped her face with a towel from her pannier.

'It's always wise to carry an umbrella, Isabel. You never can be too sure, even in August.'

'I won't melt, Álvaro. Markham sounded agitated when he called, so I thought I'd best come over, but I don't want to crowd your space.'

'How very considerate of you,' he replied with sarcasm. He looked about them. 'Judging by the deplorable state of this courtyard, Markham had already begun work on the house refurbishment.'

She nodded. 'Where is he?'

'In the living room being interviewed by one of my officers. It looks as if Bridget Kelly died of natural causes. She'd evidently wandered into her garden sometime last night in an intoxicated state and fallen down steps.'

'Who says?'

'The next-door neighbour just came by. He reported seeing her wandering drunkenly about on her back terrace at around eight-thirty last night, and later he heard her singing and laughing.'

'Was she on her own?' Isabel asked.

'He couldn't tell, but apparently, the woman was always drunk and falling over in her garden. Regrettably, this time it proved fatal. Doctor Ramis and the coroner are on their way.'

'Have you managed to secure the scene, given all this rain?'

Capitán Gómez narrowed his eyes. 'I don't think we'll be treating this as a crime scene, Bel, though I took the precaution of alerting Massip. He'll be here soon to check over the body. We managed to set up a forensics tent before the rain started.'

'Can I take a look at the corpse?'

He folded his arms. 'Strictly speaking, you know you shouldn't be here at all, but your evaluation might prove helpful.'

Isabel gave a curt nod and entered the house. She removed her sandals and replaced them with the white booties that she had stowed in her pannier along with a forensic suit. When she was prepped, she turned to Capitán Gómez.

'Are you coming too?'

He shook his head. 'Once was enough. I'll wait for the rest of the cavalry to arrive.'

With a sigh, Isabel walked through to the conservatory and back terrace, where she left Furó to wander about. It was only a few years previously that Bridget had invited her over for tea. They had sat chatting in the cosy kitchen which overlooked the pretty tiered garden and Tramuntanas beyond. Isabel had enjoyed the visit, though she had been concerned by the number of bruises that covered the elderly woman's arms and legs. Her humorous hostess had made light of it, blaming her posse of cats for constantly tripping her up, but it was obvious that she was a heavy drinker and often lost her balance. At the time, Isabel had worried about her living alone in such a large house, despite the regular cleaners and maintenance staff popping by throughout the week.

Now, she made her way gingerly down the slippery steps to the bright blue tent which had been positioned midway over a flight of stone steps. Though secured on both sides with aluminium pegs, it listed drunkenly to one side as if in irreverent mockery of the alcohol-infused body that lay within. A Guardia officer stood at the entrance, a blank expression on his face. The rain had stopped as quickly as it had begun, but the sky remained threatening and sullen. Isabel pulled on her latex gloves and thanked the officer as he pulled back the plastic curtain.

'Be careful,' he cautioned. 'The steps and ground are on a slope, so it was a bit difficult erecting the tent, especially as the rain had just started.'

Isabel looked around the cramped space. 'Despite that, you've preserved the scene well. I don't see any water contamination.'

He nodded. 'We were lucky. A minute later and she'd have been floating in the pool.'

Alone inside, Isabel squatted down next to the inert form and winced. The body lay face down on the steps, legs akimbo, the left arm tucked under the chest, the other reaching stiffly forward. Rigor mortis had set in, and a deathly pallor had settled on the corpse. Isabel pondered whether the woman had tripped before falling heavily and knocking herself unconscious. Even though the corpse lay on its front, the head was slightly turned, enough for Isabel to see a nasty gash on the pallid and damp forehead. Below the head, a mass of gore had pooled and dried in a rocky crevice, while droplets of dried blood stained the grass and edges of the stone steps. Isabel wasn't surprised, as with the extreme heat the blood would have dried within an hour. The woman's hair was dyed with henna, but the telltale signs of ageing could be seen in her white roots. It appeared that she had been on her way to bed, as she was wearing a long floral cotton nightdress. Isabel took a magnifying glass from her pocket and inspected the woman's fingers, which proved bruised and grimy. Under the fingernails of the right hand, there were flakes of dried blood and what looked like soil fragments. Had she gained consciousness at some stage and tried and failed to steady herself by grabbing at the grass? Isabel gently lifted the right shoulder to retrieve a mobile phone that had found its way there. The glass front was cracked but a luminous ray emanated from it. She pulled out a sample bag and sealed it inside, then examined the pale, inert feet, which were streaked with dried blood. She noticed that a pair of flimsy, open-toed slippers lay close by. They were the last thing Isabel would have worn to walk on stone steps at night. After a few moments of contemplation, she rose and walked out of the stuffy tent.

'Not a pretty sight,' commented the local police officer. 'Horrible way to die.'

'There are worse,' Isabel replied with a grimace.

She stepped carefully onto a nearby patch of lawn and knelt down, searching the ground around her. She expanded her search until her eyes alighted on the broken fragments of a wine glass and a pair of gold metal bifocal glasses. Carefully, Isabel picked up the spectacles and the pieces of glass and placed them in sealed bags. She stood up and stretched her back and walked in slow, ever-widening circles around the grass. She let out a small cry. Just a few metres from the path, hidden behind a clump of plumbago blooms, was a grey-white feathery wing.

The police officer strode over and bent down. He frowned.

'It's a bird of some kind.'

Isabel stepped forward. 'A yellow-legged gull.'

'You think? I'm not good on gull species.' He pulled a face. 'Shall I get it out?'

'No. Let me do it. It must be preserved intact.'

With care, Isabel lifted the leaves of the bright blue flowers and gently pulled out the dead bird. She examined it thoroughly and transferred it to a large specimen bag.

The police officer looked somewhat perplexed. 'You think it's relevant?'

'Everything is important in a potential crime scene until it's proven otherwise,' she replied. 'Please ensure that this find is only revealed to the forensics team – no one else.'

He gave a solemn nod and relieved her of the bird, placing it in a large holdall.

She heard voices and saw the coroner, Doctor Ramis, and Llorenç striding towards her, wearing lugubrious expressions. Behind them, Capitán Gómez and Pedro Massip formed a huddle with two forensic officers. The cavalry had evidently arrived.

Adam Markham sat opposite Isabel on the terrace of Bar Castell, his face crumpled in grief and shock.

'I know it sounds absurd, but somehow, I feel responsible for everything that's happened. It's obvious that Borras, Tous or someone else with a grudge is out to get me and you can't help wondering about the untimely deaths of Juan and Bridget.' With a shaky hand, he picked up his glass of Spanish brandy and took a slug. His eyes filled with tears. 'I just don't want to be the cause of any more tragedies.'

'Why do you say that? As Doctor Ramis confirmed earlier, Bridget drank a great deal. She was a closet alcoholic who'd been admitted six times to accident and emergency at Son Espases Hospital in the last year alone.'

'Fair enough, but what about the dead gull? Surely it's yet another sinister message.'

Isabel sipped thoughtfully on her *cortado* and shrugged. 'I've no idea. We need to wait for the forensic report.'

'I feel I'm at a crossroads. It's been bad enough losing Juan's project and being out of pocket but now this. Maybe I should just call it quits and leave the valley before anything else bad happens.'

Isabel chose her words carefully. 'You seem a little lonely at the moment. Is your girlfriend still here?'

He shook his head. 'Liv is visiting her parents in the Netherlands for a while and frankly I'm relieved. I don't want her knowing too much about all this. She gets really stressed and upset about conflicts and that partly sets off her psoriasis.'

'I understand, but she surely needs to know what's happening.'

Rafael appeared in the doorway, a tea towel slung over his shoulder. 'Can I get you anything else?'

Isabel cast her gaze on her empty plate. Only minutes earlier, it had been an object of culinary joy, sporting scrambled eggs, fried mushrooms and tomatoes and a pile of toasted sourdough bread.

'Maybe a croissant and a little mountain honey? And what about another coffee for the road?'

Rafael tittered. 'Coming up.'

Adam Markham gave a sniff. 'Another brandy and an espresso, thanks.'

Rafael nodded and headed back to the bar.

'I always feel he doesn't like me,' he said quietly, cocking his head in Rafael's direction. 'We foreigners are always under scrutiny.'

Isabel frowned. 'It's all a question of attitude. The more open-minded and friendly you are, the easier it will become.' She smiled.

'But you have a history in the valley, so you speak some Spanish and have old friends here.'

He shrugged. 'Yes, I had magical childhood holidays in Biniaraix, but many of the old crowd have died or moved on.'

She attempted some levity. 'Do you remember old Milo who lived with his wife in a shack up the hill behind the washstands in the village? You would have been in your teens at the time. He had long white hair and a beard and she always wore dungarees. They had a little *ratero* dog.'

He hesitated and then beamed. 'Of course. They had a farm and used to serve up great lamb and pork dishes to hikers.'

'Didn't they leave the area?'

Adam nodded. 'That's right. They sold up and moved to the mainland. In fact, my old dad was invited to their farewell party, and we all pitched up. It was such a fun night.'

His eyes grew misty and his voice cracked. 'I'll never forget it.'

Isabel brightened up when Rafael returned bearing a tray with their drinks and two plump, freshly baked croissants and a jar of local honey.

Gratefully, she sipped at her coffee and raised it in Adam's direction.

'Here's to happy memories.'

He offered her a watery smile as he clinked his glass of brandy against her cup. 'Here's to Juan and Bridget too. May they both rest in eternal peace.'

Isabel sat in her office flicking rubber bands at the wall while Furó slept soundly in his basket. She cracked open another sunflower seed and threw the husk onto a growing mound of shells on her desk. Minutes earlier, she had called the archivist at Soller town hall for a favour and had sent him a few images from her iPhone.

He promised to get back to her the following day. Pep marched in and with arms folded, stared disapprovingly at her.

'What's up with you?'

Isabel swatted a bead of sweat on her forehead and sighed heavily. 'I think I'm losing my grip. This whole Tía Maria case has really got to me. Nothing seems to be coming together and Pedro Massip appears to be slow in getting any forensics back.'

'This isn't like you. What about contacting those scholarship students?'

She offered a weary nod. 'I'm going to do that now.'

'Well, what's stopping you?'

'Nothing, but it's not just Maria's death that's frustrating me. Things are really turning ugly in the valley, and I don't feel Capitán Gómez is taking it all seriously enough.'

'Is there anything I can do to help?'

Isabel broke into a grin. 'Actually, there is. Can you drop in on Tomeu Tous and pretend you're thinking of getting married and looking for a property in the valley? You know, get him talking about what's been going on and his views on Adam Markham.'

'I'll do it, but don't get ideas about me and Angélica.'

'As if.' Isabel tittered. 'Another thing. Can you do some research about any seagull groups on the island? I'm particularly interested in yellow-legged gulls.'

Pep seemed bemused. 'Sure. Meanwhile, I'll make an appointment to see Tomeu tomorrow morning.'

As he disappeared from her office, the phone rang. It was Nacho. Isabel could hardly hide the delight in her voice.

'Tell me you're coming back to the office soon.'

He laughed. 'I'm ringing you from there now. Alice had to get back early to perform an urgent procedure for a patient who'd been in a car accident. The joys of being a surgeon.'

'Could no one else do it?'

'It was a complex back operation, and they needed her specialist skills.'

'I take it you had to cut the holiday short.'

'Only by a day. To be honest, our hotel was really noisy, and the island was packed to the gills with tourists. We're happy to be back.'

'I'm happy you're back too.' Isabel gave a sigh. 'While you've been absent, Pedro Massip has been dragging his heels.'

'So I see. I've just caught up. He still hasn't got the results back on the contents of that locket that belonged to Maria Rosselló, or the two dead seagulls from the crime scenes in Sant Martí.'

'That's not all. We urgently need Juan Jaume's toxicology report.'

'I'm on it. Give me until tomorrow. I get the feeling Massip doesn't think there's anything untoward going on in either of these cases.'

'You're right about that.'

Nacho gave a cough. 'And what's your view?'

'I feel like the lone cowboy, because Tolo and Gaspar aren't completely convinced that Maria was murdered, and Capitán Gómez is dismissive about the deaths of Juan Jaume and Bridget Kelly. My instinct tells me that we've got three potential murder cases on our hands.'

Nacho was silent for a few seconds. 'For what it's worth, I trust you. You've never got a case wrong to date, so why should this be any different?'

When she was alone in her office, Isabel bit nervously on a nail. She was relieved that Nacho had her back, but what if she was wrong? She felt butterflies in her stomach and a cold sweat came over her. She bent down and put her head between her knees just as Pep breezed in.

'Is this some kind of yoga pose? Come on, Bel, stop messing around. We have work to do.'

Isabel raised her head and managed a weak smile. 'You're right, Pep. This is no time for fooling about.'

The church of Sant Bartomeu appeared to be in fine fettle again. At one o'clock on the dot, Isabel heard a single chime and looked up from her computer. She was feeling more animated and hopeful. She had called Manuel Borras and robustly demanded a meeting within the hour and had rung both Frank Rendall, Maria's former therapist, and the practice of Doctor Blando in Palma to arrange appointments. Meanwhile, she had put a call in with Patricia Clos and organised to meet her the following day. Pep smiled when he heard about her progress.

'You see, it's all coming together.'

'Is it?'

He narrowed his eyes. 'What about the other scholarship students, though?'

Isabel swivelled in her chair. 'I left a message on the house phone of Lucia Berganza's family, which appears to be a Galician number. I spoke briefly to Juana Ballister, also on the mainland in Asturias. She wasn't very useful.'

'How's that?'

'For one thing, she denied knowing anything about the poisonous mushrooms and claimed not to have had any contact with her former fellow scholarship students. When her family relocated to Asturias two years ago, she studied at a local music school there but got pregnant and is now married with a baby.'

'Ah, okay. But did she have any intel?'

Isabel nodded. 'One thing interested me. She told me there were rumours that Maria was having an affair with Matías Camps.'

'You're kidding!'

'I'll tell you something, Pep. The more I hear about Maria, the more I think she was a woman who had many secrets.'

'Perhaps one that might have got her killed?'

Isabel raised an eyebrow. 'Exactly. Maybe like doomed Icarus, colourful and exotic Tía Maria flew too close to the sun.'

EIGHTEEN

As Isabel parked up on a piece of grubby scrubland beyond Manuel Borras's shack, she became aware of loud rock music and what sounded like someone swearing and cursing. Did Manuel have company? She walked up to the front porch and pounded on the partially open door. The music stopped abruptly, and Manuel appeared in a crumpled T-shirt and tattered jeans, his light brown hair falling over one eye. He was barefooted and had a cigarette clenched between two fingers. He offered a manic grin.

'Welcome to my palace and take a seat.'

Isabel stepped over a black plastic sack and several heavy-duty tools strewn on the floor and made her way into the living room area. She opted for an old wicker chair, the only seat devoid of clutter, and looked around.

She gave him a long stare. 'I thought I heard someone shouting. Have you got company?'

He threw his head back and howled with laughter. 'Company? I haven't had anyone up here in twenty years. Just you, some stray cats and pine martens.' He took a drag on his cigarette. 'That's why I talk and cuss to myself. Best conversation I usually have. Don't you ever talk to yourself?'

Isabel set her pannier down on the floor and nodded. 'Yes, often. For example, only this morning I asked myself whether you were responsible for your father's death and that of Bridget Kelly or perhaps were someone who always seems to end up in the wrong place at the wrong time.'

He cocked his head. 'And how did you answer?'

'I told myself that you might be an idle and hot-headed drunk and junkie, but I doubted you were murderous. Was I wrong?'

Manuel Borras scowled for a second and sat down heavily on a couch littered with papers. He flicked some ash into a filthy plastic beaker on the table in front of him. 'I'm not lazy, just bored. I drink and take drugs to forget that I was ever born.'

'That's a bit dramatic. You've had more opportunities than many in this village. Juan cared deeply about you, as did your mother when she was alive.'

He stretched out his legs. 'I guess they tried too hard. I hated school and wasn't sharp enough for college, but they kept pushing. All I've ever wanted to do is just sit in the sunshine with a beer, puffing on a joint and listening to music.'

It was Isabel's turn to laugh. 'Now that would drive me mad with boredom. Besides, who did you expect to finance your apathy?'

He shrugged. 'My old man did for years. I do a few cash jobs here and there, but without his monthly cheque, I'd have been living on bin scraps. As you know, he's left a huge chunk of his estate to some harpy in Asturias, which won't help my finances. I reckon he had some mistress, sly dog. My poor ma was certainly played.'

'Maybe he's done you a favour. Isn't it time to get yourself straight?'

He ambled over to the fridge. 'Want a beer?'

She shook her head and pulled a bottle of water from her pannier. 'I'll stick to this.'

Manuel returned and took a long draught. 'Thing is, Bel, I'm not sure I want to get straight. I don't want some boring job and a family with whining kids.'

'Something must interest you aside from getting trashed.'

He suddenly stood up. 'Come and see something.'

Isabel followed Manuel out of the kitchen to the backyard, where he unlocked a rusty bolt on a large wooden shed. Her eyes popped when she looked inside. A long trestle table ran down the centre of the room filled with wooden models of ships and yachts in various sizes. Metal shelves on both sides of the shed were stacked with more boats. Isabel picked up a miniature ferry and marvelled at the detail and the presence of tiny figures sitting inside. She looked up at him.

'Did you make all these?'

He nodded. 'When I was twenty, I got a cleaning job on the Palma to Eivissa ferry and got interested in boats. A few years later, I cleaned yachts in Puerto Portals and started making models of them out of driftwood on the beach.'

He stepped out of the door and pointed to the forests beyond. 'Now I've got as much wood as I like here. I still go down to the harbour in Soller and draw the boats that I like and come back and make models of them. Sometimes, I visit other beaches and harbours on the island.'

'How long does it take you to make one?'

He shrugged. 'Depends on the size, but anything from a day to several months.'

He pulled open the drawer of a large wooden chest. 'Here are some of the drawings I've worked from.'

Isabel inspected them closely. 'These are fantastic. Do you ever sell these models?'

'I doubt anyone would be interested.'

'I think you're wrong.'

He beckoned her outside and headed towards a scruffy-looking garage. 'Here's the biggest I've made. It's a traditional *llaüt*. Actually, it's seaworthy. I've sailed it around Soller bay.'

Isabel noticed a gleam in the man's eyes and realised that she'd found his passion. She felt a stab of regret and shame that she had always dismissed him as a drunken layabout, reminding herself that no one had the right to judge anyone without being apprised of all the facts.

'You have a rare talent, Manuel. You need to exploit this.'

Manuel locked up the garage, stubbed his cigarette on the wall and returned to the house. He pulled another can of beer from the fridge and fixed his eyes on Isabel. 'What do you mean?'

'Instead of wasting your life with booze and drugs, why not turn this into a business?'

He chuckled. 'I wouldn't know how to do that, and no one would want anything off me. Everyone hates me in this village.'

'You're not Mr Popular, that's true, but you don't really go out of your way to make friends. It hasn't helped that you were abusive to your father before he died.'

Manuel ran a hand through his unruly hair. 'I say a lot of things I don't mean when I'm high or drunk.'

Isabel eyed him intensely. 'I'm prepared to help you, but I need you to clean up your act once and for all. That also means going into rehab.'

He groaned. 'I'm not sure I could handle it.'

Isabel gave him a steely stare. 'I'll help you every step of the way, but you need to want to change.'

His eyes filled with tears. 'I miss my dad badly.'

Isabel sighed. 'I know. Here's the deal. You get straight and I'll promote your business via my clients and elsewhere. I'll also get my cleaning team to make this place shine.'

'Why would you do that for me?'

'Because you're going to tell me everything I want to know about the deaths of your father and Bridget Kelly. I also need to see Juan's will.'

He grabbed the papers on the couch and pulled a few pages free. 'Here's his will. It was sent to me by his lawyer on the mainland.'

'Do you have the man's name?'

'Augustin Suarez.' He proffered a document. 'Take it. I've got another copy.'

Isabel placed it carefully in her pannier. 'Tell me about your whereabouts the night Juan died.'

Manuel scratched his nose. 'I already told that Guardia captain everything. I went round to see my dad about seven-thirty. We began talking about the sale of the house over a couple of whiskies and then it got heated. My dad told me I was a disappointment to him, and he didn't want to entrust me with the house. He called me a drunk and an addict. I lost my cool and stormed out.'

'What time was that?'

He gave a sigh. 'I dunno, maybe an hour later.'

'Did you notice any of his medication in the kitchen that night?'

'He took his pills like clockwork at nine-thirty in the evening, just before bed, but I don't remember seeing them.'

'Did you share a bowl of crisps with Juan that night?'

He shook his head.

'You left your glass on the table when you left?'

He frowned. 'No, I remember dumping it by the sink.'

Isabel took a sip of water from her bottle. 'Tell me about Bridget Kelly. How long did you work for her?'

Manuel's face fell and he looked sombre. 'About five years. I just did a few hours of gardening once a week. We'd have a cup of coffee together before I started work.' He grimaced. 'She was an old soak like me. We needed all the coffee we could get.'

'Were you at the house yesterday?'

Taking a cigarette out of a packet, he wedged it between his teeth and fumbled with a match until it was alight. 'The last time I saw Bridget was two days ago. I watered her pots at the front and back of the house and added water and chlorine to the pool.'

'I thought she had a pool man?'

'She did, but he's been on holiday. I found that the pump wasn't working, and so Bridget rang Adam Markham and he organised for a pool engineer to come over early this morning. Bridget didn't speak much Spanish.'

'How did she seem?'

He sighed heavily. 'She was chatty as usual, but since her husband died, she was very lonely in that big house. I felt sorry for her.'

'So you speak English?'

'I had to learn the basics when I was cleaning yachts. Most of the foreign staff spoke English but not Spanish.'

'Have you any idea who'll inherit her house and estate?'

'Not a clue. Bridget had no relatives that I know of, and her only friends here were the kind of retired British expats that drink all day.'

'Are you expecting to inherit anything?'

'Why would I?'

Isabel took a Chupa Chup from her pannier, unwrapped it slowly and popped it into her mouth.

'I hate those things,' Manuel said. 'They rot your teeth.'

'So everyone keeps telling me.' Isabel smiled. 'When you visit island beaches and harbours, do you ever come across dead gulls?'

He frowned. 'Not often. Last year I saw one floating on the water near Cala Tuent. Why?'

'Just wondered.' Isabel rose and pushed a damp strand of hair back from her forehead. The intense sun was shining directly on her face. 'Do you have the key to Bridget Kelly's house?'

He nodded. 'She gave me a set.'

'Can I borrow them?'

Manuel walked over to a chest of drawers and pulled out a ring of keys. 'You can keep them. I've got no use for them now.' He paused. 'But no one can enter the house. It's got police tape across the drive.' He laughed. 'But of course you work for the police.'

'Indeed, I do.'

Isabel took the keys and stashed them in her pocket. She stepped out onto the porch.

As she started the engine, she smiled to see a pine marten dart from the roof of Manuel's shack and tentatively pop its head around the open front door. Two visitors in one day. Perhaps Manuel was becoming Mr Popular, after all.

Isabel spent the afternoon making phone calls and dealing with the water tank problems of various holiday renters. One of the disadvantages of the summer was the lack of water if the previous autumn and winter had yielded little rain. Often the reservoirs were only half full and water had to be ferried to the homes in Sant Martí by truck. Some of Isabel's clients found it astonishing that the houses they rented had to have water pumped into tanks so that washing and cooking was possible. They often used so much water that the tanks ran dry and a water lorry had to be organised. On occasion, Isabel had to be stern with clients about the taking of baths, explaining that showers were far more environmentally friendly and weren't such a drain on the valley's precious water supplies.

Capitán Gómez had called her briefly to report that aside from the gull, and assorted items she'd found, nothing had seemed untoward following a thorough forensics search by Pedro Massip and his officers of Bridget Kelly's garden. He told her that Massip had suggested that the most likely cause of death was a severe knock to the head while in an intoxicated state. The final report, he confirmed, would be issued by Nacho now that he was back on duty. Isabel felt a sense of relief.

After Pep had left for the day, Isabel sat down to have dinner on her patio. As usual, Florentina had stashed various mouthwatering dishes in the fridge and a few sweet titbits in the pantry. Later, she took Furó for an evening spin on her mountain bike, which was specially adapted to accommodate his carrier, making sure to pass Bridget's drive on the way back. With satisfaction, Isabel saw that a thin line of police tape had been secured across the ungated entrance, meaning that later, she'd easily be able to duck underneath it or scale the low side gate into the garden.

Isabel took a hot shower and changed into a dark T-shirt and pair of shorts. She slipped into some comfortable plimsoles and wedged her long hair under a black cap. She wanted to have a good uninterrupted snoop around Bridget Kelly's house now that the forensics team had already examined the place, but she would wait patiently until nighttime.

As the sky turned dark and the air cooled, she called Tolo for a brief catch-up. Having enjoyed a relaxed July, spending more time together than usual, they were both suddenly working long hours again. While Tolo was determined to wrap up the rest of the cold cases he had been toiling over, Isabel wanted to prove to herself that her instincts were once again right about both the cases she was now involved with. Tomorrow was Friday and at least Tolo would be staying overnight, and they would have the chance to talk through recent events over a relaxing supper. Isabel put on a light jacket and called to Furó just as the church clock struck midnight. Together, they slipped down the stairs and out of the house, with a full moon guiding their steps as they walked quietly along the dark street. As they reached the end of the village, Isabel pulled a torch from her rucksack and tucked Furó inside her jacket. A small *ratero* pattered by, his eyes nervously darting towards a distant garden where a gruff dog released a series of long and mournful howls. Isabel kept to the shadows and ten minutes later turned left along a narrow lane which led to open countryside and Bridget's isolated home. As she looked towards the property, she frowned, convinced that she saw the fleeting glimmer of a light in one of the downstairs windows. She stopped, turned off her torch and looked again. This time, the house appeared to be shrouded in velvety darkness. Isabel shrugged and carried on at a fast pace, her mind soothed by the familiar hooting of a nearby barn owl and the aromatic fragrance of dry rosemary and lavender.

The strip of police tape by the main entrance gleamed in the light of the torch as Isabel lifted it gently at one side with a gloved hand and effortlessly ducked under it. She tutted as Furó whined and wriggled out of her jacket and began scuttling up the path in the balmy night air. Isabel reached the front door and, in some frustration, tried the various heavy keys that Manuel had given her until finally she found one that fitted the ancient lock. The door creaked open, revealing a dark and silent passageway. Isabel was tempted to turn on the hall light, but she thought better of it. Instead, she used a discreet head torch from her rucksack. If any villager was on a late-night walk in the vicinity, they might be concerned to see lights on, thinking that someone had broken in. All the same, she reasoned with a smile, the likelihood of robbers infiltrating Sant Martí was as remote as a pride of lions attacking the village. Isabel navigated her way silently along the corridors until she reached the kitchen. She knew what she was looking for and began a systematic search of the drawers and cupboards in each room. Furó followed closely behind, sniffing along the wood panelling and scratching at cupboard doors.

'Stop that,' Isabel hissed. 'I don't want you leaving any marks. This is still a potential crime scene, whatever our esteemed Capitán might think.'

For some minutes, she sifted patiently through drawers full of kitchen implements and cutlery, and moved on to the living room, lounge and conservatory. Having found nothing of interest in any of the rooms, she approached the study cum library. A musty and stale aroma hit her as she entered the room, which was flanked by tall wooden shelves of books on all sides. As the light from her head torch bored through the gloom, it briefly settled on a patch of decaying cobwebs that drooped from a wood beam and a mortuary of desiccated ants by a skirting board. Isabel headed for a large mahogany desk and carefully slid out drawers, examining papers and documents, until finally she found what she was looking for: the elderly woman's last will and testament. It was contained in a neat plastic folder and looked clean and new, unlike the other dishevelled and dog-eared papers and files she'd sifted through. A large wooden chest caught her eye. Inside was a huge jumble of old documents, photos, and memorabilia. While Furó pattered about the room, sneezing and snuffling, Isabel slowly examined each document. At one point, Furó gave an uncharacteristic growl, but she was so engrossed with her task that she ignored him. After a few minutes, she pulled out a handful of photos that she'd selected and dusted down a creased and fragile document contained in a manilla envelope. As she stowed them in her rucksack, she smiled at Furó.

'We may have struck gold here.'

It was her companion's turn to ignore her. He stood silently, nose twitching, his dark eyes fixed agitatedly on the upper ceiling. Immediately, Isabel knew something was wrong.

'Did you hear something?'

They stood still in the darkness. Furó suddenly hissed as a loud creak came from the room above.

Isabel whispered to him, 'Seems like we have company, after all. I did see a light earlier.'

Isabel opened the French windows that led into the garden and checked that she'd left everything in order. Together, they crept from the room and along the silent corridor, stopping to check that no one was about. Isabel had turned off her torch, so she used her knowledge of the house's layout and light from the windows to grope her way towards the entrance hall. It was at that moment that she heard light and furtive footsteps descending the stairs and was able to make out the shadowy form of a man. He was clutching something in his right hand, perhaps some kind of weapon, and looking warily about him. Instead of entering the hallway, Isabel gripped hold of Furó and crouched low behind a heavy bureau in the nearby sitting room. The dark figure passed like a shadow along the corridor and began inspecting the nearest rooms with the light from a soft-beamed torch. Isabel stayed completely still, nuzzling Furó and trying to regulate her heartbeat as he stole through the rooms on the ground floor. Some minutes later, she heard windows being closed and the man returned briskly and headed for the front door. He opened it noisily and slammed it behind him, as if of the opinion that he was alone in the property. Isabel didn't dare move until she heard the engine of a car revving some way off. She released Furó from her embrace and returned to the study to find the French windows now closed. The man had evidently been taken in by her ruse, believing that a rival intruder had left via the garden.

An hour later, Isabel was back home, sipping on a cup of hot chocolate. The air was hot and damp, but she felt an inner chill gnawing at her bones and a deep sense of unease that she simply couldn't shift.

NINETEEN

The front door of Ca'n Moix lay wide open, allowing a wave of golden sunlight to engulf the tiled floor of the *entrada*. Isabel stood in the doorway, observing Florentina and Doctor Ramis as they chatted on the front porch in their exercise gear. Idò, kitted out in blue overalls and carrying a heavy toolbox and a net, emerged from the kitchen and kissed Isabel on both cheeks.

'Wish me luck,' he muttered ominously.

Isabel smiled. 'You'll do a brilliant job.'

'Enjoy your frog catching!' hooted Doctor Ramis, as he good-naturedly elbowed Idò's arm. He began wandering up the path. 'I must say, Idò, you do have a job of infinite variety.'

'That's one way to describe it.' Idò uttered a cynical guffaw. 'The trouble with these holidaymakers is that they think you can just stop nature in her tracks. You can't. As soon as I scoop up the little devils and stick them back in the pond, they'll be hopping back to the pool.'

'You'd think that chlorinated water wouldn't agree with frogs,' mused Florentina.

'Maybe they see it as an adventure,' Doctor Ramis replied. 'I suppose your clients don't see it that way, though.'

Idò tutted and set off behind him towards the gate. He kissed Florentina on the cheek. 'Thanks for breakfast, sis. Enjoy your yoga class.'

Florentina laughed. 'We're going to Alfonso's art class first. Can you imagine doing yoga on top of such a large breakfast!'

Isabel bid them all farewell and sighed with relief when she heard the gate clang shut behind them, then closed the front door decisively. She preferred to keep her house as cool and dark as possible during the hot months and also welcomed a little silence in the morning to collect her thoughts. All the shutters were tightly closed around the home in the summertime, although she liked to keep both her shutters and windows wide open in her own office whatever the weather and season. The sight of her busy hens and the Tramuntana mountains always filled her heart with joy, even in blistering sunlight or inclement weather. At night when the temperature cooled, she would tentatively reopen the shutters around the rest of the house to allow in fresh air, just as her neighbours did. All the same, the summer nights were always pulsating with heat, and many locals succumbed to air conditioning or at least fans.

Isabel carried her *cortado* upstairs to the office and grinned at Pep. 'All quiet on the Western Front.'

He frowned. 'What does that mean?'

'It was the English translation for the title of the German war novel *Im Westen nichts Neues* by Erich Maria Remarque.'

'I've never heard of it.'

'Perhaps if you read a book now and then, you might come across it, dear Watson.'

He pulled a face at her. 'By the way, Nacho just called for you.'

Isabel settled herself at her computer and offered a few endearing words to an oblivious Furó, who was curled up in his basket. She rang Nacho.

'I've good and bad news, Bel.'

Isabel's eyebrows knitted. 'That's got me confused.'

'As you know, I hurried the toxicology report for the contents of that heart locket worn by Maria Rosselló, and I've got the results back.'

'That's great.'

'It is, except the lab discovered that the locket contained a catastrophically high dose of fentanyl. About four grams – that could wipe out about 1,200 people. It's serious stuff.'

Isabel pulled a Chupa Chup from a colourful bowl on her desk and distractedly began unwrapping it. 'Was she planning a massacre? I'm guessing she got it from a dealer.'

'Or the dark web. There was also evidence of xylazine, the non-opiate sedative. A really lethal combination.'

'I know about it. It's called tranq on the street. It's a muscle relaxant, isn't it?'

'It also depresses the central nervous system. Such a toxic mix would prove fatal even in small quantities. Was she ever a user?'

'Maybe in the past. I'm visiting her therapist later today, who might shed some light on the matter. Have you had the results back from the fabric analysis in Barcelona? If there was any trace of finger or glove prints on Tía Maria's nightwear, it would prove a gamechanger.'

'Massip told me that it's taking time.' He breathed heavily into the receiver. 'I've been trying to push him on a lot of fronts since I got back. He's let the grass grow in my brief absence.'

Isabel laughed. 'That's your punishment for taking a holiday.'

'Too right.' He paused. 'Moving onto those cases closer to your neck of the woods, DNA has been detected on the gull that you found at the house of Bridget Kelly.'

'But nothing on the gull that was discovered in Juan Jaume's kitchen?'

'Off the record, I'm not even sure that Massip got round to it, but I'm going to conduct my own thorough tests.'

'I'd appreciate it if you did. I have a feeling you'll find something.'

He gave a grunt. 'Why do you say that?'

'Call it a hunch.'

'I have one other important titbit. The toxicology report on the contents of Juan Jaume's stomach shows that he had consumed Nembutal, presumably for insomnia, and also methaqualone, a sedative and powerful drug which, as you'll know, is similar to a barbiturate.'

'Presumably that heady mix could prove fatal for a man with pre-existing low blood pressure and Addison's disease?'

'A dangerous combination, especially given his age. He also had a lot of alcohol in his system.'

'You've informed Capitán Gómez?'

'Of course, but I got the impression that he was hoping there would be nothing untoward about the pensioner's death.'

She rolled the lollipop around in her mouth. 'That figures. Anything that involves extra work will always make him unhappy.'

'But not you.' He gave a hollow laugh.

'Just before he died, Juan mentioned to a neighbour who'd come to his aid that he'd been tricked and mentioned the number 7033. I discovered that this was a number printed on his daily fludrocortisone tablet, so I was expecting this outcome. Someone must have switched his normal meds for methaqualone and Nembutal. If he'd been drinking heavily and was accustomed to

241

taking one fludrocortisone tablet and an ibuprofen pill each night, he most probably didn't notice they'd been swapped.'

'I'm sure that's the case, especially as methaqualone is white and small in size. Nembutal is yellow in colour but if he was in his cups, maybe he only noticed when it was too late,' he replied.

'There's something sinister going on in my village and we need to nip it in the bud.'

Nacho tutted. 'And there you were, talking about a quiet summer.'

'It started well.' Isabel gave a cough. 'Anything more?'

'Actually, yes. Massip was of the opinion that the elderly woman, Bridget Kelly, fell and died by misadventure. In fairness, it did seem that way. She was heavily intoxicated and wearing inappropriate footwear, as you know. All the same, the pathologist believes that force of impact when she hit the stone step was most likely caused by an external factor. The trauma to the head was severe.'

'By external factor, you mean she was pushed from behind?'

'Precisely, and then her head was smashed violently against stone. The velocity of impact was unnatural. Normally, people act reflexively to a fall and put out their hands to protect themselves but not in this case. There were no abrasions to Bridget Kelly's palms or fractures to her forearms. It's most likely she was taken by surprise and had no time to react.'

'And of course, she was inebriated, in the dark, and carrying a glass. What could go wrong?'

Nacho yawned. 'The whole science behind falling bodies is fascinating – for example, how the physics of gravity is slowed by air resistance. You know so much can be deduced by using physical dummies and computer analysis too.'

'Might it come to that in the case of Maria's death?'

'No. In all honesty, we need evidence of finger or glove prints on her nightwear or hard proof that someone was physically in that bathroom.'

Isabel's call with Nacho ended and she pottered into the main office. She talked everything through with Pep, admitting to him that she'd also visited Bridget Kelly's house the previous evening. He sat quietly, absorbing every detail, his eyes sparkling with excitement.

'So, from what Nacho has said, it's very likely that poor Bridget was deliberately pushed down the steps to her death. Meanwhile, you found two wills last night, one new and the other old.'

'That's right.'

'I shall try to overlook the fact that you were totally irresponsible and took a huge risk searching her home last night. Whoever was in the house when you visited was probably her murderer and could have killed you too.'

'Let's not be overdramatic, Pep.' She tutted. 'We've no idea who or why someone was there, although I have a suspicion.'

'Care to share, Sherlock?'

Isabel grinned. 'That all depends on whether you make me a *cortado* and bring me a slice of orange cake.'

She laughed as Pep jumped from his desk and hotfooted it down the stairs to the kitchen.

Isabel found herself in a labyrinth of narrow cobbled streets in the old town of Palma. She stood still and looked about her, smiling when she spotted a discreet cut-through that led into a small *plaça*. It was here that she discovered Teatre des Nins, the Children's Theatre, where Patricia Clos, one of the scholarship students of the Conservatori, now worked part-time. As she walked into the quaint lobby of the terraced building, she congratulated herself on arriving on time. She didn't need a watch to know that it was midday. A young woman with long red hair approached her. Isabel immediately recognised her as the mystery guest who sat alone in the chapel at Maria's funeral.

'I take it you're Isabel Flores from the National Police?'

'Just call me Bel. I think I saw you at Maria's funeral?'

She nodded. 'I popped by to pay my respects. Can I get you a coffee in the staff room? There's no one about.'

'It's very quiet. Where are the kids?'

Patricia laughed. 'They're all at school. I devise creative programmes here two days a week. The rest of my time is spent teaching drama at Sant Felip's, a local secondary in town. In fact, I was at the school the morning Tía Maria died.'

In the sunny staff room, Isabel took a seat while Patricia fixed them coffees.

'Her death must have come as a shock to you.'

'Absolutely. To be honest, none of us really liked Tía Maria, but we did respect her. She was a brilliant woman.'

'I get the impression from Gemma and Georg that you all found her quite a taskmaster.'

Patricia's brows knitted. 'I suppose she was tougher on us because she believed in us most. We'd got into the school purely on talent and she wanted us to prove ourselves.'

'So why did you leave the course?'

She shrugged as she passed Isabel a *cortado*. 'I couldn't handle the pressure. The truth is that I had a part-time job here in order to make ends meet and juggling the Conservatori and work simply became too difficult.'

Isabel eyed her sympathetically. 'So you still struggled financially even with the scholarship?'

'My parents both died of different cancers two years ago and I've basically had to make my own way in the world. I don't have siblings and few relatives left.'

'I'm so sorry to hear that.'

She exhaled deeply. 'That's life. Anyway, a year ago, the headteacher of Sant Felip offered me a job that I could do in tandem with the theatre, so I decided to leave. Three of us left. My friend Juana and her family relocated to the mainland. She's got a baby now.'

'Yes, I have spoken with her. And Lucia Berganza?'

She took a sip of coffee. 'I didn't hang out with her much, but she was the most exceptional student at the Conservatori. She had the most beautiful voice and could really act too. Tía Maria adored her but also made her life hell.'

'How?'

'She wanted Lucia to be the next big operatic star but was always on her back. Lucia was really shy and sensitive and became increasingly stressed by the mounting pressure. Tía Maria insisted she practise vocals and piano for hours when she got home and also forced her to do classes privately. She had no time to herself.'

'So when did Lucia leave?'

'It all came to a head three years ago when Lucia was implicated in the poisonous mushrooms incident. Do you know about that?'

Isabel nodded. 'Had Lucia sent the mushrooms to Tía Maria?'

'Well, there's no point in lying to you as Lucia is dead,' she replied. 'After the drama died down, Lucia admitted to me that she'd done it as a joke to get back at Tía Maria. She swore me to secrecy.'

'Those mushrooms were highly toxic. They could have killed her.'

'It was a really stupid thing to do, and Lucia regretted it. She never intended to kill her. To be honest, Lucia was a bit unhinged at that stage and taking antidepressants.'

'Do you think Matías Camps knew it was Lucia?'

'I'm sure he did. Anyway, Lucia left the college and the whole scandal was covered up. I heard she committed suicide not long after.'

'Do you know much about Lucia's family?'

She folded her arms. 'Lucia told us her parents were divorced and that her mother was from Galicia. I heard she relocated there a few years ago. I never met either of them.'

Isabel drained her coffee and stood up. 'This is an odd question, but did you think Tía Maria and Matías Camps were close?'

She laughed as they walked back to the entrance of the theatre. 'All the students thought something was going on romantically between them. I often saw them leaving the Conservatori in the same car at night.'

Once back in the bright and sun-dappled *plaça*, Isabel made a quick call to Josep Casanovas. She headed for Clinica Casa de Salud in a nearby street. The clinic had been run by the mysterious Doctor Blando until his death two years previously, and she had arranged a meeting with the new director. Isabel dearly hoped that the deceased doctor's client files on Tía Maria had been preserved and might fill in some puzzling gaps in the story of the fallen opera singer.

It was early afternoon by the time Isabel finished her impromptu lunch. She had popped into the quaint restaurant of Caixa Forum on La Rambla for the *menu del día*, which she'd demolished with relish. Having tucked into vegetable spring rolls followed by grilled sea bass, she finished with a scrumptious crema Catalana. Duly satiated, she strolled through the old town, stopping on Calle Sant Feliu to buy one of her favourite notepads at the stylish Rialto Living store, and made her way past Es Baluard contemporary art museum to Sa Feixina park. She dawdled a while by the fountains, watching a group of young mothers playfully splashing their toddlers with water who giggled gleefully. A few young children came and talked to her as she sat on the edge of the fountain, sucking a Chupa Chup. Their smiling parents wandered over and gratefully accepted the Chupa Chups and packets of sunflower seeds she produced from her pannier. Isabel laughed when the children jumped up and down with excitement as they were handed the gifts. Realising that she was nearing the hour of her appointment, she waved goodbye to her new friends and walked briskly through Santa Catalina to Carrer del Vinyet. Frank Rendall's office was squirrelled away on the fourth floor of a characterful old house that had no lift. Isabel had a natural distrust of such contraptions, so despite the oppressive heat, she was more than happy to run up the eight flights of steps. Besides, she reasoned, this should be viewed as useful training for her forthcoming triathlon with Pep. Having impetuously signed up for the event, she realised that there was no way to wriggle out of it without incurring the wrath of her assistant. As she pondered the matter, a door swung open and a flamboyantly dressed figure extended a hand.

'Isabel Flores, I presume. I'm Frank. You do speak English, I hope. My Spanish is elementary.'

'I get by,' she replied with a grin. 'Do call me Bel. Thank you for agreeing to meet.'

'Not at all.' He politely ushered her into a large and modern open space.

'Please take a pew while I get us a coffee, or would you prefer something cold?'

'A *cortado* would be great, and a glass of tap water.'

He smiled at her. 'Your English is so good. How's that?'

'Thank you. I come from a family of linguists. My father taught me the English expression, "practise makes perfect".'

Frank laughed. 'Well, he was right about that.'

Isabel stood admiring the white wooden rafters and plush white sofas. The room had a minimalist feel, with honey-toned wooden floorboards, sparse decor and large windows offering tantalising views of the sea and the old town.

She wandered over to the kitchen area and watched as Frank busied himself with a coffee machine. His white cotton shirt with rolled-up sleeves and linen shorts revealed arms and legs covered in red flower tattoos. His highlighted fair hair fell in heavy waves down his back and diamonds twinkled in both earlobes.

Isabel offered him a smile. 'I love your office. It's so spacious and peaceful.'

'Thanks. Actually, I live here too. I bought the place eight years ago when the whole house was being gutted and redeveloped into apartments. It's quite a schlep climbing all those stairs, but it's worth it for the terrace. Come and see.'

Isabel took her cup and followed him up a helter-skelter wooden staircase to a large roof terrace cluttered with terracotta pots of all sizes, overflowing with lavender and rosemary. They headed for a table and chairs housed beneath a shady pergola heavy with purple Bougainvillea. Isabel took a sip of her coffee and gratefully accepted a glass of water.

'I believe you were Maria Rosselló's therapist for some years?'

Frank swept his hair over his right shoulder. 'A client gave her my details and she called me three months later. She seemed to be living in a state of turmoil and I wanted to help.'

'When was this?'

'It was about four years ago. She visited me regularly but always in furtive fashion, either early morning or late evening.'

'Why was that?'

He took a long draught of his coffee. 'She told me that it was the best way to avoid press intrusion, but in truth I think she had become paranoid and had lost a grip on reality. She was a very complex and intelligent woman but showed sociopathic tendencies.'

'In what way?'

'She lacked empathy and had a compulsive personality. She had immense charm but was calculating and appeared to use her charisma to control those around her, including her husband and pupils.'

'Can I ask how you helped her?'

He shrugged. 'I listened more than anything. She admitted to having marital problems and to having had an affair and hinted at some dark incident that had happened shortly before we began our sessions. I was never able to find out what that was, but she was evidently traumatised.'

Isabel's brow furrowed. 'Did she ever reveal who she was in an extramarital relationship with?'

He shook his head. 'No, but she was very angry and bitter about their break-up. I'd say she was close to hatred, and I urged her to seek reconciliation or to put the pain behind her. I offered her various natural therapies, but she seemed hell-bent on revenge of some kind.'

'That sounds quite menacing.'

He gave a sigh. 'To be honest, she began to frighten me. In my last session with her, about three months ago, she told me she intended to put things right before her European tour. It sounded more like she planned something reckless and even sinister. I told her that we couldn't continue our sessions unless she sought peaceful solutions.'

'What was her response?'

'She cut me out of her life instantly. In effect, I was cancelled.'

Isabel pulled a bag of sunflower seeds from her bag. 'Do you mind if I crack a few?'

He laughed. 'Be my guest. The sort of clients I have usually opt for crack cocaine.'

Isabel tutted. 'That's sad.'

'Most people who come here are fighting demons of one kind or another. Drugs are the most common of them all.'

She nodded. 'It's good that you're here to help.'

He smiled. 'I'm a trained clinical psychologist and a former addict, so I am quite an expert on the subject.'

'Did Maria take drugs or antidepressants of any kind?'

'She told me she'd been a recreational drug user in the past. I know she used to see a doctor named Blando here in Palma. He prescribed her antidepressants, but she told me she had stopped taking any medication in the last year.'

'What about fentanyl?'

He rubbed his forehead. 'She never mentioned taking it. I'd be surprised.'

'How easy would it have been for someone like Maria to get hold of a drug like that?'

Frank raised an eyebrow and offered a half smile. 'If you have the money and know the right people, you can get anything here. Maria had contacts everywhere.'

Isabel chewed thoughtfully on a seed. 'Do you think she was capable of violence?'

Frank Rendall puffed out his cheeks. 'As I say, she had become increasingly unhinged, though she was a brilliant performer. She fooled the world with her polished appearance and dazzling smile. I think she was capable of something very scary.'

She looked him straight in the eye. 'Even murder?'

Frank Rendall was silent for a few moments. He offered her a tense expression. 'Even murder.'

TWENTY

Isabel was sitting in her office throwing small colourful balls in Furó's direction. He leapt on each one, chasing them under the desk and beneath a bookcase, where they foundered. Squeaking and whining in frustration, he squeezed his lithe body under the base, his tail wagging excitedly when he managed to push them back out of their hidey hole.

'Don't get stuck under there,' Isabel cried.

Her door sprung open. Pep strode in and flung himself on a chair.

'I've just got back from seeing Tomeu Tous. He's a good bloke. Mind you, he really dislikes Markham.'

Isabel smiled. 'That figures. Did you find out anything useful?'

He nodded. 'I asked him if he knew of any seagull groups on the island, and he said that the most popular was the Gavinas Club on Facebook. He said he's not a fan of the birds, but he gave me the link. It's run by an ornithologist called Mateu Gonzales and they have a few hundred members.'

'Excellent. Find out exactly what they do and if they carry out clean-ups and rehabilitation of gulls. I'd be grateful if you could request names and images of all the members. He can email me for police authorisation.'

'What's so important about people who like seagulls?'

'Engage that brain, Watson. A lot of dead seagulls are pitching up in our village. Someone's got to have a ready supply.'

The penny dropped and he nodded. 'Got it. So you think one of Gonzales's members could be the culprit?'

'It's one line of enquiry.'

He looked up at her. 'The archivist at Soller town hall called when you were out. He says he's got some useful info for you.'

Isabel's eyes shone with excitement. 'Just what I wanted to hear. I'll ring him back.'

'Is it important?'

'It could be. I'll let you know when I've caught up with him.'

'How did your meetings go in Palma?'

Isabel took him on a journey of her meetings and spent some time describing the dishes in her *menu del día*. Pep laughed.

'I suppose food had to feature on the itinerary.'

Isabel laughed. 'Careful, or I'll have you for insubordination.'

He pushed a hand through his glossy hair. 'In conclusion, then, according to Patricia Clos, Maria was most likely having an affair with Matías Camps and Frank Rendall confirmed the same.'

'Not at all, dear Pep. Tía Maria did not divulge to Frank Rendall the name of the person she'd had an affair with.'

'But surely it has to be Matías Camps. Who else?'

'Who else indeed. Remember, there were rumours about her having a liaison with the minister of culture, and maybe there were others.'

Pep stared at her. 'I wonder where she found the time and energy. And what about Clinica Casa de Salud? When did they say they'd get back to you?'

Isabel rapped her fingers on the desk. 'The director was sympathetic but they're a wholly new team there. She's going to find out from the medical team if there are any of Doctor Blando's confidential client files still on the system. They would have been archived.'

'What are you hoping to discover?'

'I'd like to know what medication Maria was taking and, more importantly, if his records can shed any light on the trauma she seemingly had five years ago. He was the only one treating her at that time.'

'Do you have any thoughts on what it could be?'

Isabel bit on her lip. 'Yes, but I could be wrong. Until I know for certain, it's better I keep my thoughts to myself.'

It was seven-thirty when Isabel emerged from her office. As soon as Pep had left to play in a football match in Soller, she had spent a few hours at her whiteboard and made calls to the mainland, the town hall's archivist and her police contact in South Africa. When she heard a loud thump on the front door, she broke into a smile and ran down the stairs, closely followed by Furó. Tolo had already let himself into the *entrada* and wrapped Isabel in a huge bear hug. He picked up a smart paper carrier bag and handed it to her. Inside was a bottle of OM red wine, a bushy aloe vera plant, and a beautifully gift-wrapped box. Isabel could hardly contain her excitement.

'A new aloe vera! I have been bereft since mine died. You're a star. We will have the wine with supper. But what's in the box?'

He shrugged and smiled. 'You'd better open it and find out.'

Isabel walked into the kitchen and seated herself at the kitchen table. She took her time undoing the ribbon and removing the lid.

She pulled back a layer of white tissue paper to reveal a pair of stylish black biker gloves.

'They're all-season kid gloves by Furygan, the brand you like, so they should suit the climate here. I know you've been after a pair.'

Isabel slipped them on, laughing at how cosy and warm they felt on a night already heavy with heat.

She offered him a smacker on the lips. 'I can't wait to take Boadicea for a spin just to try them out. How lucky I am to have you.'

'Absolutely true. So how about a reward of a glass of red? It's been a tough week.'

Isabel presented him with the bottle of OM, two glasses, and a bottle opener while she rustled up some salted almonds and green olives in garlic oil. She placed them in earthenware bowls on the table and laughed as Furó jumped on the table and began tunnelling inside the gift box. Tolo and Isabel clinked glasses.

He scrunched her free hand. 'Here's to the weekend, *cariño*.'

Isabel placed a griddle on the stove. 'Make yourself comfortable while I cook and talk.'

'Talk about what?'

'About Maria, of course. I have a theory that I need to discuss with you.'

Tolo grinned. 'And there was I thinking Friday night might be off-limits.'

She winked. 'Do you want to hear or not?'

'I'm all ears.'

It was gone midnight when Isabel's mobile buzzed. At first her eyes remained stubbornly shut, but finally she rolled over and looked at its illuminated face. Keen not to waken Tolo, she jumped out of bed and carried the phone into the hallway.

'*Diga?*' she asked sleepily.

'Isabel Flores Montserrat?'

'Who is this?'

Her eyes opened wide at the word 'Interpol'. Some police agent she didn't know was telling her the impossible: that Hugo, her long-lost uncle, would be coming home. She slumped against the wall of the corridor, barely able to digest the news.

'All you need know at this stage is that Hugo Flores Romero is safe and well. This has been a long and complex international police operation, involving multiple criminal intelligence agencies.'

Isabel stumbled on her words. 'What operation? Are you saying Hugo isn't guilty of a crime?'

'Crime? Without your uncle's willingness to make sacrifices, even risking his own life, we would never have been able to bring this to a fruitful conclusion.'

'But I don't know what you're talking about. I need to understand what is going on.'

'Everything will become clear soon. In your capacity as an operative of the National Police, you must understand that this is a highly sensitive matter and discuss it with no one. The Ministry of the Interior will debrief you in due course.'

Isabel returned to the bedroom, but her mind was whirring. A sliver of moonlight wriggled through the internal shutters, casting a strip of white light onto the bed. She listened to the monotonous whine of the fan overlayered by Tolo's gentle snoring and pottered downstairs.

In the kitchen, she stood by the open window breathing in the fresh and balmy aromatic air, pondering the phone conversation she'd just had with an unknown police operative. And if it was true that Uncle Hugo was not implicated in any crime and really was on his way home, how would Florentina react? Would it open up old scars and cause her great pain, remembering the moment she and Isabel's father, Juan, heard of Hugo's abduction? Juan had spent his last years desperately trying to discover what had happened to his beloved twin, only to die of a heart attack. Isabel suddenly thought of her father and her eyes welled with tears. How she missed him, even with his serious, brooding, and inflexible character and exhausting perfectionism. If she were honest, as a teenager she had resented the academic discipline he enforced at home, and yet, as she got older, she understood that he had only had her interests at heart. Thanks to his ruthless desire to see her and her brother, Eduardo, succeed, they had both excelled academically and successfully found their own paths in life. Florentina, by contrast, had been the one to dole out hugs and kisses, tenderly clean grazed knees and engender a love of home cooking and the enduring power of the family and local community. Isabel blinked and felt warm, heavy tears coursing down her cheeks. She loved her Uncle Hugo and wanted him home badly and yet, when she saw that familiar face, however altered, she knew it would be a mirror reflection of the father she had loved and also lost.

TWENTY-ONE

A leaden sky hung like the wing of a bat over the Soller valley as Isabel and Pep tucked into a hearty cooked breakfast on the terrace of Bar Castell. There were a few droplets of rain, but they were so engrossed in their feast that they took little notice. Having risen early for a swim followed by a ten-kilometre run, Isabel was feeling tired. She'd had a restless night following the mysterious phone call and had been woken at five when Tolo's own mobile began bleating. Isabel yawned.

'This training is really boring. Remind me why I agreed to do this triathlon?'

Pep took a long sip of orange juice. 'Firstly, it's good for our fitness levels, and secondly, we're raising money for the Palma children's home, and thirdly, I read online that this sort of thing is good for team bonding.'

Isabel chewed thoughtfully on a piece of olive oil-smothered bread. 'If this is supposed to be about team effort, then Furó, Florentina, Idò and the cleaning team should be taking part too.'

'How ridiculous. None of them would stay the course.'

'That defeats the third objective, then.'

Pep folded his arms and rolled his eyes. 'Okay. Let's just stick to the first two goals if it makes you happy.'

'Accuracy is important, Watson.' Isabel gave Pep a good-natured shove.

'What's happened to Tolo?' he asked.

'He had a call from the commissioner early this morning. A German tourist was fatally stabbed in Arenal in the early hours. He had to return immediately to Palma.'

'You two don't get much quality time together.'

Isabel smirked. 'Where did you pick up that sort of expression? Online, I suppose?'

Pep gave a sniff. 'Actually, I've subscribed to a healthy lifestyle website, and it has some interesting articles about relationship building.'

'Perfect for you and Angélica, I'd imagine.'

'I shouldn't have said anything.'

Isabel giggled. 'Anyway, how have you got on tracking down that Facebook group?'

'You'll be pleased to know that Mateu Gonzales contacted me yesterday evening. He needs you to authorise the request for private details of his members, but other than that he's very happy to cooperate.'

'Did you learn anything interesting?'

Pep nodded. 'Apparently, the group go all over the island identifying and monitoring the gull population. Sounds a bit boring to me. Anyway, he told me that there are eleven species here in Mallorca and that the yellow-legged gull is the most common. They do have yellow legs, you know.'

Isabel grinned. 'You don't say.'

'They find a lot of dead yellow-legged gulls around the coastline and in nature parks and dispose of them sustainably.'

'What kills them?'

He shrugged. 'Maybe they just die of old age or boredom.'

Isabel shook her head and laughed.

'He told me his favourites were the rarer black-headed gull and Audouin's gull.'

'I'm partial to them too. You know that Audouin's was named after the renowned nineteenth-century French naturist and ornithologist, Jean Victor Audouin?'

Pep looked disappointed. 'So you know all about gulls already?'

'Not at all. Only a few. The information you've given me is very important.'

'Really?' he replied doubtfully.

Isabel nodded. 'Excellent intelligence, Pep. Now, I'd better head back to the office. What are you doing today?'

He got up and stretched. 'Lunch with Angélica's family and watching football this afternoon with Llorenç.'

'A perfect way to spend a Saturday.'

As they reached the counter, Pep offered to pay, but she pushed the note back in his hand.

'This was a working breakfast, dear Watson. It's all about teamwork.'

Rafael offered her a smile. 'Fancy a slice of my mother's almond cake with her special icing?'

Isabel's face lit up. 'Do you have to ask?'

'What about me?' Pep tutted.

Rafael pottered back to his kitchen and returned with two small cardboard boxes. As he handed them over, he smirked. 'Don't eat them all at once.'

By the time Isabel and Pep had reached the *plaça*, warm rain was pelting down. They exchanged kisses and Pep sought sanctuary in his car, parked on a yellow line, while Isabel ran back to her house, joyously splashing in puddles all the way home.

Isabel was sitting in front of her computer answering emails when her phone rang. In some anticipation, she saw that the call was from Galicia.

'Hola, Isabel, I am Rosa, the aunt of Lucia Berganza. I saw that you'd left a message for my younger sister, Tina, but sadly she died last year from cancer.'

Isabel gave a sharp exclamation. 'I'm so sorry. I'd just wanted to ask her a few questions about her daughter, Lucia.'

The woman gave a sigh. 'Tragically, Lucia committed suicide eighteen months ago, and shortly after that, Tina was diagnosed with breast cancer. She was destroyed by Lucia's death and rapidly went downhill. I persuaded her to come and live with me here in Galicia and thankfully, I was able to care for her until the end.' She paused. 'What did you want to know?'

'I wondered why Lucia left the scholarship programme.'

'The summer before she died, Lucia had been invited to join an avant-garde opera company for a tour in Europe. It fell in the Conservatori's holiday period. Lucia was excited and flattered, but when her tutor, Maria Rosselló, found out, she was furious. Apparently, the woman didn't approve of contemporary opera, even though this company was well established on the mainland.'

'What happened?'

'Lucia decided to perform with the group during that summer, but Maria Rosselló complained to Matías Camps, that weasel of a director, that it was in breach of scholarship rules, and when Lucia returned, she was thrown out of the Conservatori. She was already on antidepressants because of Rosselló, but this drove her to take her own life.' The woman blew her nose loudly and sniffed. 'Excuse me. Such a waste of a beautiful girl and she was so talented too. I blame both of them.'

Isabel bit her lip. 'I'm so sorry for your loss, Rosa.'

She gave a cough. 'I heard that Maria Rosselló recently committed suicide. What an irony.'

Isabel scribbled some notes. 'Yes, Señora Rosselló is dead.'

'That's no loss. She made Lucia's life hell.'

'Would you know the name of the opera company Lucia joined?'

'It was called New Xanadu. I always thought it an odd name.'

'Does Lucia still have family in Mallorca?' Isabel asked.

'On her father's side. Of course, they were in pieces when she died. I haven't seen them since Tina left us. Although Tina and Lucia's father, Miquel, were divorced, they remained good friends. He and his elderly parents flew here to lend me support at the funeral, but they seemed broken.'

'Do you have the family's address in Mallorca? I'd love to touch base.'

'I don't have it to hand, but I can text you the details. Why are the police so interested in Lucia now? At the time, her death seemed to be pushed under the carpet by that awful Conservatori. The director was so unsympathetic to poor Tina. He told her that Lucia was a very unstable girl and her suicide was not unexpected.'

'I'm very shocked to hear that.' Isabel issued a sigh. 'To be honest, we just want to talk to anyone who was in regular contact with Maria Rosselló.'

She gave a hoarse cackle. 'It sounds like you think her death was suspicious. I wouldn't be surprised if she was bumped off.'

'Why do you say that?'

'That woman must have made so many enemies. Tina told me that according to Lucia, she and the director of the Conservatori were having an affair. The husband had probably had enough, and could you blame him?'

'She is believed to have committed suicide,' Isabel replied. 'But obviously the police are carrying out a thorough investigation.'

Rosa gave a cynical grunt. 'Well, it strikes me, Isabel, that maybe she finally got her comeuppance, and I can't say I'm sorry.'

Early afternoon, Isabel heard a ping from her computer and saw that Mateu Gonzales, whom she'd emailed earlier, had efficiently sent her a list of all the members of his Gavinas Club Facebook group. She printed the pages off and began studying the names and individual profile images carefully. An hour later, she made a few calls. First up was Mateu, to enquire about the last few island gull monitoring trips he and his group had made. She was particularly interested in one member. Next, she left a voicemail on the answerphone of New Xanadu Opera in Palma, and finally she rang Pepe to ask whether she could pop by the house that evening. He seemed pleased to hear from her and invited her to come at whatever hour. The front door would be open.

Isabel made herself a *cortado* and rang Tolo to let him know her plans. He sounded tense.

'Are you sure it's wise to go over to Can Rosselló alone at night? Pepe Serrano is still our chief suspect. Can't it wait until Monday and Gaspar can accompany you?'

'I'll be fine. I really need to check something out.'

'I'd come along, but I'm stuck here at the precinct. We've made a number of arrests in Arenal in connection with the murder last night.'

'Was it a drunken brawl turned ugly?'

'The German lad was trying to negotiate a price for drugs from a group of Albanian dealers and it didn't go so well for him. He was only twenty-two and out of his head with alcohol. Such a waste.'

Isabel gave a groan. 'I don't want to hear about another young life lost today. So many families are torn apart by these senseless deaths.'

'I know, but at least in this case, we've caught the killers. Listen, if I can get free tomorrow, I'll come over. Please be careful tonight. I hope you're not taking the *moto* in this rain.'

'As if!' she replied.

Isabel stood by her whiteboard, hurriedly making notes in heavy marker pen. When she'd finished, she wandered over to the office window and looked out onto the street. A group of young revellers were strolling along, laughing and singing, while loud music boomed from Jordi's Bar in the *plaça*. She heard a warning grumble of thunder and a flash of lightning zigzagged across the sky. If the rain started, lightly attired holidaymakers would be forced to flee into bars and restaurants until it subsided. Few anticipated rain, believing that the sun always shone during the summer months on the island, so they were ill-prepared and thrown into panic when heavy rain did fall. She estimated that it had just gone five o'clock and debated whether she had time to make two more calls. One was to Catalina Grimalt, and it wasn't a conversation she was looking forward to. She hesitated momentarily and grabbed her mobile.

Despite her assurances to Tolo, Isabel decided to ride Boadicea over to Moscari. It would give her a chance to try out the new leather gloves that he'd gifted her, and if she were honest, she loved to clock up some fast kilometres on her smooth Ducati. Furó sat happily in his carrier, occasionally chuntering to himself as warm air rippled through his glossy coat and tickled his ears.

The sky had cleared, and the air was still. She relished the idea of coursing along the dark and peaceful country roads away from the habitual noise and hubbub of activity in the *plaça* of Sant Martí on a Saturday night. By the time she'd left the village and negotiated her way through the evening traffic on the MA-11, she was greeted by orchards of oranges and almonds and verdant pastureland. Once through Santa Maria, she headed towards Inca, peeling off when she saw the sign for Moscari. It was then that Isabel saw a flash of lightning and the sky turned grey and threatening. Dark clouds gathered in a sullen cluster on the horizon and thunder grumbled from afar. A wild wind sent dust and debris along the road and rain tumbled from the sky. Isabel tutted loudly. Turning into the drive of Can Rosselló, she was relieved to see the illuminated porch ahead of her. She parked up and with Furó snuggled inside her leather jacket jogged over to the front door. She politely rang the bell and pounded the door, but when no one answered, she sought sanctuary in the *entrada*. After all, Pepe had advised her that the door would be left open. Taking a cloth from her rucksack, she wiped the rain from her face and tentatively called out *hola* a few times, but there came no reply. She released Furó from her jacket and wandered into the kitchen and living room, but both were empty. Furó padded behind her, sneezing and whimpering until she picked him up.

'I'm cold too, so ferret up!'

With a grin, she carried him back to the hallway and gave him some kibble and stroked his head.

'Come on, let's head up to Maria's floor. I've no idea where Pepe is, but I'm sure he'll turn up soon.'

Isabel ascended the stairs two at a time, popping her head around the first corridor and calling out a greeting, but no one responded. Her eyes gravitated to the solemn historical portraits of Maria's ancestors, and a slight shiver ran down her spine. The house had a dark and sombre air and it made her feel claustrophobic and on edge. Normally, she enjoyed a sense of calm and peace, but the property's unremitting silence made her uncomfortable and jittery. As she reached the top floor, thunder rolled furiously across the sky and lightning illuminated the landing. The sound of incandescent, hissing rain and a fretful wind momentarily stopped Isabel in her tracks. She instinctively headed for the bathroom. An elegant mahogany door had replaced the broken one. It had a stylish, vintage wrought-iron handle and she wondered whether Pepe had chosen it himself.

Once inside, Isabel peered around the gloomy space. Nothing had changed since her last visit, although now she felt a new sense of resolve. She was certain that some of the answers she was looking for lay in this understated room, perhaps right under her very nose. She needed to think laterally, as if hunting for the missing piece of a particularly difficult puzzle. Furó pottered around the room, sniffing along the skirting board and inspecting the wardrobe. A hanger clanged to the floor as he tramped along the hemline of a silk nightdress. Isabel felt her heart miss a beat. She called to him.

'Come out, Furó. There's nothing in there.'

He re-emerged and began sniffing along the bottom of the French windows. Buffeted by the wind, they shook and creaked as tears of rain slid down the panes of glass. Against her more impetuous instincts, Isabel decided against opening the doors. Doing so hadn't ended so happily for Maria, and with such atrocious weather, it made sense to stay dry. Engrossed in her thoughts, she stood by the basin, staring at her face in the mirror. Her long dark curls were still damp with rain and her sun-kissed face seemed strangely gaunt and pinched in the harsh lamplight.

She picked up the pestle and mortar and held it to her chest, as if expecting it to offer up some magical solution. When Furó gave a low growl, she blinked and turned her attention to him, curious to see him sniffing along the edge of the bath. In an instant, she was crouching on the floor, pulling wildly at the bath's wood-panelled surround while Furó pranced excitedly about her feet. The block of stylish grey panels wouldn't budge, so she searched in her rucksack until she located her scissors. Carefully, she used them to lever open the wood under the bath's broad marble surround until the section came free. With her hands, she gently pulled off the whole panel and stared into the dingy space behind. Isabel wondered why, when the bath's elaborate wood and marble surround had been constructed, the recess behind had been made so large. Her answer came when she saw a series of water pipes running along the interior wall together with a pump and tool cupboard. She took out her torch and inspected the underside of the bath, and the generous space around it. If her current thinking was right, it was indeed big enough to accommodate a human being lying down. Although tempted to slip into the space herself, she decided against it and pushed Furó back. Forensics would need to inspect the area. Donning her latex gloves, she probed around the bath's base, using her torch to see into the darkest recesses. She felt the rustle of plastic against her hand. In some excitement, she unearthed a carrier bag secreted behind a pipe. Sitting back on her heels, she looked inside. Her eyes opened wide as she withdrew a beautiful paper mâché mask, which she presumed must be the one missing from Pepe's collection. In wonderment, she studied the tragic white face, and with her iPhone she took a few images. She couldn't be sure, but with its elaborately plaited hair which stood out in relief, hollowed-out eyes and sad, turned downed mouth, it had the look of a Greek goddess about it. Who might that be and what did it signify? Contemplatively, she pulled a large sample bag from her rucksack and placed the mask gently inside and sealed it. What was it doing under the bath and had whoever placed it there lain in wait for Maria that fateful morning? On the other hand, maybe the mask had no connection with Maria's death and had been put there for another purpose entirely. As she sat pondering her find, she became aware of Furó's bright eyes darting towards the bathroom door. Isabel spun round and uttered a small gasp. Looming large behind her was the towering form of Pepe in a long white apron, a large glistening knife gripped in one hand.

TWENTY-TWO

Pepe quietly observed Isabel. Something thick and viscous dripped from the knife he was holding. Isabel dropped her gaze to the floor.

'Is that olive oil?' she asked, eyeing him steadily.

He nodded. 'Extra virgin from the Aubocassa estate near Manacor. I was in the basement earlier and thought I heard a voice, but when I returned to the kitchen, no one was there. Then, as I was cutting up anchovies, I heard a noise and came upstairs to investigate and here you are.'

'Why were you cutting up anchovies?'

'To make a savoury paste to add to a puttanesca sauce. I add extra oil for more flavour.'

He paused and looked down at the sample bag at her feet.

'That's my missing Melpomene mask. What's it doing here?'

'A good question. I found it under the bath,' Isabel replied.

He placed the knife in the basin and picked the bag up, peering inside.

'Do you know who Melpomene was?'

Isabel shook her head and rose to her feet. 'A Greek goddess of some kind?'

'Melpomene was one of nine muses: the muse of tragedy. Some believe she was the mother of sirens who sang songs of mourning for the eminent after their deaths.'

Pepe handed the sample bag back to Isabel as his eyes explored the displaced wood panels.

'What made you decide to excavate under the bath?'

'I always felt we'd missed something important in this room, which is why I returned, but it was Furó's keen nose that led me to search there.'

He looked down at Furó and smiled. 'Ferrets are remarkable creatures. I believe they are descended from the European polecat.'

'Spot on. They've likely been around for 2,500 years. An interesting local fact is that back in 6 BC, Caesar Augustus used ferrets in the Balearic islands to control rabbit plagues.'

'That is curious. Now then, are you hungry?'

Isabel nodded. 'Most of the time.'

'Good. Let's discuss ferrets and masks over *pasta a la puttanesca* and salad.'

'A deal, although I do need to ask you some more questions.'

He shrugged and set off towards the staircase. 'Ask away.'

Just before midnight, Isabel and Furó set off back home to Sant Martí. She had spent several hours with Pepe and to her surprise had found him to be a masterly cook. In fact, she could rarely remember enjoying a puttanesca sauce quite so much. The next time she made it, she would add anchovy paste according to his specific instructions. Perhaps more surprising was the fact that Isabel felt with certainty that she had discovered how and with whom Maria had spent her last few minutes of life. All she had to do now was prove it.

Mrs Buncle and her busybody fellow hens were strutting around the corral, their feathery coats looking bleach white in the early morning sunlight. As Isabel unbolted the wooden gate, they formed an expectant little cluster on a patch of grass, anticipating the delights hidden in the bucket in her hand. She closed the gate and strode over to the feeding area, feeling like the Pied Piper as they followed quickly in her steps, clucking in excitement. If there was one thing that her greedy girls loved, it was leftover spaghetti. As they fell on the sticky strands with great fervour, Isabel could only imagine that they believed they were appetising worms. No sooner had she unleashed the pile of pasta than her mobile rang. As the hens danced about her feet, she pushed back her hair and looked up at the sun. She divined that it was just after seven-thirty, so this was no social call. She pulled the phone from her back pocket and Llorenç's name flashed up on the screen. They were due to meet later that morning to discuss final arrangements for Alfonso's birthday.

'What's up?'

Llorenç's voice was hoarse. 'Bel, sorry to disturb you so early, but unfortunately, we will need to reschedule our meeting today. It doesn't rain but it pours in this village.'

'With so much sunshine, I'm not sure I agree,' Isabel quipped. 'Why, what's happened?'

'The elderly Swedish couple at C'an Mas were found unconscious this morning.'

'The Petersens?'

'Yes. It seems that they arrived in the early hours from Sweden, turned on their water heater, and it leaked carbon monoxide while they slept.'

'Who found them?'

'Luckily for them, the housekeeper arrived at six o'clock this morning with groceries and discovered them inert. There was also an open window, otherwise they'd have been dead. They were rushed to Son Espases, but they're in a bad state.'

'Do you want me to come over there?'

Llorenç sounded alarmed. 'It's good of you to offer, but this is surely just the case of a faulty boiler.'

'Maybe, but it's a bit uncanny how it's happened on the back of Juan and Bridget's deaths.'

'The local police and Guardia have just left. Capitán Gómez had an electrical engineer there who believes the culprit is an old oil-fuelled water heater in the basement. They'll be sending over an expert to examine it later this morning.'

'But they never had a problem before, presumably?'

'Not that I know of.'

'I'm assuming that Manuel Borras is in charge of house maintenance when they're away.'

Llorenç clicked his teeth. 'Apparently so.'

'That makes things clearer.'

'How?' he asked.

Isabel walked briskly back to the corral gate.

'I'd like to take a look at the house, if that's okay.'

Llorenç sighed wearily. 'Be my guest.'

The Petersens' old detached house dominated the top of a hill on the northside of the village. When the sun wasn't quite so fierce, Isabel would bound up the zigzag of cobbled steps, two at a time, and weave through the stony alleyways until she finally reached the front gate. Now, even at such an early hour, she took her time, occasionally stopping to take in the views of the majestic Sierra de Tramuntana and listen to the birds' early morning chatter. The air was as heavy as the pelt of a bear and Isabel found herself exhaling deeply as she plodded on uphill, her mind replaying her conversation the previous evening with Pepe Serrano. Isabel didn't know the Petersens well, but despite their quiet demeanour and love of privacy, she found them friendly and liked how they supported village events whenever they returned to the valley. It was horrific to think that they had been hospitalised a mere day after arriving in Sant Martí for their holidays. A Guardia officer gave her a smile as she approached the front garden. She noticed that all the front windows of the property were flung open.

'What's going on in Sant Martí? There seems to be a new drama every day.'

Isabel wiped a bead of sweat from her forehead. 'Living here certainly isn't boring. Is Capitán Gómez still here?'

He nodded. 'He's leaving shortly. The medical examiner was here earlier with an engineer. It looks like the water heater was to blame.'

She donned her forensic suit and latex gloves and stepped into the dark corridor where she almost collided with the Guardia captain.

'I'm not quite sure why you're here, Isabel. This is a Guardia matter and a fairly straightforward case of carbon monoxide poisoning.'

'Surely it's too early to say, Álvaro?'

He issued an impatient sigh. 'An hour ago, meter readings showed high levels of carbon monoxide in the house. The Petersens were fortunate that a stream of air was entering the property from a small skylight, but nonetheless, they are seriously ill. It's frankly a miracle they're still alive.'

'Was only one window open?'

'Bizarrely, the rest were all closed and shuttered.'

'What did the housekeeper have to say?'

He shrugged. 'She claimed that the day before she'd left all the windows open and only closed the external shutters. The small skylight was one she couldn't reach, so she left it open. As for the water heater, she maintained that they were precise about servicing it. Mind you, they probably used Manuel Borras to maintain the appliances on the property, so they were asking for trouble. He may be held culpable.'

'For what?'

'I have an expert arriving soon. If he finds that it was poorly maintained or tampered with, Borras could find himself in deep water.'

'No pun intended.'

He frowned and in a moment of levity, offered her a snake-like grin. 'Indeed, Isabel.'

'Mind if I have a quick poke around?'

He shook his head. 'You never give up, do you? Go ahead, but please respect the usual protocols. I'm off to enjoy the rest of my Sunday.'

Isabel watched as the erect figure ducked under the slack police tape that ran along the entrance and spoke with his officer. Both turned in her direction. No doubt Gómez was telling his duty officer to keep a beady eye on her.

With no one to bother her, Isabel slipped into her forensics suit and inspected the kitchen cum living room. Isabel noticed a wood burner in one corner that looked in good repair, though, of course, it wouldn't be in use during the summer months. She bent down and examined the flue. All seemed in order. As she straightened up, her eyes fell on a small, square patch of white paint. It was brighter than the paint on the rest of the wall, leading her to conclude that something had recently been removed. She ran a gloved finger over its surface and discovered that something sticky had been attached either side, most likely adhesive strips for a smoke or carbon monoxide detector. Isabel took an image on her mobile and walked down the three stone steps that led to the basement. In an unusual arrangement, it gave onto a bedroom where the couple appeared to sleep. The husband walked with a stick, so perhaps they had decamped downstairs for ease. On a wall, she discovered the water heater and examined the upward-sloping duct that led into a standard vent. A nearby door led onto a small walled patio. She unlocked it and walked along the wall until she found where the vent exited. Nothing seemed awry until she crouched down for further inspection. Lying on the ground was a tiny scrap of silver *cinta Americana*, the strong and hard-wearing duct tape that Isabel always carried in her rucksack for emergencies. Once it had proven a lifesaver when the sole of her trainer came loose on a particularly dangerous stretch of mountain during a snowy winter climb. She picked it up and placed it in a sample bag. Normally, exhaust gases from an active water heater would travel through the pipes to the outside vent, but should it become blocked, harmful fumes would be trapped in the basement with no means of escape. With no ventilation, the build-up of carbon monoxide could prove a killer.

Isabel called Capitán Gómez to offer him her thoughts. He sounded distinctly grumpy.

'I shall pass on your observations to the technical team, but a small piece of *cinta Americana* proves nothing at this stage. Likewise, we have no idea what was previously mounted on that internal wall. Go home and relax, Isabel.'

With a loud tut, Isabel stomped up the basement stairs and came face to face with a technician from the Guardia team. He smiled broadly. 'If it isn't Bel!'

He stepped forward and embraced her. Isabel grinned.

'So you're the expert Capitán Gómez mentioned. Good to see you, José. The last time we met was when you managed to crack open that safe in a notorious Magaluf drug den.'

He laughed. 'I remember. Crack's the right word. It was full of crack cocaine too. Quite a find. So, what brings you here?'

Isabel brought him up to speed, outlining her theory about the vent and wall detector. José listened intently and offered a morose expression.

'It doesn't sound good. Thanks for the heads up. Earlier this morning, Gómez called and told me this near tragedy was the cause of a faulty water heater, but your findings indicate otherwise. He obviously jumped the gun.'

'A case of wishful thinking on his part,' Isabel replied. 'I think our current dramas in Sant Martí are taking their toll on him.'

José laughed. 'Then maybe he's in the wrong job. I'll fill him in on my findings when I'm done. Good to see you back with a badge.'

On her way home to Ca'n Moix, Isabel popped by to see Lluc, the local electrician. His workshop was located on Calle Amar, close to Can Busquets. Her mouth watered as she passed the slate menu board which highlighted the lunchtime specials in white chalk. Her eye was particularly caught by the grilled artichoke and prawn dish. Maybe she could squeeze an hour at lunchtime for a quick dish or two? As she stepped into Lluc's workshop, her heart sank to find Señora Coll in deep conversation with him. By contrast, the elderly woman seemed delighted to catch sight of Isabel.

'How opportune that you're here, Bel. I popped by Doctor Ramis's house earlier, but he appears to be out. I've had a bad pain in my left foot for some days and I fear it could be something serious. Could you ask him to pay me a visit?'

Isabel exchanged furtive glances with Lluc. 'Can I take a look at your foot, Señora Coll?' she asked.

Obligingly, the woman took a seat and unfastened her shoe. Isabel removed the fleecy sock.

'Isn't this a bit too warm to wear in the height of summer?'

The elderly woman shrugged. 'The heat rarely affects me, *cariño*. I keep the shutters closed and the house shady.'

Isabel examined her toes. 'I think the problem lies in your nails. They are so long that they are cutting into your skin.'

She issued a long sigh. 'At my age, bending down to cut them is very difficult and my eyes aren't as good as they used to be.'

'Give me a minute.' Isabel took out her phone and called Marga. She finished the call and smiled.

'I've arranged for you to see Marga's chiropodist who comes to the salon every week. Luckily for you, she will be there tomorrow. Is nine-thirty okay?'

Señora Coll seemed flustered. 'Is that another sort of doctor?'

'She's a foot specialist. I'll pick you up and take you there. This one is on me.'

'Thank you, dear Bel, but you will let Doctor Ramis know, in case he feels it's something more serious.'

'Of course.'

As she hobbled out of the workshop, Lluc grinned. 'Miguel owes you.'

Isabel laughed. 'He certainly does.' She paused. 'You've heard about the Petersens?'

He nodded. 'Terrible. Are they going to be okay?'

'We're still waiting to hear from the hospital. Meanwhile, could you help me?' Isabel took out her mobile and showed Lluc the image she'd taken of the wall.

'That's where I fitted a carbon monoxide detector last year. The Petersens were very particular about keeping their house safe. I installed smoke detectors in all the rooms too.'

'But this detector has been removed. Do you know why?'

He shrugged. 'No idea, but it could explain why they were oblivious to the gases seeping from the water heater. All the same, that heater was in good condition and serviced by the manufacturer every six months. It had a vent to the outside patio, so it's a mystery how any back drafting happened.'

'What if someone tampered with it?'

'It's easy enough to do. You just have to seal up the vent. Mind you, why would anyone do such a thing?'

Isabel sucked her teeth. 'Why, indeed?'

As Isabel walked back through the *plaça*, she heard footsteps and turned to see Manuel Borras. He appeared sober and wore a pained expression.

'I want you to know that I had nothing to do with the Petersens,' he blurted.

She stared at him. 'What do you mean?'

'I was at Bon Día, and Jesus told me that the Petersens had been found unconscious. I looked after the garden and house when they were away, but I never touched the water heater.'

Isabel frowned. 'Jesus should not be discussing this matter. I shall have to speak with him. As for you, please make sure you have an alibi for the last few days.'

He shrugged. 'I don't need one. I've been staying at the private clinic in Palma the last few nights.'

Isabel raised an eyebrow. 'Why is that?'

'I'm going to be entering into its rehab programme later this month. My doctor suggested I come in for a few nights to acclimatise myself. Apparently, my father privately allocated funds for my treatment there.'

'He couldn't have given you a better gift.'

He nodded. 'I guess so. I'm going to give it my best this time.'

Isabel smiled. 'I'm happy to hear that. In the meantime, keep a low profile and stay out of trouble. Why not make me a boat?'

'Really?' he asked brightly.

'I want to commission you to make me a unique *llaüt* with blue and red sails with a small figure on deck. I need it as soon as possible.'

His face flushed pink. 'A deal. I could make a start on it today.'

'I'll text you a few further details for the spec.'

He offered a flicker of a smile and strode off. Isabel might have imagined it, but she discerned a certain pride in every step he took.

Back in the office, Isabel sank into her leather swivel chair and grabbed a handful of sunflower seeds, cracking furiously on the shells until a mound of husks toppled onto her keyboard. As she swept them away into a bin, her heart melted to see Furó snoring gently in his snug basket, his paws partially covering his face and his tail curled up under his favourite blanket. Isabel drummed her fingers on her desk. She called first Llorenç and then Capitán Gómez. She suggested that they urgently get together at the town hall the next morning to discuss her findings. Neither seemed particularly enthusiastic, but she was convinced that what she had to tell them would liven them up considerably. She walked into the main office just as her phone pinged and saw that she'd received a message from Rosa in Galicia. Lucia Berganza's aunt had provided the telephone number and address of the girl's father and grandparents. She would pop by when in Palma.

It was late afternoon when Isabel heard the front door slam. She wasn't expecting Tolo until later that evening so assumed that it must be Florentina delivering a variety of sumptuous dishes for the week ahead. Instead, she heard Pep's familiar tread on the staircase. Somewhat deflated and with a rumbling stomach, she turned from her whiteboard to greet him.

'So what are you doing here on a Sunday?'

'My mother baked you an apple pie, so I thought I'd pop it round. Don't tell Florentina.'

Isabel grinned. 'Mum's the word. Actually, Mama's been very preoccupied with Doctor Ramis of late. They're always off galivanting to Palma or doing exercise and painting classes.'

'I feel romance in the air,' Pep said with a wink.

'Maybe you're right,' she replied thoughtfully.

'You don't seem that happy about it,' he replied.

She hesitated. 'It's not that. Of course, whatever makes Florentina happy is fine by me.'

Pep wandered over to the whiteboard.

'It looks like you've been busy.'

'There have been some developments.'

'Oh?'

'Have you time for a catch-up?' she asked.

Pep laughed. 'Why do you think I brought the apple cake? I'll go and get us coffee.'

As he turned towards the stairs, he offered her a quizzical look. 'By the way, when I was walking up Calle Pastor just now, I saw a red Fiat 500 parked across the street, but as soon as I got closer, it roared off.'

'Not very subtle. Could you identify who was driving?'

He shook his head. 'No, but it was definitely a woman.'

'How do you know?'

'I saw the flash of a hand on the wheel. It was definitely female.' He smiled. 'The good news is that I managed to get an image of the registration. Take a look.'

Isabel studied the image carefully, enlarging it on the screen to better see the number. To her confusion, the last three letters appeared to be KGN.

She turned to Pep. 'The last letter isn't Z.'

He peered at the screen. 'That doesn't make any sense. You must have made a mistake about the last letter on the registration of the red Fiat 500 you saw before.'

Isabel eyed him doubtfully. As he plodded downstairs, she stood by the shuttered window, peering through the wooden slats at the quiet street below. She knew that she was right about the registration number of the cars she'd seen at the Conservatori and near Campos, which could only mean that two identical red Fiat 500's with different plates were following her. What could it possibly mean?

TWENTY-THREE

It was rare for Isabel to miss her early morning swim with Furó at Can Repic beach, but she was feeling tired after having enjoyed little sleep. Tolo had arrived late the previous evening, and they had talked late into the night about Maria's death and recent developments, as well as the carbon monoxide poisoning of the Petersens. Although Tolo was not involved in the latter case, Isabel valued his opinion, even if they differed in opinion as to the next steps she intended to take. She sat sleepily at her desk reading emails, while Furó pottered about the room and main office, awaiting Pep's arrival. Moments later, the front door slammed, and Isabel heard the familiar 'Coooeeee!' of her mother. Florentina burst into the office, clamping her ample chest with her hand and exhaling deeply.

'That staircase doesn't get any easier!' she cried.

'I thought you and Miguel had become a real-life Popeye and Olive Oyl now with all your training.'

'I don't know about that,' she said rather primly, 'but those steps are very deep.'

Isabel offered a smirk. 'I haven't seen much of you the last week.'

AUNT MARIA'S LAST ARIA

'Life's been busy. Miguel and I have had so much going on and I've become completely absorbed in our family tree too.'

'Any interesting revelations yet?'

She winked. 'I think there will be. The genealogist who's helping me is just waiting for some historic records from London.'

Isabel laughed. 'I don't think we have connections in London, Mama. Most of the family hail from Castilla-La Mancha on my father's side and your family has its roots here.'

'Don't be so sure,' she replied. 'Anyway, let's have breakfast. You look pasty faced. All this police work is taking its toll.'

Isabel yawned. 'Tolo and I were up late talking. I need more coffee.'

'You need a hearty breakfast and a decent night's sleep, my girl. Come on. I'll make us a nice mushroom omelette. I've brought you a freshly baked lemon cake and some dishes for lunch.'

'You're an angel. After breakfast, I've got to take Señora Coll for a session with the chiropodist over at Marga's salon, so I need all the strength I can get.'

As they descended the stairs, Pep arrived.

'Good timing, young man. I'm just making breakfast.'

He nodded. 'Great. Angélica's on another diet so she's banned bread in the house and the fridge is full of low-fat yoghurts. It's horrible stuff.'

'All this low-fat nonsense. It does you no good. Just tell Angélica to eat less and exercise more. That's my advice.'

Pep grinned. 'No way am I going to tell her that. She'd eat me alive. I just keep my mouth shut until she gets bored and starts eating normally again.'

Isabel guffawed. 'Good plan, Pep.'

As they entered the kitchen, Florentina turned serious. 'Any news on the Petersens?'

Isabel shrugged. 'I'm meeting Capitán Gómez and Llorenç this morning so will hopefully find out more then.'

'A shocking business. Everyone is saying the water heater must have been worn out.'

Isabel placed plates and cutlery on the table and began cutting slices of bread. 'We're not sure of the facts yet, Mama. It's best not to listen to idle chatter.'

Pep winked at Isabel and put his arm around Florentina's shoulders. 'Let's wait for the police to file the report. Meanwhile, are you cooking eggs? I'm starving.'

The mayor's office was buzzing with activity. There had been a mix-up on the booking of meeting rooms at the town hall and two groups of angry local councillors stood before Llorenç's desk, pleading their cases. Isabel and Capitán Gómez watched on in bemusement from their seats at the conference table while Maria, Llorenç's long-suffering secretary, bustled about making coffee and taking calls. Llorenç spread out his arms and addressed the throng.

'Listen. It isn't for me to sort out who has priority. There is one spare room available, and you should decide among yourselves who should have it. It's a sunny day so the other group can have their meeting on the internal patio.'

This created uproar. A corpulent bearded man addressed him.

'But Llorenç, our group is discussing a series of highly sensitive issues, so we need a private space.'

The mayor passed a weary hand over his face.

'You're discussing new installations for the village play area and what sports equipment we need for the creation of a village gym. The only sensitivity is who's paying.'

The other group laughed and jeered, but Llorenç faced them with a serious expression.

AUNT MARIA'S LAST ARIA

'As for all of you, you are launching a new campaign for next year's orange *fiesta*. Why can't you meet the local press in the patio?'

'But we need to show them a PowerPoint and video presentation,' grumbled a young woman.

Llorenç thumped the desk, and all were silent. 'The most important meeting at the town hall this morning is here in my office, and we are now running late. So, here is my solution for you.'

He pulled a two-euro coin from his pocket and flipped it, slamming it down on his desk. He turned to the young woman.

'Heads or tails? King Felipe VI or the two-euro sign?'

'I'm a socialist,' she replied proudly. 'So I'm not going for the royal.'

Llorenç frowned in disapproval as Capitán Gómez shook his head and tutted loudly from the table. With his beady eye fixed on the gathering, Llorenç lifted his hand from the coin to reveal the head of King Felipe VI. He turned to the woman.

'You chose unwisely. That means your group has to conduct the presentation on the patio.'

The bearded man erupted into laughter and cheered. 'Next time you should be more of a royalist!' he scoffed.

The woman rolled her eyes and, with her associates in tow, swept out of the office. The other group followed and suddenly peace reigned. Maria let out a sigh and placed a pot of coffee, cups and *ensaïmadas* on the table.

'Now that the village circus is over, do you think we could progress with our meeting?' asked Capitán Gómez coldly. 'I have rather pressing matters to deal with back at base.'

'No more pressing than here,' Isabel replied as she pulled a coffee towards her. 'As I explained by phone, now is the time to act before we have any further deaths in this village.'

The mayor stirred sugar into his cup. 'Any news on the Petersens?'

The police captain nodded. 'Still in intensive care, but as we all agreed by phone, best to keep this to ourselves until this whole ghastly matter is hopefully put to bed.'

Isabel nodded and took a large file from her pannier. 'Perhaps I can take you through my findings before we finalise our plans for today.'

Capitán Gómez tapped the table with impatient fingers. 'This better be good, Isabel. I've got the team on standby, but I won't activate my officers unless I am utterly convinced by your hypothesis. Remember, we are still lacking some crucial forensic evidence.'

His phone rang and as if swatting a gnat, he silenced the volume button without registering the caller.

As she opened the file, Isabel's mobile rang too. Seeing that it was Nacho calling, she decided to answer.

'Any news, Nacho? I'm here with Capitán Gómez and Llorenç.'

After listening in sombre silence for some minutes, she thanked him and hung up.

'That was Nacho trying to reach you just now, Álvaro. There is now irrefutable forensic evidence to suggest that Bridget Kelly was pushed down the staircase in her garden and her head smashed against a stone step. As I suggested when we spoke yesterday, this was a case of murder, not misadventure.'

Llorenç groaned. 'Did they find anything useful on her mobile? Could she have arranged for someone to come round that night?'

Capitán Gómez shook his head. 'There was nothing of relevance on her mobile. We'll never know if she had planned an assignation.'

Isabel eyed the plate of *ensaïmadas* and thought better of it. She looked across at Capitán Gómez. 'What did your technician have to say after visiting the Petersens' property yesterday?'

He took a sip of coffee. 'It was sabotage, as you surmised. The housekeeper also confirmed that the carbon monoxide detector fixed by Lluc, the local electrician, had been removed from the wall. As you predicted, they also discovered another yellow-legged gull. It was in the dustbin. You might find this of interest too.' He pulled a file from his briefcase. 'My officers found a pristine will in the Petersens' office. The date is this June.'

'And who are the inheritors?'

He looked up at her with a blank expression. 'That is what I'd like to know too.'

It was late afternoon when Isabel and Furó arrived at Bar Castell. Rafael offered her a complicit nod as she walked through the empty interior towards the terrace. She looked down at the *plaça* where she saw Padre Agustí in deep discussion with Jesus outside Bon Día. Groups of tourists clustered about the fountain, while others sat enjoying fresh orange juice and coffees on the patio of Café Jordi. The clock chimed five-thirty. Isabel stepped back inside and chose a table in the corner of the room, close to the French windows, and settled Furó on the seat next to her, where he promptly fell asleep. She examined her mobile, made some adjustments to it, and returned it to her pocket. Soon she heard footsteps and Adam Markham appeared before her, a large smile on his face.

'Where's everyone gone? It's like a morgue in here.'

Isabel smiled. 'I think everyone prefers to be out in the sunshine at this hour, not cramped up in a bar.'

Rafael ambled over to their table. 'What can I get you?'

'A *cortado* and water for me,' she replied.

Adam nodded. 'Same for me.'

As Rafael returned to the bar, Adam turned to her with a concerned expression.

'Any news on the Petersens?'

She inhaled deeply. 'I'm afraid it's not good news. Both are severely ill in intensive care.'

'I'm sorry to hear that. The family must be so worried.'

'Actually, they don't have children or any other family members.'

'How sad.' He hung his head. 'My heart goes out to them. I pray another dead gull wasn't found at the property?'

Isabel tapped her lip. 'I shouldn't mention it, but yes, one was found. It is being analysed for DNA. It seems to be a calling card.'

Adam eyed her intently. 'It does indeed. I trust the expertise of the Guardia and police teams, but everything points to Manuel Borras. After all, he was the handyman for the Petersens. Then again, maybe he and Tomeu Tous have been working in cahoots.'

'We don't want to jump to conclusions, but it is troubling.'

Rafael returned and placed their drinks in front of them just as Isabel's phone rang. She listened intently and returned the mobile to her pocket.

'Terrible news, I'm afraid. The Petersens have both died.'

'Really? What a tragedy. I'm lost for words.' Adam stared at her in seeming disbelief. He shielded his eyes with both hands. After a few moments, Isabel broke the silence.

'Anyway, how are you bearing up?'

His looked at her dolefully. 'The truth is, Isabel, that I've decided to leave the valley. It's been a rollercoaster, but Liv and I no longer feel safe. It started with those dead seagulls I found at the office and on our doorstep. And now I've lost money on so many deals thanks to my clients being targeted by unknown sinister parties. I'm throwing in the towel.'

Isabel nodded sympathetically.

'When will you leave?'

'We're going to head back to South Africa tomorrow. Liv is staying with her mother in the Netherlands so will fly from there.'

'It's a shame that it hasn't worked out for you both,' she replied. 'You know there's a saying here about how people come to Mallorca either in search of something or to leave something behind and reinvent themselves. Which are you?'

He shrugged. 'I guess I came here in search of something that I didn't find.'

'Oh, I wouldn't say that,' Isabel said brightly.

Their conversation was interrupted by Rafael. 'Would you like anything else?'

Isabel gave him a wink. 'Almond cake is always welcome.'

He nodded. 'Coming up.'

'Almond cake in this heat?' Adam asked.

'As far as I'm concerned, it's good in all weathers,' she replied. 'So, Adam. Tell me about the yellow-legged gulls in your freezer?'

He stared at her uncomprehendingly. 'Sorry, what? I'm afraid you're speaking in riddles.'

Isabel folded her arms. 'The only riddle is you, Adam, or should I call you Agustin?'

His face drained of colour.

'When you first told me about the dead seagulls left at your house and office, I found it perplexing. It's really not the sort of thing locals do these days, even if they want to make a point. When more birds pitched up at the houses of Juan and Bridget, it became obvious to me that someone had a ready supply. That got me thinking. Maybe there were groups that collected or disposed of dead gulls.'

He eyed her coolly.

'Before I continue on that trajectory, let's look at the clients you signed contracts with here. Firstly, they were all elderly, and secondly, they had no discernible heirs. Quite a coincidence. Juan's son Manuel was the odd one out, but he had a poor relationship with his father, as you were aware. You also knew that he had connections with both Bridget and the Petersens.'

'Where are we heading with this?' he asked impatiently.

'Let's take one step at a time. According to Manuel, after Juan died, he was contacted by his father's lawyer on the mainland, who told him that the old man had divided his assets between Manuel and an unknown woman in Asturias. I found that odd. Why had Juan, a simple man of the village, employed a lawyer on the peninsula? Who was this mysterious woman and why would he leave half his estate to her, rather than to his only son? They often fell out, but they remained close. When Manuel recently gave me a copy of the will, he mentioned the lawyer's name was Agustin Suarez. I made a mental note and did some investigations via a lawyer contact on the mainland who works at the Spanish bar association, Abogacía Española. It took her some time, but she eventually found Juan's lawyer. However, she informed me that on file, his full name was Agustin Adam Markham Suarez. It turned out that he was a partner in the Suarez Pujol practice in Madrid. He operated it with a female lawyer named Esperança Pujol Bos, but guess what? Her second Christian name was Liv. Ring any bells? It transpired that she had Spanish nationality, but her mother was actually Dutch.'

Adam took a sip of water and sat back in his chair. 'I'm listening.'

'You seemed devastated at the death of Juan, but in reality, you just shed crocodile tears. On the night of his death, you must have known that Manuel was going to see his father. You lay in wait and when he'd left, you let yourself in. After all, the door was always left open and no doubt you had a spare set of keys from Juan anyway. You shared a whisky with Juan and a bowl of crisps. That was careless, as earlier that night, Manuel had also had a whisky with his father and had left his empty glass by the sink, which forensics later discovered bore his fingerprints. Neither of them had eaten any crisps. That told me that someone else had been there after he'd left, especially when one glass was found to have Juan's prints, but the other had been wiped clean. You'd hardly have wanted your prints to show, would you? Still, you should have replaced the glass by the sink with Manuel's prints with the one you'd wiped clean on the table. You could have washed it up and we'd never have known that Juan had entertained two different people that night. I'm guessing that when you saw Manuel leave, you slipped into the house to see Juan on the pretext of needing to discuss the house project with him. While you fixed the drinks that night, you switched Juan's bedtime medicine with methaqualone, a harmful barbiturate, and Nembutal, for insomnia. Although one was yellow in colour, both were small pills, very similar in appearance to his other medication. For an elderly man with Addison's disease and low blood pressure, who was also fairly intoxicated by then, this would have proved fatal. You had got to know his daily routine well, and doubtless knew when he took his pills. Juan collapsed in his own kitchen and while he was dying, you coldly planted a yellow-legged gull behind a shutter. Why? To implicate Manuel.'

'This is absurd.'

'Let me continue. Before you left that night, you locked the door to Juan's home. That too wasn't clever as he never locked his front door. You evidently didn't know that.'

Adam scowled at her. She continued.

'When I saw that Juan's will had been made quite recently, I was suspicious but thought that if someone had forged it, surely, they'd have ensured that all the money would go to a new party. But you were devious. You kept Manuel in the will, even if it was only for half the estate, to put any snooping cop off the scent. Instead, you implied that you yourself had lost a lot of money that had been invested in Juan's refurbishment. I found out from Juan's bank that you were yet to sign off on transferring funds. In reality, the mysterious woman who apparently hailed from Asturias and was a beneficiary of the estate was none other than Liv Bos using her Spanish name. You and she drew up the new will in your shared legal practice in Madrid, believing that no one other than Manuel would contest it. By ensuring he inherited half the estate, you assumed he'd accept the situation.'

Adam laughed. 'Have you any idea how ridiculous this all sounds? I'm a South African estate agent, not a lawyer.'

'But that's simply not true. My contacts at SAPS, the South African police force, told me that there is a Woning real estate business in Cape Town, but it's not yours, and that the bogus website you set up connects to a shell company. Your South African father, James Markham, and Spanish mother, Marta Suarez, divorced when you were young, and you were brought up by your mother in Madrid, where you eventually studied to become a lawyer in Spain. Your father died some years ago. There were no idyllic family holidays here in the Soller valley, as you claimed.'

'Of course I came here as a child. We stayed in Biniaraix.'

Isabel shook her head. 'I found out from the archivist at Soller town hall that some months ago, a man named Agustin Suarez had asked to see old archival images of Biniaraix from the era when you would have been a teenager. The mysterious man even sought out our two local newspaper offices for archival reports from that era. I sent the archivist an image of you, and although the man he met wore sunglasses and a cap, he was convinced that you and Agustin Suarez were one and the same. You made a big error, though.'

'It seems I made several.'

'I deliberately mentioned old Milo, the well-known Biniaraix resident, to you. At the time, there had been an erroneous article in one of the local newspapers that he and his wife were leaving the village and intended to hold a farewell *fiesta*. In the end, they stayed. You maintained that you had known them and that you and the family had attended their farewell party. There never was one. I should know, as Milo was a close friend of my mother's family. You had taken the news report at face value, but it was wrong.'

'Well, aren't you the clever one?'

'That's not all. You got close to the widow, Bridget Kelly, an alcoholic Irish expat and abused her trust. You knew she was short of money and so persuaded her to let you handle the refurbishment and sale of her property. All you really wanted was to get rid of her and create a new will, just as you had with Juan Jaume. I can only assume that when you came to research the valley, you also sussed out large properties with elderly owners. You chose those with no known heirs and made them tantalising financial offers that they simply couldn't refuse. We know from forensics that the night Bridget died she was heavily intoxicated. No doubt you plied her with alcohol and pushed her violently down that flight of stone steps. But that wasn't enough. You smashed her head on a step to ensure that she couldn't survive. And of course, you left another dead gull.'

'For what purpose, Isabel?'

Isabel grimaced. 'I'm coming to that in a minute. I visited Bridget's house at night because I wanted to find her will. Little did I know that you were also in the house. I'm presuming you had gone there to place a new counterfeit will in her chaotic library. Predictably, it left her entire estate to a woman in South Africa – I'm presuming Liv had set up a false identity. But unbeknownst to you, I also found Bridget's original will in a wooden trunk in which she left all her worldly goods to a female friend in Ireland.'

'This all seems like wild speculation to me.'

Isabel ignored him. 'And now we get on to the Petersens. Both had recently signed a house refurbishment project with you. That is why they'd arrived sooner than usual in the village. You knew the exact time that they were arriving and made your move. They were killed in their sleep due to carbon monoxide poisoning and again, a dead gull was discovered in their home. The carbon monoxide detector had been removed from the wall and *cinta Americana* had been used to block the outside vent. A pristine, newly drawn up will was also found in a desk draw by the Guardia, leaving everything to an unknown woman in the Netherlands. I wonder who that might be? Conveniently, the Petersens had given you a set of keys to the property, so you were able to set your plan in motion the night they returned to the house. You also ensured that all the windows were closed, rightly surmising that the pensioners would be tired and not bother to open them all until the following day.'

'Listen, Isabel. I know nothing about the will or its contents. I appreciate that you help out the local police, but your fanciful imaginings are really too much. At the end of the day, you're just a hick ex-cop running a village holiday rentals business.'

'In that case, as a hick ex-cop, I'm intrigued that you and Liv spent so much time monitoring my movements. You or Liv followed me to Manuel's shack, and Liv even stationed herself outside my home last night.'

'I'd love the proof of that.'

Isabel smiled. 'Well, my clever associate took an image of the red Fiat 500 she was driving. The number plate ended in KGN and was traced by the Guardia this morning to a rentals company at the airport. The registered driver is none other than Esperança Pujol, in other words, Liv Bos.'

Adam Markham's face darkened. 'Is that all you've got?'

'Far from it. I need to bring you up to speed on the dead yellow-legged gulls. You see, we managed to find a Facebook group called the Gavinas Club. Mateu Gonzales, the ornithologist running it, was very helpful and sent me images of all the members. Imagine my surprise when I saw your face next to the name Agustin Suarez. He told me that the group cleared up dead gulls around the island and disposed of them safely. On the last few excursions, you were tasked with disposing of ten gulls. Instead of doing so, you ripped one up and placed it outside your own office and another at your rented home in Biniaraix, attempting to make it look like a sinister action by a resentful local. Furthermore, when you killed your elderly victims, you placed dead gulls in their homes, having ensured that DNA from either Manuel or Tomeu Tous would be discovered. You were hoping to implicate either or both. You slipped up, though, on the morning Bridget's body was discovered. You mentioned to me, while we were sitting here in Bar Castell, the finding of a dead seagull at her house, but you couldn't possibly have known that as I had made sure that it wasn't made public knowledge. You knew about it because you'd planted it in the plumbago bush.'

His eyes simmered, but he remained silent.

'In fact, you even stole Tomeu Tous's jacket from his office in order to get DNA from it.'

Adam Markham froze. 'How could you possibly know that?'

'How indeed?' she goaded.

'Borras and Tous were both complete cretins. They were perfect fodder for being set up.'

'All the same, the dead gull motif seemed a little gauche to me. I think you overegged it.'

'It would have worked if you hadn't been around,' he snapped. 'You were the spoke in the wheel.'

'I'll take that as a compliment,' Isabel retorted. 'So, while we've been having our pleasant chat, Guardia officers have raided your home in Biniaraix, and discovered the remaining yellow-legged gulls in your freezer. No doubt you originally had plans to murder more elderly clients in the valley and place a gull at each crime scene, implicating both Manuel and Tomeu. But I reckon you and Liv felt that things were starting to unravel and decided to cut loose before you got caught. You must have seen me the night I visited Bridget Kelly's house and thought I was on to something.'

'I had a bad feeling about you from the day I met you.'

'The feeling was mutual.'

'I warned Liv that you could be trouble. You seemed to have fingers in too many pies.'

'Alas, I have to agree with you. I really should spend more time tending my garden. So, to continue, you lied about Liv being in the Netherlands. She has just been apprehended by the Guardia at Palma airport trying to board a plane to Madrid with a connecting flight to Cape Town. The red Fiat 500 hire car has been found in your garage.'

'That's not possible.'

'I'm afraid it is. When Rafael popped by the table just now, asking if we wanted anything else, it was just a sign to let me know that the Guardia had successfully completed their operation at the airport and at your home.'

His eyes blazed.

'I also must confess that I told you a fib. The Petersens are alive and well. When you closed all the windows at their property, you had missed a small skylight which remained open and undoubtedly saved their lives. It helped that their housekeeper arrived early the next morning too. I'm sure they'll be as curious about the new will left in the desk at their home as the Guardia has been.'

Adam Markham offered her an insolent stare. 'I suppose you think you're really smart.'

Isabel shook her head. 'Sometimes, one can put two and two together and make five, but on this occasion my instincts were right about you from the word go. What I don't understand is why you did it. According to the Spanish bar association, you and Liv had a successful practice. What changed?'

He gave a coarse cackle. 'You cops are always hell-bent on finding motive, aren't you? It was just greed, pure and simple, Isabel. I can't take credit for the idea. In Cape Town, a notorious conman pulled off a similar idea and made millions. Liv and I had just met there at a law conference and discovered that we had similar luxurious and expensive tastes. The idea of aping the fraudulent scheme really appealed to us. We both had good law degrees and Spanish citizenship, so we set up a legal practice in Madrid while working on the concept. It helped, of course, that we had interchangeable Dutch and South African surnames and an air of respectability. We identified various countries where we might operate. More recently, we researched the Soller valley because of the high real estate prices and the plethora of wealthy elderly homeowners, many living alone.'

'So cold and calculating.'

He smirked. 'We are, Isabel. Liv and I both had turbulent childhoods and dysfunctional families who showed us no love. Frankly, we were prepared to sacrifice a few old people for a life of limitless pleasure. None of them had much to live for anymore.'

'I'm guessing you're serial offenders and have pulled off this kind of scam in other places.'

'Now that would be telling.'

'I suppose Liv never really had psoriasis,' she said flatly.

He laughed. 'No, that was just for a sympathy vote and a reason for pitching up here.'

'Did the police apprehend the South African conman?' she asked.

'He had a blast of a life before the law caught up with him.'

'But the point is that the law did catch up with him in the end and now they will with you. Your luck is about to run out, Adam.'

Isabel jumped up from her seat.

Adam grabbed her violently by the neck, pulling a small, glinting knife from his pocket with his free hand. 'I had a feeling you might pull a stunt, Isabel.'

Glowering, he held it to her throat just as Capitán Gómez and several officers piled into the room. Adam looked at them all.

'Don't do anything stupid or she dies. I've got nothing to lose. We are going to walk out of here and you're going to stand back and let us through.'

Capitán Gómez shot a look at Isabel, who offered an uncomfortable nod of the head. Adam forced Isabel to her feet, and with the knife shaving her throat, took a few steps forward. The group of officers began to clear a path.

Capitán Gómez held up a hand. 'There's no way out, Señor Markham. Let her go. You cannot escape.'

'That's where you're wrong. I'm leaving via the kitchen exit. If anyone follows me, she's dead.'

Isabel's eyes fell to the floor, and she gave a cough. 'I don't think so.'

'Shut up!' Adam commanded, but his words were followed by a screech of pain as Furó pounced, his teeth sinking into the man's bare leg. Isabel used the commotion to break free, but Adam lunged at her, yanking her hair. An explosion of sound erupted from nowhere and Isabel felt Adam suddenly relinquish his grasp. He thundered to the floor, his arm bleeding profusely. Capitán Gómez stood at some distance, a smoking gun raised in his hand.

Isabel was shaking with adrenalin. She scooped up Furó and scrambled to safety among the nearby officers. Adam lay writhing on the floor, screaming in agony, his leg and arm streaming blood, until he was brusquely hauled to his feet and led away.

Isabel and Capitán Gómez exchanged glances.

'You potentially saved my life, Álvaro.'

A ghost of a grin spread across his face. 'Another fine scrape you managed to get yourself in, Isabel, but I enjoyed your entertaining conversation with Markham. How he squirmed. The earpiece worked splendidly, and everything went according to our plan. I'd like to take the credit for your survival, but I think we have this little creature to thank.'

He gave Furó a stiff pat of approval with his gloved hand. 'I've never thought about it before, but maybe a ferret on our force might not be a bad thing.'

He strode towards the bar as Isabel gathered up her pannier and followed in his wake.

'When you feel ready, can you pop by my office to file a report?'

Isabel nodded. 'Of course. I'll come in later.'

He shook his head. 'Tomorrow morning is fine. In the meantime, I think young Furó deserves a particularly large plate of meat.'

TWENTY-FOUR

Isabel sat on the shady terrace of Hotel Can Alomar overlooking leafy El Borne, savouring a frothy cappuccino and a breakfast of poached eggs and avocado slices on toast. She had relished the exotic fruit salad and smoothie and now nursed the hot coffee in her hands as she contemplated the previous day's excitement and her meeting earlier that morning with Capitán Gómez. Despite their many differences, their joint operation had almost gone without a hitch, though neither could have predicted Adam Markham's violent outburst. Still, Isabel knew only too well how felons could turn savage when cornered like rats. Some would meekly accept defeat, while others would put up a fight to the bitter end, often with tragic consequences. Happily, aside from a cut she had sustained on her neck from the sharp blade of Adam's knife, she had suffered no ill effects from the drama.

After her meeting with Capitán Gómez, she had visited the Petersens as they continued their recovery at Son Espases Hospital. Both had seemed utterly bewildered by Adam Markham's actions, insisting that he had seemed like such a trustworthy individual. When Isabel showed them a copy of the new will he and his partner in crime had created and left at their home, with Liv as a beneficiary under a false name, they were incredulous. They admitted having entrusted the keys to their home with him, as had most of his other clients. Isabel pondered how a handsome face, confident air, and sharp dress sense could so easily fool people into trusting an inveterate conman. She and Capitán Gómez had no idea whether Adam Markham and Liv Bos had pulled the same stunt in other parts of the world, but Interpol was now involved and would investigate. On the surface, she had found Adam a likeable figure, but years of detective work had given her an innate instinct for those with inherent criminal traits. It still baffled and disturbed her that two intelligent and talented individuals were prepared to commit heinous crimes with no other motivation than money.

She gave a long sigh just as Maribel, the hotel's marketing director, walked by. The young woman stepped forward to give Isabel a kiss on both cheeks and expressed mock surprise.

'Are you drinking a cappuccino? What about your *cortados*?'

Isabel laughed. 'I felt like a change. A daring move, I know.'

'We've just baked some fresh croissants. Would you like one?'

Isabel shook her head. 'I have more than enough here, thanks.'

Maribel scrunched her nose. 'I'll bring you a few anyway. You can always take them back to the office to share with Pep.'

Moments later, she deposited a small, delicious-smelling package on the table. With a wink, she strode back into the hotel.

After finishing her leisurely breakfast, Isabel was about to leave when her mobile buzzed. Josep Casanovas was calling.

'Josep, what a surprise.'

A cackle. 'I don't think so. Come on, Bel. Spill the beans about this Markham fellow and his moll. Are they really accountable for at least two deaths in your village?'

Isabel rolled her eyes. 'You know I'm not at liberty to answer that. Have you spoken to Capitán Gómez?'

'It's like talking to a stone.'

'What do you expect? He's wrapping up a complex case. Be patient. I'm sure he'll be setting up a press conference soon.'

'I heard that you unravelled the whole case, but of course, I know you'll deny it as always. I'm glad you're okay. One of my Guardia contacts told me you'd been wounded.'

Isabel guffawed. 'For heaven's sake, of course not. I'm not sure I'd trust your sources if I were you.'

He gave a cough. 'Actually, I'm calling for another reason. It's about Tía Maria. I had a boozy night with one of the cultural minister's stooges and he confirmed that she'd had an affair both with the minister and Matías Camps a few years ago. Apparently, there was some other high-profile lover before that, but my contact never knew of the identity. Is that at all helpful?'

'It's what I have suspected, but it's useful to hear it from another source.'

'Who do you think the other guy was?'

'I have a clue, but whether that helps us in the case or not is debatable.'

'You still think she died under suspicious circumstances?'

Isabel was quiet. 'Put it this way, Josep, things are gradually slotting into place.'

'I was thinking of running a spread on her turbulent life with open-ended questions about her death. My readers would love it.'

Isabel tutted. 'Can you hold off for now?'

He laughed. 'Okay, but I'm expecting to be first in the queue on the outcome of this case.'

'That's up to Tolo Cabot, not me.'

Josep let out a whinnying laugh. 'Cabot never cuts deals with me, as you know. I'll trust you not to let me down. In return, I'll wait to run a story.'

'Appreciated,' Isabel replied.

She finished the call and plopped the mobile and the sweet package into her pannier. It was eleven-thirty and she had a meeting with the director of Clinica Casa de Salud, who had managed to retrieve Maria's personal medical file from the clinic's archives. Isabel was not looking forward to reading the contents. With a heavy heart, she got up and made her way to the lift, thanking the bar staff on the way. She had a few calls to make en route to the clinic, not least the two main veterinary practices in Lloseta and Inca.

Isabel sat facing Adriana, the director of New Xanadu, in the opera company's bright and welcoming lobby on Carrer d'En Morei. She had spent the previous hour at Clinica Casa de Salud learning about Maria's medical history five years prior to her death. Although not surprised by the revelations, she felt a profound sense of sadness and, despite herself, pity for the deceased opera singer. Now, she listened intently as Adriana told her about her dealings with Lucia Berganza, whom she believed would have become a rising star in opera had her life not been cruelly cut short.

'It's a joy to talk about Lucia, if I'm honest. She was a rare talent but also a very vulnerable soul.'

Isabel studied the kindly face opposite her. Adriana was middle-aged and a former opera singer herself, who had created the concept of New Xanadu. Make-up free and wearing a simple grey linen dress complemented by a neat, silver-streaked bob, she exuded an air of calm.

'You asked me about the opera *Melpomene*, Isabel. A few summers ago, Lucia came for an audition, and I chose her to perform in it. It's a chamber opera suitable for a single performer, and with Lucia's magnificent voice and stage presence, we knew it would succeed. Our group is well established on the mainland, and we had many venues booked for that summer. Lucia performed superbly, as expected.'

'What was the opera about?' Isabel asked.

'It was based on the tragic myth of Melpomene, the muse of tragedy. Lucia loved the sense of drama and despair. For a soprano, it is a unique part.'

'What happened when your group returned here?'

She put a hand to her mouth. 'Poor Lucia discovered that she'd lost her scholarship place at the Conservatori due to some draconian rule banning students from taking on commercial work while studying. We offered to employ Lucia, but she was inconsolable, and her confidence evaporated. She cut off contact with us and then shortly afterwards we heard that she'd committed suicide.'

'Do you know how she died?'

Adriana nodded slowly and pushed a tendril of hair behind her ear. 'It was about eighteen months ago. She jumped from her bedroom window in Palma. Her poor mother found her dying in the garden below.'

Isabel thanked Adriana for her time and made her way thoughtfully towards La Rambla. Later, she had a meeting with Tolo and Gaspar at the precinct, but first she needed to pop by Lucia's family home and also to speak with Enrique Dias. She would place a call with Matías Camps. The director of the Conservatori certainly had a lot of explaining to do.

As Corc placed more coffees on the table in Tolo's office, Isabel stretched out her arms and yawned. She suddenly felt exhausted and realised that she'd been existing on adrenalin the last few days. Gaspar sat next to her, hunched over a thick pile of papers, while Tolo roamed the room, a frown etched on his face. He shooed a fretful Corc out of the door and addressed Isabel.

'This case has turned out to be far more complex than we ever imagined. You've done such a thorough job, Bel, but we still need a few more pieces in the jigsaw before we act.'

Gaspar looked up. 'Actually, I agree with Bel on this one. I think we need to move fast. What more do we really need?'

Tolo leant against his desk and eyed him impatiently. 'I'd feel happier if we waited until Nacho came back with the forensic report on the mask that Bel found under Maria's bath.'

Nacho shrugged. 'Even if it has DNA, which is unlikely, Bel has proven her case. Nacho also confirmed this morning that glove impressions were detected on Maria's nightgown. We now know conclusively that she was murdered, and thanks to Bel, who killed her. The missing piece of the jigsaw is a confession and Bel's plan works for me.'

'I think it's risky, and after Bel's unwise heroics in Sant Martí the other day, I'm unhappy about sending her in.'

Isabel knew that Tolo was still smarting about her intervention in the apprehension of Adam Markham. Although she knew that he cared deeply about her, his at times macho attitude rattled her.

'Her? I'm still in the room, Tolo, and this is my call. Without my investigation on this case, it could have been recorded as a suicide.'

Tolo's eyebrows knitted. 'That's unfair. I've trusted you all the way on this case, but instinct, as you know, is not enough to nail a killer.'

'As for the honey trap in Sant Martí, Álvaro and I did everything by the book and carefully assessed the risks.'

'But neither of you reckoned on Markham having a knife. Gómez should never have exposed you to danger.'

'It was my choice, and the only casualty was Markham himself.'

'You got a cut on your neck.'

Isabel laughed. 'It was a graze, as you very well know. What would you prefer I do, sit at home knitting?'

Gaspar clapped his hands together. 'Come on, guys, can we stop bickering and concentrate on the operation in hand? Bel is the best person for the job. She has Pepe Serrano's trust and knows her way around the house. We'll have earpieces and be ready to make our move.'

Tolo flung himself on his swivel chair and ran a hand through his hair.

'I apologise, Bel. I just worry about you. You can be impetuous and too blasé about your own safety. On the other hand, we'd never have got to this point without your superb policing, so Gaspar's right, you're the best person for the job.' He eyed her imploringly. 'All I ask is that you assess the dangers carefully and don't take risks.'

She gave a curt nod. 'Understood. Now, let's discuss the next steps.'

Isabel sat on her patio under a sooty sky encrusted with white stars. The air had cooled, and the only discernible sound was the distant call of a scops owl. It had been another long day and yet she knew that she was on the last lap, like a marathon runner on the final few kilometres of a race. Tomorrow would hopefully bring the strange and sad case of Tía Maria to its conclusion. There were still unanswered questions, but Isabel felt she was on solid ground. She was apprised of most of the facts, but she still needed an encounter with Maria's assassin to confirm the whole truth. Anything Nacho subsequently discovered would be the icing on the cake. She yawned and was about to blow out the candle on the table when her mobile buzzed. Earlier, she had left a message for Enrique Diaz and now he appeared to be ringing her back.

He issued a sigh. 'Señora Flores, I got your message. I've been thinking about it and feel it's time to come clean.'

'I'm pleased to hear that.'

'You asked if Maria and I had arranged to meet when I returned to the island. The truth is that she had found out that I was visiting Catalina Grimalt and asked if we could clear the air and meet up for a negroni.'

'Am I right in thinking that you and Maria were having an affair that ended when she was on tour with you on the mainland five years ago?'

'We had an affair that lasted just over two years. She visited me several times on the pretence of organising future opera dates. My wife and her husband knew nothing about it.'

'You're sure about that?' Isabel asked.

'I have no reason to think otherwise. On that last tour, we fell out. She had become totally hysterical and unreasonable, demanding that I leave my wife and that we set up home together. I told her I wanted to end the relationship.'

Isabel gave a cough. 'But you had already begun a relationship with Catalina Grimalt?'

After a long silence, Enrique clicked his teeth. 'That makes me sound fickle. Catalina and I had grown increasingly close when working on projects together. It just happened.'

'Maria knew about it?'

Enrique exhaled deeply. 'I think she suspected, even though we were very discreet.'

'What happened after you ended things with Maria?'

'Nothing. We stopped communications and made sure not to work together on any forthcoming opera tours. Catalina and I became serious in our relationship. In fact, my wife and I are divorcing.'

'I see. You don't have children?'

'I don't know why you need to know that, but no, my wife couldn't have kids. That's partly why our relationship began to fall apart.'

Isabel took a sip of water. 'Where were you and Maria due to meet the day of her death?'

'That was bizarre. She wanted to meet in a remote rural spot just beyond Esporles. It wasn't far from where I was staying. She offered to pick me up at the entrance of the hotel and drive me back afterwards. She swore me to secrecy.'

'Is that where you were going to have your negronis, then?'

He snorted. 'She could be quite eccentric. Her idea was to take a walk in the woods and have a few negronis and a picnic away from the public gaze.' He paused. 'But of course, sadly we never made it to our rendezvous because she died. I will forever feel wretched about that.'

Isabel contemplated how Enrique Diaz's fate could have been so different had Maria not died that day. It was obvious to Isabel that, far from seeking atonement, the opera singer had determined to unleash a lethal dose of fentanyl in Enrique Diaz's negroni. As he succumbed to the drug, Isabel imagined that the singer had planned to leave him in the woodlands, his corpse left undiscovered for some time.

Isabel was distracted by the rustle of a gecko and focused back on the call.

'I appreciate your honesty, Señor Diaz. We can never predict what will happen in life. Just cherish the happy memories you had with Maria. Perhaps fate decreed that it was best for your two paths not to cross that day.'

'I guess you're right. Maybe we'll meet in another life.'

Isabel ended the call, hoping for both Maria and Enrique's sake that such a spiritual encounter might never happen.

TWENTY-FIVE

Isabel finished her last piece of toast and fretfully cast her copy of *El Periódico* aside. At least Josep Casanovas had been true to his word and not published a kiss-and-tell feature about Maria. Isabel imagined that local and international media would have a field day when the whole sorry story was revealed. She took a last sip of coffee and made a quick call to Pepe Serrano. His voice was characteristically calm.

'Everyone is present and correct, Isabel, as you requested, and Fermin will be here by eleven-thirty. Is that all?'

'Thank you. I'll be with you in the next hour or so.'

She stood up and swung the pannier over her shoulder. Florentina had agreed to look after Furó for the day and Pep would be manning the office phones while Tolo, Gaspar and the team waited for events to unfold. Isabel picked up the key to Boadicea, feeling a twinge of guilt for neglecting Pequeñito once again, but with the summer traffic, it was so much easier to take the *moto*. As she left some coins on the counter of Bar Castell, Rafael cast her an ambiguous look.

'Try to keep out of trouble today, Bel. You know how your mother worries.'

'I'll do my best. Besides, Tolo is staying over tonight and we're having supper at Can Busquets, so I will definitely be back for that.'

'I'd hope so,' he said with a grin.

Once she'd retrieved Boadicea from outside Ca'n Moix, Isabel headed off towards Moscari. As she sped along the country roads, her mind doggedly recalled the unsettling words 'something nasty in the woodshed' from *Cold Comfort Farm*. Inexplicably, the previous night the book had entered her dreams and she had found herself wandering in a peaceful wooded glade, reminiscent of the Otzarreta beechwood forest she'd once visited in the Basque country. In the dappled sunlight that cut through the towering trees, she had seen in the distance a lone wooden shed, but in order to reach it, she first had to cross a stream. The water had felt icy on her bare feet as she waded across, and it was only then she had realised that she was wearing just a flimsy cotton nightshirt. To her frustration, the wooden shed had just one small, grubby window and the door was locked with a huge padlock and chain. It was impossible to see clearly through the glass pane, but she caught sight of a dusty table in the centre of the room on which stood a pristine white package trailing blue ribbon. Desperate to get inside to take a closer look, Isabel had found a large rock and had begun pounding at the lock. After several minutes, it had fallen apart, and she had hastily pulled the rusty chain free. Tantalisingly, as she reached forward to open the door, she had found herself being pulled backwards with the force of a giant magnet. Her body was no longer in her control and soon she was flying over mountains and cities, until finally with a tremendous thump, she was dropped back in her own bed in Sant Martí. Her eyes had opened and with a gasp she had sat up and glugged back a glass of water while beads of sweat formed on her forehead. In that moment of wakefulness in the dark and sticky night, she had realised, with relief, that her misadventure had merely been the stuff of dreams. All the same, it had been unsettling and eerie.

Now, she focused on the road before her, shaking the unnerving images from her mind. Soon, she turned into the driveway of Can Rosselló and parked under a shady pine. As she removed her helmet and stood on the gravel, she took several deep breaths, closed her eyes briefly, and turned towards the house. She found Pepe in the kitchen, blending aubergines. He smiled as she observed him from the doorway and killed the machine.

'Isabel, how nice to see you. I am making baba ghanouj. Roberto has grown so many aubergines in the garden that I need to be inventive.'

'I love any kind of aubergine purée, and the more garlicky, the better.'

He nodded. 'I agree, but the key ingredients with this recipe are obviously tahini and lemon juice.'

'And virgin olive oil, of course.'

'Naturally,' he conceded.

While Pepe washed his hands under the kitchen tap, Isabel wandered about the kitchen, her mind elsewhere.

'As you requested, Raquel and Roberto are here,' Pepe remarked. 'Roberto is working in the garden and Raquel is cleaning on the first floor.'

'Good,' Isabel replied. 'I suppose Fermin will be here shortly.'

As if on cue, there was the sound of a gnawing bike outside.

'That will be Fermin,' Pepe replied without the slightest inflexion in his voice. 'Shall we all go upstairs?'

Isabel locked eyes with him. 'Yes, let's do that.'

Fermin entered the *entrada* and shook hands with Isabel. He briefly offered Pepe a tentative hug.

'How can I help?' he asked.

Isabel smiled. 'I'd like you to accompany us to Maria's bedroom.'

As they made their way up the extravagant staircase, Fermin smiled wistfully. 'These portraits take me back. So many of my ancestors are here on these walls.'

'I imagine so,' Isabel replied.

On the top landing, they entered Maria's unlocked room. It resembled a static museum display. Nothing seemed out of place since Isabel's last visit. Ludicrously, she half imagined positioning stanchions and ropes around the enormous antique bed, as if paying visitors might pop by at any time just like in a stately home and try to touch the artefacts. Fermin broke the silence.

'I know this room so well. When I was a nipper, we used to play hide and seek, and I used to hide in the big wardrobe here.' He gave a sigh. 'Of course, in those days, Maria and I were close. Things changed.'

Isabel eyed him intently. 'You told Pepe that the wardrobe held secrets. What did you mean?'

He laughed. 'That sounds more exciting than it is. My grandfather – well he was Maria's too, of course – had an expert carpenter build that wardrobe. It's got a special sliding double panel at the back where we used to hide mementoes and sweets. You know how kids are.'

Isabel was tense. 'Can you show us this panel?'

Fermin frowned. 'Surely Maria showed it to you, Pepe? You've lived here long enough.'

Pepe shook his head. 'When Isabel asked me if there was anything unusual about the wardrobe, I didn't know what she meant. It was only when you told me that it had a secret panel that I understood.'

Isabel stared at him. 'To be honest, I didn't know what I was hoping to find in there, but I felt we'd missed something.'

Fermin sighed. 'I hate to disappoint, but I don't think you'll find anything still there.'

'Maybe not, but I need to satisfy my curiosity. I've had strange dreams of late.'

Pepe eyed her in some bemusement. 'Me too. What was this dream of yours?'

Isabel's face flushed. 'It was about something nasty in the woodshed.'

'*Cold Comfort Farm* by Stella Gibbons. You think there's something rotten in the wardrobe?'

'It sounds absurd, I know. It's just that my ferret found a ladybird button in there that didn't seem to relate to any of the outfits on display. I had a bad feeling about it.'

Pepe approached the heavy wooden door and glanced at Fermin. 'There's only one way to know what might lie beyond. Can you locate this panel?'

The man took a torch from his rucksack and, crouching low, felt inside. 'It's hard to see with all these garments. The panel has a fingerhole and you just slide it back.'

He began removing hangers bearing exotic dresses, evening wear and suits as Isabel and Pepe looked on. Finally, he eyed them brightly.

'Got it!'

Isabel could hardly breathe. A cold and irrational fear engulfed her as she watched him pull back the double mahogany panel to reveal a gaping hole. She stepped forward and grabbed his arm.

'Fermin, it might be better if I look inside.'

The man touched his beard thoughtfully and nodded. 'Of course.'

Isabel waited until Fermin joined Pepe at the foot of the bed. Wearing latex gloves, she took the torch and leant as far inside the wardrobe as she could. Flicking the light around, she at first saw little more than a mound of cobwebs in the hidden space, but as she peered inside, a small padlocked black metal chest came into view. It took Isabel some time to pull it into the interior of the wardrobe, and once she had, she carried it carefully over to Maria's desk. The two men gawped at her find and said nothing until Fermin offered to break the lock. Isabel shook her head.

'Thanks, but I have a feeling the key may be in here.'

She opened Maria's voluminous antique wooden jewellery box, with its exquisite marquetry, and carefully examined the contents. She discovered several small keys, but one with a tasselled fob perfectly fitted the lock. With shaking hands, she pulled the padlock free. There was silence as Isabel slowly opened the lid. Inside, she discovered several worn leather-bound journals, a miniature blue cardigan and matching ribboned booties, and a pristine, white linen baby's romper suit. Evidently none of the infant clothing had been worn, as the Parisian branded cardboard tags were still intact. Underneath the stiff cotton Peter Pan collar on the romper suit were three glass ladybird-shaped buttons. The fourth was missing; only loose threads remained. Isabel now understood the significance of Furó's find. Elaborate smocking and blue hand embroidery formed a rectangle on the chest area. The last remaining item, a large, soft blanket, contained a velvet drawstring bag that appeared bulky. Isabel instinctively stopped in her tracks and turned to the two men.

'Would you both mind leaving the room? I apologise, but as this is a police investigation, it's more appropriate that I examine the contents alone. I'll meet you back in the kitchen.'

Both demurred and stepped into the corridor, quietly closing the door behind them. Isabel braced herself. Her dream once again came back to haunt her and, in that moment, she felt a compelling desire to flee the room too. She took a deep breath, bowed her head, and uttered a short prayer.

She gently pulled out the contents. Rather like unwrapping a Russian doll, there were three more outer cloth bags. Isabel removed the last one and her heart stopped. Inside was an elaborately folded piece of white silk, secured with a navy velvet ribbon. Isabel slowly undid the bow and opened the parcel to reveal a tiny, shrivelled form. At first, she wasn't sure what she was seeing, until it became abundantly clear. In horror and revulsion, Isabel realised that before her were the skeletal remains of a tiny baby.

Isabel carefully placed the contents back into the metal chest, stopping to leaf through the journals. They took the form of diaries with entries written in an extravagant hand in burgundy-hued ink. She was tempted to read them there and then but accepted that there would be no denouement without her. She locked the box and placed it on the desk, putting the key in a zipped pocket in her pannier. Next, she pulled out her mobile and called Tolo. It was important that he knew that all was in place.

He sounded tense. 'This is an important find, Bel. Well done. We too have made some progress. I'm happy to say that we've discovered the red Fiat 500. It was where you'd indicated we'd find it.'

'It ended in Z?'

'6667JVZ, to be exact. Everything's going to plan. Now, just hold fire and wait for us at the house and we can make a formal arrest. We'll be with you shortly.'

Isabel threw the mobile in her bag and walked along the silent corridor to the bathroom. She opened the French doors onto the terrace and took some long deep breaths. Holding the railings where Maria most likely stood that day, she looked down at the fractured greenhouse and gave a sigh. The sky was a radiant blue and a hot white sun blanched the lawn and bark of the trees. How could such beauty be marred by so tragic an event? A sudden creak, maybe that of a floorboard, caused Isabel to turn and she found herself staring into the dark eyes of Roberto, the gardener. He offered her a gentle smile and ran a hand over his beard.

'I thought I'd find you up here, Isabel. Tío Pepe called both Raquel and me last night and asked us to make sure that we were at the house all morning. He didn't say why, but I had a feeling that you and the cops would probably be coming to make an arrest.'

'Does Pepe know you're up here?'

He shook his head. 'He thinks I'm in the orchard, but don't worry, I'm not going to interfere with your plans today.'

'That's considerate of you,' she replied.

'We've only properly met once, but I feel as though I know you, Isabel.'

She nodded. 'Well, you've certainly become quite a shadow in my life, Roberto, or should I call you Miquel?'

He shrugged. 'Roberto is my name. My family and ex-wife always preferred to call me Miquel, my second Christian name, because Roberto is also the name of my father, and it became confusing sometimes.'

'Why did Lucia take her mother's surname of Berganza and not yours?'

He chuckled. 'Lucia admired the famed opera singer, Teresa Berganza, and thought the name more stylish than Pons. They actually shared the same birthday, though they were born decades apart, of course.' He stared at her. 'When we spoke that day in the kitchen, I had a feeling that you weren't convinced by the suicide theory. That's why I decided to keep an eye on your movements.'

'A good plan in theory, but you weren't very subtle. I saw your car parked at the Conservatori and in Campos. I'm presuming that was you in the crematorium car park in Inca too, the day of Maria's funeral?'

'Correct. You and your male colleague took me by surprise. I tried to make a quick getaway, but it was messy.'

'Yes, that's why he suggested you were a female driver, which was rather sexist of him. By the way, the police have found your red Fiat 500. I guessed you must keep it in the family garage in Palma.' She paused. 'Rosa, Tina's sister, gave me the address of your family and I popped by there the other day and saw the garage. She also gave me your home address near Moscari, but when I drove by there, I noticed there was no lock up for a car.'

'I rent the place cheaply and there's no garage. Besides, I had a feeling the police might do some checking of household staff, so I made sure it was never on view at either address.'

Isabel felt the sun boring into her shoulders. 'Perhaps we could go and talk inside away from the sun?'

Roberto shook his head. 'I'd prefer to stay here. I want to talk to you before the backup cops arrive to take me away. I've bolted the bathroom door so they can't come and disturb us.'

'Why do you assume that anyone's coming?'

'I might be careless, but I'm not stupid, Isabel.' He turned and pointed to a free-standing folded parasol standing against a wall. 'I can pull that over here.'

As he drew it towards them, Isabel leant against the railings, thinking fast.

'So you and Lucia's mother, Tina, divorced some time ago?'

He raised the shade and with relief, Isabel no longer felt the sun's harsh rays.

'We divorced four years before Lucia's death, but we remained on good terms. Lucia lived with her mother and, as you'll know by now, I worked at the Conservatori as the caretaker. Lucia didn't want her friends to know that I was her father, not out of shame, but in case they assumed she'd got her scholarship through nepotism. It was nothing of the sort. I'm assuming that Matías Camps told you all this?'

Isabel nodded. 'Yesterday when I asked him about you, he told me the truth about Lucia's suicide, your role at the Conservatori, and his relationship with Maria.'

'Everyone knew they were having an affair, but it didn't last. None of Maria's lovers hung about, by all accounts.'

'Matías Camps also told me that when Lucia committed suicide, he suggested that you take some leave. He felt the memories would be too painful if you remained at the Conservatori.'

'It was a year and a half ago. I intended to leave, but maybe out of guilt, Maria offered me the post of gardener here. I almost laughed. Imagine being under the same roof as the woman who caused your daughter's death?'

'Matías Camps told me. I presume that you thought it offered the perfect opportunity for revenge?'

He was quiet for a moment. 'I didn't know how I'd destroy her for what she did to Lucia, but in the time I worked here, it came to me. I knew that, like clockwork, Maria sang on this terrace every morning at the same hour, always looking down at her beloved grandfather's greenhouse. She entrusted me with the spare set of keys to her bedroom and I was free to roam the house. A few months ago, I came up here to fix a drip under the bath and pulled out the bath panel. That's when I had the idea. I realised that there was ample room to squeeze inside and wait for the moment when she took her morning shower before I made my move. It seemed fitting that she should die in the same manner as my beloved Lucia.'

'And you wore the mask of Melpomene to remind Maria in her last moments of Lucia. After all, Maria's anger at Lucia performing with New Xanadu in the opera, *Melpomene*, was possibly the trigger for your daughter's suicide.'

'It was the trigger,' he replied passionately. 'Anyway, one day, Tío Pepe showed me his mask collection and in passing mentioned that one of the white masks was a depiction of the Greek muse, Melpomene. It was a perfect way to torture the witch moments before her fall.'

'Did she know that you were her killer?'

He flinched. 'I'm not sure, but that wasn't important. It happened quickly. By the time she knew what was happening, I'd pushed her over the railings.'

'It was clever of you to bolt the bathroom door. It nearly foxed me.'

'What made you suspect that she hadn't killed herself?'

'Instinct. Also, I felt that someone was trying to frame Pepe. He didn't strike me as killer material. When we first met, he told me he still suffered from a herniated disc. I couldn't imagine a man of sixty-five with a back complaint having the strength to physically push someone over railings, even low ones. And yet by smashing open the bathroom door and thoroughly exhausting himself, the poor man left himself open to scrutiny, even with Raquel's evidence confirming that it had been bolted from the inside.'

'I felt bad about that, as I've always liked Tío Pepe. He's a good man, if a bit strange. But what was I to do? I was hoping that the police would record her death as suicide, but if they were in any doubt, I needed someone else to carry the can and he was the perfect fit. He and the witch didn't get on and lived increasingly estranged lives. And of course, he'd inherit everything in the event of his wife's death, so he would be the prime suspect.'

'Or Fermin, who had been trying to make a claim on the house and had an acrimonious relationship with Maria.'

'Yes, he was my second-best bet. All the same, it's a shame you didn't just buy into the suicide theory. It would have made things so straightforward.'

Isabel ran a hand over her hot forehead. 'You had a third bet too: Enrique Diaz. It was you who removed the police tape from Maria's bedroom door and entered using your spare set of keys. You deliberately rearranged the photos on her desk and positioned the ones showing her with Enrique Diaz at the front. The day I returned to Can Rosselló, I could see that someone wanted to implicate Enrique in some way. Why? What had he done to you?'

'Nothing, but I knew he and Maria were close and had had some kind of bust-up on the mainland some years ago. By luck, I heard her on the phone to him a few days before I killed her. She mentioned Esporles and I worked out that they were planning to meet, but I couldn't hear when. I thought he'd make another convincing suspect if I needed one. Call it an insurance policy.'

'As I said before, I didn't believe Maria committed suicide. She was on the eve of an important opera tour and was in the most stable mental state she'd been in for some years and was no longer taking antidepressants. Her ego craved the trip. I subsequently discovered that she had agreed to meet someone that evening.'

'I'm guessing it was Enrique Diaz?'

'Yes, it was. A pity you didn't catch the date and time of their proposed meeting when you eavesdropped on Maria's phone call. You'd have realised that she'd hardly commit suicide on the morning of the day she'd arranged to meet someone. Not just anyone, either. He had been her lover and was returning to Mallorca for some days.'

Roberto gave a cynical grunt. 'You can't win them all.'

Isabel continued. 'So, I formed a theory that some enemy of Maria could have found a way to hide in the bathroom with the intention of killing her that fateful morning. But what was the motivation and where would they hide? The next question was how someone could make the murder look like suicide? By bolting the door from the inside, the police would naturally assume suicide and a fall from the balcony was the most obvious way Maria might kill herself. But if her assassin was wily enough and could find a way to exit the bathroom undetected while the door remained securely locked from the inside, they'd possibly be able to get away with murder. It was a hugely frustrating puzzle. Other than using a rope to descend from the balcony – a near impossible task except, perhaps, for an experienced mountaineer – I could see no way to leave the bathroom except by the door. Then I had a breakthrough and discovered the large space under the bath, partly thanks to my intuitive ferret, and all that changed. My next task was to narrow down who had access to the bathroom that morning and to address motive.'

Roberto folded his arms. 'Tío Pepe could have done it.'

'He certainly had time to get up the stairs while Raquel was sorting fruit in the kitchen cellar, as he'd popped out for some minutes. This would possibly have allowed him time to hide under the bath undiscovered, push his unsuspecting wife off the balcony and then return to the kitchen. The problem would have been that the door would no longer be bolted from the inside, making suicide look less certain.'

Roberto said nothing but kept his eyes fixed on her. Isabel gave a cough and resumed.

'I suppose in theory Pepe could then have feigned surprise when you rang Raquel to report having seen an apparition fall from the balcony, rushed up the stairs with her as a witness and broken open the door while pretending that it had been locked from the inside.'

'So why didn't you stick with that hypothesis?'

Isabel rested her back against the balcony railings.

'For one thing, Pepe is very tall. It would have been nigh impossible for him to squeeze under the bath. You, however, are slightly built.'

Roberto shrugged. 'True.'

Isabel exhaled deeply. 'Of course, your biggest mistake was lying about your dog.'

Roberto frowned. 'What do you mean?'

'When we met in the kitchen the day after Maria died, you mentioned that your Labrador pup, Brut, had been sick on the Monday and that on the Tuesday, the day of the incident, you'd had to leave him at home, following a visit to the local vet. Later, as things began to fall into place, I decided to check out vets in this area to find out whether that was true.'

'Why? How could that be important?'

'You see, if you had planned on killing Maria, what would you have done with the dog? Apparently, he came to the house with you every day. You could hardly have hidden a boisterous dog under the bath with you.'

He shook his head. 'I was a fool to mention it.'

'This week, I contacted all the vets in the area. One of them turned out to be yours and had given your dog his vaccinations. He told me that the dog was a picture of health and you hadn't visited for some time.'

Roberto laughed. 'Well done. You trumped me.'

'So, to conclude, having murdered Maria, you called Raquel to say that you were in the orchard and had seen something fall from Maria's balcony. You were, in fact, still in Maria's bathroom.'

He nodded.

'Then, when Pepe broke down the bathroom door, discovered Maria wasn't there and ran to the garden below with Raquel, you released yourself from under the bath, and left the house via another exit undetected by either of them.'

He smiled. 'It worked like a dream. I knew they'd exit by the front door, as it's closest to the greenhouse. I waited till they'd gone and left the house via the kitchen door.'

'You told me when we first met that it took fifteen minutes to walk from the orchard to the house. I tried it myself when I popped by Can Rosselló on another visit, and it only took me five minutes each way. So, I'm assuming you hid in the garden a short while before suddenly emerging from the direction of the orchard, supposedly out of breath and in shock. You then joined Raquel and Pepe at the greenhouse.'

'You've summed it all up perfectly, Isabel. We have reached the grand finale.'

Isabel gave a sad shake of the head. 'Whatever you thought of Maria, she didn't deserve to die.'

He frowned. 'As far as I'm concerned, she killed Lucia.'

Isabel shrugged. 'Maria undeniably caused Lucia pain, but your daughter had mental health issues and so we'll never truly know what drove her to commit suicide. But you decided to play God, which was wrong.'

Isabel's mobile rang from her pannier. With her eyes trained on Roberto, she went to answer it, just as banging came from outside the bathroom.

'Shall we open the bathroom door now, Roberto?'

He shook his head. 'I don't think so, Isabel. I've chosen how this is going to end.'

He ran towards the railings. Isabel dropped her phone and grabbed at his arm. Aggressively, he pushed her away and, gripping the top of the railing with both hands, propelled himself upwards. Isabel got to her feet and put her hands in the air.

'Come on, Roberto. Don't do this. Think of the hurt it will cause your parents. They've already lost their daughter-in-law and granddaughter.'

Edging closer, Isabel cast a quick glance down into the garden, where Gaspar and several police officers stood looking upwards. Someone was wrestling with the bathroom door.

'Stop right there, Isabel, or I'm going over.'

Isabel stood still. 'Okay, let's talk about this. Think about Lucia. She'd want you to live and to honour her memory in some way.'

For a moment he hesitated, but he shook his head and grimaced. 'I've nothing left to live for, Isabel. The only two people I ever cared about are dead and I don't want to spend the rest of my days in prison. Please look out for Brut.'

Isabel lunged forward just as the bathroom door burst open and Tolo and two armed officers appeared in the doorway. With one last look at Isabel, Roberto flipped headfirst over the railing.

A candle flickered on the white linen tablecloth and cast a golden glow on the glasses of white wine that flanked Isabel and Tolo's place settings. After the harrowing aftermath of Roberto Pon's suicide at Can Rosselló, the pair had spent time at the Palma precinct before returning, exhausted and subdued, to Sant Martí. They decided to stick with their original plan, and to share a comforting meal at Can Busquets. Isabel took a long sip of wine as she toyed with her salad.

'I keep thinking that I could have done more. If I'd held fast to his wrist, I could have prevented his death.'

Tolo shook his head and reached for her arm.

'Listen, you did everything you could. Who could have predicted his actions? In some ways, it was for the best.'

Isabel's eyes opened wide. 'How can you say that? A man's life was needlessly lost today. I feel responsible.'

'Be honest. What life did Pons have to look forward to? He made his decision when he murdered Maria. There was no coming back from that.'

Isabel offered him a glum look. 'The sun is shining and life goes on, and yet it's been the worst few weeks I can remember. Poor Juan and Bridget are dead, thanks to their hiring a fraud to help with their house refurbishments, and now this. The irony is that Maria hired Roberto at her home as a way of making amends. She evidently felt she was partly responsible for Lucia's suicide.'

'And so the moral of the story is entrust your home and house keys at your peril. The hired help could be the death of you,' Tolo quipped.

Isabel couldn't help but smile. 'You're such a cynic. Well, given that just about everyone has access to my home, and the door is rarely closed, I'm sunk.'

Tolo chewed thoughtfully on a chunk of tomato. 'We'll need to run the DNA on the foetus you found in Maria's wardrobe. It's the last piece in the jigsaw.'

'I think we can guess who the father would have been, but let's wait for the forensics report. Tomorrow I'll read through Maria's journals to see if there's a clue. I guess you'll need samples of the prime candidates, if they're willing?'

Tolo nodded. 'It's going to cause a rumpus and I'm not sure if we'll get cooperation from the minister of culture, if it comes to it.'

'Tomorrow Tío Pepe's daughter is arriving from South Africa. I've been invited over to meet her.'

He grinned. 'I wonder how that reconciliation came about. You had nothing to do with it, of course?'

Isabel offered him a coy smile. 'I might have found her details via my police contact in Joburg and given her a call.'

'And what might you have said to her?'

Isabel shrugged. 'To reconnect with her father, given that he missed her and was lonely following Maria's death.'

He laughed. 'That's what I love about you. You flagrantly break the rules and yet I can't get mad because it's always for the good of others. You're incorrigible. We'll keep this episode between us. I hope it works out for him and his daughter.'

Isabel brightened as Fabian appeared with a traditional metal *paellera* brimming with seafood, meat, and saffron rice.

'I suppose life must go on, Tolo. The day after tomorrow we have Alfonso's sixtieth birthday party at the town hall and Furó's new playpen arrives.'

As Fabian passed Isabel and Tolo steaming plates of *paella*, he laughed good-naturedly.

'Believe it or not, Alfonso's booked himself a birthday dinner here just for himself on Thursday night. Of course, I pretended to take the booking. When he discovers that he'll instead be spending the night with the whole village, he'll be in shock.'

Isabel smiled. 'It's important he knows that he is loved in the village. He's still mourning his beloved husband, Darius, but we will always be here for him.'

Fabian touched her arm and winked. 'Since he won't be having dinner with us on Thursday night, we've rearranged it for Saturday, and Llorenç, Doctor Ramis and your mother are attending. It's our birthday treat for him.'

Tolo beamed. 'A wonderful gesture. No wonder Bel tells me that this is the best village in the world. What a community.'

Fabian laughed. 'It's also got the best restaurant serving the best *paella*. Now eat up before it gets cold.'

TWENTY-SIX

As Isabel approached the porch of Can Rosselló, the front door swung open and Brut, his tail wagging happily, came over to greet her. She whisked the cream puppy into her arms and laughed as he began enthusiastically licking her face. A tall and slender woman with a gentle expression appeared in the *entrada*, and as Isabel released Brut from her arms, she came over and shook her hand.

'I am Juliette, Pepe's daughter. We spoke on the phone.'

Isabel smiled. 'Yes, of course. It's so good to finally meet you.'

The woman pushed her long fair hair behind her ears and led Isabel into the house. 'My father is in the kitchen waiting for you. Let's have coffee.'

Isabel found Pepe at the stove in a white chef's apron, stirring something spicy. 'Any anchovies in there?' Isabel teased.

He turned to her and smiled. 'Actually, no. I'm making a spicy passata.'

He lowered the flame and came over to greet her. 'I see you've met Juliette. We have you to thank for bringing us together.'

Isabel scrunched her nose. 'You both made it happen. I just helped to reconnect you.'

'The fact is, Isabel, I realise that I just didn't know how to change my life while Maria was alive. I felt so diminished and humiliated and had lost sight of who I was. I took comfort in my job and my—'

'Anchovies,' Isabel cut in, trying to lift the mood.

Both he and Juliette laughed. She placed a hot coffee and homemade almond biscuits in front of Isabel.

'He'd become quite a fish obsessive,' Juliette replied. 'Last night when I arrived, he showed me his massive anchovy tin collection.'

Pepe returned to stir the pan. 'I want you to know that I am relocating to Cape Town, Isabel.'

'Gosh, that's a big decision. What about Can Rosselló?'

'I'm giving it to Fermin. He is the rightful heir. He has promised to care for Brut and will keep Raquel in her position. I am leaving with my daughter at the end of this week.'

'This is such wonderful news, Pepe. How good of you to make Fermin's dream come true.'

Juliette smiled. 'My husband and I have a large farm and so we want Dad to live with us. He can do all the cooking!'

Isabel noticed how animated and happy Pepe appeared to be. It was as if a huge burden had suddenly been lifted from his shoulders. His eyes watered. 'I will meet my young grandchildren for the first time.' He gave a sniff. 'And as a small gesture of appreciation, Isabel, I am delivering all my fish to your home.'

She gave a small gasp.

'That's not necessary, Pepe, much as I appreciate your kindness.'

He shook his head stubbornly. 'It's all arranged. It will arrive by van tomorrow morning. Do you have some kind of store?'

'I have a shed in the garden and a large pantry.'

'Good. That sounds perfect.'

'Thank you. I'm sure my family and friends in Sant Martí will be delighted to share the bounty. So, what will you do about Maria's memorial service at Bellver Castle next month?'

He shrugged. 'I've decided not to attend. I feel it is not appropriate. In the light of your finds yesterday, I realise that my life with Maria ended at least five years ago. All the same, I am the inheritor of her estate, and I will ensure that her music and recordings live on.'

An hour later, Isabel stood on the porch and reached forward instinctively to give Pepe a hug. She passed him a small package and watched as he opened it and dangled Maria's gold locket before him.

'Maria may have been flawed like us all, but I hope this memento will serve to remind you of happier times with her.'

He nodded slowly and went to put it in his pocket.

'Before you do that, did you know that it has a secret compartment at the rear?'

His brow furrowed. 'I had no idea.'

Isabel took it from him and slid open the back.

'It's empty but a curiosity, all the same.'

He smiled. 'I wonder if Maria ever hid anything in there.'

'I guess we'll never know,' Isabel replied hastily. 'Keep well, Pepe, and enjoy your new life. You're a good man.'

His eyes glistened. 'Thank you for always believing in me.'

Isabel set off towards her bike, turning when he called to her.

'By the way, your colleague, Tolo Cabot, sent over an officer to get a DNA sample earlier today. Unless the remains of that poor premature child were languishing there for many years, it cannot be mine. Either way, I would rather never know.'

As Isabel rode off on Boadicea, she took one last look at the picturesque façade of Can Rosselló, a house of immense beauty that harboured more than its fair share of dark secrets.

Late that afternoon, Isabel parked Pequeñito in front of a modest terraced house in Inca. Josep Casanovas sat in the front passenger seat, combing his highlighted locks and checking his complexion in the mirror in front of him.

'My job is certainly taking its toll on my face. I can see new lines every day. This is the gift one gets for unselfishly serving one's community.'

Isabel resisted the urge to giggle. 'You still look handsome. Come on, let's do this.'

He wrinkled his nose. 'The girl's house isn't very palatial, is it?'

'Stop being a snob.'

He grinned. 'Remember, Bel, this is a huge favour and I'm expecting pay back.'

Isabel rolled her eyes and opened her door. 'You'll get your pound of flesh, Josep. Tolo has agreed to give you the heads up as soon as the investigation concludes. You'll get the lead story.'

He nodded. 'Okay. Just so we're clear.'

Isabel knocked on the front door and was greeted by a shy Gemma Palau. She beckoned them into the *entrada*, where her mother and stepfather stood in awed silence. Isabel made introductions and turned to her.

'So, Gemma, as I explained by phone this morning, this is the editor of *El Periódico*. Josep is very excited to hear all about your starring performance as Minnie in *La Fanciulla del West* next month.'

Josep breathed heavily and his mouth broke into a well-rehearsed toothy smile. 'Oh yes, I'm a Puccini fan and an admirer of the Conservatori. Your director, Matías Camps, told me yesterday that you are one of his up-and-coming scholarship students and this opera will mark the beginning of a great career for you.'

Gemma's mother gave a sharp intake of breath. 'Is that so? Gemma never told us about this. We're so proud.'

'We'll be sitting in the front row, pleased as punch,' her stepfather rejoined. 'Will this be in the newspaper?'

Isabel subtly nudged Josep. 'It will be in tomorrow's edition, won't it?'

'Indeed, it will, with an image of Gemma. Naturally, the reporter handling the newspaper's cultural section will also attend on the night.'

The girl's cheeks turned pink. 'This is like a dream. Thank you for organising this, Bel.'

Isabel smiled. 'You said you had a small garden, Gemma? How about we take some quick shots there and then Josep can interview you?'

'I've made coffee,' enthused her mother. 'We'll leave you in peace to interview her after that.'

As she bustled through to the kitchen, Isabel saw her place an arm around her daughter's shoulders.

'We're so proud of you, Gemma,' she whispered.

Isabel felt a lump in her throat. She gave a hoarse cough and followed the student and Josep out onto the sunny patio.

It was midnight and Isabel gave a hearty yawn. She was sitting on her patio, the last dregs of a glass of red wine in front of her. Despite the intense heat, there was a light breeze that fluttered the pages of the leather-bound journal in Isabel's hand. She had spent the previous few hours immersed in the five journals that she had discovered behind the sliding panel in Maria's wardrobe. Sombrely, she closed the cover and returned it to the stack on the table. Now, the final piece of the jigsaw had been revealed. She would have a lot to tell Tolo the next morning. With a sigh, she rose and scooped up Furó, whom she found sniffing animatedly around the corral. She kissed his furry head.

'Tomorrow, you will have your own playpen and won't need to disturb the hens anymore. And now, it's time for bed, my little friend. It's been a long day.'

Furó nestled into her neck and gave a little yawn. He closed his eyes as she snuffed out the candle and closed the kitchen door. Isabel stood quietly by the window. A full moon cast its gentle gaze on the orange and lemon trees and the wild ivy tendrils hanging from Isabel's wrought-iron pagoda. She smiled and turned out the kitchen light, reminding herself of the healing power of nature.

TWENTY-SEVEN

Isabel was still wearing her cycling gear when Tolo arrived. He made them both coffees and pottered about her kitchen making a cooked breakfast while she showered. Then he set the table on the patio and called for her. Isabel returned with a towel, which she used to dry her long curly tresses, and joined him in the sunshine.

'This looks incredible. Scrambled eggs and crispy *jamon serrano*. After that excruciating ride, that's just what I need.'

'Where did you go this time?'

She tutted. 'You know Pep. He insisted we head up to Escorca on the American Road. Even early morning, you end up sweating buckets.'

He took a bite of toast. 'True. This heat is pretty insufferable. We're nearly at the end of the month. September will be better.'

Isabel took a forkful of egg and regarded him solemnly. 'So, what's the news from Nacho? Gaspar phoned me yesterday afternoon to say he'd rushed through the results on the foetus.'

'First things first. Nacho confirmed that the only DNA found on the white mask of Melpomene was that of Maria. We can only assume that she had reached out and touched it before Roberto Pons pushed her from the balcony.'

Isabel gave a groan. 'She must have been so terrified.'

He nodded. 'However unpleasant and messed up the woman was, she didn't deserve that.' He took a sip of coffee. 'Nacho also wanted me to fill you in on the last findings of the cases here in Sant Martí. He's already spoken to our dear chum, Álvaro. Apparently, the DNA of Manuel Borras was present on the yellow-legged gull at the homes of his father and Bridget Kelly, while a hair from Tomeu Tous was found on the specimen left at the Petersens.'

'That figures. Adam Markham had stealthily taken DNA from both. He must have removed a hair from Tomeu's jacket that he'd stolen from his office, and he could easily have got Manuel's DNA from his father's house where he often stayed.'

'So back to Maria. The foetus proved to be male and had Enrique's DNA. He provided samples in Barcelona the day that the remains were found. He needs to be told the news.'

Isabel nodded. 'I thought as much. Maybe I should do that?'

'As you have built some kind of trust with him, it makes sense. The baby was twenty-one weeks old and had been delivered naturally. It was most likely stillborn.'

Isabel rested her hands under her chin.

'I stayed up late last night reading Maria's diaries. She wrote that her relationship with Pepe was over a few years before she fell in love with Enrique. As he was married, they decided to conduct their affair secretly, but when Maria went on tour five years ago, she demanded that they come out in the open, divorce their partners and marry. He refused and they split acrimoniously. However, not long after she returned to Mallorca, she discovered that she was pregnant with his child.

Although filled with hatred for Enrique, she was ecstatic, as she had desperately craved a baby for years. She confided in Blando, her private doctor, who visited her regularly. It was at this time that she had the five locks fitted on her bedroom door as she didn't want Pepe or the household staff to see that she was pregnant. She records the day when she unfortunately lost the baby. That is when she appears to have struggled with depression. The journals become increasingly filled with hateful rants against Enrique and a desire to make him suffer for her loss. Maria seems to have blamed him for the baby's death, as if his rejection of her was the cause. Later, she alludes to Doctor Blando prescribing her medication to deal with her manic episodes. It's obvious that she became paranoid and clinically depressed and increasingly mentally unstable.'

'When do you think she decided to murder Enrique?'

'In the journals, she mentions Catalina Grimalt and seems to have got wind of her romance with Enrique. She fantasises about seeing him die and talks about giving him a high dose of fentanyl served in a negroni.'

'The woman must have been truly deranged in the end.'

'Grief seems to have tipped her over the edge. She meticulously describes in one of her last entries how she intends to stow the fentanyl and xylazine in her locket, and lure Enrique with the promise of a truce to a remote piece of woodland near Esporles. She mentions how, once there, she'd pour him a negroni with a fatal dose of the drugs. In a final twist of the knife, she vowed to tell him about the baby, which she'd christened Enrique posthumously. She mentions that as Enrique and his wife couldn't have children, it would devastate him before he died.'

Tolo put a hand to his face. 'It's hard to believe any person would be capable of such hatred.'

Isabel sighed. 'And yet, look at Roberto, another damaged and hate-filled soul. But he wasn't always like that. Grief and hatred make lethal cocktail ingredients.'

Tolo clicked his teeth. 'Maria's memorial at Bellver Castle is going to be interesting next month. Do you reckon all these ghosts from the past will pitch up?'

'I don't know, but I for one will not be attending.'

There was a bang at the front door. Tolo and Isabel sprang to their feet and walked through to the *entrada*. On the doorstep they found a cheery delivery man.

'I've got a load of tins to deliver to Señorita Flores.'

'That's me.'

He laughed. 'Good. Well, in that case, all I can say is that I hope you like fish.'

It was five-thirty and Florentina's kitchen was buzzing with people. Boxes and platters of food sat on the long wooden table while her hands danced about a worktop, putting the finishing touches to a huge, tiered chocolate cake. Doctor Ramis cheerfully issued instructions to the various villagers who'd popped by to help with carrying items over to the town hall. He was careful to ensure that the children carried only the least delicate items in case of mishaps along the way. Meanwhile, Marga and Rafael had been sent by Llorenç to collect Alfonso from his home, on the pretence of attending an urgent meeting at the town hall that would have ramifications for his next course of art classes. Isabel had felt this might panic poor Alfonso, but Llorenç insisted it was a good plan. Padre Agustí had been invited to give an uplifting address, while Llorenç would perform master of ceremony duties. It seemed that the majority of villagers would be attending, although Jordi offered to keep his bar open to keep the tourists happy. He would slip out later for an hour to join the festivities, leaving his manager in charge.

Out in Florentina's garden, Tolo was crouching on the grass peacefully watching Furó as he hurtled around his new playpen, ringing bells, splashing in water and wriggling through long plastic tubes. Isabel came outside to escape the din in her mother's kitchen and laughed to see Furó's antics.

'It's been bedlam in there. I think half the village turned up.'

'It just shows how popular your village artist is.'

Isabel nodded. 'He's got a heart of gold and is so unassuming. Anyway, Mama is serving us a quick glass of *cava* before we set off, so shall we go inside?'

They walked back into the kitchen just as Idò and Pep arrived, swerving to avoid the rest of the helpers as they left the kitchen clutching the remaining platters.

'Who's carrying the cake?' asked Pep.

Florentina eyed him sternly. 'You are, so if you drop it, I'll be after you with a rolling pin.'

Idò gave a raucous chuckle. 'It'll all end in tears.'

Pep pulled a face and gratefully accepted a glass of cool *cava*. 'I always get the bum jobs.'

Isabel patted his shoulder. 'At least you have a wonderful boss.'

He laughed. 'In your dreams.' Pep took a sip and offered her a serious expression. 'I'm still reeling about Maria. You haven't filled me in.'

'Let's talk about that tomorrow. Tonight is all about celebrating life,' Tolo replied.

Pep nodded. 'Okay, so talking about celebrations, Florentina, do you and Miguel have anything to tell us?'

'Whatever do you mean?' asked Florentina, her eyes darting towards the doctor.

Isabel looked askance. 'Well?'

Her mother wiped her hands on a tea towel, her cheeks flushing pink while Doctor Ramis lowered his head and chuckled.

'We were waiting for the right time to bring it up, and our plan was to tell Bel first, but the truth is that we have become more than friends.'

A brief and awkward silence followed until Isabel grinned. 'It's been fairly obvious that you've become attached.'

Idò slapped the table. 'Well, well. Sister, that makes me very happy. Even better to have a doctor in the family.'

Florentina tutted. 'We don't want a fuss, but we are very content together.'

Isabel leant forward and gave both her mother and Doctor Ramis a hug. 'In that case, we're thrilled for you, Mama. You are both special people and deserve every happiness.'

'Hear, hear!' yelled Pep. 'What a night this is proving to be.'

As Tolo congratulated the pair, Florentina suddenly grinned. 'I have another little revelation for you, Bel.'

'Really?' asked Isabel warily.

Florentina placed her glass on the table and laughed. 'It's about your grandmother, Ana. You know, Juan's mother.'

'What about her?' interrupted Pep.

'I don't have the full facts, but it's very likely she was British.'

Isabel's eyes popped open. 'What? Don't be silly. Juan's mother was Spanish.'

Florentina shook her head. 'Not according to my genealogist. Apparently, her name was spelt Anna, not the Spanish way.'

Tolo looked at Isabel and winked. 'Well, you do speak excellent English and you have a thing about Chelsea boots and English furniture.'

Pep and Idò looked on in stunned silence just as Padre Agustí appeared in the doorway. 'Llorenç has asked that we all gather before Alfonso arrives. He'll be there in thirty minutes.'

'Quick,' said Florentina, as she finished the dregs of her *cava*. 'Let's not be late.'

Isabel eyed her wryly. 'We'll discuss this genealogy matter further. I'm not convinced.'

'I don't have all the details yet, but it's true, Bel. The genealogist told me that she has copies of historic records from the UK.'

As they left the house en masse, Pep struggled to carry the enormous cake in his arms. He gave Isabel a cheeky grin. 'If it's true that your dad's mother was English, that means you're only half *Mallorquina*, a quarter Castilian and a quarter English. We'll never let you live that down.'

Isabel narrowed her eyes. 'If that cake wasn't for dear Alfonso, I might just be tempted to push your face in it.'

Alfonso, flanked by Marga and Rafael, blithely opened the door to the events hall. He stopped in his tracks and his mouth dropped open. He looked around him in disbelief as countless familiar faces swam before his gaze. Emblazoned on a wall in front of him, in large colourful letters, he saw his name and the words 'HAPPY 60th BIRTHDAY', and trestle tables groaning with treats. Unable to contain themselves, his fellow villagers sang '*Feliz Cumpleaños*' at the top of their voices and burst into applause. Marga and Rafael gently led Alfonso to meet the mayor, who embraced him warmly while friends and neighbours huddled about him, offering hugs and kisses. The village's regular oompah band struck up and locals began queuing for drinks at the bar, while others tucked into food.

Capitán Gómez and Josep Casanovas walked in together. Isabel nudged Tolo. He gave a groan.

'Both my favourite people. How wonderful is that.'

Isabel grabbed his arm and led him over to them. Capitán Gómez offered a stiff smile.

'This all looks very calm, although these village affairs so easily get out of control.'

'Yes, hopefully we won't have to make any arrests, Álvaro,' quipped Tolo.

With a straight face, the police captain nodded. 'I shall be keeping a close eye. This village is full of undesirable characters, as has been clearly demonstrated in recent weeks. As for that Adam Markham...'

'In fairness, Álvaro, he was not from our village,' Isabel retorted.

Josep offered Tolo an obsequious smile. 'As Isabel probably told you, I stuck to my end of the bargain regarding Tía Maria, so I look forward to your full cooperation in the next few days.'

Tolo scowled and turned to Isabel just as she whipped a copy of *El Periódico* from her pannier and stuck it under his nose. He studied it for a few seconds.

'Is this one of Maria's students?' he asked.

'It is indeed,' Isabel replied. 'Her name is Gemma Palou and Josep kindly interviewed her yesterday about an opera she'll be performing in next month. You and I will be attending.'

'We will?' he asked in some bafflement.

'Most certainly.'

His brow furrowed. 'What has this got to do with me?'

Isabel soothingly drew him towards the drinks table. She grabbed a glass of red wine and thrust it into his hand.

'I'll explain everything shortly,' she hissed. 'Oh look, the speeches are beginning, and I have a surprise for Alfonso. I'll be back.'

In some confusion, Tolo watched Isabel weave through the happy throng and step onto the small stage. She whispered something in Llorenç's ear as he approached the microphone with Padre Agustí at his side. Llorenç smiled and gave a nod as Isabel mysteriously disappeared from the room. Josep Casanovas positioned himself near the stage, his camera at the ready. The beloved artist took his position next to Padre Agustí. Despite his usual timorous demeanour, Alfonso was smiling broadly, his eyes brimming with happiness. As an excited hush fell on the room, Isabel sidled back into the room, this time accompanied by Manuel Borras. He was holding a magnificent hand-crafted model of a *llaüt* that he solemnly carried up onto the stage with Isabel's help. Together, they presented it to Alfonso to great applause and whistles and placed it on a small table. He examined it carefully, and with tears in his eyes, gasped to see a miniature figure of himself at the helm. He hugged them both and, at Llorenç's invitation, took hold of the microphone and smiled at his fellow villagers.

'This is simply one of the best surprises and nights of my life and I will be eternally grateful to Llorenç and all of you for making my sixtieth such an occasion to remember and cherish. I am privileged to live in Sant Martí among people who mean so much to me.'

He paused and cast a reassuring smile in Manuel's direction.

'And I thank Manuel, who recently lost his wonderful father, Juan. He has been through a great deal and yet has found time to make this beautiful boat for me. It is an exact replica of my own *llaüt* and surely proves to us all what an astonishing talent he has. I feel this will beckon a new career – one that all of us villagers will wholeheartedly support.'

Isabel smiled to hear the loud clapping and roars of praise. Hopefully this would mark the beginning of Manuel's rehabilitation in the village.

Llorenç returned to his duties at the microphone, announcing that Padre Agustí would make a speech. When the *padre* had finished, Isabel made her way over to Tolo, who was now enjoying much banter with Marga, Pep and a bunch of locals. She looked about the room, her heart swelling with joy to see such mirth and harmony after such a turbulent period. As she took a sip of her *cava*, her mobile blared from her pannier. She tutted. Excusing herself, she headed for the door. Once outside in the quiet corridor, she checked the number. It was unknown to her and had a Barcelona code.

'*Diga?*'

A rich and velvety voice filled the void. It sounded strangely comforting and familiar. 'Is that you, Bel?'

In some agitation and with a catch in her throat, she asked, 'Who is this?'

There was a long pause, followed by a deep sigh. 'It's me, Bel. Your Uncle Hugo. I'm home.'

Acknowledgements

Writing a book and seeing it come to fruition is all about team work and I could not have brought my fourth adventure to light without my longstanding talented partner in crime, illustrator, Chris Corr, expert designers, Chris Jones and Ben Ottridge, and hawk-eyed editors Lucy York and Laura Burge. A special mention to my agent, Francine Fletcher of Fletcher Associates, for her continued friendship and guidance.

It goes without saying that big hugs are due to my hugely supportive husband, Alan, son Ollie, and sister, Cecilia, for their constant cheerleading and encouragement. My nephew, Alex, has gone the extra mile and invested his time and energy into Burro Books for which I am eternally grateful.

Finally, immeasurable thanks to you, my readers, for having supported me thus far on my publishing journey. Without you, it simply wouldn't have been possible.

Download Anna Nicholas's audio guide walking tour of Soller via the VoiceMap App (https://voicemap.me) here:

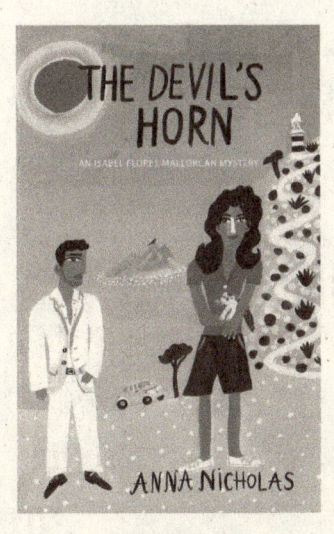

THE DEVIL'S HORN
An Isabel Flores Mallorcan Mystery

Anna Nicholas

Paperback: 978-1-9996618-4-7
Ebook: 978-1-9996618-5-4

When 33-year-old Isabel Flores Montserrat quits her promising career with the Spanish police to run her mother's holiday rentals agency in rural Mallorca, her crime-fighting days seem far behind.

Basking in the Mediterranean sunshine with pet ferret Furó, she indulges her passion for local cuisine, swimming in the sea and raising her pampered hens.

However, in just a few days, the disappearance of a young British girl, violent murder of an elderly neighbour, and discovery of a Colombian drug cartel threaten to tear apart Isabel's idyllic life.

Together with local chief inspector Tolo Cabot, an old admirer of her unorthodox methods, Isabel must race against the clock to untangle a sinister web of crime and restore peace to the island once more.

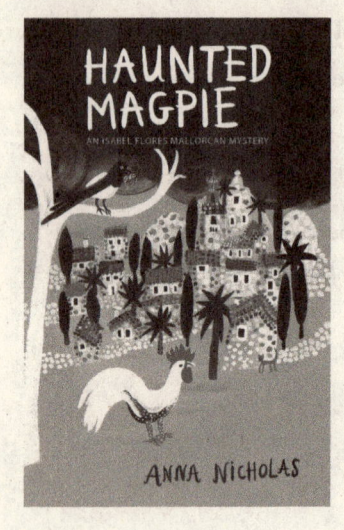

HAUNTED MAGPIE
An Isabel Flores Mallorcan Mystery

Anna Nicholas

Paperback: 978-1-9996618-4-7
Ebook: 978-1-9996618-5-4

When a young florist vanishes at night, the only evidence found is a tiny wooden heart. With nothing else to go on, Mallorca's police chief calls upon unorthodox former detective, Isabel Flores Montserrat, to help.

But a second disappearance confirms a connection with a series of sinister cold cases. Suspecting that a serial killer has resurfaced, Isabel races to uncover the link between past and present, the meaning of the wooden heart, and the identity of the culprit.

Meanwhile, trouble is brewing in Isabel's own village with a spate of mysterious animal disappearances. Could it all be connected?

FALLEN BUTTERFLY
An Isabel Flores Mallorcan Mystery

Anna Nicholas

Paperback: 978-1-9996618-4-7
Ebook: 978-1-9996618-5-4

With political tensions running high due to a controversial new motorway scheme, the chilling and ritualistic murder of a high-flying local government minister sends shockwaves through the island.

When her home is ransacked and another brutal killing occurs, Isabel Flores Montserrat, unorthodox former detective, joins up once again with Mallorca's police chief, Tolo Cabot, in a perilous race for answers.

Meanwhile, fear and distrust grow in Isabel's village as fake signs and cairn markers send disorientated hikers plunging off cliffs. Is this mountain mischief the work of environmentalists or is something far more sinister afoot?

burrobooks
www.burrobooks.co.uk